THE TREASURE OF MONTE FUEGO

THE TREASURE OF MONTE FUEGO

A Novel

Claude M. Jonnard
Author of Bimini Man and Caribbean Conspiracy

iUniverse, Inc.
New York Lincoln Shanghai

THE TREASURE OF MONTE FUEGO

iUniverse books may be ordered through booksellers or by contacting:

iUniverse
2021 Pine Lake Road, Suite 100
Lincoln, NE 68512
www.iuniverse.com
1-800-Authors (1-800-288-4677)

This is a work of fiction. All of the characters, names, incidents, organizations and dialogue in this novel are either the products of the author's imagination or are used fictitiously.

This book is a sequel to two earlier works of fiction: Bimini Man and Caribbean Conspiracy.

ISBN-13: 978-0-595-39426-5 (pbk)
ISBN-13: 978-0-595-83822-6 (ebk)
ISBN-10: 0-595-39426-4 (pbk)
ISBN-10: 0-595-83822-7 (ebk)

Printed in the United States of America

To my family and friends,

whose support, patience and understanding

made writing this book possible.

SYNOPSIS

This third book of the trilogy, The Fictional Biography of a Hit Man, takes place in the present in Connecticut, Florida and the Caribbean. In this final book, Amison Jones, after his rescue from a storm at sea, inherits a piece of an old mining company, West Indian Mines, on the island of Monte Fuego, and is immediately marked for death. He finds that West Indian is actually a cover for an international ring of jewel thieves who are looting Holocaust victims' valuables from government warehouses in Europe and selling "conflict" diamonds from Africa to finance a right wing conspiracy. Amison discovers the strange truth tying the gang's diverse operations together and is faced with betrayal and deceit by his friends and associates as he exposes the gang in an explosive climax when a dormant volcano erupts on Monte Fuego.

Part i

▼

THE
INHERITANCE

Prologue

The big cruise ship was now abreast of the island's barren western side. Sid was out on the balcony of their cabin suite, peering through the binoculars at the smoking mountain and the gray cloud above it. Through the glasses could be seen the remains of a sprawling town and what was once its harbor.

"What's that I'm smelling?" asked a voice from inside the cabin.

"Hydrogen sulfide," replied Sid. "It's called 'rotten egg gas.' It comes from the cloud above the volcano. The wind is blowing it to the ship."

He adjusted the glasses as the ship drew nearer to the island.

"Get your kids. They should see this."

No action was necessary. The captain had already announced that the vessel was being slowed to give passengers a close look at the havoc wrought by the volcano a few months ago. Charlotte's two teenagers ran into the cabin from their inside stateroom and hugged the balcony rail for a better view.

"Twenty thousand people once lived on Monte Fuego," the captain told his passengers in a rich European accent over the intercom. "Most of them lived in La Fortuna. You can see the city's remains from the starboard side of this ship. It looks almost as if it was leveled by an ariel bombardment.

"Today, less than two thousand are left on the island. They live in scattered communities east of the mountain where damage was lighter.

"The people of Monte Fuego were very lucky. Most were evacuated before the eruption and few lost their lives. However, the volcano is still active, and it is not known when people will be able to return to their homes."

A pause. And then the captain continued.

"In the center of the city can be seen the burned out shell of a dome on top of the ruins of the presidential palace on the main square facing the harbor. A tall needle like obelisk in the square was miraculously left intact. Behind the dome can be seen the remains of the Excelsior, La Fortuna's main hotel. And on a hill to the left of the city is an old fortress called La Fortaleza. It was the only structure untouched by the firestorm from the lava filling the Rio Blanco that flowed through La Fortuna into the harbor. Molten lava covered the city and harbor and extended into the sea before it stopped and solidified."

One of the teenagers pointed La Fortaleza.

"Isn't that where all the gold that your friends wanted is buried, uncle Sid?

Sid shook his head.

"There was no gold, and our friends were looking for something else. They were lucky to get out alive, and so were we."

"Sidney wanted to build a resort hotel on the island," Charlotte explained. "On a grander scale than the ones he has back in the States, but it didn't work out like we expected."

She turned to Sid.

"We should get ready, dear," she said. "We can tell them over dinner what really happened."

"This sad Monte Fuego business started while Amison Jones was still lost at sea," Sid Stone began when they had settled down for dinner. "We called him Jonesey, but his real name was Amison Rubin Jones. He occupied a suite at my hotel, the Riverside, in Fort Lauderdale, when it started. Someone had broken into his apartment and stolen a gold watch. Ordinarily, a robbery in south Florida would have attracted little attention, and this particular thief would have grown richer by one gold watch. Also not a big deal. But this was different. This robbery ended up being a very bad move for the thief, a fatal error in fact.

"For some reason, he happened to be on the deserted pedestrian walk along the New River behind the hotel shortly before dawn when he was shot dead in a drive-by shooting. I was asleep when it happened and Frank Hoffman was in his pad on the second floor of the Sagamore House overlooking the river. Anastio Petropoulos, one of the partners at Hamburger Haven on the boulevard, was waiting for a cab at the hotel's livery entrance to take him to the airport for the early morning flight to New York. He saw the commotion, but he was gone when the police arrived…"

Frank was up and dressed when he heard the sirens shortly after dawn. He opened a bedroom window and poked his head out to see what was going on but all he could see was the reflection of police lights from squad cars as they converged near the Cheesecake Factory restaurant outside his range of sight.

Rain was falling, a drizzle at first, and then a downpour.

He had an early morning meeting and was already dressed. Adjusting his glasses and bow tie, he put on his seersucker jacket, grabbed an umbrella and went out to see what was going on.

Whoever was shot had crawled to the Cheesecake Factory's locked doors before dying. When Frank arrived, he found the police roping off the area from the hotel's Las Olas Boulevard entrance all the way to the Cheesecake Factory on the corner. Jerry Goodman, his beefy body sandwiched between the steering wheel and the seat of his EMS van, was already there and Jake Santana from the Broward County sheriff's office pulled up in his unmarked sedan driven by Teddy his chauffeur, moments later.

Jake stepped out of his car, yawned and tugged at his red suspenders under his suit jacket. Popping a hard candy into his mouth, he sauntered over to the van and rested his arm on the open window. Teddy threw Frank a wave from inside the sedan.

"Hey Frank, how are things?" The burly driver called out.

"Wet, Teddy. How's the family?"

"Have we disturbed your beauty sleep?" Jake asked Frank before Teddy could answer.

Frank laughed lightly and looked at his watch.

"It's ok, inspector. I have a meeting at the hotel in about an hour."

Jake rubbed his moustache and turned to Jerry.

"What do we have, amigo?"

Jerry Goodman smiled and replied in his wheezy voice,

"A single shot to the head and tire marks on the street. We're talking one shooter and a driver, maybe a third person. And oh, the deceased had a gold watch in his pocket, the one reported stolen yesterday from Jonesey's suite."

He produced the watch from a plastic sandwich bag.

Jake looked at Frank.

"It looks like yours," he remarked.

"It's identical," said Frank, holding his up. "There are three watches. Luis Santiago has one; I have one; the third is for Jonesey, if he ever shows up again."

"Trophies?"

"Tokens of appreciation. Who called the cops?"

Jake shook his head.

"Don't know. A concerned citizen, maybe? It was an anonymous 911."

"A random drive-by shooting?"

"Maybe. Robbery certainly wasn't a motive."

"Did you see the body, Jerry?"

The EMS worker nodded.

"You know him, Frank. It's Sammy Luke, a small time jewel thief."

"Shit! He used to work for us as a cat burglar and he was damn good. Why the hell would he have wanted to rob Jonesey?"

Jake Santana sighed.

"Beats me. Doesn't a dog sometimes bite the hand that feeds it?"

He handed the evidence bag to Frank.

"Well, he just had his last meal. Here. You take it. At least the robbery is solved. Anything on Jonesey?"

"Nothing. But we're hopeful."

A police officer walked up and asked for instructions.

"Find the shell casing and send it to ballistics," Jake ordered. "I also need to know more about those tire tracks. I want to find the car they were under."

"Who would want to kill Sammy? The officer asked.

"That's what we need to find out. Robbery sure wasn't a motive."

"It would be nice to find out how and why Sammy broke into Jonesey's suite in the first place," said Frank. He must have known all along about the watch. Either that or someone must have put him up to it."

"Good point," agreed the police inspector. "We'll do that. And maybe you can help us at your end. Speak to Sid and some of the other folks running the hotel. You know your way around that place."

Night passed and the rain continued to fall.

Rain or shine, Las Olas Boulevard's sidewalk cafes opened early every day. The ones at the Riverside, set under the hotel's second floor balcony were no exception and four men in suits and ties were already seated at a table away from the rain discussing business over coffee and doughnuts.

CHAPTER 1

▼

The Obits

Jorge Ramirez, trim in a freshly pressed white jacket and apron, stood by the two aging telephone booths near the door and greeted the day manager as he walked into the hotel. It was the start of a rainy, dreary, melancholy day.

"Long night, Felipe?"

The day manager, a young man of medium height and build with dark curly hair, grimaced. His hand pointed to the ground with its thumb down.

"Too long."

"Will Al Garcia be working the bar today?" Jorge asked.

"He has to. He can't afford not to show his face."

He nodded in the direction of the door.

"Better take care of those guys outside. They're important."

Felipe went to his office and Jorge poked his head out of the hotel entrance to see if his customers needed anything. They were engrossed in conversation and ignored him. He looked right to see if Hamburger Haven next door was open. It was. He waved to Dimitri who was busy pulling chairs and tables into the street under the eatery's canopy with Angelo, his brother.

On the corner was the Europa café. It was open and people were braving the rain for an early breakfast under table umbrellas. On the other side of the street, partially concealed by the drooping foliage of rain drenched trees on the divider separating Las Olas Boulevard's two opposing lanes of traffic, were more restaurants. They were still closed, but they never opened before the noon. He looked to the left and could tell that the Cheesecake Factory was open by the hand full of people standing on the corner waiting to be seated.

Jorge began sorting napkins and silver at a counter behind the two mustard brown cast iron lions that guarded the hotel's street entrance. The four men at the table were steady customers and he wanted to eavesdrop. The big tall one with the pockmarked, hound dog face, heavy jowls and droopy eyes was Sol Weinberg, CEO and Chairman of Centurion Insurance's board of directors.

Next to him sat someone too dapper and well spoken to be American. His nose was too sharp, his slicked back hair was too coifed, and his dark custom suit and cuff linked shirt was too out of place in Fort Lauderdale. The waiter also did not care for his sharp eyes. The foreigner was either Belgian, French or German. Jorge could not place the accent. His name was Jacques Leroux.

The waiter smiled inwardly. He enjoyed snooping for Felipe. The trick was not to be obvious. He knew the third man, Frank Hoffman, who lived across from the hotel's rear livery entrance on Southeast Fourth Street. He headed up Horizon Research, a small market research firm on contract to Centurion, or so went the scuttlebutt. He liked Frank. He was polite and courteous and addressed him as Mr. Ramirez, and not by his nickname, Jose, as everyone else usually did by mistake. And when Frank spoke to him in Spanish and called him by his first name, he used the correct name, Jorge. Frank was a good man, but slightly absent minded. Jorge felt an obligation to protect him.

Frank was more like a college professor than a business executive. He even looked the part, tousled hair and steel framed glasses. It was rumored that he was a past president of Las Olas University and checking up on Frank was on Jorge's 'to do' list when he was not so busy. He mused often about Frank's seersucker suit. It was all he ever wore and Jorge was beginning to think it was his only suit.

The fourth man, squarely built and dull faced with thinning hair was Max Zimmer, who occasionally met his associates at the hotel bar and engaged the waiter in long conversations on all sorts of subjects. One of those associates was someone named Calvin Bard. The waiter recalled only two things about Calvin Bard. He had thin lips and his eyes were icy blue. He had once stalked angrily out of the bar after threatening to fire Max. The waiter thought they were drug traffickers.

What was going on? Jorge Ramirez heard a cell phone ring and looked up. Frank Hoffman took the call, mumbled something and left the table. Passing Jorge on the way into the hotel, he winked at him. Where was he going? What was he going to tell Felipe when he asks? Jorge wanted to stay on Felipe Gutierrez's good side and kept him posted about the goings on at the hotel. He had even eavesdropped on a board meeting where Sol Weinberg discussed a new insurance company, Alliance, a joint venture between Sol and Harold Levy, someone recommended to him by that foreigner, Leroux, In fact, Alliance had already bought Centurion's underperforming assets for $500 million.

Sol was to remain Centurion's board chairman, giving up the CEO's post for the Alliance chairmanship. Harold would be Alliance's president with a CEO to be named later. The seven member Centurion board, hungering for the money, unanimously endorsed the move when Sol produced a certified check from the Miramar bank of Miami and Monte Fuego for $500 million.

In return for the money, Centurion's equity in several companies, namely, the Emerald House Jewelers chain, Boucher & Salieri, the Parisian precious gems firm, and a venture on the island of Monte Fuego called West Indian Mines were transferred to Alliance. Except for West Indian operation, these businesses had never made money and for the Centurion board, it was good riddance to bad rubbish. Moreover, it had been agreed that the money would be pro-rated among the board members in terms their equity participation in Centurion.

For example, Sol and Raman Salva, each of whom owned 40% of the stock, received $200 million apiece, while Max Zimmer, with 2.5%, pulled a check for $12.5 million. Jorge knew all the board members since they always met at the Riverside. There was Keith Bates, the short, stocky white haired diamond merchant. He had a 5% interest in Centurion. So did Sid Stone, the owner of the hotel, and Victor Duncan, the president of Emerald House. Their take was $25 million each. Leroux owned 2.5% of the stock, like Max Zimmer. He too walked away with $12.5 million.

Frank Hoffman was not a board member but Jorge made a point of keeping him informed about the Centurion-Alliance deal. Frank had thanked him and gave him a $100 tip.

He was not that friendly with Sid Stone who, besides owning the Riverside, owned the Delmar in Connecticut and the Brittany in San Juan, Puerto Rico. Sid was a pharmacist turned innkeeper and a self-made millionaire who, like like Ramon Salva, had backed Sol years ago when Centurion was a startup. Jorge was privy to other trivia. Keith Bates had two beautiful, blonde twin daughters, Denise and Danielle. Danielle was married to Victor Duncan and Denise was married to Felipe's father, Emilio Gutierrez. Emilio was in his sixties and Victor was in fifties; the twins were in their thirties as was Felipe, and Jorge could not help but wonder how long those marriages were going to last. Felipe said nothing, but Jorge noticed that Felipe was Denise's constant companion when Emilio was away.

Keith Bates also had a lunatic son, Quentin, who was in his twenties. The only thing Jorge knew about him was that he headed a private militia group called the White Knights and that he was currently languishing in a Cuban prison.

The waiter jumped to attention when someone in a tan blazer over an open white shirt appeared at the door to see what was going on. Tall, swarthy and with a cynical expression glued to his face, he nudged the waiter and nodded in the direction of the table.

"See if they want more coffee, Jose," he said. "And then go to the kitchen and help out. The dishwasher never showed."

"Yes sir, Mr. Stone. Right away, sir."

The man in the tan blazer waved casually at the men around the table and then ducked back into the hotel.

Jorge was greeted by incoherent grunts when he approached the table and interpreted the sounds as a call for more coffee and rolls. A busboy came to clear away the leftovers with Jorge in tow for replenishment.

Sol Weinberg had three papers open in front of him, the Miami Herald, the Sun Sentinel and the San Juan Daily News.

"Here's the Sun Sentinel piece on Jonesey," he said in a low, monotone.

"Amison Rubin Jones (no age given), of Fort Lauderdale, died Labor Day in a drowning accident during a fishing trip to the Bimini islands. He was the manager of the Riverside hotel and a long time resident of Florida. Born in Louisiana, educated at Harvard University, he served in the Marines before moving to Florida. Married to the former Dolores Alvarez Santiago de Silva of the Dominican Republic who died at childbirth, he is survived by a son, Gordon, and a daughter, Deborah Delaney, and two grand children."

"Is that all?" The man with the foreign accent asked.

Sol looked up.

"You want more, Leroux? We're not even sure the guy is dead. Here's the stuff on Hank Lawrence. It's in the Herald."

He continued to read.

"William Henry Lawrence (again, no age given) died after a short illness in Puerto Rico over the Labor Day weekend. He became an analyst for Horizon Research in Fort Lauderdale after graduating Harvard University and serving in the Marines. He is survived by a half-brother, Sidney Stone, who owns the Riverside hotel in Fort Lauderdale and other hotel properties."

Sol smiled at Leroux.

"At least we know that guy is dead."

The Frenchman scowled and exchanged glances with Max Zimmer.

"I had no idea Hank went to Harvard," said Max.

"He went there with Frank and Jonesey," said Sol. "They went to school together and served in the Marines together."

Frank Hoffman returned to the table at that point and sat down.

"That's right," he confirmed. "We were brothers even though we weren't related."

"In what way were Sid and Hank half-brothers?" Max asked.

"Different fathers, same mother," replied Sol. "The interesting thing is that Sid has just hired a private eye to find his brother."

"What about Luis Santiago?" Max Zimmer asked.

"Frank and Jonesey met him in the Dominican Republic," said Sol. "He had a sister, Dolores, who Jonesey married. That too was a long time ago."

Sol looked down at the newspapers.

"Here's the one on Bienvenido. It's in the English language San Juan Daily News."

Frank excused himself again, went indoors and Sol continued reading.

"Bienvenido Salvatore de la Maza, age 39, died in a fishing accident off the Bimini islands on Labor Day. Born in the Dominican Republic, he moved to Puerto Rico as a child where he grew up to inherit the Barberi business and fortune in Ponce and Miami."

Sol sighed.

"Well, that's where we are. We won't miss Hank and Bienvenido much; they were never with us. But we lost good assets in that Culebra mission."

"There's good and bad news here," Max said.

"How is that, Max," said Leroux.

"It's like I said in Bimini," Max replied. "You won a big one for Europol and the CIA by derailing that insurrection. Isn't that so, Jacques?"

Jacques Leroux allowed a thin smile to escape his lips.

"Yes," he replied. "The Horizon team certainly did a fine job for Europol and the CIA and Centurion can be proud. Now, Max, the bad news?" "Jonesey has many enemies and I'm afraid there'll be a price on his head if he surfaces," answered Max. "How do we handle that?"

"Carefully," answered Leroux.

"Amen," responded Sol. He looked at the rain cascading through the trees on the divider running down the center of the boulevard.

"Now, on another note," said Sol. "The Sun Sentinel is carrying a story on what we already know. 'Horizon Research has acquired 15% of West Indian Mines of Monte Fuego in the eastern Caribbean in accordance with the terms of a will left by Armando de Silva who died a few days ago at the age of 90. Mr. de

Silva is survived by a brother, Roberto de Silva, who lives in Puerto Rico. Another 15% was left to a Mr. Bienvenido de la Maza of Puerto Rico.' The piece goes on to list Amison Jones, Frank Hoffman, Hank Lawrence and Luis Santiago as Horizon's owners."

Jacques Leroux asked to see the article and Sol passed him the paper.

"An interesting mix," Sol reflected. "West Indian owns 50% of Emerald House and Victor Duncan in turn owns 20% of West Indian. Centurion had a 30% share, but that now belongs to Alliance."

His sorrowful eyes stared off into the distance.

"West Indian also sits on a gold mine, but it's always been dry. No gold."

Leroux looked up from the article.

"Europol does not usually meddle in business relations, but, if I may be so bold to ask, monsieur Weinberg. Since monsieur Lawrence is dead, to whom do his shares go?"

"Horizon's by-laws are clear, director," Sol answered. "These are limited partnership shares. With Hank dead, his shares are divided among the other stockholders. If Jonesey never returns, his action goes to Frank and Luis, and if they die, since I originally set up Horizon and financed it, everything goes to me. Last man standing wins all."

"What about Bienvenido's share?" Max asked.

"His estate will have to deal with that if he's dead," answered Sol.

The response failed to satisfy Max.

"Do counter insurgents and terrorists make good corporate executives?"

Those guys are trained killers."

"We're all trained killers turned business executives," Sol reminded Max. You're here because of your CIA position. Leroux is on the board because the CIA sends missions too hot to handle to Europol who farms them out to Centurion who in turn assigns them to Horizon. The other Centurion board members are in the same boat. Salva is an arms dealer and Victor and Keith have important global connections vital to the execution of our missions."

"Who are the other West Indian stockholders?" Max asked.

"They're no strangers to us," replied Sol. "Emilio Gutierrez holds 10% for his brother, Juan Duarte, the president of Monte Fuego. Victor Duncan owns 20%. Hernando Gomez, Estrella's father has 5%; Black Star Trading, that's Keith, has 5%; and Bienvenido has 15%. With the distribution of Armando's stock; Horizon has 15%. And of course Alliance has Centurion's 30% share. Too bad the mine is worthless. I'd have regrets otherwise."

"What did Horizon do to inherit Armando's piece of West Indian?"

"Those shares were held by the de Silva family of the Dominican Republic. Jonesey's former wife was a de Silva as was Luis. They took care of her folks when Dolores died at childbirth. Jonesey's mother-in-law died several years ago and Armando, his father-in-law, wanted to leave his share to Luis and Jonesey. He left it to Horizon to reward Frank for his long friendship with the family. Horizon was Frank's idea and Armando wanted to make sure it had a steady cash flow in between assignments."

Sol got up.

"Anyway. This is where we stand."

He beckoned to Sid and Max to follow him inside while Jacques Leroux waited for Frank and then followed him to Hamburger Haven where Dimitri ushered them into the converted garage behind the restaurant's kitchen that doubled as a storage and meeting room. Luis Santiago was having coffee and packing gear with Angelo at a corner table when they walked in. He got up and pulled Frank aside for a moment.

"Weather is clearing in the Biminis," he whispered. We're taking Red Fish out. You coming?"

Frank nodded and sat down at another table as Luis returned to his chores.

Leroux had apprently overheard or guessed what was afoot and said, "Send me the bill when you're done. And stop in North Bimini. Cecil Fergueson has a package for me. Now, let us talk. Any thoughts about your inheritance?"

"Should I have any?"

"West Indian Mines has always been a mystery to me, "Leroux said. "But the mystery concerns illegal trade in precious gems and priceless heirlooms that seems centered in Monte Fuego. This is a new development that leads me to believe that Armando de Silva's shares in West Indian may be worth more than they seem. This is peaking my curiosity."

"You have a point, director," Frank noted. "Is there something else?"

"Yes. If my hunch is correct, Horizon Research may be bought itself a new mission and perhaps even a small war."

"We could use a new mission," said Frank. "But not a small war."

"In connection to which, monsieur Hoffman, who hired the new waiter?"

"Jorge? Felipe Gutierrez hired him but I don't trust him."

"Neither do I. Nor do I trust Felipe."

Frank's voice sank to a whisper.

"But you know what? If he steps out of line, we'll kill him. We can kill Felipe too, but that will be a more delicate matter."

The rain fell harder.

CHAPTER 2

▼

Red Fish and Blue Eagle

"Red Fish, Red Fish. This is Blue Eagle. Come in, Red Fish. Over."

Amison put down the VHF radio and closed his eyes. His mind wandering off to a place somewhere between life and death where the departed rose up to face him in ghostly lineup. They were all there, including Harold Levy.

Whatever happened to Harold Levy, Amison's role model? He had thrown him out a window from the Alliance building in Philadelphia during a winter storm when he found out that Harold had participated in the murder of his second wife.

Yet it was Harold Levy who had once put their lives in perspective.

"The intelligence community is an extended family living in an onion. The outer skin is smooth and sweet smelling. Here we find the diplomats and cabinet ministers in their penguin suits carrying out foreign policy. Peel off that layer and we have find senior intelligence officers engaged in very high level espionage through diplomatic, corporate and celebrity functions. In a deeper layer are the professional assassins and special mission specialists like us. And finally, at the onion's rotten core are the thieves, hookers, swindlers and mercenaries who keep the outside skin of the onion smelling sweet. Our role is simple. The CIA calls Europol who calls us. We do the heavy lifting. We're the killers of last resort."

Amison came to with a start. He tried the radio again but it was gone. He opened his eyes and saw ceiling fan blades rotate slowly over him. The note that he wrote to Luis? Where was it? He never should have written it. If he was alive, then Phoenix sank with the note on it. If it did, no one would be any the wiser. But was he alive?

His hands felt the soft sheets surrounding his body. He was in bed, near an open window. He turned his head to the window and his eyes followed the sheer curtains that billowed from the breeze wafting in from outside through the windows and open French doors leading from the balcony over Las Olas Boulevard. Amison blinked. He was in his suite at the Riverside.

His hands wandered back from the bed sheets and felt his throbbing head and then his aching body. A faint smile crossed his thin lips. He was alive when he should have been dead. The last thing he remembered was hanging to Blue Eagle's life lines in the middle of a storm...

...Amison stared at a black eternity of bone drenching hell. He closed his eyes and only then did the memory of a vision emerge. His brain reminded him that he was lost at sea somewhere between the Biminis and the Straits of Florida. A suicide hit? In the Zodiac he had snuck up behind the big Hatteras and tossed his grenades over the yacht's transom. The Hatteras exploded and he saw Bienvenido swept overboard by the same steep wave that overturned the inflatable.

Amison clung to the Zodiac's lines until another swell righted the raft, and then with super human effort, he hauled himself back into the Zodiac and lay face up, dazed and panting. He groped for the raft's survival kit and retrieved an oil skin sweater and storm slickers, wriggling into them during a lull in the storm.

Somewhere out there was his catamaran, Phoenix. He also knew that the trawler, Red Fish, had been standing by. But where the hell was it? Why was he just now being haunted by pictures of Erica and Janice? He had not seen them in years. Was he dead?

Erica had dropped him for the security of marriage and went to live in some house owned by Hernando Gomez in some godforsaken island in the eastern Caribbean. And Erica's crazy cousin, Janice? She dropped Frank when Erica dropped Amison. But that was ok. Amison took up with Denise and Frank made it with Danielle. That too ended when they married.

Where in blazes was Frank anyway? And Denise, Leroux, Danielle and Harold. Well, Harold Levy was dead. Amison knew that for a fact because he had killed him. But good old Luis Santiago was alive, Amison was sure of that. He could see that bald head and broad Cheshire cat smile under a pencil thin moustache exposing a gold tooth along with the diamond pinky and his wardrobe of silk suits and lizard skin loafers.

The sea tossed the Zodiac from wave to wave like a cork. Debris from the Hatteras swept by, a banquette seat, a splintered outrigger, a cushion and a fighting chair. A portable freezer drifted by, its door open with food dangling out like entrails and for the first time in the years that he could remember, Amison leaned his head over the side and threw up. What a way to die, but at least it was a total release and relief. The problem is that he did not die; but the storm did end that night, and at dawn Amison peeked over the top of the Zodiac at the rising sun.

Not far off was something bouncing about in the shrinking swells. It was a large white flotation cushion with a body curled around it. It approached and an arm, slightly bent at the elbow, followed by a hand, its fingers curled as if ready to grasp a carousel ring, reached out.

Amison wrapped one arm around a safety harness for leverage, stuck out a free arm and hooked it around the out-stretched limb. His hand closed like a vise around the body's arm above the elbow at the same time that his own arm was seized in a steel grip. The body on the flotation cushion moved and the head to which it belonged turned to Amison with dark, smouldering eyes.

"Damn!" Amison yelled. "Bienvenido de la Maza. I thought I had sent you straight to hell!"

Bienvenido gasped.

"Hell would be too lonely without you, old man. Pull me in!"

"Call me 'old man' again, and I'll let you drown."

"Fine. I will call you senor Jones from now on. Now pull me in."

Amison braced himself, and with all his remaining strength he pulled the younger man into the Zodiac where the two men lay panting on its wooden floor boards.

Bienvenido was hurt and could barely move. His breathing was labored. "Agua? Da me agua!" Water? Give me water."

"I have two bottles. I can share one, even with a terrorist."

Bienvenido glared at him. He gasped but still he managed to cry out.

"I am not a terrorist."

"A terrorist and anarchist!"

"No anarchist," he moaned. "I am a revolutionary. And you have stopped my revolution. But I will live and I will succeed."

He took the bottle from Amison but could not remove the cap.

Amison grabbed the bottle from him, twisted off the cap and returned it.

"Nurse it," he said, "Or you won't live to see anything succeed."

His own anger was dulled by fatigue.

"I will win," Bienvenido whispered.

"And what will you win?"

"The right to be like you, senor Jones. The right to be just like you. That is the American way, is it not?"

He closed his eyes and his voice was almost inaudible.

"We are all bastards, senor Jones. We might as well die rich bastards."

"Is that what this fight is all about?"

Bienvenido laughed.

"No, senor Jones. Only in part. It is also over women."

"Women?"

"Si. La senorita. Denise Bates. You stole her from me."

"No way," Amison protested. "She left you for Jacques Leroux and then she left him for Emilio Gutierrez. I had her during the intermission between Leroux and Emilio. I never spoiled your act."

Bienvenido passed out and Amison cursed. He removed the VHF radio that was strapped to his waist and issued another distress signal.

"Red Fish, Red Fish. Come in, Red Fish. Over."

No answer.

He shut the radio down in disgust and closed his eyes.

Red Fish was actually near. The trawler had slugged its way over the Gulf Stream and began canvassing the waters off the Biminis in a light rain. Mike Quinn was at the helm and Virgil Holmes and Tucker Andersen worked the GPS and radar systems, taking turns on the radio with Chico Alvarez.

"Blue Eagle, Blue Eagle. Come in. Blue Eagle. Come in. Over."

No response.

Frank ducked in from the deck and threw off his slickers. His steel rimmed glasses were fogged and he had to wipe them off. He chanced to look at the gold watch on his wrist, one of three handed out by Ramon Salva on behalf of the CIA for their work in the Culebra mission. Luis wore his, but the third lingered in Frank's pocket. It was for Amison if he was ever showed up alive. It was almost dinner time.

"Anything?"

"Nothing."

"We have to find the boss," Chico kept repeating. in rapid fire English laced with a pronounced Hispanic accent.

"Jonesey's not dead!" Frank insisted.

Luis Santiago came in behind Frank. His bald head glistened from the rain and his slickers were drenched. His broad frame filled the doorway. His usual smile was gone and his lips were pursed, hiding his gold tooth. His thin black moustache was tinged with moisture.

"He's alive, I say," he growled. "We stay until we find him."

Virgil Holmes offered a more practical approach.

"Or until we run out of fuel," he added in his soft Louisiana drawl, his craggy face expressionless. He adjusted the pony tail band behind his head and said to Tucker, "I'm going up the tower, You coming?"

Tucker Andersen stroked his heavy beard, pushed his grizzly bear frame away from the table and followed his lankier partner on deck as Mike Quinn surrendered the helm to Chico.

Mike threw them all his enigmatic Irish smile. His heavy, red hands began working the wheel and communications equipment in the main cabin with the delicate touches of a professional harpsichordist.

They docked in Alice Town in North Bimini briefly to collect the package Cecil had ready for them and set off again when the sun went down, settling on the western edge of the Bahama Banks under a full moon. Red Fish kept its lights on and the vessel glowed like Christmas tree in the night. The effort was futile and the search resumed in the morning under a bright, hot sun. The noon hour came and the trawler heated up like a kettle. The sky was still and below decks, the faithful diesels chugged on. Only the tap-tap of their pistons broke the silence of the motionless sea. Frank stuck his head out the cabin door and yelled up at Tucker who was in the tuna tower.

"Anything?"

"Nothing. Some birds on the horizon off the starboard bow at two o'clock."

Mike Quinn had taken his customary post at the wheel and turned to Chico.

"Where's that?"

Chico studied the compass on the console above the chart.

"One hundred and five degrees."

He stared more intently at the chart.

"That t would be five miles due west of South Bimini."

"How far from here?" Frank asked.

Chico hit some buttons on the GPS next to the radar.

"About five miles."

Luis Santiago stuck his head out another porthole.

"How are they flying?"

"Circles," Tucker responded.

Chico and Mike exchanged glances and Frank's voice went up a notch.

"Let's move! One, zero, five!"

"One, zero, five! Mike repeated.

"That's it. One, zero, five!"

He dropped his hands on the throttles and pushed them forward. The big trawler groaned and barreled ahead at hull speed, cutting a path through the flat water. Twenty minutes passed and the birds were now easily visible. It was a band of sea gulls.

"Try the radio again," requested Frank.

"Blue Eagle, Blue Eagle. Come in, Blue Eagle? Over."

The men grit their teeth and said nothing until they were only a hundred yards away from the gulls who were cawing and shadowing a floating object. Tucker blinked and let the binoculars drop and dangle from his thick neck on their strap. He barked hoarsely from the tower.

"Something in the water!"

Suddenly, the ship's radio crackled.

"Red Fish, Red Fish. This is Blue Eagle."

"Boat!" Virgil hollered. It was the Zodiac.

Amison rubbed his eyes and found himself facing a rust stained hull. The bottom rungs of a rope ladder dropped over his head and moments later he and Bienvenido were being hauled up by several pairs of anxious arms.

Chico greeted him with a big grin and tears in his eyes.

"Welcome back, boss," he said.

Amison and Bienvenido were given water and sedatives and were asleep when Chico yelled, "Vessel coming astern, Mr. Hoffman."

Frank went out on deck and looked up.

"What's up?"

"Coming up fast!"

Frank and Luis ran out on deck to look. A boat was closing, It was a long nosed racer, throwing geysers into the air as it tore through the water. In the wheelhouse, the radio was receiving another signal. It was Jimmy Wales in one of Mike Quinn's cutters warning that a go-fast boat lay between it and the trawler. The tumult awoke Amison who went out to join the others. He braced his tall thin frame on the hand rail along the gunwales and waved at Chico who slid down from the tuna tower and handed him his binoculars.

"It's after us, boss," he said.

Amison looked through the glasses. The low profile racer barely touched the water, leaving a foaming rooster tail in its wake. He gave the glasses to Tucker who took one look, saying, "It must be doing fifty knots. Drug boat?"

"No. If it's drugs or cash they're after, they know slow trawlers don't carry much. They aim to take us down. Someone's on to us."

"Wales just signaled," said Mike Quinn. "He won't reach us in time."

"What the hell do they want?" Frank yelled anxiously.

"Beats me," Mike answered glumly. "I only own this tub. Frank. You're the man of the moment. You tell us. Who else knows we're here?"

"You don't understand, guys," Frank answered. "Our communications must have been breached."

"Breached big time," remarked Amison, looking around.

"Any guns around?"

Chico pointed to the main cabin.

"A shoulder mounted rocket launcher and one shell. No seconds."

"What are you going to do, Jonesey?" Frank asked.

"It depends on where we are," said Amison.

"Near the Stream," replied Tucker.

"Then, let's get into it. We can hide in the swells."

Tucker relayed Amison's instructions to Mike Quinn who immediately gunned the engines. The powerful diesels under the deck shook and snorted, and the trawler lurched forward into the Gulf Stream's fast rolling swells.

"This tub can't do more than twelve or fifteen knots," Mike complained.

"Don't matter," Amison said, running to the wheelhouse with Chico to retrieve the launcher and the missile. "The chase boat can't move any faster in the high swells than we can. That will even the odds."

Chico located the weapon, passed it on Gonzo who loaded it and gave it to Amison. Machine gun fire burst out but the rounds fell short and moments later, they were in the Stream, running in the troughs between the swells.

"What now?" Frank asked.

"You're the best shot here," Amison said. He handed the rocket launcher to Frank. "You go up the tower."

Frank appeared stunned. "Moi?"

"Yeah. You. Take the elevator if you can't climb."

"Fuck you, buddy. I'm too old for this."

"Right. And you won't get older if you don't get your ass up there."

Frank cursed, grabbed the loaded launcher and climbed up the tuna tower.

The racer was close but had to slow down for the swells. The trawler crew heard something like a pop followed by a whoosh. But nothing happened. It was a louder exploding sound that shook everyone on board. A water geyser mixed with smoke and flames shot upwards and the racer was gone.

Chico looked up at Frank, yelling, "You hit the fuel tank!"

"I didn't hit shit," Frank growled, huffing and puffing his way down to the deck. "It was a clean miss."

He returned the weapon to Chico and borrowed his binoculars to have a better look. An old converted cutter decked out as a research vessel appeared in the swells with Jimmy Wales manning a rocket launcher on the foredeck.

The cutter positioned itself on the trawler's port side and sent a boarding signal. The cutter kept its distance to avoid a collision in the swells and sent an all-clear signal.

Amison took the glasses from Frank. He could clearly see Jimmy Wales, a big grin on his face. With him was Desmond Lyons, the owner-manager of the Golden Lyon grill and restaurant at the Riverside. At the helm on the bridge house above the deck was Sid Stone.

CHAPTER 3

▼

The Inheritance

Amison was wide awake now. He remembered the parcel Frank had picked up from Cecil Fergueson in the Biminis. It contained twelve flawless, blue white two carat diamonds, each worth at least $100,000 to any wealthy buyer of precious gem quality jewelry.

The story, according to Frank, was that they were purchased by Black Star Trading from Kinshasa Export, a shipping company in Africa, and had been re-sold and re-consigned in Nassau at a markup to an Emerald House boutique in the city of La Fortuna on the island of Monte Fuego. It was while awaiting transhipment from Nassau to Monte Fuego that the diamonds were seized by the Bahamian customs people for Europol on a tip that they night be African conflict diamonds, that is to say, diamonds stolen by warring armies and then sold to finance military operations.

Frank was vague as to how Cecil had gotten his hands on the diamonds, and that worried Amison. Frank was great at the big picture but tended to be fuzzy on the details. What was clear was that $1.2 million in high quality stones had changed hands. Someone would be happy and someone would be pissed.

He raised his head and looked around. He was back in Fort Lauderdale, in bed in his suite at the Riverside hotel. How long was he here? How long was he sleeping? Where was everyone?

Where was Estrella Gomez and the million dollars in cash that had been stolen from Bienvenido's drug dealers. Where was his son, Gordon? How about Deborah, his daughter, her husband Mitch and their two kids? What were they up to? Was he still the hotel's general manager?

He assumed he still was since Sid had a special understanding with Frank Hoffman. He let Amison, Frank, and Luis use his hotels in return for 10% of Horizon's income received from its missions. If Horizon made money, Sid made money, and as an added bonus, Amison turned out to be a very good hotel manager.

"Your home base doesn't matter to me," he pointed out at a meeting once. Amison remembered being there, with Frank and Luis. "You're welcome at any of my places. You make money and I make money. I own the Delmar in Greenwich, Connecticut and the Brittany in Puerto Rico. They all work out for me and for you. But the best place is right here where we have connections with the police and Europol. Luis cultivated that relationship over the years when he was police inspector and now Jake Santana, his cousin, carries the torch as Europol's Florida coordinator.

"Besides, the Riverside is in the center of town between the New River and Las Olas Boulevard and is an easy in and out by water or by land. Frank lives next door. Centurion occupies the high rise above Jackson's Steak House a stone's throw from the Cheesecake Factory and Jacques and Max have offices in the opposite direction near the Floridian diner. Your boats use Mike's boat yard up the river and the hotel's bulkhead slips by the Sagamore House and we're minutes away from the airport. All our people work here and at Las Olas University where we park assets and where Emilio Gutierrez is its new president. I say we stay put."

Amison sat up and drew his legs over the side of the bed. Well, at least he could move. He pressed his bare feet upon the bare floor and tried to stand.

Success. His next move was to toss on the bathrobe lying on a chair next to his bed and then tried to take a few wobbly steps. More success. Now for a serious test. He made his way carefully to the combination living-dining room where a table had been set with breakfast foods, coffee and tea. How nice. Someone must have thought he would be hungry.

With somewhat more self assurance, he went to the tall open window on the long balcony. He took a deep breath and looked out upon the hustle and bustle on Las Olas Boulevard below.

"A Paris street with palm trees," Leroux had observed when he first set up his office in town.

Amison had agreed. It was downtown Fort Lauderdale's only full service hotel and was a goldmine and kaleidoscope in constant motion. Guest rooms and function facilities were booked solid all year around; business was brisk and restaurants were full. The boulevard, filled with clubs, flashy boutiques and sidewalk cafes, was a Mecca drawing a global crowd. Leroux had called it right; Paris with palm trees.

Amison could visualize the front entrance under the balcony, guarded by the two mustard colored cast iron lions. Flanking them were the sidewalk cafes belonging to the hotel's Golden Lyon and Indigo restaurants. It was early, but already from his suite's tall french windows he could see throngs of people strolling along the boulevard.

A loud triple knock interrupted him. Amison staggered on wobbly legs over to the door, opened it and in walked Sid Stone, followed by Frank Hoffman and Luis Santiago. Bringing up the rear was Sol Weinberg, hunched over a tray of breakfast treats that he clumsily pushed in front of him.

No words were necessary. They embraced like long lost soul brothers.

"Well," said Sid at last. "Are you ready to get back to work?"

Sid Stone was in his usual tan blazer, but while Frank favored seersucker suits and bow ties, Luis was back in one of his custom made silk suits. He had a big smile on his face.

"Brother-in-law. Welcome back to the world," he declared.

Amison drew his robe closer about him and drew cigarette from its pocket, lighting it with the gold lighter lying on the dining room table.

"How long have I been here?" he asked, inhaling deeply.

"A week," replied Sol. "You were dehydrated and had some hyperthermia, according to the doctors. Otherwise, you're good to go."

"What about Bienvenido?"

"Back on his feet and taking inventory of everything he inherited from his late wife and father-in-law. Centurion holds the policies on his estate and the first thing he did when he came to his senses is make a premium payment. So I'd say his fighting days are pretty much over."

Sol Weinberg, a good six and a half feet tall and wide in his rangy gray suit and red tie, amply filled the space in which he stood. His voice was deep and he spoke deliberately and slowly.

"Anyway. We're stuck with him as he is with us."

Amison's lips formed a weak smile.

"You think? What makes you say that?"

He was still a bit dazed but was gradually coming back to life.

"His late father-in-law, Acting on Armando de Silva's advice, put up the money for Alliance to buy up Centurion's underperforming assets early this summer. Since he's dead, the money is owed to Bienvenido."

"Why would Barberi have done that?"

"Because Armando convinced him that several rich veins of untapped gold lay under the West Indian Mines property and he needed a majority of all the stockholder votes to tap the mine. I didn't want Centurion to be involved, and I still don't. But I don't give a damn what Alliance does. So the $500 million buyout made sense. I made out as did Ramon Salva and the other Centurion stockholders. Alliance planned to vote with Barberi and Armando to force West Indian to start mining for gold this Fall. But with Barberi and Armando dead, I'm not too sure what's going to happen."

"This is a tough one, Sol," said Amison. "Can we eat and talk?"

"Great idea, but first we have a little something for you," said Frank, pulling a shiny object out of his pocket.

Amison finally had his gold watch and lost no time putting it on his wrist.

"Your wish is our command," joked Frank, making a mock bow.

They sat down around the table. Luis passed around the coffee and tea and they began working on the rolls, making small talk and catching up with each other's trials and tribulations.

"Any progress on your mom and brother?" Amison asked Sid.

"Nothing yet," answered Sid. "But I'm hopeful. Anyway. Stop talking and eat. You look like shit."

"I have to say, guys," Amison finally admitted in his thin Louisiana drawl after downing a cup of coffee and several doughnuts. "I never thought I'd see daylight again."

And then he abruptly shifted gears.

"Are my clothes still here?"

"Bedroom closet," said Luis. "Chico had them cleaned and pressed."

"What about my piece?"

Sol pulled a thirty-eight caliber revolver from inside his jacket.

"You should trade this relic in for a semi," he suggested. "You can get more shots out of it."

Amison took the weapon and examined it.

"One shot is all you get in this business," he explained. "This will do."

"Talking about getting shot, Jonesey," said Frank. "Sammy Luke broke into your suite while you were away and was shot dead a day later with your watch on his wrist. Jake Santana wants to see us about it."

"It might have been a case of mistaken identity," Sid added.

"Whatever," said Luis. "We're down a good second story man."

"What possessed him to rob me in the first place?" Amison asked.

"I kind of remember that he was hanging around the hotel when Salva gave us the watches," recalled Frank. "Maybe he got greedy."

"Or someone thought he was you," suggested Luis. "You're both ugly."

"Well," said Amison. "I'm more worried about the Red Fish stuff. We're in someone's short hairs, and I want to know who and why. Who knows. Some idiot just could have mistaken him for me if I'm on an active hit list."

With no satisfactory answer forthcoming, he changed the subject.

"What happened to the diamonds?".

"Leroux thinks they're conflict diamonds from Africa," answered Sid.

"With luck, we'll get to keep them," said Frank. "But that's his call."

"That would be nice," noted Amison. "How did Cecil get them?"

"He didn't say," said Luis. "We'll have to ask him.".

"And Kinshasa Export? What's that?" Amison asked.

"We have to find out," replied Luis.

"And who blew your cover?"

"Don't know," replied Frank.

Amison said nothing. He busily devoured a buttered roll and downed a cup of coffee while he carefully eyed his friends.

"So, what's been going on while I was gone? Where are my kids?"

"They're fine, and they know you're alive," answered Luis. "Gordon is in Asia with Mitch on a Europol assignment and your daughter is in Canada with Mitch's folks. Your grand kids are in school there."

"What about Estrella?"

"She went to Armando's funeral in Miami after opening her beauty parlor at Charlie Hand's barber shop," said Luis. "She flew to Monte Fuego from there to see her father."

"Hernando?" Is she staying with him? That place is a shack."

Frank looked at Amison with some trepidation.

"No. You'll never guess, Jonesey."

"Try me, Frank."

"Remember Erica Brown? Estrella is staying with her while she's looking into opening a beauty parlor in La Fortuna."

"That sounds like trouble waiting to happen."

"Easy, Jonesey. Erica is changed. She's not the same woman anymore. She owns a clothing boutique in town."

"Well, Estrella has my money. Those two broads are probably having one hell of a time spending it."

"Women are thieves," said Luis. "They're worse than us."

Amison shook his head in dismay.

"If Erica is around, Janice can't be far. You hear from her, Frank?"

Frank's nervousness increased and he let Sid answer.

"She manages the Brittany," he said. "I thought we'd give her a fresh start."

"You trust her?"

"She's mellowed out," insisted Frank. "I'll tell you more later, but right now we have more important things to talk about."

Amison noticed the scruffy growth of beard on his face in the wall mirror.

"You guys talk while I go shave," he said with disgust in his voice.

He dropped the revolver in his robe's pocket and left for the bedroom from where, moments later, they heard the sound of an electric razor.

"So, what do we have, guys?" Amison asked from the other room.

"For starters, Horizon owns 15% of West Indian Mines," Luis announced.

Amison's voice trailed in over the razor's buzz.

"I figured. What's the catch?"

"No catch," said Sol. "If Horizon isn't into foreign investments, it could sell its share."

"Was gold ever found?"

Luis snickered.

"Many rumors but little gold."

"The gold may or may not be there," Sol explained. "West Indian is also a holding company. It owns half of the stock in Emerald House and half of the stock in Boucher & Salieri. On top of dividends, it gets 50% of their gross revenues in the form of a management fee. That makes West Indian a cash cow for its owners."

"I like that," Amison yelled from the bedroom. "How did Bienvenido make out in Armando's will?"

"He got 15%."

"So, tell me again, why did Centurion sell out?"

"Why not?" Sol snapped back. "Everyone made out. It put $200 million in my pockets and $200 million in Ramon Salva's pockets overnight. The other Centurion board members can't complain either. Keith Bates, Victor Duncan and Sid here each got $25 million and Zimmer and Jacques Leroux ended up with $12.5 million apiece. That's better than monitoring a cash register at long distance that's in the hands of thieves we can't trust."

"Fair enough. So now that Alliance owns 30% of West Indian and Horizon has 15%, and Bienvenido has 15%,. What happens?"

"Nothing unless a majority wants to resume mining. The old guard opposes any mining operation," Sol called out. "They have Juan Duarte's support who prefers resort hotel development over mining."

Sid agreed.

"It's something to consider, Jonesey, if the mine is dry. The place is ripe for resort development and West Indian could get in on the ground floor. I might even make an investment."

"How does Emerald's equity distribution work?" Amison asked.

Sol counted on his fingers.

"Let's see. Victor Duncan has 20%; Keith Bates and Boucher & Salieri each have 10% ; West Indian has 50% and Centurion had 10% which now belongs to Alliance."

"And Boucher & Salieri?"

"Paul Boucher and Louis Salieri each own 30% of the company for a total of 60%. Black Star Trading has 10% and Carib Financial has another 10%, with Centurion's 20% share having been moved to Alliance."

"I have a stupid question for you, Sol."

"Shoot."

"Who owns Alliance?"

"I own 50% and my new interim CEO owns 50%."

"Does this new interim CEO have a name?"

"Harold Levy."

Amison guffawed so loudly it could be heard in the livingroom.

"I have one more stupid question for you, Sol."

Sol Weinberg's eyes turned to the sound of Amison's voice.

"What's that?"

Amison emerged from the bedroom, freshly shaved in a shirt, blazer and slacks and with a wide grin on his face.

"How come people I kill never stay dead?"

CHAPTER 4

▼

Strange Bedfellows

Amison was back in top form a few days later and went to have breakfast with Frank and Luis at their office quarters in Hamburger Haven's converted garage. It was a combination storage, meeting room and pizza kitchen where the ovens, vented through the ceiling, stood in a corner. The space had once accommodated two cars, but its garage doors were locked from the inside. A fire door, also inside bolted, was the only way out into the parking lot behind the restaurant.

Amison took one look at the grimy surroundings and grinned.

"It's good to be home again," he remarked.

It was to be a busy morning. Dimitri and Angelo caught Amison on the way in to say that they were worried about their brother, Anastos.

"The night Sammy Luke was wasted," Dimitri said, "Ernie was supposed to be catching a cab to the airport. He never boarded that flight to New York and my relatives up north never saw him. We're worried, Jonesey."

"Did you file a missing persons report with the police?" Luis asked.

"Here and in New York," answered Angelo.

"Doesn't Klondike Pete do the graveyard shift on airport service?" Frank wondered aloud.

"I'll speak to Virgil," said Amison. "Klondike is Max Zimmer's driver and errand boy. Virgil can snoop around and ask some questions."

Teddy, Jake Santana's driver, came by trying to raise money for one of his sons who was college bound.

"Whatever you can do for me, I'll appreciate," said Teddy. "And I'll always pay you back; you know that. I'll even pay points."

"Forget the points," replied Amison with a wave of his hand. "Maybe you can work it off. We can use good help."

"That would be great," Teddy responded. "It's hard to get by on what the county pays."

Pete Kowalsky came by next to welcome Amison for Max Zimmer who was busy at another meeting. Big and fat, he was called Klondike Pete by the people he worked with.

Angelo came in from the kitchen as Pete was chatting with Amison, giving him a large brown bag of hamburgers-to-go with all the trimmings.

"Here," he said to Pete. "This is the lunch Max ordered."

Virgil, who was in the room, laughed.

"They're all for you, Pete. But save one for Max."

Angelo wanted to speak with Pete, but Virgil waved him off. He unlocked the fire door and let Pete out into the parking lot.

"What's going on?" asked Pete.

"It's about Ernie," replied Virgil. "Did you take him to the airport?"

"I got the call," said Pete. "But he wasn't there."

Virgil returned to the room and relayed Pete's words to Amison, saying, "I think he's lying."

Sol Weinberg and Sid Stone arrived, but were kept waiting in the restaurant until Amison was done with his business. When they were finally allowed in, Sol immediately brought up the subject of Harold Levy.

Amison put up his hands to slow him down.

"I do have reservations about him," he stated, "But they're part of broader issues facing Horizon Research. You want to tell him, Frank?"

Frank cleared his throat.

"This concerns our equity in West Indian Mines, Sol. Do we keep it, sell it, or adopt a wait and see attitude?"

"Wait and see," Sid suggested. "You might be pleasantly surprised."

"Then, there's this thing with Sammy Luke's murder and the strike against Red Fish," continued Amison, turning to Luis.

"That's right," said Luis. Santana tells me that a casing found near Sammy's body was military ordnance. Now, I had a private lab check out the casings on Red Fish. They also were military issue; standard fifty caliber shells."

"What about bugs at the hotel?" Amison asked. "Government issue, too?"

"No. Plain Jane security stuff. They're all over," replied Luis.

"That's right," confirmed Virgil. "Al Garcia and I keep getting rid of them and they keep coming back. But the hotel is clean as of now. For how long, I don't know."

"How about background checks on all hotel employees?"

"That's being done. We're also updating our data base on Centurion, West Indian, Emerald and B&S stockholders."

"Not good enough. I want everyone profiled," insisted Amison."

"Everyone?"

"Damn right. Everyone. Stockholders, directors, employees, relatives, even friends and lovers. Even Zimmer and his boss, Calvin Bard."

"That takes time," said Sol.

"And money," Sid added as a reminder.

"So what," said Amison. "We have time and money. These hits are the work of someone who issued a contract on us. We need to find out who and why."

Dimitri stuck his head in the doorway to announce that Charlie Hand had dropped off an envelope. Amison nodded and Dimitri came in and gave him a fate, sealed brown envelope.

"Thanks, Dimitri."

But instead of leaving, Dimitri went over to the ovens.

"Do you guys mind if I get these going?" he asked. "People are going to be ordering pizza for lunch."

He opened up the ovens, scraped away some hardened soot with a long iron poker and started them up. On the way out, he took another envelope that was tucked away inside his apron and gave it to Amison as he was leaving.

"Before I forget," he said.

Sol couldn't help but notice the exchange of envelopes and asked, "What's going on?"

"I made investments," answered Amison simply. "I need a steady cash flow in my old age."

Luis smiled.

"Jonesey is reason why Charlie Hand's barbershop and Hamburger Haven are in business."

"He also bankrolled Mike Quinn's boatyard," said Frank.

Amison leaned back in his chair and looked carefully at Sol.

"Talking about old age," he began. "Let's consider Hernando Gomez. He has 5% of West Indian and is no youngster. What happens when he dies?"

"Estrella Gomez inherits his estate?" Luis responded by way of a question.

"And if she dies?"

"Maybe she has a will," suggested Sol.

"She's too young to be into wills," Amison snorted.

Frank snickered.

"You'll make sure to keep her alive," he said.

"I'm glad to hear that we're all so eternal," said Amison sarcastically. "But assuming that we're mortal, shouldn't we consider the folks who have become our new sweethearts at West Indian, Emerald and Boucher & Salieri?"

Sol placed his big hands on the table.

"I admit we have strange bedfellows but we're stuck with them. Keith Bates is a diamond merchant with global contacts. His Black Star outfit is the glue that keeps Emerald and B& S together. Those outfits couldn't buy costume jewelry without him. We need him despite his politics and his kids."

Amison helped himself to the appetizers brought by Angelo.

"Is that why he's on the Centurion board?"

"That's one reason. The other reason is because he and I have a special deal going. We also use his daughters on occasion. They're cat burglars and great jewel thieves."

"They aren't a problem for me, Sol," Amison pointed out. "We've worked with them. I also like Ramon Salva and get along with Keith. But Quentin, his kid, is a loose cannon. How long is he going to be in that Cuban prison?"

Sid Stone coughed, making Amison stop.

"Quentin was set loose a few days ago in a prisoner exchange deal with Havana."

Amison shook his head.

"Not good. We had him put away in the first place after he and his White Knights gang shot up a town outside Havana. He's going to come after us the first chance he gets and his dad is going to back him up."

"You're over reacting," said Sid. "I'm sure Keith is reasonable. He knows his kid is crazy. Business is business."

Amison was not convinced.

"Maybe," he responded. "Business is business, but blood trumps money."

"Jonesey may be right," Frank noted. "But we'll have to wait and see. At least Denise and Danielle are almost sane."

Sol smiled.

"Marginally. They're kleptomaniacs. They like to steal but they're not quite as crazy as their brother. We use them to recover stolen merchandise insured by Centurion. Didn't you guys have a fling with them a few years ago?"

"It was a one night stand for me and Jonesey. That's all," said Frank. "It's not even a memory for us."

Amison shrugged.

"I don't know, Frank. Men forget, but women never forget."

"It doesn't make any difference what they do for a living and what you did to them," Sid stated. "We've used the twins on some of our missions and they were a big help and they can be helpful again."

"I'm sure," continued Amison. "It's their role in West Indian that worries me. Let's not forget that they're trophy wives. Denise went from Bienvenido to Leroux and then bounced off to marry Emilio Gutierrez."

"That's right," added Luis. "And Danielle left Harold Levy at the hospital door to marry Victor Duncan. If we're stuck with Emilio and Victor, we're stuck with their spouses, If Emilio and Victor die, they enter the scene from stage right, If something happens to Keith, they and brother Quentin enter the same scene from stage left, leaving us stuck in the center."

Sid nodded.

"That's assuming that the guys all die in short order. What are the chances of that happening?"

"You have a point," said Luis. "But Jonesey has a point on the inheritance thing. Estrella's dad is a diabetic with a bad heart and is old. If he dies, we have no guarantee that his daughter will continue to see things our way. It's pretty much the same way with Denise and Danielle. If their husbands die, they take over their estates, and I imagine Quentin gets a piece of the action if his dad dies. If all that happens, then what?"

Sol dismissed Luis's concerns.

"Victor is still relatively young," he said. "He's in his forties and healthy.

Emilio is older, but he too is healthy. The girls are going to have to wait a while before their husbands keel over."

Amison was about to reply when Chico showed up at the door.

"Can I speak to you for a moment, boss?"

He rose from his seat and chatted with Chico in the doorway for a few moments. Chico nodded, smiled at the others and left.

"Mike Quinn wants Chico and Virgil for one of his salvage jobs," Amison informed the group. "I told him it's ok but not to get lost. But getting back to this so-called inheritance. Since it's a done deal, let's move on. Besides the mine, what else is in Monte Fuego?"

"Monte Fuego is a small, round, hilly island in the eastern Caribbean," Sid explained. "It has a kidney shaped harbor on its western side. I was there a few weeks ago and met with Juan Duarte Gutierrez, Emilio's brother. He was recently re-elected president and I was interested in buying land for a hotel."

"Where's the main city?"

"La Fortuna? It's the island's port and capital and lies along a narrow plain under the hills around the harbor. It's an old city of narrow streets dating back to the Spanish conquest. Behind the downtown area around Avenida Nacional bordering the harbor are slums crawling up an uneven slope to the suburbs in the hills. A river. The Rio Blanco, divides the city but a bridge joins the two sides. The executive palace and parliament buildings are on Avenida Nacional on the river's north side and Europol's new Caribbean offices, the shopping district, hotels, clubs, restaurants and casinos are on the south side and extend all the way to the new container terminal and hospital at the south end of the harbor. There, Avenida Nacional turns inland and makes its way around the dead volcano to the airport and the other side of the island."

Luis's eyes opened.

"Did you say La Fortuna has casinos?"

"Yep. Monte Fuego is a laissez -faire society with gambling, prostitution, everything. It's also a tax haven."

"What about the volcano?" Amison asked.

"It's called El Diablo, but it's quite dead. It rises up from the center of the island and the river runs westward around it through the hills until it reaches the city and empties into the harbor."

"How about the mine? Is it near the volcano?"

"No. I mentioned it because the airport is on the mountain's eastern side and is a two hour, bumpy car ride over a bad road around El Diablo to La Fortuna. The mine starts at the north wall of an old fortress and former prison on top of a hill facing the Caribbean on the north side of the harbor's inlet. I was at the fortress and from it you can see across the breakwater at the mouth of the inlet to the hospital at the other end. The mine property covers about a square mile of land. And by the way, the old fort is called La Fortaleza by the locals."

"Does the mine include La Fortaleza?"

"Negative. It's Juan Duarte's executive residence right now. I met with him when I visited and he said the fort belongs to the government and that it's for sale. I think it could easily be turned into a classy resort hotel. I'd like to buy it if the price is right."

"What about Hernando? Doesn't he live on the property?" Luis asked.

"Yes. He has a hut over a cave on a spit of land jutting out into the sea at the bottom of the cliff under La Fortaleza. Water flows into the cave from the sea at high tide, but that's besides the point. Juan Duarte tells me that Hernando is making noises about being the mine property's owner. He's saying also that he owns La Fortaleza."

"He may be looking for a payoff," said Luis.

Amison's mind was on another tack.

"Sid, how much money are we talking about for your dream project?"

"Lots. I want something bigger than the Atlantis in Nassau."

"You have that kind of money, Sid?" Amison asked.

"No, but control over West Indian gives us enough equity to collateralize a construction loan once we show some earnest capital. Keith and Salva might be interested."

"Keith has cash," said Sol. "But his politics are to the right of Attila the Hun and I don't need that kind of connection. It's bad for business. Ramon Salva is even richer but we're not friends. I'd unload him if I could. But I need money to do that." Sol placed his big hands on the table. "I need to ease Bates, Salva, Duncan and Zimmer out of Centurion. That's where Alliance and Harold enter the picture."

A long moment of silence followed.

"I knew I should have done a better job killing him," moaned Amison

"Listen Jonesey. I know you have your own gig going and that's good. But I need you and I need Harold and Bienvenido who's backing him. And you're going to need us. Let's make this a go."

"Will Keith keep supplying Emerald and B& S?" Luis asked.

"I'm sure," answered Sol. "He gets paid on delivery and he likes money as do his daughters. As for Quentin, we will have to watch him."

Dimitri came in from the kitchen at that moment with a large tray filled with platters of Greek salad.

"Here's what you ordered, boss." he said, placing the tray on the table. "Thanks, Dimitri."

They started eating while Dimitri stood idling at the door. Amison noticed that he was not leaving and asked, "What?"

Dimitri hesitated at first, looking at Sol and then at Sid.

"It's all right," said Amison. "What is it?"

"It's those visa applications for my brothers back home…"

Amison interrupted him, saying, "Done while I was gone, including the employment contracts. Have your brothers check our embassy in Athens."

Dimitri's face was beaming.

"Thanks, boss."

The Greek restauranteur turned and left without saying another word.

"How come he called you boss?" Sid asked.

"Everyone calls Jonesey the boss," explained Luis, giving Amison a toothy grin. What do you say, boss? It's worth a try. We're all behind you."

"I say it's a go," added Sid.

Frank was equally positive.

"Why not, Jonesey," he said. "If it doesn't work out, you can always kill Bienvenido and Harold again."

"Fine," Amison finally agreed. "Let's do it. Now, what do we do?"

"How about you and Frank paying a visit to Monte Fuego."

"You can also stop and check things out at my hotel in San Juan," said Sid.

"And maybe you'll want to pay Erica a visit," Frank suggested meekly.

"Eat your salad, Frank."

CHAPTER 5

▼

La Fortuna

A brief tremor rippled through Monte Fuego while Amison and Frank were en route to the island. Damage was negligible but it triggered a land slide from a hill on the West Indian Mines property. The slide buried the only mine shaft and destroyed Hernando Gomez's home when the cave over which it stood collapsed into the sea. Luckily, he was away when it happened.

Jacques Leroux put the matter in perspective as he drove Amison and Frank from the airport to La Fortuna where he was in town to supervise the opening of Europol's new Caribbean office.

"Monsieur Gomez is lucky and so are you," he said. "He is alive and so you have no need to worry about the disposition of his shares. Furthermore, the issue of what to do about the mine is moot until a way is found to get into it."

"I guess that word of our inheritance is out," Amison mused.

Leroux grinned from the driver's seat.

"Of course."

He swerved to avoid a cow crossing the road and Amison grabbed his seat for dear life. But the Europol director drove on, pointing to an old billboard that announced, "Welcome to Monte Fuego, Your Caribbean Paradise."

"The mine closing will stalemate everyone for months, and that makes me happy," he said.

"Why?" Frank asked.

"West Indian Mines will need a court order for permission to re-open the mine and I know that Juan Duarte Gutierrez will fight it because his brother, Emilio, wishes to keep it closed."

"Emilio must have reasons," Amison said.

The smile disappeared from Leroux's lips.

"Could be. But Emilio also listens to Denise and she has her own agenda."

"She may be listening to her dad."

"On occasion. Not always. She is meaner, and crazier."

"Well, you must have a handle on her. Weren't you both an item once?".

Leroux's lips curled at Amison's question.

"Denise was my ruin. It began with lunch and a glass of wine near my office in Paris and pretty soon I was keeping her in a Miami apartment until my wife found out. Denise cost me my wife, my family, a fortune and got me farmed out to the Caribbean. I wanted to marry the woman and gave her an expensive four carat diamond ring from Boucher & Salieri in Paris. She turned me down and kept the ring. She turned me down for Emilio. She said she was going to marry him because he could keep her better. And now I hear that she is having an affair with one of her father's diamond suppliers."

"Sounds like you miss the woman. Maybe you should try to get back with her," said Frank.

Leroux waved a hand in disgust.

"Never," he replied. "She stole my honor, my love and my money. I want her dead. Perhaps you can arrange that as a personal favor to me."

They arrived at the foot of La Fortaleza where he left them in the hands of the security guards at the gate.

"This is Juan Duarte's executive residence," said Leroux. "Perhaps you can visit my new office on the Avenida Nacional before you leave Monte Fuego. It is in the presidential palace on the square next to the Rio Blanco."

"How long will you be here?"

"Until tomorrow. Then it's back to Fort Lauderdale. Good luck with Juan Duarte, senor el Presidente."

Frank asked Amison what he thought of Leroux's story as they were being escorted up the path to the old fort.

"It's a human condition," he responded. "No man likes to lose a woman to another man.".

Juan Duarte Gutierrez, a portly, pleasant faced man in his fifties, met them personally at the door of his villa that was built into the fortress's ramparts behind the battlements facing the sea and the harbor. He gave them the usual sweep-of-the-hand tour, proudly pointing out the new container terminal and hospital at the far end of the harbor past the breakwater. Inbound traffic used the channel directly under La Fortaleza and outbound vessels exited through the channel from the container terminal.

"A gift of your government," beamed Juan Duarte after sitting them down on the veranda. And he proceeded to tell them how the economy had picked up with the opening of the terminal. Even the crime rate had dropped.

"Speaking of crime, we had a recent event," he said.

"Looting as a result of the earth tremor?"

Juan Duarte shook his head.

"No. A boat was attacked and sunk a few miles outside the breakwater. It was reported to us by returning fishermen."

"Did anything happen to Hernando?" Frank asked.

Juan Duarte shook his head.

"No. He was in town and knew nothing."

Amison fished a cigarette from his blazer jacket and lit up, cupping a hand over his lighter against the afternoon breeze.

"What about the fishermen who reported the incident. Are they around?"

"They said they were from Antigua and left after being questioned. I doubt that we'll ever find them again. Antigua is a day away by boat and many boats from Antigua and other nearby islands throw their nets in our waters. At any rate, the story is that two fisherman were in a sailing skiff just out of sight of land when a great white yacht come to a stop two hundred yards away. It had been seen several times in the same spot over the past few years but no one had an explanation for its presence.

"The witnesses claim they saw the yacht lower a tender that powered past the skiff toward the cave under Hernando's house. It returned two hours later and again passed the skiff. Then, two helicopters lifted off the yacht and sank the skiff and tender with rockets. The choppers returned to the yacht which then sailed away."

"Did the incident take place at high water or low water?" Amison asked. "Low water," answered Juan Duarte. "The witnesses were concealed by the reef which is submerged at high water. If the attack came at high water, they would probably not have been left alive. Of course we have no evidence of anything having happened. Our witnesses are gone and the cave is gone. All I have is an anecdote."

Amison puffed away on his cigarette and gazed out to sea.

"Put enough of these anecdotes together and pretty soon you have a story."

"Perhaps," said Juan Duarte. "It would be nice to locate that yacht."

"There are many large yachts on the ocean, Excellency;" noted Frank. "But a yacht that size with armed helicopters is a warship. It needs a port of call for fuel and maintenance. Where would it find it?"

Juan Duarte scratched his head.

"Not here. We're too small. Maybe in the larger islands."

"Any ID on the yacht?" Frank asked.

"Nothing reported. Why would such a yacht want to blow up its own tender along with an innocent sailing skiff?"

"To eliminate witnesses," replied Amison. "If the yacht was here before, it must have important business worth killing for. That cave sounds more and more interesting."

Juan Duarte agreed.

"We shall have to find out. I have sent a dive team out to retrieve whatever evidence can be found and we are trying to dig our way into the cave. In the meantime, your friend, Dr. Alstrum, was here last week to give me annual physical examination," he continued. "I find his energy amazing. He is still making his rounds to see his patients, especially those insured by Centurion. I like him and your Sid Stone who feeds me the latest gossip from the States."

Amison put out his cigarette.

"Is Sid Stone interested in Monte Fuego, Excellency?"

Juan Duarte leaned forward and stroked his gray handlebar moustache as a servant approached with a tray of rum cocktails and placed it down on the table. Frank was about to lift his glass when it began to shake ever so slightly.

He blinked, adjusted his glasses and examined his drink before he finally raised it to his lips. On the narrow beach a hundred feet below the veranda, a flock of birds screamed and flew away in a flurry of flapping wings.

"I am sure he spoke to you about his desire to promote tourism in Monte Fuego by turning the West Indian Mines property into a resort. He also has ideas about La Fortaleza that my government is willing to sell to him or to West Indian at a very attractive price."

"He certainly has ideas," Frank echoed.

Juan Duarte relaxed. Changing the subject again, he asked, "And how is my brother, Emilio?"

"He's doing well at Las Olas University," Frank responded. Then, sensing an opening, he countered with his own question.

"Where does Hernando Gomez live now that his house is gone?" Amison inquired.

"Here at La Fortaleza. He wants to stay and says that his property includes West Indian Mines and La Fortaleza. But he is old and does not know what he is talking about. However, word of his claim must have spread because when Julio Maldonado flew Ramon Salva's jet in a few days ago, he had with him a passenger from France who came to see Hernando about buying his house."

"Julio? Estrella's ex-husband is here?"

"Yes. With the Frenchman. But about Hernando's home; it was more like a shack than a house and it is difficult to see why anyone would have wanted it unless it was part of a larger tract. The house alone is useless. Only a dirt path connects it to the main road at La Fortaleza. It was fine for Hernando and his bicycle but a car could not negotiate that path. Dear old Hernando. He always avoided our century."

"How's his health?" Frank asked.

Juan Duarte sighed.

"Getting older, like us. Henry Alstrum says his diabetes is under control, but his heart is bad. Julio, Estrella and Ramon keep an eye on him when they're around but that's not often enough. It is too bad we have so few commercial flights. If we had more, it would be easier to care for the sick and elderly. It would be good for tourism as well. That is what stunts our development. No non-stop flights from America or Europe. Not everyone has a private jet like Ramon. There can be no tourism without non-stop flights."

Frank nodded and pointed to the harbor south of the veranda.

"What about cruise ships?"

"Your navy makes courtesy calls, but cruise ships hardly ever stop. Most tourists are not attracted to dead volcanos."

Frank took a sip of his drink.

"Where's Julio now?"

"With Hernando and the Frenchman."

"Who's the Frenchman?" Amison asked.

"Paul Boucher of Boucher & Salieri. This whole affair is bizarre."

"I'm wondering," Frank said. "You mentioned that Ramon Salva visits on on occasion. Does he have interests in Monte Fuego?"

"He has a vacation home here and I hope to cultivate his interests," replied Juan Duarte. "But he is not our only visitor of note. Keith Bates also owns a home on the other side of the island. We met a few times and according to him he would like to expand the Emerald and Boucher & Salieri stores in La Fortuna. I told him I would give the companies special tax breaks if they did that."

Amison and Frank exchanged sidelong glances while Juan Duarte looked at the sun sinking in the west.

"Quien sabe. Who knows? Maybe someone will find that legendary gold."

Frank's eyes opened wide.

"Gold?"

Juan Duarte laughed.

"Easy, my friends. That is the way Ramon Salva and Keith Bates reacted as well when they came here. I assured them that no gold is here. The gold lies in tourism. La Fortaleza was originally built as a prison to keep slaves shipped from Africa until they were sold in the Americas. It is rumored that gold at one time was stored in caves carved out of the rock below us until it could be shipped to Spain. The problem is that the caves and the gold have never been found."

He lifted his glass at the last rays of the setting sun, saying, "Salud.".

Amison and Frank raised their glass together.

"Health," they echoed.

"Well, here in Monte Fuego," concluded Juan Duarte. "We have health and love but no pesetas."

A very nervous servant suddenly appeared in the doorway.

"Con su permiso, Excellency," the servant began. "With your permission, Excellency, Hernando has been taken to the hospital."

Juan Duarte sat up in his chair.

"What happened?"

"He took ill an hour ago. Shall I call your chauffeur?"

"Si. Yes, yes. By all means. Right away."

He looked at his guests.

"Care to join me? I could use the company."

The road from La Fortaleza took them to Avenida Nacional that circled the harbor on the way to the hospital. They passed the presidential palace facing a great square overlooking the harbor. Its golden dome deflected the last rays of the setting sun into a tall, needle like obelisk that rose from the middle of the square. As they crossed the bridge over the Rio Blanco dividing the city, they saw an American destroyer and warships from England, France, Holland and Spain in the harbor.

"Your country is important to us," said Juan Duarte. "Without your foreign assistance, we would cease to exist."

The drive from the far side of the bridge to the El Convento hospital took another hour along a promenade and seawall that separated Avenida Nacional from a narrow beach where couples and groups of young people now gathered under graceful palms to catch the early evening breeze. Sunset gave way to a warm humid dusk that turned into night as the presidential motorcade reached the emergency room entrance.

Juan Duarte left his police escort at the door and rushed inside with Amison and Frank. They were immediately ushered through the emergency rooms to a corridor where Hernando Gomez lay on a bed. Two men stood by nervously and as a nurse and doctor checked his pulse.

The old man was thin and his leathery skin looked pale under the overhead florescent lights, and yet he was wild eyed, alert and defiant.

He raised his head when he saw Juan Duarte and waved his free arm.

"El Dorado," he cried out. "I have found El Dorado."

Juan Duarte grabbed his hand and tried to calm him.

"Take it easy, my friend. Try to rest."

Hernando would not be deterred.

"It's gold, Excellency! Gold! I even found diamonds!"

The nurse lay the old man's pulse hand down on the stretcher and shook her head.

The doctor took a reading and then examined the fisherman's chest.

"Heart attack," he said.

"From a diabetic seizure," she added. "He is delirious."

Juan Duarte turned to one of the two men.

"Did you bring him here, Julio?"

The man called Julio nodded.

"Yes," he replied. "We were meeting with this gentleman here," and he pointed to his companion, "when Hernando collapsed. We drove him to the hospital."

The president looked at the other man.

"And you are?"

"Paul Boucher of Boucher & Salieri."

"Oh, yes, the Paris jewelers."

"Yes." Paul Boucher confirmed.

"What brings you to our small island nation?" Juan Duarte asked. "We are but a tiny speck in the Caribbean with nothing but bananas and sugar."

"I wish to buy his home," he replied. "But of course that will not happen."

Juan Duarte scowled.

"Are you two gentlemen friends?"

Julio Maldonado shook his head.

"No, Excellency. I flew him in at my boss's request."

Juan Duarte now turned his attention to Paul Boucher.

"Ah, tell us, senor Boucher. What is so special about Hernando's house?"

"I was looking for a house on water for a good price," Paul said.

"Not so," cried Hernando. "He wants my gold. I saw the treasure with my own eyes. It even shines in the water at low tide."

He started coughing, breathing heavily at that point, and the doctor gave him a sedative mixed in a glass of water that the nurse quickly brought over.

Amison disliked hospitals in general and this one in particular, He thought they were death chambers. Here, he found the long corridor with the yellow walls and vinyl tile floors oppressive, and now he was stuck with a dying man.

Hernando was growing weaker. His face was gray and his frail body was barely concealed by the ill fitting hospital frock. His arm, the color of chalk, trembled as his hand reached out and grabbed Juan Duarte's sleeve.

"El Dorado," he gasped, looking anxiously at Paul Boucher. "I cannot talk here. I want my daughter. Where is Estrella. She will help me."

The jeweler began sweating. Amison remembered him now. He had met him in Paris when he accompanied Emilio to buy Denise an engagement ring. He smiled, recalling the fling he and Denise had behind Emilio's back during the course of a mission for Centurion. In any case, Emilio and Denise married and he never saw the jeweler again.

Two pictures lingered in his mind's eye. Denise was a beautiful, blue-eyed blonde with dancers' legs and Paul Boucher was sweaty and shifty eyed. The jeweler was now in a blue suit and plain brown tie that Amison swore was the same outfit he wore in Paris.

Paul adjusted the tie under his jacket, pulled a handkerchief from the rear left pocket of his trousers and wiped the sweat off his brow. His small beady eyes followed Hernando's every move behind thick, steel rimmed glasses.

"What does he mean?" Paul asked.

Amison thought it best to ignore the question.

"I don't know," Julio replied.

"Neither do I," said Juan Duarte.

He was on the verge of crying and tried to avoid the old man's eyes. It was clear that he was dying.

"I am sorry, old friend," whimpered Hernando. "We will talk at a better time."

"No problem," said Juan Duarte. "First things first. The treasure can wait."

"What's going on?" Paul demanded to know. What is he saying?"

He leaned over the stretcher as if he expected to learn something new.

Hernando smiled feebly and squinted.

"There is nothing. Nothing."

He was suddenly seized with another coughing fit.

"My God," he cried. "I am dying!"

He lay there helplessly and looked imploringly at Amison while the nurse summoned two passing attendants.

"Tell my daughter I love her," he said.

Amison seemed slightly embarrassed.

"Don't worry," he replied. "I will."

"And take care of Estrella. She is the flower of my life."

He pointed to a cloth bag at his feet.

"Please give it to her."

Amison nodded and took the bag.

All they could do was to watch the two attendants roll the stretcher through the operating room's swinging doors at the end of the corridor.

Juan Duarte was left standing alone with his two guests and Julio and Paul Boucher. They walked slowly down the hallway and sat down on chairs near the operating room to wait, their voices echoing strangely in the hallway.

Amison thought he heard a faint hollow sound in the distance followed by a slight vibration or tremor that seemed to come from a furnace starting up. The corridor lights dimmed but not long enough for anyone to notice.

"Is she the one who once worked at the Riverside hotel where the memorial luncheon for Hank Lawrence is to be held?" Juan Duarte asked.

Amison turned to Frank.

"What memorial luncheon, Frank?"

Frank grinned sheepishly.

"We've been talking about it," he replied. "We even thought you'd do the eulogy. But I think the function will be at the Brittany."

"Amison raised a hand in protest.

"Count me out. And if it happens, don't invite me."

Juan Duarte tried to be diplomatic.

"Of course my attendance depends on my official schedule. But in any case, Hernando's daughter is here in Monte Fuego. She should be informed about her father's wishes."

"We can do that later," Frank said.

Juan Duarte promptly turned his attention to Paul Boucher.

"So, you want to buy in Monte Fuego."

"I thought it might be a good idea," Paul responded.

"Let me tell you something, Paul. We are a small pancake in the middle of the Caribbean. From the center of this pancake rises a sleeping volcano. We have sugar, bananas and palm trees. East of the volcano is desert inhabited by lizards and cacti. West of the mountain we find jungle, rain forest, large bugs and strange animals. Twenty thousand of us live in Monte Fuego, and most of us are here between the rainforest and the sea because this is the only part of the island with drinking water. This is the land that God forgot."

"Is Monte Fuego so poor?" asked Boucher.

"Yes," Juan Duarte confirmed. "You would do better elsewhere. But if you want to buy something here, you must first consult with our government. We can direct you to better opportunities on the east side of the island."

"Personally, I'd stick to jewelry," said Amison. "Like the African diamonds you deal in."

"You must speak to Keith Bates about that. He buys for us and for Emerald House."

"I thought Emerald House dealt directly with Boucher and Salieri."

Paul shook his head.

"No. They buy from Keith Bates at Black Star Trading. We only appraise diamonds and have them authenticated and certified."

"Does he sell conflict diamonds?" Frank asked.

"No. Of course not. We would not certify them otherwise."

The doctor and his nurse emerged from the operating room at that moment.

"Senor Julio Maldonado? Senor Bouchard? Your Excellency?"

Everyone stood up.

Hernando Gomez was dead., but Juan Duarte was seething.

"I want the body examined," he fumed.

CHAPTER 6

▼

The Proposition

"It was murder," said Frank over the cell phone. "With three suspects: Julio Maldonado, Paul Boucher and Estrella Gomez. Where are you anyway?"

"San Juan, at Sid's hotel," Amison replied. "Where are you?"

"I'm still in Monte Fuego. How come you didn't stop to see Erica when we were in La Fortuna?"

"Oh, I don't know," responded Amison somewhat defensively. "Sometimes it pays to leave the past alone." Besides, I don't have a good feeling about that damn place."

"La Fortuna?"

"La Fortuna and the whole island. There's an air about it that bothers me. It smells like death warmed over. When are you leaving?"

I'm flying out tonight. How are things in San Juan?"

"At the Brittany? Fair to middling. I saw Janice. Why didn't you tell me that you two were an item again?"

Amison could feel Frank hesitating.

"I thought about it," he replied at last. "I'm not getting younger. My wife is gone, my kids hate me, I have no pets and I want to settle down. Do you have any plans, Jonesey?"

"I hate plans, Frank. Long term relationships never worked out for me, and they've worked out worse for the women I was with. The lucky ones drifted away and the others died. I don't know why but it seems that I always leave a trail of blood in my wake when it comes to women."

"You're over reacting, man," said Frank.

Amison tried again to rationalize his position.

"Maybe. But if you recall, those women almost cost us our careers and our lives once when it turned out that they were hooked up with the wrong side."

"That's true," replied Frank. "But the girls were greedy and I was running a con game and got blind sided. Things are different now."

"You think?"

"Everyone deserves a second chance." As an afterthought, Frank added, "If you speak to Janice, don't talk about Keith Bates and his daughters. Erica and Janice know the twins. They went to school together."

"That's another thing, Frank. I did a number on Denise and you had a thing with Danielle in Connecticut until Victor Duncan came into the picture."

"Good point, Jonesey, and Harold had her before me. But what the hell, life without a tightrope would be boring, wouldn't it, Jonesey?"

"I guess. But tell me. What's new in Monte Fuego?"

"Juan Duarte had an autopsy done on Hernando's body and tells me that his medication was switched to induce a diabetic seizure. That's what brought on the fatal heart attack."

"What about Julio Maldonado and Paul Boucher?"

"Flew off with Estrella that night. Juan Duarte called Leroux for Europol to issue an international warrant for the three of them but Leroux convinced him to hold off until after they could be questioned. I think he wants to wait until he finds out more about yacht with the choppers. Right now, they are persons of interest."

"Estrella too."

"Especially Estrella since she inherits Hernando's piece of West Indian. It's a good thing for us that you have a cozy relationship with the woman."

Amison laughed.

"It's good for her too and we'll have to see how that plays out, Frank. How about the incident with the yacht and choppers? Anything?"

"Juan Duarte's divers came up with some shell fragments and turned them over to Europol. If he's half right, we're talking about a single vessel strike force equipped with two attack choppers. Unless it's part of some country's navy, we're talking about a filthy rich maniac with big toys trying to protect something very important."

"How many filthy rich maniacs do we know, Frank?"

"Enough to fill a police lineup, Jonesey."

Amison sighed.

"Luis needs to start tracking down the boat and choppers," he said. "And we need to find a way into the mine."

"Luis is working on the boat," replied Frank. "The mine is another problem. It's sealed tighter than a drum. I heard a rumor that the cave under Hernando's house led to the mine but it's rubble now. Juan Duarte ordered has equipment is on order but it's going to take months to arrive. As matters stand, there's no way in and no way out."

"Do you think Hernando actually owns La Fortaleza and the mine?"

"Good question. A title search might give us an answer. I asked for one. I may have more information more when I see you in Florida."

"Want to know what I think?"

"What's that?"

"Someone is upset at West Indian's new stockholder organization and at the noises that Hernando has been making. That makes the attack on Red Fish, the chopper attack on the fishermen and Hernando's murder related."

"I'll buy that," said Frank. "Now, prove it. I'll see you back in Florida."

Denise Bates Gutierrez lived in a penthouse apartment in a flashy high rise building facing the Brittany hotel. It was also a stone's throw from the Caribe Hilton that rose high above the old fortifications of San Jeronimo on the edge of the lagoon that separated Old San Juan from the Condado's tourist district along Ashford Avenue. Amison could not understand why Sid bought the old hotel but was pleased to see from the books that it was full.

"It's a great location," Janice said when they went over the books. "We get the overflow from the Hilton and, except for our suites, rooms here cost less.

By the way, How's Jorge Ramirez doing at the Riverside?"

"Why do you ask?" The question caught Amison by surprise.

"Oh, nothing. We used to date when he worked here. He wanted to be in Florida so I introduced him to Felipe who hired him. We're still friends."

Amison dismissed the conversation as small talk and moved on.

"I noticed a beach between the Brittany and the Hilton. Do the guests have beach access?"

"Yes. It's public and a problem for the Hilton. Its hotel security can't stop outsiders from walking through the hotel to and from the beach. There's also open access to San Jeronimo."

"How come you know so much?" Amison asked.

"I'm a part time tour guide at the San Jeronimo," she answered simply.

Janice was a pretty woman. Long, brown hair tied back in a bun and a shapely figure tucked into a blue jacket and skirt ensemble gave her a smartly attractive appearance. But her voice was humorless and distant. It grew only slightly more animated when she gave him Denise's phone number. It was funny, but there was always something about Janice that left him cold.

He called Denise at dinnertime.

"Quien es?"

"I have come to take you away from all this," Amison answered.

"Ruby! This is a surprise. What are you doing here?"

"I'm at the Brittany," he replied, "going over the books."

"You're always going over the books," she said. "If you took care of your women the way you take care of Sid's books, you'd still have one today."

"I'm willing to make a fresh start. How about dinner at the Ritz Carlton on Isla Verde near the airport?"

"Are you paying?"

"Why? Have you blown your husband's allowance?"

"Close. I'm blowing dad's allowance. I'll see you downstairs. Get a cab."

Denise, blonde hair, great legs and all, showed up in a dark cocktail dress and stilettoes. With her hair pulled in a bun over her head, she stood eyeball to eyeball with Amison,

"Great hairdo," he said, giving her a light kiss on the cheek.

"Is that the best you can do?"

Their second kiss was longer, almost passionate.

"That's better. Now, I'm ready for dinner. "And by the way, Estrella did my hair. She also does Danielle's hair. I'm glad you like it."

A twenty minute cab ride dropped off them under the Ritz Carlton's canopy. They went directly to the hotel restaurant inside and were given a corner table where they ordered drinks.

"I hear that Frank is back with Janice," Denise began. "How is he doing?".

"Ask him," answered Amison. "He waited until today to tell me."

"I thought he was still interested in Danielle."

"He was until she bounced over to Harold and then married Victor."

Denise smiled.

"Do you miss me?"

"I can't sleep without you."

"You're such a great liar, Ruby."

"Always. But say, what have you been doing? Any great gigs?"

She shook her head.

"Pickings are slim, sweetie. Something is going on between dad your boss, Weinberg, leaving me and Danielle dry. I need work, So, I've become a sales associate for Boucher & Salieri at their Hilton boutique. Emilio arranged it."

"Oh? I was wondering about that."

"Emilio says it'll keep us going until things get straightened out."

"Do you love Emilio?"

"It was a marriage of convenience. Danielle and I went to school with Erica and Janice. We went our separate ways after graduation until we met at a party a few years later. By then Erica was working for Emilio while he was at the University of Puerto Rico in Rio Piedras. One thing led to another and you know the rest. I thought he had money and married him. I never realized that dad was calling the shots for Emilio as he was for Victor Duncan. Whatever they have, they have through dad. Life's good, but I want me own action. Do you have any suggestions?"

Amison could not contain his curiosity.

"What about Danielle? Is she also on the job market?"

Denise threw him a knowing look.

"We're both on the job market. But you know my sister, Ruby. She likes to lie low until the price is right. She's playing housewife but that's about to end. She's going to divorce him just like I'm going to dump Emilio the first chance I get."

"I don't follow."

"Emilio and Victor have been screwing around."

Amison tried hard not to grin.

"How shocking."

Denise took his hand in hers.

"Don't be, sweetie. They were playing the field before we married and they still are. Emilio is screwing Erica and Victor is doing Janice."

"Such a small world. I'm sorry to hear that."

"You're not sorry and neither am I," said Denise. "Anyway," she went on. "It works out fine. Neither Emilio nor Victor are great in bed. They're like hard boiled eggs. Three minutes and they're done. They're no bargain and no damn good to us."

"How do you know all that about Danielle?"

"We're sisters, sweetie. We talk."

Amison decided not to pursue the subject. He had his hand in hers and she placed her other hand over his.

"We had great times, Ruby," said Denise. "You should have called sooner," "I was busy."

That's a copout, Ruby. We're birds of a feather. We belong together. I told you that we should have run off together when we did that job in Paris."

"We should have, I guess."

"We were going to run off to the islands with the stuff we stole and live happily forever after. What happened?"

"Nothing. We're here, aren't we? And you're doing good. Look at the way you're living, a condo in a luxury high rise, the clothes…"

Denise frowned.

"Danielle and I are the female ends of brokered marriages that dad set up. His deal with Sol Weinberg is stalemated, and we're stuck in the middle."

Their drinks arrived and Amison raised his glass in a toast to lift her spirit.

"Here's to your next gig."

Denise giggled and raised her glass.

"To us."

She stopped smiling and turned serious.

"Tell me, Ruby. I know you're still in the business. Are you here to hit on me or to make a hit."

Amison feigned shock.

"That's not fair, Denise. "This is a business trip."

"Bullshit, Ruby! I know you. You're a hit man. Pepito told me."

"Pepito?"

"Yes. Bienvenido de la Maza. He's a former lover, in case you've forgotten. He's here in Puerto Rico pulling together the businesses he inherited from his late wife and father-in-law. I hear you had a hand in their deaths."

"That's an old story," said Amison. "The old man caught me together with his daughter. He shot her by mistake and someone shot him in the back. I was a lucky innocent bystander. I never had a contract on them. And I don't have a contract on you, your sister or your brother."

"Ah hah! Then you admit to still being a killer!"

Amison stiffened in his chair and his nostrils flared.

"If that's what you want to believe," he snarled, "that's fine with me." Fishing some some money out of his pocket, he threw it on the table and started to get up. But Denise grabbed his hand and forced him to sit down.

"Damn it, Ruby. How are we going to make it together if you have such a thin skin? Besides, Pepito also told me that you saved his life after you tried to kill him. He said you intended to kill yourself too."

"Who the hell told him that?"

"Your brother-in-law, Luis Santiago."

"He did? And did Luis or Bienvenido tell you that we're partners in a mine in Monte Fuego?"

"Yes. West Indian Mines."

"What else can you tell me about it?"

"So, you're here on business after all."

"Ok. You win. Business and pleasure."

A waiter came over for their dinner order.

"If I tell you about the mine, will you be nice to me?" Denise asked when the waiter had left.

"Promise," replied Amison.

"Liar. And will you make sure that Danielle doesn't get hurt?"

"Always. Here's the thing," he continued. "Luis Santiago, Frank and I have been sitting ducks ever since we inherited a part of West Indian. Someone in our circle wants us out and we need to find out who that is."

"It's not anyone in your circle," said Denise.

"How do you know that?" Amison asked.

"Because of that deal dad has going with Sol Weinberg and you guys are part of it."

"You mean Frank's asset recovery scheme that has you women stealing high end jewelry?"

"Right, sweetie. But only jewelry sold by Emerald and insured by Centurion at its original invoice cost. We've been turning the loot over to dad who then sold it to Emerald's South American branches at a double markup over Sol's reimbursement cost using Ramon Salva's contacts. Things in South America usually sell for twice as much as they do stateside because of import taxes.

"It was beautiful and everyone made out. It also enhanced Sol's reputation, enabling Centurion to sell even more insurance policies on jewelry certified, authenticated and appraised by B&S You made out too."

"You're right," agreed Amison. "I was wondering why the action stopped. Horizon always handled the claims investigation for Centurion."

"That's how I know your friends aren't after you guys. The whole scheme can't work without Horizon doing the claims to keep everything legitimate. You're indispensable. Sol would be hard put to replace you guys. It's Emilio and Victor who are making a fuss and trying to force dad to cut them in for a piece of the action. That's why it all stopped."

The waiter returned with dinner and a bottle of wine and Danielle changed the subject.

"With Hernando Gomez dead, I imagine your girlfriend, Estrella, inherits his home and 5% of West Indian,".

"She's a good friend."

"Bull shit, Ruby," exclaimed Denise. "Estrella does my hair, remember? We talk, and Pepito says you like brown meat. Does she have better moves than white women?"

"Different," he replied.

Denise smiled suggestively.

"We'll see," she said. "Take me home after dinner. If I'm in a good mood in the morning, I'll tell you more."

They awoke in the morning to a tropical sun that lit the bedroom in brilliant colors.

"So, how was your night?" Amison asked.

"Too short," Denise replied.

Amison got out of bed, dressed and lit a cigarette.

"You should cut down on your smoking," Denise remarked.

Nag, nag! But he extinguished the cigarette anyway.

"What are you doing today?"

"I'm helping B&S set up their display for the San Jeronimo jewelry show."

"Anything interesting?"

"You bet," answered Denise. "They're featuring the Menorah of Titus. That thing is three feet tall, solid gold with two carat diamonds all over it."

Amison whistled and Denise smiled.

"It's a copy of the original that the Romans moved from Jerusalem during the reign of Titus. The original was worthless compared to the copy. It's on loan to B&S for the jewelry show by the Louvre in Paris."

"Who holds the insurance on the menorah?"

"Centurion."

Amison whistled again.

"It's a billion dollar policy." she said, grinning. But let's talk about us. You can solve my problem by killing Emilio and Victor. You have what it takes."

"Why not use Quentin?" Amison asked.

"He's a killer but not a hit man. You are."

"I'll take that as a compliment."

"So, I have a proposition. Let's trade. You kill them and I'll tell you who's really after you and your friends. You also get my pussy as a bonus."

▼

CHAPTER 7

Interlude

Amison returned to the Riverside from Puerto Rico in the early evening and hid the bag Hernando had given him in his suite. In the lobby, he encountered a highly apologetic Al Garcia who stopped to say that Luis Santiago had been shot and might be dead. Amison felt the blood drain from his head as his heart skipped a beat.

"It happened when he was playing golf with Jake Santana yesterday," said Al.

"Where is he now?"

"At the hospital on life support. I'm sorry, Jonesey. We'll miss him."

Amison mumbled something and went to Hamburger Haven where he found Virgil in the back room checking the security system.

"Glad you're back, Jonesey," he said without looking up. You've got a busy schedule ahead. Estrella is back and looking for you and Felipe left word that Max Zimmer wants to see you at Charlie Hand's barber shop tomorrow morning. He wants to meet with you alone at eight."

Amison felt like screaming.

"What about Luis?"

Virgil looked up in surprise.

"Who the hell said anything about Luis?"

"Charlie Hand just told me he was shot and might be dead."

"That's sheer bullshit, man. And how would he know Luis was shot?"

"You mean he's not dead?"

Virgil guffawed.

"It was a flesh wound. He's fine."

Amison began to breathe more evenly.

"How did it happen?"

"He was golfing with Jake Santana," said Virgil, "when a bullet nicked his arm. He went to the hospital for stitches and a sling. He'll be fine and should be here tomorrow."

"Where was Jake?"

"On the far side of the fairway. That bullet had Luis's name on it."

"How did you find out?"

"Luis's wife called me and I'm telling you now."

"Does anyone else know?" Frank, Sid, Felipe, Charlie Hand, anyone else?"

Virgil shook his head.

"Frank's away and doesn't know yet, and Jake and I thought we shouldn't say anything until we figure out what's going on. Besides, Felipe's off today. He's hasn't been here since last night."

"What about Jorge?"

"He's not due back until tonight."

Amison scratched his ear.

"Strange. How did Al Garcia know Luis was shot and who the hell told him that he might have died? Listen. Keep checking our security. Information is reaching people before it gets to us and that's not good."

"We've had problems since Charlie joined us," Virgil noted. "Do you know that since I set up the new system here last year, it's never been breached?" "I know," said Amison. "Frank also doesn't care for Felipe and Jorge."

"Give the word, boss. We can make those guys go away,"

Amison shook his head.

"Not yet. I want to know who they're talking to. Anything else going on?"

"As I said, Estrella is back. She has something for you."

Amison smiled.

"Good. How are the accounts? Are you on top of them?"

"You bet, boss. The only guy behind is Charlie Hand. Should we send him a reminder?"

"Not before I get a haircut tomorrow," said Amison. He suppressed a yawn and returned to his suite. It was late, he was tired and he looked forward to a good night's sleep. In bed and daydreaming his thoughts were interrupted by a knock at the door and a soft female voice.

"Senor Jones?"

"Estrella Gomez!"

Amison jumped out of bed, threw on some clothes and rushed to the door. He opened it without giving any thought to how unshaven and disheveled he must have appeared.

Estrella stood in the doorway in a new beautician's frock over a plain white dress, white socks and sneakers, a coffee cart next to her. When did he see her last? A week or a month ago? It felt like a year. Pleasingly plump, her thick, dark wavy hair in a pony tail, and the fullness of her breasts forcing her to keep her dress's top buttons open, she was attractive in a sensual way.

"Essie!" He could not forget the hours they had spent together in her trailer on the outskirts of Fort Lauderdale before he had left for the islands on the last mission. After a passionate hug and lingering kiss, she dropped a small satchel that she held in her hands.

Finally, he managed to blurt out in between their kisses.

"Essie. I thought I'd never see you again."

They stayed locked in each other's arms until he happened to glance down at the floor.

"What's this?" he asked, breaking away.

"Have you forgotten?" She said. "This is the million dollars that was stolen from Bienvenido's dealers. You left it with me before you went away. I have come to return it."

He kissed her again and placed the satchel in the hall closet safe, retrieving at the same time Hernando's bag while Estrella pulled the coffee cart into the living room.

"Your father gave me this for you," he said.

Estrella began to fight back tears.

"He was murdered," she cried. "Why would anyone want to kill him?"

"Maybe the answer is in the bag," replied Amison.

"Did you look?" Estrella asked.

"No. It's yours. You look. Has the Monte Fuego police contacted you?"

"The police can wait until we take care of our business," she said.

"Our business?"

"Si."

She opened the bag on the dinner table. It contained a few personal effects, a small leather pouch and a neatly folded map. Turning the pouch upside down, its contents spilled out.

Estrella gasped.

What looked like six, gem quality blue white diamonds, an assortment of gold wedding bands and bracelets fell on the dark mahogany table top.

"Your father was in the jewelry business?"

"No," she said. "But he always said gold and diamonds were on his land."

Amison took the folded map on the table, opened it and spread it out.

"Que es esto?"

A map," Amison explained. "An ordinary street map of La Fortuna from the hospital to La Fortaleza. Nothing unusual about it. Your dad knew his way around town. Why would he need it?"

He took a closer look at the map and noticed a series of seemingly random letters scrawled along the margin. The writing was faded and scratchy, is if recorded in a rush with a dull pencil. Amison held the map up to the light and read the letters out loud to Estrella.

"A, F, E, I, E, O, D, O, C, O, D, O. Do the letters mean anything to you?"

She shook her head.

"Is that his hand writing?"

"No. It is Roberto de Silva's writing."

"Why would Hernando keep a worthless map tucked away with jewelry?"

"My father and Roberto once worked together at West Indian and searched for an underground passage used to move slaves from the city to La Fortaleza. They thought it might go to the mine but I do not know if they ever found the passage."

"Where can I find Roberto now?"

"I hear he owns a small restaurant in Puerto Rico. But I plan to go to Monte Fuego to find out more," she stated bravely. "I will also speak to the police."

"We'll see," said Amison.

He put the map and jewelry back in the bag and placed it in the safe next to the satchel.

"It's too soon for you to travel to Monte Fuego. Your father's funeral can wait until I check a few things out."

Estrella breathed a sigh of relief.

"I knew you would take care of me," she said.

"I'll do that."

"And now, since you are my pirate, I want you to treat me like pirates treat their women."

Without another word, he took her to the bedroom.

"I am here to collect for watching over your money," she said with an air of rising self confidence.

"Oh? And what is it you wish to collect?"

Estrella drew back a few feet. Her softness in her voice turned became low and husky.

"I need you to take care of me the way you did the night before you went away, and then we can talk about the future."

She hiked her dress up above her thighs, let her panties drop half way down her thighs and spread her legs in front of him.

Amison tried to be nonchalant about the whole thing but his body tingled with exhilaration and anticipation that mingled with some apprehension. He had learned many years ago that while an occasional feast might be pro bono there was in fact no free lunch. There was sex for pay and there was free sex. From experience he understood that sex for pay was infinitely less expensive than free sex. But moments like this left no room for second thoughts. At his age, all return calls were welcome.

When they awoke early the next morning, she re-heated the coffee from the cart in the kitchen while he showered, shaved and got dressed.

"What will you do with the cash?" Estrella asked suddenly when he sat down to drink his coffee.

"You tell me," he answered. "The money is good but I don't need it at the moment. Do you want it?"

"Thank you," she murmured. "But I want you to keep it. I trust you. If my plans do not work out, I may need help."

"What plans?"

"I am going to marry."

The announcement stunned Amison.

"I don't follow."

"Of course you do, senor Jones. The women who know you well call you Ruby. I will never have that pleasure because I would want to be with you forever. A woman needs to be owned by a man and you will never want to own a woman forever. But I need to be owned by someone. I need a husband. I met a rich man. He proposed and I accepted. He will take good care of me."

"Is he nice?"

"Si. Yes. He is el senor Keith Bates. Last night was your wedding present to me."

"You may be making a mistake," Amison suggested.

"A mistake? Will you marry me, Ruby?"

Amison was speechless. This was the first time he had been asked such a direct question and called by his nickname, both at the same time.

"Right now?"

"You see? Commitment is not your middle name. La senorita Brown told me all about you. She wanted to make you hers but was unsuccessful. You should marry her, you know. She loves you."

Estrella leaned over the table and kissed him on the lips.

"I must go," she said.

"Will I ever see you again?"

"I will be easy to find if you need me. And I will find you if I need to. We will always help one another. I want only one thing."

"What's that?"

"I want to call you Ruby, like all your other women."

Amison sighed.

"You can call me anything you wish. How come you and Julio divorced?"

Estrella smiled coyly.

"No children."

"By choice?"

"No. Miscarriage. The doctors said I could not have children. Julio wanted children and so our marriage ended. But we remain good friends."

She stared wistfully off into space.

"It is good to be free, but it is also sad to be incomplete as a woman. It is like your loss of your friend, Hank Lawrence. Something is missing. I hear a memorial luncheon is being planned. Will you be doing the eulogy?"

Amison looked at his watch and a horrified expression came over his face. He jumped to his feet.

"You hear too many things, woman. I could never eulogize someone who tried to kill me? Not on your life. Not on anyone's life."

"Still, he was once your friend," she insisted.

He finished dressing, threw on a blazer and headed for the door.

"Will you remember me?"

A smile returned to Amison's lips.

"Always."

He gave her a lusty kiss and left her sitting in the kitchen as he bolted out the door into the hallway and ran down the stairs to the lobby.

Marry Keith. What a stupid idea, Amison thought. He wondered how long that relationship would last. Of course, Keith was after Estrella's inheritance.

He passed Felipe in the lobby. Standing nearby was a short, heavy set man with sun glasses in a knee length leather jacket. Amison mumbled something about forgetting his billfold and bolted up the stairs to his suite.

When he returned, the stranger and Felipe were gone and Virgil was waving a finger at him from the management office door.

"Going to the barbershop?"

"To meet Max. Have you seen Luis yet?"

"He's picking up Frank at the airport," answered Virgil. "Maybe you should wait. Why would Max want to see you at the barbershop alone?"

Amison stopped short.

"In my suite," he said. "You'll find a bag of jewelry and a map and one with $1 million in cash, Make copies of the map, get the jewelry appraised and then put it away with the cash in Hamburger Haven. And send backup to Charlie's. One more thing, get word out that Frank is offering $1 million for information leading to Sammy Luke's killers. Tell Frank when he gets here."

Virgil nodded and Amison headed for the barber shop.

CHAPTER 8

▼

The Haircut

Charlie Hand's barbershop catered mainly to the Riverside's management personnel and selected guests. Its street entrance was a defining landmark and the talk of the neighborhood: a massive brass lined revolving door salvaged from a defunct bank. Charlie was an air conditioning technician turned barber. When not at the barbershop, he took care of the hotel's cooling systems.

Charlie counted Amison, Frank, Luis, Sid, Sol and Felipe Gutierrez among his steady customers. Luis was bald but had his shoes shined and moustache trimmed at Charlie's. Felipe had a full head of hair (probably highlighted, or so Amison and Frank thought) and paid Charlie weekly visits. Chico Alvarez, Virgil Holmes, Mike Quinn and Tucker Andersen went there. Jacques Leroux, who had his own regular barber in Paris, would make an appearance when he was in town, as did Keith Bates, Victor Duncan and Raman Salva.

Amison needed no haircut and had no desire to see Max. He did however realize that Max's position trumped his. Not only was Max on the Centurion board, he was also a member of its advisory council that included Horizon's executive managers, Amison, Frank and Luis. It made no sense to snub him, especially since the CIA had proven generous in feeding missions to Europol that were passed on to Horizon. Besides, how long could the meeting take? But still, he had misgivings about it.

It was midweek and the shop had opened an hour earlier and only Charlie Hand was there. Max liked brevity and Amison thought this meeting would be undoubtedly nothing more than a short debriefing session.

Max was already there, sitting with his back to the window and reading a newspaper. He put it down when Amison arrived and sat down next to him. Charlie had a broom in his hand and was sweeping the floor.

"What's up, Charlie?"

"Same O, same O," replied Charlie. "Things are a little slow. How are you doing?"

"Not too bad. Have you taken care of Max yet?"

"Can't you tell? He should come here more often."

Max Zimmer managed a weak smile.

"I was waiting for you, Jonesey."

"Well, you guys chat while I go clean up."

Charlie left and Max gave Amison a sidelong glance.

"Sol says you and Frank went to Monte Fuego," said Max.

Amison nodded, saying, "I guess you heard."

"Sol updated me. However, I'd think that a homicide in Monte Fuego with foreign suspects would be of more interest to Europol than to the CIA."

Max Zimmer's flat, monotone voice was devoid of feeling and his roundish, expressionless face and light, watery blue eyes revealed nothing. Amison felt no need to tell him about his meeting with Denise in San Juan, with Estrella at the hotel and about Hernando's bag of goodies. It was clear that Max wanted the deflect everything away from the CIA.

"Oh, I agree, Max. Juan Duarte has already brought Europol into the picture and I'm sure the CIA need not be involved. But Horizon is involved since it owns a piece of West Indian Mines that seems to be worth killing for."

"That's a tall assumption, isn't it? Have you spoken with Victor Duncan?"

"Not yet, but I will. Have you?"

"Yes," said Max. "He believes West Indian has potential but that it needs professional management. And that's what I'd like to pass by you, Jonesey. I've been thinking about Horizon's equity in West Indian and about my own position. I've also been thinking about all the years you guys have been out there putting your lives on the line for us. I think it's high time for you to cash in your chips and get out before you all get hurt or killed. I can cut you a deal that will put you and your buddies on easy street for the rest of your lives."

"Why the generosity, Max?"

"I want to retire. Jonesey, and I want to invest in West Indian. Do you want to hear more?"

"Of course."

"I just finished speaking with Sol Weinberg and he agrees that Horizon may be over its head. The CIA can use a cover in the Caribbean and West Indian may be the ticket. I think I can arrange to have you bought out."

"How much?"

"For argument's sake, shall we say $10 million apiece for you, Frank and Luis? That's a good price for worthless land."

"I don't know, Max. What about Bienvenido?"

"I met with him and made him the same offer. He wants to think about it."

"You have that kind of money up front?"

"Don't worry about my end. You get cash deposited out of the country the moment you give the word."

"What about your position at Centurion?"

"That's not your worry. The CIA needs a Caribbean window and Horizon is that window."

"Have you consulted with Calvin Bard?"

"Yes. He's enthused like I am."

Amison feigned confusion.

"Are you saying that all of West Indian Mines is worth $200 million if all the shares are tallied equally?"

"You're a good mathematician, Jonesey."

"As you say, that a lot of money for worthless land."

"I'd jump on the deal if I were you," Max urged.

"I'm sure. But I want to see West Indian's financial statements before doing anything. I also need the Emerald House and Boucher & Salieri financials to see if West Indian might be worth more."

Max's voice went up a notch.

"On top of the cash, I can make sure you personally get a pension at a bird colonel's rank in military intelligence," he offered.

"That's mighty generous, Max. Do spooks have status in the Army?"

"It's paperwork. I can arrange it."

That sounds like retirement to me," Amison noted.

"Exactly. And that's what I'm coming to. We need new blood. Not that you guys are old, but there are other options open to us."

"I thought you were quitting the Agency."

"I am, Jonesey, I am," Max replied quickly. "I want to arrange everything before I leave. Besides, there's one more thing."

"What's that?"

"I'm aware that a contract is out on you, Frank and Luis. I might as well tell you that it includes Harold Levy and Sid Stone."

Amison looked at Max sharply.

"Is that your doing, Max?"

Max shook his head.

"I have nothing to do with it. And I can't stop the contract and I can't call off the dogs. But I can tell you who issued it and give you the names of the dogs. That will give you a head start at retirement."

"I can't give you a decision right now," said Amison.

Charlie Hand came out from the back, a barber's cape over his forearm.

"Too bad," Max replied pleasantly. "Maybe you'll feel differently later." He picked up the paper and continued reading.

Amison thanked him again and went over to the barber's chair.

"Trim?"

He sat down and stared at his reflection in the mirror. He wanted to see past his shoulders out into the street where three men were lounging near a parked car, but his line of sight was partially obstructed by Charlie Hand.

"A trim is good," agreed Amison."

He sat down and Charlie draped the cape over his body.

Ten minutes later when Charlie was about done cutting his hair, he looked at Max.

"You sure you don't want a haircut"

Max raised his hand.

"Maybe. I want to finish the paper first."

He turned the chair around to let Amison off and inadvertently gave him a clear view of the street. Sure enough, the three men he thought he had seen in the mirror were still out there. One of the three was wearing sunglasses and Amison recognized him as the stranger at the Riverside. He nicknamed him 'Shades.' The second man was wearing boots. 'Boots,' he called him. The third had on driving gloves. Amison decided that he was the driver and named him 'Gloves.'

Shades walked over to the barber shop door while Gloves climbed into the car and started the engine. Boots followed Shades, gripping his jacket to keep it closed while Charlie Hand, humming a tune, left for the back room. Shades entered the revolving door and Boots waited for it to turn to come in behind

Shades. The revolving door swung around and Shades stepped into the shop brandishing a machine pistol in his hands.

But his timing was off. Amison dropped to one knee, revolver in hand, as the machine pistol went off over his head, shattering the wall mirror. Shades never had another chance. Amison fired and Shades fell against the revolving door, trapping Boots between the panels.

Shades sank to the floor, blood oozing from a hole in his forehead and Max Zimmer ducked under the table, a knife falling out of his pocket as he dived.

Amison blinked when he saw Luis Santiago wave to him from outside. A second shot rang out and the glass in the revolving door behind Boots broke into pieces. Boots teetered out and fell on the sidewalk.

A very tall shape that Amison did not at first recognize suddenly appeared behind Luis. He was over six feet tall, dark featured and very solidly built. He sported an over-the-trousers, short sleeve tropical shirt that exposed a pair of long, muscular, tattooed arms. Close cropped, salt and pepper hair over dark, reptilian eyes and a wide nose defined a handsome face except for the lips that curled in a sneering grin. It was the big Jamaican, Harold Levy.

Harold fired a round over Luis's head at Gloves who had emerged from the get-away car to help his friends. The shot caught him squarely in the chest and threw him back against the car door. His legs gave way under him and he was dead by the time he crumpled to the ground.

Inside the barbershop Max Zimmer was still hiding under the table. Amison calmly tucked his weapon back into the holster set in the small of his back under his trousers, wiped the loose hairs from his shirt and helped Max to his feet. He picked up the knife Max had dropped and threw it in his own pocket.

"You can tell Charlie it's safe to come out now," he said. And then he added as an afterthought.

"I don't know if retirement is for me yet, Max," he said. "But I sure as hell will take your kind offer under advisement."

He left Max inside and gingerly stepped out into the street over the dead body and through the smashed plate glass of the revolving door.

The police arrived in a wail of sirens within minutes and the entire area was was cordoned off. An EMS van and a squad car from the Broward County's sheriff's office arrived moments later with a plain, blue unmarked sedan. Out of the vehicles stepped Jerry Goodman and Jake Santana.

Luis went over to greet his cousin.

"Jake. Jake Santana," he called out over the heads of the police officers and bystanders who were milling about.

Jake turned and a wide grin filled his face. He popped a piece of hard candy into his mouth, pulled at his suspenders and made his way to Luis.

"So, Luis. Are you and your buddies making trouble on my turf?"

"Not at all, cousin. This was self defense."

"Should I thank or curse you, cousin? You were supposed to keep the peace in your former turf. Is this the price pay to be a police inspector?"

"Chief homicide inspector," Luis reminded him. "That's how I retired from the force, You'll make that rank too if you play your cards right."

Jake slapped his back.

"Don't worry, cousin. I'm aiming for that too."

"Inspector Santana. I like that," said Amison. He threw sidelong glances at Charlie Hand and Max Zimmer who finally ventured out of the barbershop, but his eyes were fixed on Harold Levy.

"Thanks for the assist. Sol said you were back in action. When did you get to town?"

"Late last night, Jonesey. Luis said you might be in trouble. I figured I owed you for the mess I created a few years ago."

"Let's not worry about that now, Harold. We have more pressing problems."

Jake looked at them suspiciously and tugged at his suspenders.

"I have dead men who can't be arrested. Should I arrest you, amigos?"

"They're clean," said Luis. "I can vouch for them."

"The three dead dudes were armed," said Jerry, coming over after checking the bodies. "It looks like they were carrying standard military issue."

"Jerry Goodwin," exclaimed Amison. "How the hell are you?"

"Oh, hi, Jonesey. Good to see you in the flesh."

"Keeping busy?"

Jerry made a wry face.

"This is south Florida. Never a dull moment. Had a truck full of bodies last week in the swamps west of here."

He turned to greet Harold. How are you doing, big guy? Long time no see."

"I hate to break up this social conversation," said Jake, "But what happened here?"

"Hard to tell," Charlie Hand began explaining. "I was cutting Jonesey's hair when the shooting started. This is a mess. My shop is ruined."

Jake looked at Max Zimmer who so far had kept his silence.

"Is that what you saw, Max?"

"I played possum the moment the fireworks started. I didn't see anything."

Jake popped another hard candy into his mouth and started chewing.

"I assume you have licenses for the arsenal you're carrying, amigos?"
Luis smiled.

"Si, cousin. We all have licenses. We would never break the law."

"Well, let's get you out of here before the media catches up," said Jake.

"What do say when the cameras get here?" Jerry asked.

"It was an attempted robbery and the shooters were killed in self defense. Also, check out the shop's security cameras. They may tell us more."

"What about Jonesey and his buddies?"

"I'll give them and Max a ride back to the Riverside."

But Max declined the favor.

"No thanks, Jake. I'll walk; it's safer."

CHAPTER 9

▼

The Cowboy Clown

Jake led them to his car and sat with Teddy in the front seat while the rest piled into the back.

"Teddy," Amison asked. "How did your kid finally make out on his college applications?"

"Got a football scholarship at one," replied Teddy. "We're waiting to hear from others. But now he thinks he wants to learn how to fly jets. I guess he wants to do what I did once. Go figure, but thanks for asking."

They took off through a side street and headed for the Riverside as Jake spoke to his passengers in the rear seat.

"Things have been tough since I took over this job," he confided. "First, we have the Sammy Luke killing, and now this thing. I can see why the shooter mistook the victim for you, Jonesey. You're both ugly. But we made progress. The ballistics report traced the shell we found to the Canaan Metal Works in New Canaan, Connecticut. The company produces specialty small arms and ordnance for the government. We haven't found it yet, but I have to assume that the weapon also came from the same company."

"Why is that?"

"A shootout in the Everglades on the western edge of the county left us with a dozen bodies and a stack of weapons made by the Connecticut outfit."

"What happened in the glades?"

"It took place at some sort of a camp, like a militia training camp where old guys go to play war. The camp dudes were Latinos and were ambushed by a gang of red neck crackers. The ambush failed and the gang was slaughtered. But one of them got away, a big cowboy who looked like a clown."

"How do you know that?"

"That's the description the Latinos gave us. We ran the ID down and it turns out to be your old friend, Quentin Bates."

"If it's Quentin," said Amnison, "those crackers must be from the White Knights."

"Who are they?" Harold Levy asked.

"A white supremacist militia," answered Luis.

"Wait. That's not all," said Jake. "That Latino militia group turns out not to be a militia after all. It was a United Nations peacekeeping training camp that was contributed by Washington. What's more, Bienvenido de la Maza owns the land and his people run the camp>"

"Damn. What's that guy up to?"

Amison shrugged and said, "We'll have to ask him, won't we? But talking about the weapons, how do you know the red necks were the ones carrying U.S. made weapons?"

"Because the Latinos used and fired Russian made AK-47's."

Jake's last statement was met by silence.

"At least we have a connection between the Sammy Luke shooting, the fight in the glades and the White Knights," said Luis at last.

"We have more than that," remarked Jake. "The shells that hit Red Fish and the bullet that nicked you on the golf course were also made by the Canaan Metal Works." He took a deep breath. "Now, it'll be interesting to see what ballistics has to say about the shootout at Charlie's. In the meantime, I'd say that you guys have a problem."

"Anything on Anastos?" Luis asked.

"Ernie? Bad news. We found his remains in a canal. His stomach was slit open and a bat was shoved up his ass. Now, I haven't connected the numbers yet, but Klondike Pete reported his cab stolen the night Sammy was killed and Ernie disappeared. When we found Ernie. we found the cab torched nearby. I think the cab was used to kill Sammy and grab Ernie because he might have been a witness. I also think Kowalsky was the driver. The tread marks on the road match the cab's tires. Man, I hope this doesn't hit the media. I'm trying to keep things quiet until I have enough to put a collar on Pete."

There was nothing more to say. Jake parked in front of the hotel's livery entrance, dropped off his passengers and walked over to Hamburger Haven to deliver the bad news to Angelo and Dimitri.

"Let's stay in touch," he said. "You want to stay alive and I want to keep my job."

Word of the incident at Charlie Hand's barbershop reached Sol Weinberg who summoned the entire Horizon cohort to his office with Harold Levy and Jacques Leroux the next day to find out what exactly happened. Max Zimmer was also invited. He declined, citing a prior engagement.

Leroux put it all together for Sol after the debriefing.

"Everything that happened occurred after the re-distribution of West Indian stock. Someone is murderously unhappy about the change."

Frank, freshly returned from Monte Fuego, shook his head.

"It's too soon to start pointing fingers except perhaps to start having a closer look at Quentin Bates and his White Knights."

"What about Keith and his daughters?" Luis asked.

"If we do that," added Amison. "We might as well include Victor Duncan and Emilio Gutierrez, and even Juan Duarte Gutierrez. That gives us too many suspects."

"We might be faced with a grand conspiracy," Leroux suggested.

Sol's brow furrowed.

"What kind of a grand conspiracy, director?"

Leroux smiled.

"I am awaiting word from Europol for permission to say more."

Amison cursed.

"This entire scene sucks big time and we're stuck in the middle with little wiggle room. And to make matters worse, we have a lunatic on the loose."

"We're running out of wiggle room," said Luis.

"What about the diamonds from Nassau?" Frank suddenly asked Leroux.

"Conflict diamonds originating with Kinshasa Export in Africa. We can talk about them later."

Sol turned to Harold.

"You realize that most of this falls in your bailiwick at Alliance," he said.

"I don't follow," said Harold.

"It's simple. These situations are unfolding under your watch at Alliance and will have to be handled by your Horizon people, including assignments sent to you by Europol."

Harold's dark eyes jumped to Leroux.

"Is that right, Jacques?"

"Yes," answered Leroux.

Harold now turned to Amison, asking pointedly, "Now that you guys work for me, what have you done lately besides trying to get killed?"

"We're offering a million dollar reward for information leading to Sammy Luke's killers," said Frank, having been briefed by Virgil on the way from the airport.

Harold blinked, asking, "You have that kind of money?"

Amison smiled and nodded affirmatively.

"In that case," said Harold, "I have a flight to catch."

After the meeting ended, Harold corralled Amison, Frank and Luis and asked them to accompany him to the airport. There, over coffee at Fort Lauderdale's general aviation terminal, he asked, "How's that reward thing for Sammy's killers going to work?"

"We hope to smoke some people out into the open. Virgil is spreading the world on the street," said Luis. "Money is a powerful drawing card."

Harold grunted and then asked Frank to tell him more about Monte Fuego and Hernando Gomez.

"Hernando has a valid claim," Frank began explaining. "The land on which both West Indian Mines and Hernando's house stands was granted by Philip II to Enrique Gomez-Avila, a conquistador who conquered Monte Fuego for Spain in the 1500's. Enrique's descendants built La Fortaleza and lived there until the nineteenth century when they rented it to the government and moved to Bolivia. The rental amount was nominal, the equivalent of about $1,000.00 a year. Successive governments including Juan Duarte's have been paying that rent without question. The amount became so insignificant over the years that auditors never caught it."

Now, Hernando, direct descendant, moves to Monte Fuego from Bolivia and promptly lays claim to the land in a court action, even though it was leased to West Indian. And guess what? He wins title to the land and Monte Fuego has to keep paying him rent which it has now for over forty years. The problem is that the written deed was never filed. It must be some place but so far it's not been found. Estrella may need that document if push comes to shove."

Amison felt it important at that point to explain that, according to Estrella, Keith Bates had asked her to marry him and that she had agreed.

"I thought she was your woman," said Harold.

"I thought so too," replied Amison. "But that's besides the point. I went to see Denise Bates in San Juan where she told me that the deal between Keith and Sol was falling apart because Victor and Emilio were trying to muscle in on their action. If the deal dies, Horizon is out of chump change and the girls are out of work. Matter of fact, Denise asked me to kill Victor and Emilio."

"So much for relationships," Frank observed.

Harold alternatively cursed and moaned, "Damn Danielle!".

"I have another scoop," said Amison. "Denise claims to know who has us in their short hairs and will tell us in exchange for their deaths, and Max said at the barbershop that a contract is out on us, you and Sid and that he'd clue us in if we retired, meaning if the Horizon gang retired. But maybe he'll agree to pay you and Sid off too if you guys retire."

Harold shook his head defiantly.

"Max is a fat rat. He's trying to muscle in on Centurion and Alliance and he doesn't care how he does it. And Denise and Danielle are snakes. Denise went from bed to bed and Danielle dropped me for Victor. They can fry in hell; I'm not dealing with them. But I'd watch Max more right now. I bet he set you up at the barbershop, Jonesey. They should all be killed before they kill us. What about Keith and the diamonds? Is the story real?"

"We have no choice but to take Leroux's word. Cecil Fergueson may know more about what's going on," replied Luis.

"Okay. I'm heading for Stamford. While I'm gone, Jonesey, why don't you and Frank pay Cecil a visit. Take Chico for backup. Luis, you hold the fort here call me if someone looks at you cross eyed. We'll meet again in one week when we have more information. And guys. Fly. Don't go by boat."

The Bimini islands were forty five miles east south east of Fort Lauderdale and a half hour away by commuter sea plane that landed them in Alice Town, North Bimini island's chief hamlet where they found Cecil Fergueson having breakfast at a local eatery.

"Good Lord!" Cecil declared when he saw them. "How did you know I'd be here?"

"Where else would you be?" Amison quipped. "Either here or fishing."

Cecil was a short, stocky Bahamian with a Groucho Marx moustache, a halo of pepper colored closely cropped hair around his head and a slightly crooked smile that gave him a comical appearance.

"Let's fo fishing," suggested Cecil after they finished telling him why they were in the Biminis.

"I could use some sleep," said Chico.

Cecil got up and left some money on the table.

"You can take a nap at my office. It's near the beach."

A few minutes later, they were at Cecil's Reel estate office, a small house on the narrow island's bluffs overlooking the sea. Chico was soon fast asleep on the sofa and they headed out to the beach.

"Someone blew your cover," Cecil noted once they had cast their lines.

"That's old news," said Amison. "But let me ask you this. How did you find out about the diamonds?"

"It was a tip from Europol's Paris office. Customs in Nassau turned them over to me when I presented my papers as a Europol agent. You know the rest. I also found that similar diamonds and assorted high end jewelry were being seeded throughout the Caribbean. I didn't want to appear brazen, so Charlotte and I booked a cruise from San Juan that made its first stop in St. Thomas where we went window shopping at the Havensight mall."

"Does Charlotte know you're working for Europol?"

"No. In fact, she stumbled on the Emerald House outlet on her own and I played dumb. Anyway, we were shown several trays of diamonds by a sales woman. They were blue, white and perfect and Charlotte offered to buy one if the woman could tell her something about their pedigree.

"The sales people at Emerald worked on salary and it was obvious she was not pushing sales. She told Charlotte that the stone had papers from the GIA certifying that it was a perfect two carat white diamond and was guaranteed."

"Is that the Gemological Institute of America in New York?"

"Yes. She dug up the certification papers and showed them to us. Charlotte examined them and noticed that the gem's certification was requested, not by Emerald, but by Boucher & Salieri. The woman told my wife that B&S was Emerald's surety for all fine gems and went on to say that a shipment was in transit to the Emerald store in Nassau and that we could buy the same quality gems there if we wanted."

Amison and Frank exchanged glances.

"Did you check stores on the other islands along the way?" Frank asked.

Cecil grinned.

"You bet. We visited Emerald shops in Antigua, St. Martens, Monte Fuego, Barbados and St. Lucia. The story was pretty much the same. Diamonds come from Africa and have GIA papers guaranteed by B&S. The largest Emerald store was in Monte Fuego. It was fully air conditioned and had a restaurant. What struck me was that B&S had a kiosk in the store from which certificates of authenticity were issued for gems bought from Emerald. I think they also did appraisals. Emerald also sold estate jewelry with no GIA certification but which were still guaranteed by B&S.

"That sounds odd," said Amison. "Any ID on the Belgian consignor?"

"The shipper? It's a shell agent representing Kinshasa Export in Africa. The consignee is an outfit called Black Star Trading and payments are confirmed by a merchant bank called Carib Financial in Monte Fuego. Do the names register with any of you?"

"Kinshasa and Carib don't," Frank replied. "But Black Star Trading is Keith Bates. How are the payments made?"

"Emerald pays with irrevocable confirmed letters-of-credit issued by Carib Financial through correspondent banks in ports where Emerald has an outlet. The beneficiary of those credits is always Black Star. I'm still working on the paper trail."

Cecil looked out at sea.

"I think Emerald and B&S are peddling conflict diamonds and hot jewelry and someone wants to keep you guys at a distance. Am I on to something?"

"You might be," said Amison. "Did you file report with Leroux?"

"Yes. You know the rest."

"Did you buy any diamonds?"

"Too expensive. My wife told them to call her when prices improved"

"Shit," said Frank. "She may have signed her death warrant."

They spent the next week fishing, trying to figure out a way to place Cecil's wife out of harm's way. This also gave Amison time to get his catamaran set for its journey back to Florida.

A plan finally materialized. Charlotte would fly to Geneva to see their kids in school, and Cecil would leave with Amison, Chico and Frank on Phoenix. On the morning of their departure, Charlotte was at home packing with Chico, and Amison, Cecil and Frank were at the beach with their fishing gear for one last attempt to catch the big one and to review their plans.

It was warm and the western sky was pale blue and the air was very still. It was so quiet that they never bothered to cast their lines. Instead, they stood silently, their eyes fixed on the distant line where sea and sky met. Not that they expected to see anything. There was not a cloud to be seen in the heat of the morning, not even a breeze to sway the palms on the beach.

Frank pointed to small flock of birds in the sky. There was an empty space in the flock's left wing, enough for one bird. It reminded him of the missing man formation used by military aircraft.

"We should have that memorial luncheon for Hank Lawrence and the guys we lost in the last mission," he said.

Cecil muttered in agreement but Amison shook his head.

"Count me out," he said. "Hank almost got us killed."

But Frank was adamant.

"So what? He's dead and we're alive. We owe him for the old days."

Amison's mood was turning sour.

"Count me out!" He repeated in a louder voice.

The birds were slowly flying south.

Further to the north, Frank saw two specks in the sky, moving south.

"They aren't birds," said Amison.

"What did you say?"

"They aren't birds. Let's get out of here. They aren't birds!"

They grabbed their gear and made a mad dash for Cecil's office, trying to escape a deep, vibrating eggbeater noise that grew progressively louder until they found themselves surrounded by roaring thunder.

They made it to door and Cecil ran in. But Amison and Frank jumped back and dove into a clump of brush and shade trees at the side of the house. In the sky, the black dots they had seen from the beach had morphed into two attack helicopters.

"Cecil!" Amison screamed. "Get the hell out of the house!"

There was no answer, and Frank drew a long barreled revolver from his gear bag.

The choppers circled like giant insects and descended. The lead chopper's doors were open and inside, next to the pilot in dark aviator glasses, sat an odd looking passenger. He wore a cream colored ten gallon hat and cowboy boots and his face resembled that of a comic book joker. High cheek bones, big, deep blue eyes and a long ski slope nose over thick lips and buck teeth defined his face.

A diamond studded pink jacket over bright green trousers over his muscular body gave him the look of a circus performer and a crop of long, yellow corn hair stuck out from under his hat like scarecrow straw. An ammo belt snaked around his broad shoulders and narrow waist and in his hands he held an automatic assault rifle.

The rear chopper veered off to Cecil's home next to his Real estate office where it swooped down and released a rocket. In a single instant the house went up in a ball of fire and smoke.

The chopper returned and the cowboy clown laughed. It was a high pitched hee-haw sound that sounded something like a cross between a hyena howl and the braying of a wild mule. He kept laughing and pointing to the flames.

The lead chopper dropped in position and the cowboy aimed his weapon, raking the area with automatic fire.

Again, that high pitched yelp.

The two choppers realigned themselves in the front and back of the hut that was the real estate office when Cecil suddenly appeared with a shotgun at the door. A salvo of rockets hit the hut and blew it up.

The cowboy tipped his hat and hee-hawed again, but his pilot was not so lucky. Frank took careful aim with his revolver and squeezed the trigger. It was a lucky shot. The pilot gripped his left shoulder and left the controls to the cowboy clown who emptied his weapon into the brush with his free hand. The choppers then circled around a few times and flew off.

CHAPTER 10

▼

Equilibrium Lost

Cecil Furgueson was dead. So was Chico who had stayed at the house while Charlotte went last minute shopping in town. Charlotte was now a widow and everything went on hold. Harold Levy rushed back to Florida from Stamford where family, friends and associates of Cecil and Chico began gathering to mourn and wait for word of a funeral.

Back in Florida, something was happening at Hamburger Haven during the the chopper attack. According to what Amison was told later, Klondike Pete showed up at Hamburger Haven to dispute a lunch delivery invoice on behalf of Max Zimmer. By then, the newspapers had a field day with the way Ernie had died, questioning his sexuality as a Greek immigrant. Klondike, basically stupid and uninformed, cracked a joke to the effect that Ernie must have died happy. Angelo was in the back room, getting his ovens started when Klondike began his bantering with Virgil who happened to be there checking Amison's accounts. Angelo went ballistic, seized the red hot poker from the oven and smacked Pete with it. Max's driver lunged at him with Virgil climbing on his back to restrain him. In an instant, Angelo plunged the poker into Pete's belly and drove it up into his chest. That night, Angelo, Dimitri and Virgil carved up Klondike Pete's body and threw the parts in garbage bags.

"Is Red Fish going game fishing anytime soon?" Dimitri had asked.

"It is now," Virgil had replied, wiping the blood off his hands.

The news reached Amison when Red Fish made a fuel stop in the Biminis.

Cecil and his wife were Bahamians and so it was understandable that he would be buried in the Biminis. Chico was a Dominican, and his wife, who lived and worked in Florida, wanted him buried in the Dominican Republic. Charlotte was distraught, in seclusion, and in no position to make decisions. And so it was left to Amison and Frank to sort things out. Guests planning to attend Cecil's funeral had to be accommodated and a flood of police queries had to be answered.

They could contribute little to the police beyond stating that Quentin Bates was the shooter they had seen in one of the choppers. Charlotte had nothing to add to their account except to confirm that Amison, Chico and Frank were Cecil's friends. What were they doing in the Biminis? Amison insisted he had come for his catamaran and the police seemed satisfied with his explanation. Bahamian officials were thrilled when told that Chico's funeral would be in the Dominican Republic and when they determined that no drugs were aboard Phoenix. Within hours, permits were granted to ship out Chico's remains and release the catamaran. And they were likewise quick to surrender the chopper attack story to the Europol agents who surfaced a few days later.

Time dragged nevertheless and another week rolled by while funeral plans were finalized and friends and relatives began trickling in to pay their last respects. Both Cecil and Chico were well known and popular. To maintain harmony, Charlotte agreed with Chico's widow in Florida, that he would be eulogized along with Cecil at the All Souls Non-Denominational Church in North Bimini. Other matters had to be addressed: the housing and feeding of guests and the memorial wake following the funeral. Charlotte also needed to find lodging for herself and her teenage children who had flown back from Switzerland.

"I'd hold off on the memorial," Sid Stone suggested to Charlotte when he arrived. "Cecil worked with us on our last mission and we're going to have one soon for all the good people we lost. It's most likely going to be in Puerto Rico. It's a good central location between Europe and the Americas and I was hoping that you would join us for the occasion. It would means a lot to all of us."

Sid solved the housing problem for Charlotte and most of the funeral guests by having them housed in vacant apartments at a new condo development on South Bimini that he owned. He also deeded a three bedroom unit to Charlotte and informed her that Cecil carried a hefty insurance policy with Centurion. Sol Weinberg, landing in the Biminis with Harold Levy in an Alliance jet, was equally helpful.

"I'm not good at mourning," he said upon meeting Charlotte. "But you need to know that you and your kids will have no financial worries for the rest of your lives."

The quiet sorrow in the furrows of Sol's face was not lost on Charlotte. "You're very kind, Sol," she said. "I know we won't have any worries. I just wish Cecil and I could have retired together."

They embraced and Charlotte went on with the funeral preparations.

That evening, an unexpected visitor arrived on the last seaplane flight from Miami. It just so happened that Amison was at Bahamian customs looking for a box of parts for his boat when he made eye contact with a radiant looking brunette in a dark blue business blazer and skirt with her done in a page boy cut. He did a double take and called out across the customs counter.

"Erica Brown,"

It almost seemed as if she expected him to meet her. She cleared customs, retrieved her roll-on suitcase and gave Amison a big hug.

"This is where it all began, isn't it?" She said when they released each other.

"Yes it is. Many years ago. What brings you to the Biminis?"

"You. I was on my way to a trade show in Miami when I heard about Cecil. I knew you'd be here for his funeral and I did want to see you."

"Well, it's good to be wanted. Where are you staying?"

"I don't have a place," she said coyly.

Phoenix was afloat by now and Amison invited her to spend the night.

"It's not much," he apologized. "But we have food and booze and I promise not to lay a hand on you."

Erica laughed.

"There was a time when you couldn't wait to lay your hands on me."

"That's right; so you better watch out. I could change my mind."

That evening, after they had finished a makeshift dinner that Amison had prepared in Phoenix's small galley, Erica inquired about Frank.

"He's staying in town, meeting and greeting people as they come in for the funeral," Amison answered without elaboration, suddenly realizing that it was difficult for him to sustain a conversation with the woman. It was a clear night and they sat quietly on the rear deck under the stars and silently sipped their drinks until Erica popped a question out of nowhere.

"How come you never called when you were in Monte Fuego?"

Amison shrugged his shoulders.

"I was busy with other business."

"Did you know that Estrella was staying with me? She has your money, you know."

"I heard, and she did return the money."

"You must be doing well, Ruby, if you can be so casual about a cool million in cash."

"I can't complain."

"Did you know that Frank and Janice are dating again?" Erica asked.

"So I heard," he replied. "What about you? What's going on in your life?"

"Not too much. I have this boutique in Monte Fuego where I sell women's and men's fashions. That's why I'm going to the Miami fashion show."

"That's nice. Are you and Janice still friendly with Denise and Danielle?"

"Yes. I'm also friendly with Emilio, her husband," she blurted out.

Amison said nothing.

"I'm having an affair with Emilio," she said. When Amison did not react, she went on to add, "And Janice is having an affair with Victor Duncan."

"Are they love interests or meal tickets?"

"You have a way with words, Ruby. They're meal tickets, if you want to put it that way. We can't possibly live the way we do on what we make. I should have hung my wash with yours when I had a chance, but that's over."

"You called the shots on that one, Erica. Whatever happened to that guy you dropped me for?"

"We got married, but it didn't last."

"Did he have more money than me?"

"No," she replied, shaking her head. "He had more promise. You were not very dependable those days. You were footloose and fancy free and I wanted a family."

"Did you ever get that family?"

"No."

"To bad. At least you're making a living. What else do you need?"

"I need the thrill of a new start. Do you remember that we were going to run off to the Keys and start a business?"

"A beer, bait and tackle shop," said Amison.

"Ice extra," she countered. "But I think you've moved on from that."

"So have you. Those threads you have on cost money."

"That's because I'm a kept woman, Ruby, like Janice. Why is it that I must remain single? It's not fair. All I wanted was a husband, kids and grand kids to grow old with. At least, you had your turn. You're a father and grandfather. When do I get my turn?"

She began crying and Amison put his arms around her.

"Listen," he said. "It's okay. There's always that beer, bait and tackle shop."

"Ice extra?"

"Ice extra. Now, tell me. What are you really here for?"

Leslie dried her tears and straightened up.

"You bastard!" She yelled. "You sure know how to break a mood. I'll tell you what Janice and I want. We heard about you, Frank and Luis becoming involved with West Indian Mines and you guys are hired guns. I want you to promise that you're not going to after Emilio and Victor. We need our meal tickets. Will you do that for me, for old times' sake?"

"I'll see what I can do if you tell me the name of the guy you married."

"Erica took a deep breath and whispered, "Max Zimmer."

Amison's smile froze in place but it never betrayed the turmoil in his mind.

"Well, maybe we should forget the past," he said.

Erica's face lit up.

"Maybe, we can talk more about that little business of ours in the Keys."

"That would be nice," said Amison. "Anything else I should know?"

"In fact, yes," she replied. "There's a Jorge Ramirez at the Riverside. Janice saw him at the Brittany where he told her he was going to St. Maarten to visit family. He claims to know who killed this guy, Sammy Luke, and.wants to meet with Frank. He knows much more too but he wants money to talk."

"How much money?"

"A million, cash, the reward money that Frank put up."

"I have it. Tell Janice to set it up. Frank will be there. Jorge trusts him."

Luis Santiago arrived in the morning with Max Zimmer, Ramon Salva and Emilio Gutierrez in Salva's jet flown by Julio Maldonado. Landing minutes later was another corporate jet carrying Chico's young widow, her two small children and Bienvenido de la Maza. Erica Brown left for Miami as their jets landed.

Bienvenido seemed in top shape, garbed as he was in a tailored mourning suit and his shiny dark hair tied back in a short pony tail. His presence took everyone by surprise and he had to take pains to explain that he had not come to make trouble.

"It is a coincidence," he said. "I reopened the Miramar warehouse in North Miami and needed employees. Rosina was looking for a job and I hired her. I had no idea at the time who she was and that Chico was her husband. When she learned of his death, she wanted to come here to bring his body back to the Dominican Republic. Since we are both Dominicanos, I felt duty bound to help her. It is also to express my thanks to Chico and to all of you for saving my life."

Bienvenido looked directly at Luis.

"I am sure you will understand as a fellow Dominicano," he said.

Luis frowned.

"She should speak to me," he complained. After all, I am Chico's cousin and you are an enemy."

Bienvenido corrected him.

"Former enemy, amigo. I have no wish to open old wounds, especially now that we are partners."

Amison muffled a smile.

"That land in Monte Fuego is giving us problems," he said.

"I hear," Bienvenido responded. "I too am beginning to feel the heat. If you are marked for death, so are your partners and so am I."

Amison pointed to the Church entrance, saying, "It's time.".

The service went fast, and when it is over, Charlotte stood at the door with the reverend to receive condolences. The sky was overcast and it drizzled on and off as she stood quietly under an umbrella, nodding without listening to the soft words of sympathy whispered by well wishers as they filed by one by one. The line moved painfully slowly but finally the Church was empty.

The reverend had already gone to join the funeral cortege, leaving her alone for a moment when a short, well groomed elderly man in a dark hat stepped in front of her.

"I am Keith Bates," he announced, removing his hat and exposing a thick shock of silver hair.

"I am the father of the man falsely accused of killing your husband."

"Why are you here?"

"I want to set the record straight and to make things right," he said. "I never knew your husband although I do know the other gentleman. I had no reason to have your husband killed. Nor did I have a reason to have the others killed. And neither did my son. I want you and the world to know that. That's all I have to say."

Charlotte did not respond. She turned her back and walked away, leaving Keith alone at the door and followed Amison and the funeral cortege to an old cemetery near the beach where only weeks ago he and Frank had been fishing with Cecil.

It was an interesting crowd and Amison could not help noticing that cliques formed even at funerals. Frank Hoffman, Luis Santiago Harold Levy and Sid Stone stood on one side of Sol Weinberg. Ramon Salva, Victor Duncan, Max Zimmer, Emilio Gutierrez and Felipe Gutierrez flanked him on the other side. And there, sandwiched between Sol and Max was Keith Bates, trying to tell everyone within earshot that his son was innocent.

Julio Maldonado stood behind Max and Ramon Salva, listening to Keith's stout defense. The two men were short. Julio was heavyset and still in his pilot's jacket while Ramon Salva was slim and swarthy in his tailored silk suit.

Seizing upon a lull in the small talk, Ramon Salva drifted over to Amison.

"What a shame we have to meet under such circumstances," he said in a low voice.

Amison nodded.

"I never had the opportunity to thank you for your work on the last mission. Have your friends given you Centurion's token of gratitude?"

Amison raised his hand and displayed the gold watch.

"I wear it everyday," he replied. "And so do my friends."

"Ah, I am pleased."

He pointed to Julio Maldonado.

"You must thank Julio who bought them in Paris and flew them over for el senor Weinberg."

Sid Stone was standing nearby and gave Julio a slap on the left shoulder that made him wince.

"Perhaps you'd like to become my personal shopper," he joked.

Ramon Salva fell back into Sol Weinberg's shadow, giving Max a chance to sidle over to Amison.

"I need your help, Jones. My man, Pete Kowalsky, went over to Hamburger Haven to settle a bill and never returned. Do you know what happened?"

"Beats me," replied Amison. "But tell you what. Find out who has a contract on us and I'll ask around."

"Speak to Frank," Max said. "He orchestrated the diamond heist in Nassau."

"The conflict diamonds."

"Stolen, I say. Do you believe in equilibrium, Jones? We're a team, Jones, and our equilibrium is out of synch, and that's too bad. It must be restored and you need to do it. Otherwise, you can say goodby to CIA missions in the future."

Max's voice had turned to ice. He was poker-faced as ever and continued to speak in a low, steady robotic monotone.

"You and your gang are overreaching, and that's not good equilibrium. That must change. And Bienvenido's continued presence is a travesty of justice and I'm beginning to question your patriotism, Jones. How come you didn't waste him when you had a chance?"

A grim smile fell over Amison's face.

"The word is called pity, Max. Look it up."

Max gestured sarcastically.

"You know, Jones. You and your friends should seriously consider cashing in your chips and retiring. My offer is still good."

Amison took Max by the arm to a clearing where they were alone.

"I have a shit list, Max," he whispered. "And your name is at the top." His hand tightened on the back of Max's neck. "So, you listen closely, fuck face. About Klondike Pete, What part of him do you want back? His balls or his ears? About the diamonds, speak to Leroux. And about those CIA missions? You can shove them."

Amison loosened his grip when Harold Levy appeared and placed a heavy hand on the lapel of Max's jacket to flick away an imaginary speck of dust. "We were discussing retirement," said Amison.

Harold gave Max a hearty back slap.

"Great idea, Max. Go for it."

The CIA operative slunk away and Harold mumbled, "I've bought myself a hornet's nest."

They moved back in with the gathering of mourners where Chico's widow and her children stayed close to Bienvenido. At the end of the funeral, when Cecil's remains had been laid to rest, Bienvenido walked up to Charlotte and introduced himself.

"I am Bienvenido de la Maza," he announced, "And this is Chico's wife, Rosina, and her two children, Carmelita and Juanito."

"Were you a friend of my husband's?"

"No, my dear senora. We were enemies. All of your husband's friends were my enemies. I am here to mourn an old warrior's death and to bring Chico's body to his village in the Dominican Republic for a proper burial."

Before she had a chance to reply, he led Rosina and her children away and disappeared into the crowd.

Charlotte was teary eyed but otherwise remarkably reserved during the entire funeral ordeal. When it was over, she left her children aside and went over to Amison, Frank and Luis.

Her voice was calm and soft.

"I know this was none of your doing. But I want you to get those bastards who murdered my husband and Chico. I'll help you any way I can."

Without uttering another word, she walked away to join her children who were standing with Sid. But Keith Bates, egged on by Max Zimmer, had other ideas. He stepped forward and confronted Amison once the crowd thinned.

"Your men stole my diamonds," he declared, wagging a finger. "I demand a meeting of the full Council."

Sol Weinberg came over in an effort to calm him.

"We'll talk in Florida," he said. "Not here."

"Yes," agreed Amison. "After all, equilibrium is important, isn't it!"

Part ii

▼

CONSPIRACY

CHAPTER 11

▼

The Woman in Red

Amison, Frank and Luis met briefly over coffee with Harold Levy, Leroux and Bienvenido before their departure from the Biminis. The one thing upon which they could agree was their experiences in common with women.

"Those dames will be a problem," declared Harold.

"How so?" Luis asked.

"All broads are problems," the Alliance chief said. "But these women are bed hoppers and opportunistic gold bricks, and that makes them dangerous to us. They're losing their meal tickets and they're going to rebound on us." Amison lit a cigarette.

"How do you mean, Harold?"

"What monsieur Levy is saying is that our four female friends suspect that the fortunes of their husbands and boyfriends are in jeopardy and are running for high ground," said Leroux. "It is something like rats leaving the sinking ship. Victor has high gambling debts on top of owing Centurion $100 million in past due mortgage notes. Emilio is in trouble for not disclosing his earnings from West Indian Mines. I believe your country and my country call that tax evasion."

Luis laughed.

"That's an interesting coincidence," he said. "Stan Short is a friend of mine at the IRS and I asked him to run down Emerald's books. Once it pays for its expenses and a 50% management fee to West Indian, it never turns a profit.

That's why it pays no taxes and why West Indian stockholder receives high dividends."

Leroux nodded.

"The same situation exists with Boucher & Salieri. The Paris firm is always destitute because of its 50% management fee to West Indian. Paul Boucher and Louis Salieri are in fact mere West Indian employees. But France is now suing for the taxes B&S has avoided paying all these years. I suspect that the women are aware of the dangers facing their male consorts. But they know as well that your own futures may be compromised, and must therefore be very careful of their every move."

"Are you suggesting that we at Horizon being targeted because we threaten to take over West Indian Mines?" Frank asked.

Leroux shook his head.

"More," he replied. "A treasure lies under the land owned by West Indian Mines. Whoever owns the land owns the treasure of Monte Fuego. You are all being marked for termination to prevent you from accessing that treasure. The women are important in the sense that they may cloud your judgement, but the challenges we face transcend our sexual peccadillos.

"What kind of treasure are we talking about, director?" asked Amison.

"I expect a release from my superiors in Paris in a few days and will tell you then. I can only say now that it is large enough to finance the most nefarious schemes of men and that it must be kept from falling into the wrong hands. I hope to be able to count on your support in protecting the treasure of Monte Fuego."

Harold got ready to board his jet.

"I speak for all of us present," he said. "Our agenda is to control Centurion, West Indian Mines, Emerald and Boucher & Salieri. Anyone who isn't with us is against us. We're being hit from all sides, guys. So let's get out there and kill someone important."

The meeting ending and Harold returned to Florida and from there he flew to Connecticut. Amison and Frank arrived a few days later on Phoenix and had Luis invite Bienvenido for lunch in Hamburger Haven's back room.

"Is this business or social?" Bienvenido asked, looking around.

"Both," said Amison. "I want us to make sure that we're working together."

"I thought el senor Levy made that clear,"

"He did make it clear, old buddy," continued Amison. "But I want to make it clear on my turf."

"You own this place?"

"Yes. Frank and Luis have interests in this and other businesses in town that provides us with alternative resources."

"I understand," nodded Bienvenido. "I have been following your moves for a long time and believe you are doing the right thing. I am comfortable with your position and I am comfortable with how the matter of el senor Klondike was habdled."

"You heard?" Luis asked.

"Si, amigo. Word moves fast on the street. But that is not my problem. You must do what is needed. My problem is that the organizations backing you are not trustworthy. I would rely more on the trust between us than the trust that I have in your associates at Centurion, Europol and the CIA."

Bienvenido laughed and raised his glass of water.

"To trust." They raised their glasses and toasted.

"Now," he said, folding his hands on the table. "You are not a man to waste time and words, senor Jones. What is on your mind?"

Amison chose his words carefully.

"Harold Levy is right when he said that the women we know cannot be fully trusted. They can't be trusted, but they can be used."

"In what way?"

Amison proceeded to tell Bienvenido about Erica's overnight stay in the Biminis where she indicated that Janice had told her that Jorge Ramirez was in St. Maarten and wanted to make a deal with Frank.

"Does this have to do with that famous $1million reward I've heard about?"

"Yes."

"Jorge is bad," said Bienvenido in his guttural voice. He and Felipe betrayed the U.N. peacekeeping trainees in the Everglades camp to el senor Zimmer"

"Why?" asked Frank.

"El senor Zimmer believed that they were terrorists and that the camp was a cover because I owned it. Jorge learned of our encampment from his girlfriend who was the sister of one of my men. He gave the camp's location to Felipe."

"Jorge is at the low end of a command chain," Luis noted. "We need to start with him. I say he goes. What do you say, guys?"

Frank nodded, saying, "He goes."

"I agree," muttered Amison. "He has to go. He's a two bit spy who knows too much. What about you, Bienvenido?"

"I will not cry when he dies," replied the Dominican. "He speaks to el senor Zimmer who is my enemy. El senor Zimmer is part of a renegade ring at the CIA backing the White Knights."

"What's your deal with the U.N.?" Amison asked.

"The United Nations pays me to train peacekeepers. We use special bivouac zones in the Everglades and teach courses set up by your government."

"Damn!"

Amison broke out in laughter that quickly spread around the table, leaving Bienvenido to think he was with three men who had lost their minds.

"Seriously, senores," he smiled shyly. "Did you truly believe I could give up my violent nature? I have a U.N. mandate to protect the world for which your country pays the bills. It is better than engaging in revolution Now, what is it that you need from me?"

"We need a fast jet," said Frank, drying his tears. "We have the pilot."

On Sunday, a week later, a meeting between Frank and Jorge was arranged by Janice and a jet piloted by Mike Quinn with Amison and Frank aboard left Fort Lauderdale for the island of St. Maarten. On Monday, they were touring the island and Harold Levy was at his Stamford office getting ready for lunch. He had much to be happy about as he studied the mantle clock on the ornate sideboard standing against the wall under a fancy painting opposite his desk. Connecticut was a long way from Florida but in the Fall the weather was quite pleasant. The mantle clock's chime announced that it was noon.

He was on the phone with Luis Santiago in Florida.

"Four things," Luis was telling him. "According to French police records obtained by Leroux, Paul Bouchard has a rap sheet."

"What for?"

"Selling jewelry stolen from Holocaust victims. He pleaded no contest in a Paris court, arguing that he didn't know that the jewelry was stolen, and was let go. The second thing is about the shooters at Charlie Hand's barbershop. According to ballistics, their weapons came from Canaan Metal Works too. Santana believes they were White Knights. The third thing is that the Anglos in the glades were from the White Knights militia in Connecticut."

Harold chortled.

"Well, what do you know! Good old Connecticut Yankees. Probably from proper suburban homes and the right families. What's the fourth thing?"

"It's the jewelry that Jonesey found in Hernando's bag when he died. Jake Santana and Europol ran a check and found out that the stuff was stolen."

"What's so unusual about that?"

"It was stolen from European warehouses where unclaimed jewelry and household effects belonging to Holocaust victims are kept. It also turns out that much of the estate jewelry sold by Emerald and Boucher & Salieri in the Caribbean is also Holocaust inventory. Cecil was right. Emerald and B&S are fencing stolen goods. And what's more, everything is insured by Centurion. It dovetails neatly into the Bates-Weinberg stolen jewelry deal. I can see why Victor and Emilio want to muscle in, especially if they're broke."

Harold was non-committal.

"Where's Frank and Jonesey?"

"In St. Maarten."

"What the hell are they doing there?"

"They're working their way up the food chain."

Harold understood.

Anything else?"

"A robbery in San Juan. Rare pieces of estate jewelry being exhibited at the San Jeronimo fortress near the Hilton were stolen an hour ago."

"Who's the exhibitor?"

"Boucher & Salieri. It should be on the police wires by now."

"Keep me posted and check with Leroux to see what he knows."

"What about Sid? Should I update him?"

"No, not yet. Now, What's the Council?"

"It's the Centurion board and Horizon. The meeting is set for Friday."

"Great. I'll be there."

"That may be difficult, Harold. You're not on the board and you're not a part of Horizon."

"I'll work it out."

He hung up and called Ray Booker, his chief information officer one floor below, asking him to brief him on the San Juan robbery.

The robbery described by Luis had taken place in a converted dungeon deep in the bowels of the San Jeronimo fortress, according to Ray who seemed to have the world's current events at his fingertips. He described the dungeon as a public museum that hosted traveling exhibits. This one was sponsored by Boucher & Salieri and a Holocaust victims group and featured a showing of French household effects stolen by the Nazis from families who perished in concentration camps during World War II. Most of the items were returned by the Allies to the French government after the war and kept in warehouses for unclaimed merchandise, Ray Booker went on to explain.

Selected pieces were displayed each year by Boucher & Salieri at different locations. These were well publicized events that also gave the firm a chance to sell its own jewelry. Their events drew big crowds and this year's showing in San Juan was no exception.

Showcased at San Jeronimo was a fancy dining room set with an elaborate service for twelve on the table. Centered in the middle was a three foot high menorah of eighteen karat gold encrusted with diamonds. It was the copy of the Menorah of Titus that Denise had told Amison about.

It was illuminated by a powerful ceiling light and sealed inside a plexiglass cubicle cordoned off from the public by an alarm wired rope barrier patrolled by armed guards. Around the barrier were counters and display cases filled with diamond necklaces, gold pins, rings, bracelets and watches offered for sale. Louis Salieri was there in person to preside over the exhibit.

According to witnesses, he was present with two sales associates who were catering to a tall, high heeled blonde woman in a flashy red cocktail dress and dark floppy hat, veil and white kid gloves. One sales associate was showing her a tray full of diamond rings while the other stood by and kept watch.

Two more salespeople worked the lunch crowd who pressed forward against the counters to view the jewelry after being reminded that the dining able, the place settings and menorah were not for sale. But something went wrong with the credit card swiping machine. Louis Salieri came over to have a look and make a phone call, but the line went down and the lights went out, plunging the gallery into darkness. When power was restored and the light went back on, the lady in red and the menorah were gone.

Harold wondered after he hung up on Ray Booker whether it was Centurion or Alliance who held the master policy covering the menorah. In any case, he had no intention of paying. He mind was made up on that. But that was only a fleeting concern. He was too busy admiring his new space. The mantle clock, the painting, sideboard and desk were gifts from Jacques Leroux's Paris office for jobs well done in the past.

Noon. He was expected at Used-To-Be's restaurant in Greenwich where he knew Victor Duncan would be waiting. A self satisfied grunt left his lips and he lit a cigar despite the no smoking ban in his building. He had several good reasons to be happy. His attorneys had just informed him that the West Indian stock transfer was a done deal. Now, the trick was for him to gain full control of Centurion, West Indian Mines, Emerald and Boucher & Salieri.

Alliance was now firmly entrenched in the new high rise office building in Stamford's corporate center. It occupied the two top floors and penthouse and Harold's private office was in the penthouse which had a three hundred sixty degree view of the city and Long Island Sound. A private elevator connected the penthouse to the operations floor on the forty second floor and another one lead to the company's general offices on the forty first floor and to the reception area near a bank of general use elevators that ran down to the lobby off the street and to the garage below the street.

Not as fancy as Centurion's digs, Harold thought, but nice enough for right now. Moreover, the rest of the building was fully rented, and that was good.

Looking west, Sol could see the upscale town of Greenwich, and between the trees and low rise buildings he could even make out the vague outline of Greenwich Avenue, the town's main thoroughfare that sloped gently down from the Boston Post Road to Used-To-Be's at the bottom of the hill across from the interstate highway and the railroad station.

It would take Tommy Hicks, his chauffeur, about five minutes to make the run to the restaurant, depending on the traffic. Sol relied on Tommy's driving instincts. Tommy was a Bridgeport native who had spent the last ten years in a federal prison for several armed bank robberies and needed a job. Sol needed a driver with local knowhow and so this was a marriage of convenience.

He lifted his rangy frame from his oversized executive chair behind the desk, stuffed the cigar between his side teeth with a swagger, triggered open a door leading to emergency stairs and bounded down to Ray Booker's office.

Harold had another reason to be happy. If his arrangement with Tommy was a mutual accommodation, his connection with Ray was fortuitous. Ray was a a handicapped computer and telecommunications expert who Sol had rescued from a dead end life in a veteran's hospital.

Ray was tuned in to a talk radio program when Sol appeared.

"Hate radio" was how Sol described that particular program.

"Who's on today?" Sol asked.

Ray turned in his wheelchair.

"Keith Bates. He's talking about forming an alliance between his Patriotic Front party and a European neo Nazi party to defend the White race against contamination by the rest of the world."

Harold shook his head.

"The problem with Keith is that he hates everyone. White isn't his favorite color; it's his only color."

Ray shrugged.

"It's a free country, Harold."

Harold snickered.

"Anything going on in the Caribbean?"

Ray swung himself around in his wheelchair and bent his stocky frame to better see the computer screens around him. He used his good hand to push some buttons and the images and data on several of the screens changed at his touch.

"Santiago's sources report that a private yacht with two choppers put in for fuel at the Navy base in Charlotte Amalie on the island of St. Thomas in the U.S. Virgin islands," he replied.

"Follow up on that, Ray. Find out who's on the boat. I'll speak to Luis about this. He must have more information. What else?"

"Jacques Leroux will be at today's meeting."

"Good. He'll also be in Washington tonight. Call me if anything else comes up," Harold said. "You know where I'll be."

"I have one question," said Ray.

"What's that?"

"What's a menorah?"

"It's a candelabra or something. How the hell would I know?"

"I thought you knew."

Harold laughed.

"I'm a Jamaican Anglican," he explained. "It wasn't unusual for slaves in the old days to adopt their masters' names. That's how I got my name, but I'm not Jewish."

Harold left the operations floor and made his way to the underground garage where Tommy Hicks was waiting with his limo. On the way down, he pulled out his cell phone and called Sol Weinberg.

"You heard about the candelabra in San Juan?"

"Menorah, Harold. Yeah. I heard."

"With whom is Boucher & Salieri insured?"

"With Centurion. I didn't transfer that account to Alliance."

Harold sighed with relief and asked, "What about the woman in red?"

"She fits the description of either Denise or Danielle Bates, but there's one small problem. Denise is in Florida and Danielle is in Connecticut."

CHAPTER 12

▼

Used-to-Be's

So, that was that. But, it was a nice day and Harold thought he might be able to get in eighteen holes of golf that afternoon if lunch went well and there was no reason why it should not be successful. Victor wanted his family holdings to be reassessed for insurance and estate planning purposes by Alliance. This was in addition to their being already insured by the company and would be gravy on the steak for Harold.

It was obvious that Victor wanted to cozy up to Harold and was offering him carrots. Sol had transferred all Emerald's mortgage based debt to Alliance and Harold planned to have Victor agree to exchange his stock in West Indian and Emerald in return for debt forgiveness plus a guaranteed income which would at least cover his impending legal expenses. He had discussed all this with Victor who had seemed amenable.

It took little time to reach the restaurant in light traffic where Tommy Hicks dropped him off and agreed to pick him up an hour later. Harold squared his shoulders, threw his cigar away and entered the popular eatery, hoping for the best.

The place was packed with the usual lunch crowd: business executives from local corporate centers like General Electric, well heeled clientele from trendy boutiques and department stores lining Greenwich Avenue such as Saks Fifth Avenue and Ralph Lauren, and young mothers with their toddlers in tow. There were window tables and a bar to the left of the door, a dining room to the right behind a dividing wall, and an outdoor seating area that was filled to capacity.

Toby Sands, the headwaiter, greeted Harold at the bar.

"They're at the table on the other side of the bar, sir," he said. "It's the best spot this time of day."

Harold nodded politely.

"Thank you, Tobias."

He followed the headwaiter past the bar where Tom Clark, a local police detective with a John Wayne face and figure, was engrossed in conversation with a female companion. Ben Olsen was working the bar and winked at the big man.

"Good to see you again, sir."

Harold smiled and looked up and down the bar.

"Where's Wayne Cabot?"

"Took a job in sunny Florida. More money, less work."

"Great," said Harold, and turning to Jack Stuart, the general manager who was seated at the bar speaking to a leggy, well built blonde woman, he asked, "How's everything, Jack, Danielle?"

"Fine," Jack answered. "How's with you?"

Danielle gave him a languorous hug that seemed slightly embarrassing.

"You look terrific, Harold. Victor is waiting for you. Three people are with him. I know Leroux, but not the other two."

"That's ok," said Harold. "Sorry I'm late. How's your sister?"

"Denise? She fine. She's in Florida." Then, she whispered in his ear. "You never returned me calls."

"I got you messages on the cell," he replied in a low voice. I thought your sister was getting back with Jonesey or Leroux or maybe Bienvenido. He's the one with the bucks."

"That's not working out so far," Danielle said. "But what about us?"

"When Victor is out of the way and I get what he has, then you have a shot." Toby led him through the maze of customers to the table past the bar where Victor Duncan was seated with Jacques Leroux facing two men whose backs were to Harold. One was a short, pudgy man in a blue suit and red tie who was introduced as Stan Mason, an Internal Revenue Service agent.

His companion, taller, in a tweed sport coat and sporting a Teddy Roosevelt moustache, rose to shake Harold's hand.

"Calvin Bard," he said, grabbing Harold's hand in a firm grip. "CIA."

"Monsieur Bard heads the CIA's Caribbean desk," Leroux said. "He is my counterpart in Washington. I invited him because of our mutual interests. I also invited Monsieur Mason who was been investigating the relationship between West Indian Mines. Emerald House and Boucher and Salieri."

Victor, seemingly oblivious to the newcomers, stretched over the table to shake Harold's hand as a waiter took lunch orders.

"How are you doing old buddy? Getting used to your new digs?"

"Sure am. I might even move up here. Are the ponies treating you right?"

Victor made a wry face.

Harold sat down at the space reserved for him.

After the small talk about the wonderful weather was done and pleasantries about nothing in particular were exchanged, Victor asked,

"I bet you guys don't know how I chose the name, Used-To-Be's, for this joint."

Harold leaned forward and cupped his hands.

"Tell us," he said.

Victor's carefully slicked back dark hair glistened in the artificial light and his eyes danced in anticipation of his guests' reaction.

"The restaurant had several owners before I bought it, and each time it had a different name. Now, there must be more than a dozen joints along this strip, some cheap and some expensive, and I bet their names are hard to remember. So I decided to call this one Used-To-Be's, and it's drawn a repeat business ever since."

"But why a restaurant?" Harold asked.

Victor grinned.

"Adjoining us is Emerald House, our main store. This is a rich market, but we find it's easier to close a million dollar deal over burgers and coffee here than at those fancy places up the street."

"How are your other stores doing?"

"Great. Our biggest business is in the Caribbean. You may want to have your guys make the rounds and get acquainted."

"We're going to do that, Victor," Harold assured him.

Harold's words gave Stan Mason the opening he needed.

"The IRS is also trying to figure out what you own," he chimed in.

"I like that," said Victor, laughing, "because when you find out, you can tell me."

Two waitresses returned with the table's appetizers.

"We'll try to save a few morsels for you when we're done, Vic," Stan said.

Harold looked at his watch as everyone else guffawed.

"That's great, people. But can we talk business now? I just want to make sure Vic understands the agreement he's about to make with Alliance."

"Shoot," said Victor.

"Good. Now my understanding is that you owe Centurion $100 million as reflected in a number of credit instruments. Is that correct?"

"Yes."

"And you understand that your obligations to Centurion have been assigned to Alliance."

"Yes, I know."

"Fine. And since those obligations are past due, I think we should resolve the issue. Here's what I propose. I'll write off your obligations in exchange for the transfer of your Emerald and West Indian stock to Alliance. In return, Alliance will guarantee you a life time annual income of $1 million. That's it in a nutshell. If you agree, I have an agreement for you to sign."

Harold patted his jacket pocket to confirm that he had the document.

Victor Duncan looked at Harold and Jacques Leroux and then at the IRS and CIA men. This was like a poker game and each player held a hand. Harold had played his hand. The IRS and CIA had not yet played their hands but he knew deep inside that after all was said and done he had the losing cards.

Victor took a deep breath and looked around the table one more time.

"Including the restaurant?"

Harold surveyed the eatery quickly with his eyes and answered, "Yes.".

"Ok. Where do I sign?"

Harold pulled the short document out of his inside jacket pocket and gave it to Victor to sign. He took more copies out of his pocket and distributed them to Leroux, Mason and Bard, saying, "You guys hang on to these copies. They make you witnesses to this transaction."

They took their respective copies, studied them briefly, put them away, and at long last, Victor Duncan broke into a nervous smile.

"Well," he said. "It seems that you guys have everything under control." His eyes wandered over to the bar where his wife had been chatting with his manager, Jack Stewart. Both were gone. Toby Sands had caught his gaze eye and came over to explain that Danielle's car was in service and that Jack had driven her home to pack for Washington where she was filling in for Denise and Emilio at a function at the embassy of Monte Fuego that Juan Duarte was hosting.

"I better get home and help my wife get ready," said Victor. "Good luck with my restaurant. It's all yours, now."

He got up and left through the kitchen.

Harold waited until Victor was gone before asking Leroux.

"I think we got what we wanted, Jacques, don't you?"

Leroux nodded.

"You have also inherited Victor's tax problems, and I wish you well. This is why I invited these gentlemen to our luncheon. Monsieur Mason, you wish to say something?"

Stanley Mason cleared his throat.

"Here's the situation, Harold. Emerald House, Boucher & Salieri and West Indian Mines are giant tax scams, as you probably guessed by now. The IRS has a solid case for back taxes, interest and penalties going back years. So do the French. In other words, I'm saying that what used to be can't be anymore, if you pardon the pun."

Harold leaned back, folded his arms and studied Stanley Mason carefully.

"Is that all?"

Stanley was not too sure Harold had understood the ramifications of his words and decided to elaborate.

"Let me put it another way," he said. "The IRS takes a dim view of trade in conflict diamonds, offshore tax shelters and tax evasion. That's what West Indian Mines and Emerald are about. So is B& S. But that's a French issue.

Now, factor in a dose of good old fashioned smuggling to the equation, and we have serious criminal counts followed by long prison sentences at the end of the rainbow."

"Smuggling?"

"Exactly," replied Calvin Bard, speaking for the first time. "Grand theft and smuggling. Our investigations with Europol indicate that Black Star Trading is using companies like Emerald House and Boucher & Salieri as fences. The CIA and Europol need your assistance"

"I thought your man, Max Zimmer, took care of things like that."

Calvin Bard shook his head.

"Max is in charge of counter-insurgency. What's more, he's about to retire. It would be better if you worked directly through my office."

"Sounds good," said Harold. "But how do you define this assistance?"

Stan Mason looked first at Calvin Bard and Leroux before replying.

"Easily," he replied. "Clean up those companies."

"That's a tall order. Are we going to be paid for that?"

Jacques Leroux nodded affirmatively.

"Messieurs Bard, Mason and I have discussed that, Harold. We propose a quid pro quo. The IRS will drop all charges in return for your assistance to the

CIA and Europol, The IRS also wants West Indian to exact from Emerald not more than a maximum management fee of 5% of revenues from today on in lieu of the current 50% and pay its income taxes on all earned income in the United States. And naturally, your mission expenses will be paid by Europol."

"And Europol will send its missions to Horizon as usual?"

"As usual."

"I suppose that this makes us partners, Jacques?"

"Of course."

Harold smacked his lips, saying, "Well, how about eighteen holes of golf?"

CHAPTER 13

▼

The Hit

Harold called Sol Weinberg late afternoon to find out if the Council meeting was still on for Friday. It was, and it was to be at the Riverside. No firm date had been set for the memorial luncheon to honor those who died in the line of duty but the consensus was that it would be at the Brittany. It was also agreed that Amison would do Hank Lawrence's eulogy.

Amison greeted the news with a curse when he was called by Luis on his cell phone Wednesday morning to summarize Harold's Greenwich meeting. He was with Erica at the Grand Hotel on Phillipsburg's boardwalk near the beach at Wathey Square. He and Frank had arrived the day before from the tiny island of St. Barts a few miles away from St. Maarten where they were flown in directly from Fort Lauderdale by Mike Quinn and Tucker Andersen, Virgil Holmes and Jimmy Wales were already in St. Barts and busy preparing two island hopping go-fast boats at a small marina owned by a local Europol agent for the short off shore passage to Philipsburg.

Erica had come in Tuesday evening from Miami on her way back to Monte Fuego to set up a meeting with Jorge Ramirez on behalf of Janice who stayed in San Juan.

Frank had a room at the Seaman's Rooming House across the road from Bobby's Marina, halfway between the city and the cruise ship terminal and a short walk from the center of town.

Their rooms were reserved by Erica under the name she used when she was living with Max Zimmer, Erica Marie Zimmer. She registered as M. Zimmer and paid cash. But unbeknownst to them, Wednesday morning, two stateside events had already transpired.

They happened simultaneously Monday evening, One was in Washington at the embassy of the Republic of Monte Fuego to honor the re-election of its chief executive, Juan Duarte Gutierrez. His brother, Emilio, was with Denise down in Florida and could not fly up in time. That left Danielle to represent both of them as well as Victor who had to stay in Connecticut to host a wine tasting charity dinner at the Delmar hotel facing Greenwich harbor.

Victor was about to propose a toast when a tall blonde in a black, cocktail dress and white kid gloves walked in with a pistol in her left hand and aimed it at Victor.

"No. No," Victor was supposed to have cried according to witnesses. "It's not me you want."

Tom Clark, the detective who was given the case, was told by these same witnesses that the woman fired point blank. Victor fell dead on his back. She then placed a shapely leg on his body, puckered her lips and blew the smoke away from the gun barrel before dropping the weapon on his belly. Turning around, she smiled and disappeared into the night.

Several phone calls and a fast police inquiry confirmed that Danielle at that very instant was in Washington and that her sister, Denise, was with Emilio in Florida.

Amison learned of Victor's death in calls from Luis and Harold and Leroux who interrupted their breakfast.

"Things are beginning, as you say in America, to rock and roll. First we have the robbery and now this murder. I suppose Alliance is a winner here since it acquires Victor's shares in West Indian, Emerald and Boucher. But it is the robbery in San Juan that is of immediate concern."

"Was the menorah valuable?" Amison asked.

"Holocaust inventory," said Leroux. "That particular menorah is priceless. However, this is but the tip of an iceberg, monsieur Jones. Europe has many warehouses filled with the unclaimed possessions of Holocaust victims. A routine inventory check of a few warehouses has found many precious items missing. We suspect this to be the work of a professional gang of thieves and believe that menorah was taken by this same gang. I believe that Danielle and Denise are in that gang but the robbery may have been for their own benefit."

"Should we put the squeeze on Keith Bates?"

"Yes, by all means. Press him at our meeting, Friday." replied Leroux

"In that case, Frank, Luis, Sid and I would like to see you."

"As soon as you get back will be fine."

When the conversation ended, Amison turned to inform Erica to whom he had not yet said anything.

"Janice may need a new sugar daddy," he said. Victor Duncan is dead. The police say that a woman answering the description of Danielle or Denise shot him."

Erica appeared stunned.

"Are you sure?"

"No," Amison replied, "Danielle was in Washington and Denise was seen in San Juan Monday, but that too would have been impossible too since she was reported in Florida with Emilio. Are you still holding out for him?"

"Do you have a better idea?" she asked in return.

"Well, I could take you away from all this. We'll sail away to the Keys and start over."

Erica gave him a friendly shove.

"You're not serious. What about Estrella?"

Amison laughed.

"She's an heiress. She'll be fine. We'll make sure she gets her due. We owe her that."

"She registered a will in Monte Fuego," Erica volunteered. "And named you as the beneficiary of her estate."

Amison sat up straight.

"Now, that's funny. Especially since she plans to marry Keith Bates. Won't he be surprised!"

Erica became very quiet. Finally, she asked, "You're serious about us going to the Keys?"

"Very serious. I'm ready to pack it in. It's time."

"Yes," she whispered. "And maybe, we'll open up that beer, bait and tackle joint we've always talked about."

"Ice, extra," Amison added. "But we need to wait a while. Today, we have work to do."

Breakfast ended on that note.

As the lunch hour neared, Erica put on a colorful long sarong style skirt, a white blouse, covering her head with a broad brimmed straw hat to shade her from the tropical sun. It was going to be a beautiful day.

While she was dressing, Amison packed and threw on a tan over-the-trouser short sleeve shirt over his slacks. Checking out of the hotel with their duffels, they walked around the corner to Wathey Square.

In his free hand Amison gripped an attache case and for once the tattoos on his long sinewy arms caught Erica's attention; a faded screaming eagle was on one arm and a striking snake on the other. She had been in his arms and seen them the tattoos many times but now they bothered her in a strange way.

His thinning hair was carefully slicked back and his gait was jaunty and yet determined and his eyes were distant and cold. He was no longer looking at her but through her as if he was waiting for something dangerously inevitable to happen. A shudder ran down her spine despite the heat and the sun above.

They found Frank on a bench under a palm tree facing a Burger King, the only American fast food eatery in the center of town.

The food service counter was off the street and the dining area and restroom was upstairs. It was easy to find and Jorge had told Erica it would make for an ideal meeting place.

Frank, who had also checked out of his quarters, was subdued despite his having on a colorful short sleeve island shirt over his chinos. He was now all business and greeted them without cracking a smile.

"I spoke with Jorge," he said. "He'll meet us upstairs. It shouldn't take more than a few minutes."

"What do you want me to do?" asked Erica.

"Wait here for us," replied Amison.

"But we were going to look at jewelry."

"We have time to kill. Let's go shop for rings now."

They left Frank on the bench and spent the better part of the hour shopping for rings at the Emerald outlet on Front Street right around the corner from the square. After examining several trays of dazzling diamonds, they focused on a shiny two carat diamond ring that the sales associate proudly stated could be their's for a mere $110,000, tax free.

Amison seemed ready to buy until Erica took him aside, suggesting that they might do better at Emerald in La Fortuna.

They thanked the sales person and took a window shopping stroll along the main street.

"I don't think you should buy me such an expensive ring," Erica finally said upon reflection. You can put your money to better use."

"I could sell this gold watch," Amison joked, showing her the watch on his wrist.

"It's nice," she said. "You deserved it and you should keep it."

"You're probably right," replied Amison. "I was actually more interested in pricing than in buying. I actually have access to a bunch of two carat stones that were confiscated from Black Star Trading that are supposedly worth at least $100,000. I want to make sure I'm not hearing things."

Erica took his hand in hers.

"You're going to be in deep shit if Keith finds out."

Amison sighed.

"I'm in deep shit already. He knows."

"Are you going to return them?"

"No. They're hot diamonds to begin with."

Erica let his hand go.

"You're not telling me everything, Ruby" she said. "This thing you're in is bringing us trouble. You don't have to do anything for Emilio, you know. I don't need him anymore. I have other options now."

"That's nice to know, But Frank, Luis and I are on a roll."

"That means you're not ready to retire, are you?"

"I am, but not today," he said.

"That's always been your story, Ruby," Erica noted sadly. "And that's the business you're in. Death is your shadow."

"I suppose. But tell me, what's Janice going to do without Victor?"

"She too has other options."

"I'm glad. You both might need them if things get nasty."

"It doesn't matter anymore, Ruby. Nothing matters. I'm in as long you're in, I have no choice. You're playing your last hand, and so am I. This is the end game for us. There is no tomorrow."

Erica wanted to shop other stores but time ran out and they had to get back to the square.

Erica followed Amison in a trance back to Wathey Square. It was now filled with tourists from cruise ships and hotels mingling with the locals in the heat of the day for a few frenetic hours of shopping. From the square could be seen the public dock and the crowded beaches. A road crew digging up a section of the square with clattering jack hammers pounded on Erica's brain and images began to blur. She saw Frank from the corner of her eye go into Burger King, but did not hear Amison as he left her at the side of a bench like a pet dog. She only saw him from the back, attache case in hand, follow Frank inside. There was now nothing else for her to do but to wait.

Inside the Burger King, Amison and Frank found Jorge, perspiring, hands shaking slightly, at the order counter. Frank passed him a twenty dollar bill and asked him to get coffee and bring it upstairs where they could talk. They waited until he had picked up his lunch and their coffees and went up to the second floor seating area where they took a table near the public bathroom.

"Do you have the money?" Jorge asked nervously as they sat down.

Amison patted the attache case and answered cheerfully, "Sure do," he said.

Jorge started eating.

"I must think of the future," he stated in between bites of food. "If I tell you what I know, I cannot return to the States. If I do, I could be killed."

"I understand," nodded Frank sympathetically before suggesting, "However, if we solve a few problems at the Riverside, there might be room for you as an assistant manager or even a manager."

A broad smile broke across Jorge's face.

"Do you think so?"

Then his smile vanished and he pursed his lips.

"No. Mr. Stone would never allow it."

"I can speak to Sid," said Amison. "He personally likes you. He simply has problems remembering names. Think about it anyway."

Jorge shook his head and replied, "No. I will stay here on the island where I have friends and family, and with the money I will open a restaurant."

"Maybe that's best," agreed Frank. "Now, what do you have for us?"

"I am not to blame for Sammy Luke's death," Jorge began. "I merely let him into Mr. Jones's suite to steal the watch that had been left for him by Carlos Ramon Salva."

"You helped Sammy break into my apartment?" Amison asked in surprise.

"Si. In a moment of weakness. We were going to sell it and make money. We thought you were dead and would not need the watch. I did not know he was going to be shot."

"Do you know who shot him?"

Not sure. Mr. Zimmer told me the morning before Sammy was shot that you were back and that I should tell Felipe. I passed the word to Felipe who told Klondike Pete. That night he, Al Garcia and another gentleman said they were going to meet you. I saw them leave the hotel together early the evening Sammy Luke was killed."

Frank folded his arms.

"Does that other gentleman have a name?"

"Si. Wayne Cabot. But I don't know him," added Jorge quickly. "I saw him only once when he was having lunch with Mr. Zimmer at the hotel and heard the name. I think he works for Mr. Zimmer. Felipe and Al Garcia also receive money from Mr. Zimmer. I have seen it with my own eyes."

Amison smiled benignly, asking, "What about Emilio Gutierrez? Does he know what his son is doing?"

"Maybe. I am not sure. Emilio is mad at his son because he caught him with his wife."

Amison and Frank laughed.

"And what happened in the Everglades, Jorge. Did you tell Max Zimmer about the terrorist camp?"

"Yes. Mr. Zimmer pays me to give him this kind of information. He says it is good for the country and that I am a true hero."

"Why are you telling us this now, Jorge?"

"I do not want to be implicated in murder," the waiter answered. "I want to do what is right."

Frank smacked his lips and looked at the bathroom door which had opened to let out a customer. Pointing to the unoccupied restroom, he said, "You've earned your keep, Jorge. Let's go inside and count the money."

The lunch crowd was gone; they were alone and Jorge was anxious to get his money. Amison nodded, rose up and walked into the bathroom with Jorge behind followed by Frank who locked the door with the inside push knob.

Jorge kept his eyes on the attache case in Amison's hand and never saw the surgical gloves he and Frank had put on. Nor did he see the switchblade knife flourished by Amison as he suddenly turned, shoved the attache case into his chest with one hand and slit his throat with the other. In one sweeping motion, Frank caught the limp waiter in his arms, easing him down on a toilet stool in one of the open stalls. The attache case was still clutched in his arms.

Amison pried open Jorge's right hand and deftly closed the fingers over the switchblade handle. He squeezed the fingers for a moment before letting the knife drop to the ground while Frank cautiously opened the bathroom door and looked out. The dining room was still empty.

"What was in the attache case?" Frank asked when they were outside.

"Travel brochures."

"Whose knife did you use?"

"It was the blade Max dropped at the barbershop."

Erica was still sitting on the bench and stood up when they approached.

Amison gave her a kiss on the cheeks and they started walking away.

"Where's Jorge?" she asked.

"He decided to stay for dinner," Frank answered.

It finally dawned on Erica that Jorge was dead and she began to cry.

"Better dry the tears," Frank said softly.

A cab pulled up on Front Street. Virgil was behind the wheel.

"Get in," ordered Amison. "We're out of here."

A tense silence marked the short ride to Bobby's Marina where they found Tucker Andersen waiting with a go-fast boat. Alongside was another racer with Jimmy Wales aboard. Suddenly, Erica burst into tears.

"This is awful," she cried. "I never thought this is how you do your work, Jorge never had a chance."

"People died because of him," replied Amison.

"You used me!"

"We need to get out of here" Frank said, checking his watch."

Clouds rolled in with a squall line and a light rain began falling. Amison felt a chill crawl down his back and was in no mood to argue. He pulled a wad of bills from his pocket and stuffed them into Erica's bag.

"What's this?"

"Ten grand, doll. This will keep you a while. You're going back to Monte Fuego today."

"Can I count it?" Erica asked tearfully.

"It's all there," replied Amison impatiently, closing the clasp on the bag.

"I...I don't think I can spend the rest of my life with you, Ruby," she said.

Amison shrugged, throwing her a fast sideways glance as he began walking away."

"You suit yourself, cookie. But have a good life anyway, you hear."

He turned his attention to Jimmy Wales, saying, "Get her to La Fortuna. It's four hours southeast of here. If you move fast, you'll get there tonight."

Hustling Erica on board, they waited until the racer had thundered off before jumping on the first go-fast boat with Tucker Andersen.

"Mike Quinn is waiting with the jet in St. Barts," said Tucker.

CHAPTER 14

▼

Carte Blanche

Except for Jimmy Wales who returned late on Thursday, everyone was back in Florida by midnight, Wednesday. However, news of Jorge's death reached Leroux and Jake Santana within hours after his body and the knife was found by a Burger King employee. The local police thought it to be a case of either murder or suicide. But since his death occurred on an island technically under Dutch control, the body was flown to the Netherlands for autopsy. The knife was turned over to the local Europol agent who examined it then gave it to the Dutch authorities.

Thursday morning, dressed and refreshed after a good night's sleep, ran into Virgil Holmes in the Riverside's lobby.

"Luis got the word from Jake about St. Maarten, boss.".

"Figures. Thanks anyway, Virgil. Anything else going on?"

"Frank's up and about if you need him."

"Tell him, Luis and Sid that I want to see them next door."

"Sure thing, boss."

Amison was a loner and rarely called meetings, and so on those occasions when he did, they tended to start promptly.

Dimitri closed the restaurant to the public and kept watch with his brothers, Angelo and Petros, at the front door, leaving Virgil to guard the rear exit.

Dimitri was short and had a thick accent. He was a Greek immigrant who found his niche with an inexpensive restaurant that featured hamburgers and cheeseburgers and assorted hot dogs in the middle of tony Las Olas. It was in keeping with the seat of his eatery's drab appearance that his brown hair was disheveled and his white tee shirt was as stained as the old apron covering his cheap chino slacks. He and his brother, Angelo, were permanent fixtures at Hamburger Haven as Anastos had been before being killed. But Dimitri came from a large family and had eight brothers and many first cousins. A cousin, Petros, was imported from a family owned diner in New Jersey, and was in place at Hamburger Haven when Amison and Virgil showed up.

The division of labor was simple. Dimitri cooked; Evangelo waited tables, and Petros did dishes and cleaned.

"New laws," said Dimitri with regret in his voice. "No more smoking in the kitchen."

Over coffee, Amison and Frank described their visit to St. Maarten to Luis and Sid.

"Jorge had it coming," Sid commented. "Felipe has to be next."

"Will Erica keep her mouth shut?" Luis wondered.

"Why not?" Frank replied. "After all, Janice set the whole thing up. They're both in on it."

Amison shook his head.

"Let's think straight, guys," he cautioned. "The girls didn't set up Jorge to be killed. The meeting was set up so that he could talk and collect the reward money. We need to make sure they don't talk and sell us out."

"How are we going to do that?" Frank asked.

"Carefully," replied Amison.

Frank tried to ease his mind.

"The saving grace is that Erica and Janice like us and want to stay in good with us. Besides, they're not virgins. Erica is seeing Emilio on the sly and Janice was making it with Victor until he died. They'll stay quiet That's the way life is. Look at Sid. He has a thing going on with Charlotte. Is she going to blow the whistle on him?"

Amison took a sip of coffee and deferred to Sid.

"That's different," Sid noted. I'm keeping company with a recent widow with kids and Charlotte doesn't have the foggiest idea that I'm working with you guys."

Amison looked up, saying, "Why? Is she stupid? All these women can be bad news. You know, Frank, I never should have taken your advice to see Erica. Do you know that in a moment of weakness I was on the verge of asking her to marry me?"

"Am I glad I stuck with one wife," muttered Luis. "One wife, three kids in college. I could use another husband around the house."

"Oh, shut up, Luis."

But Luis was not to be deterred.

"I told you and Frank many times. Scorpions don't make good house pets."

"You're right," said Amison. "And in this instance, we're with women who are screwing their best friends' husbands and their best friends want their own spouses murdered."

Frank countered. "You mean Danielle and Denise. Who cares? A woman is a woman and so on. We're not eunuchs. Besides, they'll end up killing each other before they kill us if we're lucky. In any case, they know things that we still need to know. So let's hope they stay afloat a while longer."

Sid raised his hand to interrupt.

"Can we get back to this Ramirez business, Jonesey? Now that he's gone, what do we do about Felipe?"

"That's what I want to discuss," said Amison. "Felipe is a trained dog. We need to find his handler or handlers before killing him."

"Emilio?"

"I don't think so. He's a side show. Keith and Max are better bets. Matter of fact, Bienvenido fingered Jorge, Felipe and Max as the guys who set up the Everglades ambush, and I'm sure Max set me up at the barbershop. But by the same token, Max isn't acting alone. He either has partners or higher ups. We stumbled onto something big when we inherited that piece of West Indian and when Cecil seized those diamonds for Europol. It's biting us big time and we can't get out."

"So, what do we do now?" asked Sid.

"That's where you come in. You've always been one of us but you've stayed in the background and given us support with your resources and connections. Can we continue to count on that support?"

Sid did not hesitate with his answer.

"Of course! You shouldn't even ask. Indeed, Leroux and I have been invited by Sol and Harold to take an equity interest in Alliance. That can be good for you."

"How did that happen?" Luis asked.

It was a stock trade. I owned 5% of Centurion and Leroux had 2.5% Sol Weinberg traded us 7.5% of his Alliance stock for our 7.5% of Centurion. That reduced his interest in Alliance to 42.5% but raised his Centurion equity 47.5% so that he can even outvote Ramon Salva. Smart move. It's good for him, good for Leroux and me and good for you guys."

"Terrific," said Amison. "Now, I want Leroux to give us his Carte Blanche. I've already asked to meet with him later today."

Sid's face paled.

"Me too?"

Frank laughed and slapped him on the back.

"No, not you. Killing isn't your specialty. We need it for ourselves. It's an insurance policy when we start hitting back."

Jacques Leroux was in his office with Harold Levy when they called to say they were coming over. They were greeted outside by Rafael Perez, Leroux's assistant who was on an errand. Amison exchanged a few words with him and then followed the others into the Europol director's office.

"I thought it would be important for monsieur Levy to be here since we are obviously reorganizing ourselves into a new team," said Leroux, explaining Harold's presence.

The Europol director began by asking the obvious question.

"What do you think of the island of St. Maarten?"

"I'm hoping to go there some day," answered Frank. "Is it nice?"

Leroux laughed and clapped his hands.

"A wonderful response," he said, continuing to tell them what they already knew. "What is strange is that a knife belonging to Max Zimmer was found near Jorge's body with Jorge's fingerprints as well as those of Max on it. It is very confusing, very confusing." Leroux shook his head repeatedly and then added. "Also, it seems that Max was on the island and stayed at a local hotel where he registered and paid cash for a room. Very strange." He shook his head again, suppressing a smile.

"Maybe Jorge and Max had a thing going and Max got jealous," suggested Harold.

"Excellent explanation," agreed Leroux. "But let us put poor Jorge's death aside to discuss more pressing matters." He began detailing the new equity relationships by reading from a set of notes inside a leather file folder.

"Centurion is completely changed. Monsieur Levy has acquired poor Victor Duncan's shares and of course monsieur Weinberg now owns 47.5% of the company. That gives the two of them a solid majority, and of course monsieur Levy is now a member of the board of directors, replacing monsieur Duncan who is deceased.

"Monsieur Levy has 50% of Alliance; monsieur Weinberg has 42.5%, with the rest going to monsieur Stone and myself. Horizon will now be working on contract with Alliance.

"At West Indian Mines, Centurion's 10% share now belongs to Alliance, and Victor Duncan's 20% share is owned by Alliance. Estrella Gomez has 20%, Horizon has 15% and Bienvenido de la Maza has 15%. That leaves 10% for Emilio Gutierrez in trust for his brother, and 10% for Black Star Trading." The Europol director looked up. "That is monsieur Keith Bates.

"At Emerald House," he continued, "Alliance now owns 40% of the chain, having acquired Centurion's and Victor Duncan's shares. Black Star has 10%, but West Indian has 50%, and of course West Indian is dominated by our side.

"At Boucher & Salieri, the story is pretty much the same. West Indian and Alliance own 50% of the company."

Leroux slammed the leather folder shut with a self satisfied grunt.

"If we are such winners," asked Harold. "Why are we being shot at?"

The Frenchman looked up and smiled.

"Ah, my friends. Not through wisdom but by chance have you tripped over a grand conspiracy."

"A grand conspiracy, Amison echoed. "In that case, we need a favor."

"Pray. What may that be, monsieur Jones?" Jacques Leroux asked.

"We need Europol's Carte Blanche."

Dark hair, thinning, slicked back, sharp eyes, a masterful nose and thin but expressive lips, a dark striped business suit over a white, French cuffed shirt and an expressive, attentive manner trademarked the Europol director, one of a rare breed of quintessential Eurocrats. His Fort Lauderdale office reflected the status of his position. Located in a gated mansion around the corner from the Floridian Diner on Las Olas Boulevard, it was decorated and furnished with period pieces reminiscent of the Empire days.

Leroux watched Amison, Frank and Luis carefully who sat impassively in front of him in the large, airy room. He opened his desk drawer and pulled out three envelopes, each sealed with the raised red and blue Europol wax seal over the lid. On the wall behind his desk was a map of the Caribbean islands.

"I assume you are asking for my Carte Blanche as special Europol agents," he said in his lyrical French accent.

"I suppose," Luis Santiago stammered, looking nervously at his friends. "I'm not sure. What does that mean?"

"A Carte Blanche is no joke, gentlemen. Your friend monsieur Jones is quite familiar with a Carte Blanche because I have given him several in the past and he has used them on my behalf. Carte Blanche is Europol's license to kill and is disbursed sparingly. It gives the bearer immunity from prosecution for all acts committed in connection with sensitive missions. Do you still want it?"

"Positive," Amison replied.

"And I assume my licence will not be used for revenge." Leroux continued.

"You must consider the circumstances since our visit to Monte Fuego," said Amison. "People have been killed not to mention the attempts on our lives."

"We need retribution," said Frank.

"We're sitting ducks," Luis continued. "Our moves are being tracked."

Leroux's lips curled.

"Retribution alone does not justify a license to kill, gentlemen. However, I agree that criminals must be punished. But before they are brought to justice, we need suspects and motives. The wishes of grieving widows must indeed be heeded, but we would not be serving them by chasing the wrong suspects. It could be that these events you describe are separate incidents growing from a common root."

"Can you explain that in English?" Sid asked.

"Yes. This goes back to the conspiracy. The fishermen who disappeared in Monte Fuego did exist. Their families reported them missing. They were done away with because their attackers thought they were witnesses to something in the vicinity of Hernando's house. We are now looking for a large yacht that can carry one or two helicopters that cruises around the Caribbean on orders from a single command center. We have been unsuccessful thus far, and I believe, monsieur Santiago, that your efforts have also been futile.

"Hernando was killed because it was suspected he knew how to access the mine from the sea, the passage used by personnel from the big white yacht. He may also have been killed to accelerate the transfer of his West Indian stock to his daughter. But in any case, whoever called for the murders of the fishermen called the hit on Hernando and is the one you must find.

"Sammy Luke's shooting, the assault on Red Fish, the helicopter attacks in North Bimini, the attempt on Luis's life on the golf course and the incident at the barbershop are connected to the change of control at West Indian, Emerald and B&S and to whatever lies buried beneath the ground on the West Indian property.

"Further, I see a connection between all these incidents and the Everglades clash. My conclusion, my friends, is that these incidents share a common root, and that root is West Indian Mines."

"What about those tax problems you discussed in Stamford?" Luis asked.

Leroux shook his head emphatically.

"Murder to hide a tax fraud scheme is silly. Plea bargaining is a better way. In fact, that is the arrangement monsieur Levy has with your IRS and it all but neutralizes the tax fraud issue."

"How does Quentin Bates figure in this?"

"Aha!" Leroux exclaimed. "That is the larger conspiracy. Are you familiar with the outrage industry? It is a global business these days."

"His guests exchanged glances.

"Allow me to explain," he continued. "People form affinity groups around issues important to them. For example, one group believes in saving the deer while another may believe that they are a traffic hazard and should be killed. There are laissez -faire groups and those who believe in totalitarianism. But whatever the group, they are well organized, well financed and lie in wait like dormant epidemics waiting to spring.

"That brings me to the hate groups. They are all over. Keith Bates belongs to a hate group, the Patriotic Front. We know for a fact that very high quality diamonds are being sold by terrorists in Africa to pay for arms. Many of these diamonds are bought at a deep discount by Boucher and Salieri and Emerald through your Keith Bates and Black Star Trading. That is how he makes his money. Sometimes, he buys and sells diamonds for his own account and most likely does not pay income taxes on his profits."

"Is that Europol's main concern?" Amison asked.

Jacques Leroux shook his head.

"No. These are minor matters of smuggling and of income and customs tax evasion. Gentlemen. We are faced with a vast conspiracy. What I need from you is a thorough house cleaning. That is the real mission."

Frank arched his eyes.

"Conspiracy? House cleaning? Can you be more specific, director?"

"Our main concern is political. Your friend Keith Bates is a member of a right wing faction in your country."

"A lobby and political action group," said Amison. "The Patriotic Front is legally registered."

"I am sure it is," Leroux went on. "And I am not opposed to free speech and freedom of expression, etcetera, etcetera. However, our intelligence informs us that the European Patriotic Front is affiliated with your Patriotic Front. In Europe, the Patriotic Front is a transnational alliance. Does it strikes a bell?"

"The neo-Nazi association of right wing parties?" Sid guessed.

"Exactly. Now consider these facts. Quentin Bates belongs to a private, right wing militia in your country, the White Knights, who you tried to neutralize a few years ago. Their European affiliates go by the same name and Intelligence tells us they are working together. That is not good for Europe and America. "Intelligence also tells us that they are being funded from sale of diamonds that flow from Black Star to Boucher and Salieri and to the Emerald stores in the Caribbean. Exactly how it happens we are unsure."

"Where are the diamonds kept prior to distribution?" Luis asked.

"That is where you come in." Leroux replied. "Your FBI has been unable so far to track the diamonds once they reach the U.S. Virgin Islands where they seem to disappear into thin air. Exactly how they end up at Emerald is what we would like to find out. But let me get back to the European White Knights. Europol believes they are behind a rash of robberies in France, Germany and in the Benelux countries that involves far more than diamonds."

"What kind of robberies?"

The Europol director's voice turned somber.

"There are the warehouses in France, Germany and other countries where the unclaimed personal possessions of holocaust victims are stored. Many are of high value, furnishings, artwork, jewelry, silverware, china, gold objects, you name it. A special section of each warehouse is devoted to items that were stolen from concentration camp inmates, gold fillings from teeth, wedding rings and watches, necklaces, bracelets, watches, everything, all the personal valuables that people would take on their last voyage away from home."

"How much are we talking about?"

"It is too much to count. Over twelve million people perished in the camps. Perhaps twenty million were imprisoned and lost their possessions. We may be looking at many billions of dollars in gold, diamonds and jewelry."

"Now, that's what I call grand larceny," exclaimed Frank.

Leroux looked up.

"I thought you would be impressed," he observed. "These warehouses are being systematically looted. And let me tell you, the thieves are brazen. They leave a business card with the raised emblem of a white chessboard knight on a black background each time they strike, like the card they left in San Juan."

"Supposing your scenario is correct," said Frank. "What is the connection between the warehouse robberies and the flow of conflict diamonds?"

"We believe they are somehow connected in a plot directed by the Patriotic Front. Our research suggests that everything is ultimately sold by Emerald to buy cocaine and heroin used to buy arms and finance campaigns to ultimately overthrow European and North American governments in favor of right wing, totalitarian Christian theocracies."

"Do you think the stuff is being warehoused in the mine?" Amison asked.

"Yes," answered Leroux.

"Who would you say runs this conspiracy?" inquired Harold.

"I have no idea. But Kinshasa Export intrigues me. It deserves a look. One thing for sure. You must find and kill the conspiracy's master architect. With this corporate reorganization, the pressure for resolution is mounting."

"What about Denise and Danielle?"

Leroux shook his head.

"Thieves and maybe killers but they are not key players. The people around us who may be implicated are players dancing to a choreographed script. Now Keith Bates and Max Zimmer may be higher up and should be watched much more carefully but not killed. At some point they will expose their leader who has money and knowhow. I need you to find the treasure of Monte Fuego and to return it to its rightful owners, and to find the grand dragon of the Patriotic Front. Find the treasure of Monte Fuego and you will find those who want to make you disappear."

"Sounds like a clear mission to me," said Harold. "How about it, guys?"

They nodded their agreement.

"Quite frankly," Leroux concluded. "I could care less if the warehouses were emptied. Most of the holocaust victims are dead and their estates are generally unaware that the inventory exists. And certainly few people worry about the origin of diamonds and other valuable objects. What frightens me more is the possibility of right wing coups in your country and Europe. It would return us to the Dark ages. The world cannot afford that."

He stood up, walked to the window and looked out.

"We need to stop the flow of life giving blood to those vampires."

Amison found Leroux convincing but Frank was skeptical.

"How does the menorah heist and Victor's killing fit in your theory?"

"Poorly," admitted Leroux. "As I said before, some people use a conspiracy to serve their own ends. You will have to solve those mysteries for me."

With those words, Leroux held out the three Carte Blanche envelopes.

"What do you think, guys?" Amison asked Frank and Luis.

"Let's go for it," Frank said.

"The letters of marque are backdated to last week," said Leroux. "And bear in mind that with these letters of mark, you answer to me. But do be careful," he added. "The truth can sometimes hide a lie."

CHAPTER 15

▼

The Council Meeting

The meeting broke up and Amison, Frank, Luis, Harold and Sid reconvened in Hamburger Haven's back room. The eatery had been closed for a couple of days in remembrance of the death of Anastos and his brothers were still quite morose over the affair. Dimitri was playing cards with Virgil when Amison and his friends entered.

"I hear you guys are in some sort of deep shit," Dimitri said in a low voice to Amison as he started for the kitchen. "You can count on us if there's any trouble."

"Thanks," replied Amison. "Virgil will keep you posted."

Virgil nodded and went to the front of the restaurant to take up his position at the front door.

"With Leroux's carte blanche, we need to do what we have to do, and that includes taking down Felipe when we're ready," Amison started.

The others grunted in agreement.

Harold turned to Amison,

"It's your call, Jonesey. But check with Bienvenido. We want to keep him in the loop. In the meantime, I have a few things for us to review. "I'm going to have the Canaan Metal Works torched this weekend. Therefore, I want the Council meeting postponed until Monday."

His statement was greeted by a dead silence.

"Is there a connection?" Frank asked.

"A big one," answered Harold. "The weapons plant is supplying the White Knights with arms and ammunition. I want its computer records and the place put out of action. Sunday night works because there'll be noone around. The news will also be fresh when the Council meets Monday."

Luis looked at Harold as if he had gone mad.

"How are we going to do that? We've never seen the place."

"Don't worry. Bienvenido's guys are doing the job. He has people working inside the plant and it's been cased for weeks. He wants payback and I need a paper trail. Canaan's order and shipping department has it."

"Once a terrorist, always a terrorist," observed Luis.

"No way," said Harold. "He trains U.N. peacekeepers. That's why the White Knights are on his case, according to Jake Santana's investigations.

"Now, about West Indian. Juan Duarte Gutierrez has been advised through our consulate in La Fortuna that Alliance has taken over the mine operation. I asked Bienvenido for help and he's sending his personal goon squad to handle things and to make sure no digging takes place until we gave a closer look. I called Juan Duarte and told him personally that he would be amply rewarded for his cooperation.

"But the real reason I'm having the Council meeting moved is to give Sol Weinberg breathing room. The Louvre museum in Paris is pressing Boucher & Salieri for a billion dollar insurance payout on the stolen menorah. B&S in turn has asked Keith Bates to pressure Centurion for payment since he owns 5% of the stock. But Sol has a cash shortfall now and can't pay. I'm positive that the robbery was an inside job designed to extort money from Sol. In any case, the subject is bound to come up at the meeting and I want to see how that scene plays out, but I need the weekend to sort things out."

In fact, Harold had no trouble convincing Sol Weinberg to have the date of the meeting pushed to Monday. It turned out that everyone wanted to get a head start on the weekend and preferred not to be in town on Friday.

On the morning of the Council meeting, Harold greeted Amison, Frank and Luis at the Riverside's registration counter, a newspaper under his arm.

"The Canaan Metal Works is gone," he announced

"How do we play Max and Keith at the meeting?" Amison asked.

"Push them. Maybe they'll crack."

Harold checked his watch.

"It's time, gentlemen. Shall we?"

The registration counter faced a wall of sliding glass doors on the far side of the combination lobby-sitting room opening into a courtyard that had been turned into a lush tropical garden. A brick walkway led through the garden to a taxi and limo stand at a cross-street. A second path circled left to the Champ Carr banquet hall where the Council was about to convene.

The hall was a mirrored ballroom with chandeliers, one of which hovered over a long conference table. To the courtyard's right was a smaller meeting facility called the Garden Room where a sales seminar was in progress.

They were interrupted by a small dapper man in a tan silk suit. It was Carlos Ramon Salva. A steely smile was fixed to his lips as he made eye contact with Amison who excused himself.

"It's good to see you again, don Carlos," said Amison, shaking his hand. "The pleasure is mine," replied Ramon Salva. "Will you be at our meeting?"

"Yes. Max Zimmer called it."

"Good," Ramon Salva said. "However, I want to remind you that some of these issues are delicate and may impact my interests."

"I can appreciate that, don Carlos."

"Si. Let me explain, senor Jones. I am Sol Weinberg's financial partner and that makes me your partner as well."

"I understand," Amison acknowledged.

"Do you? I am glad, because I need two things. First, I need you to keep an eye on Alliance Insurance; its course is different than that of Centurion's."

"I thought you were the one that urged Centurion to unload unprofitable accounts like West Indian and Emerald to Alliance."

"Si, senor Jones. But Alliance is moving too fast. Harold Levy is your old friend. Please see what you can do for me."

Amison smiled blandly.

"What is the other thing, don Carlos?"

"I am looking for a map that Hernando Gomez had. My niece, Estrella, told me about it. It is an antique map of historical importance. Do you have it?"

Amison nodded.

"Yes. It's yours. I'm sure your niece won't mind."

Just then Frank came up to announce that the meeting was starting.

The Centurion Council's meeting was open to the Centurion board and to the Horizon stockholders and guests. Harold Levy now had a vote, having taken over for Victor Duncan, Jacques Leroux and Sid Stone. Ramon Salva and Sol Weinberg were there with Max Zimmer and Keith Bates with one vote apiece. Leroux and Sid were present but they no longer voted since they no longer owned stock in Centurion. Felipe was on hand as recording secretary, and Emilio Gutierrez, who showed up as a non-voting guest, was immediately appointed to be the ad hoc meeting chair. Bienvenido de la Maza, invited by Harold, walked brazenly into the banquet room and sat himself down on a straight back chair near the door.

Outside, Amison ran into Virgil Holmes.

"Weapons, boss?"

"Just in case," Amison replied.

. By the time he entered the banquet hall, he was pleased to see that Virgil and Desmond Lyons had placed blue binders at the various place settings on the table before taking their places near the door with Jimmy Wales.

Very fancy, thought Amison, taking a seat at the table as Keith Bates walked over to shake his hand.

"Still active in politics?" Amison asked.

"Sure am, Jonesey. I intend to purify America. Let me tell you, my friend.

The White man made just two mistakes in this world when he sent rabbits to Australia and black people to America."

"A refreshing insight, Keith."

"Nothing personal, Jonesey. But are you ready for a fight?"

"Always, Keith."

"You understand that I have to protect my interests and my family."

"Fully," replied Amison.

"Then may the best man win."

Emilio banged his gavel and called the meeting to order.

He sat at the center of the oblong table facing the wings and Sol Weinberg sat at the far end facing the door to the courtyard. Amison and Sid took their places on either side of Sol while Frank. Harold, Leroux and Luis sat with their backs to the wings facing Emilio who was flanked by Ramon Salva, Max Zimmer, Keith Bates and Felipe. The chair with its back to the courtyard door, which ordinarily would have been filled by Victor Duncan, was left empty.

The bright light from the chandelier above the conference table cast a warm glow and Max Zimmer complained that the hall was too warm and that the air conditioning should be turned up. Felipe explained the cooling system was not working well and that the courtyard door should be opened.

Virgil opened the door and cool air began filling the hall, giving Amison a good view of the Garden Room across the courtyard where he noticed that the windows had gone dark.

"It's late," Emilio declared. "We must begin."

They all sat quietly as Emilio slowly and methodically went through a voice roll call dutifully recorded by his son, Felipe.

"We have two questions to discuss," began Emilio. "The first is the bible reading and benediction at the memorial luncheon to be held at a date yet to be determined. Any volunteers?"

Keith Bates raised his hand.

"I carry a bible," he offered. "It's in English. I can read a verse."

Sol objected.

"We will have Latino guests," he said. "We need a few words of Spanish."

But Keith held his ground, saying, "Why? If English was good enough for Jesus, it should be good enough for everyone!"

Emilio interrupted them to avoid an argument.

"Let's settle that question later. The second question concerns several recent events. Max. Do you want to start?"

Amison gave Max Zimmer a long hard look for the first time. Except for his watery blue eyes he left no impression. He had the look, shape and dress of a man who was hard to define and who would easily be lost in a crowd without a propellor glued to the top of his head. It was hard to believe that this was the jerk with whom Erica once rolled in the sack.

Max talked from where he sat, without emotion or feeling.

"I'll pass to Keith Bates," Max said.

Keith thanked Max and addressed the group from his seat in a voice that was loud and clear.

"My son-in-law, Victor, has been murdered. I will stand here for him and his rights as a shareholder in Emerald House and West Indian Mines."

Sol Weinberg interrupted him.

"That might be difficult, Keith. Harold here bought him out and Sid Stone and Jacques Leroux have traded their Centurion shares for Alliance stock.'"

Keith's mouth dropped as Harold referred everyone to the blue binders that included copies of the agreement signed by Victor at Used-To-Be's.

Keith's face reddened and he banged his fist on the table.

"I'll see you in court about that," he declared.

"Right Keith," countered Harold. "You have lawyers and I have lawyers."

Keith straightened his tie and tried to regain his composure and looked to Max for assistance.

"We should vote to see who represents Victor," he suggested.

Harold nodded politely.

"Oh, I agree fully, Max. But this is a scheduled meeting of the Council with all members voting. Look around. Do you want to force a vote today?"

"Are you suggesting that you are a board member by fiat?" Salva asked. "You'll have to figure it for yourself, pal," replied Harold coldly. "The file in the binder covers everything, the changes at Centurion, Alliance, West Indian, Emerald and Boucher & Salieri and reflect the equity positions of the new stockholders. My side controls West Indian Mines, Emerald and B&S and Sol and I together own more than half of Centurion. Your 40% aside, Salva, what alse do you own?"

Harold's pronouncement left the table stunned.

"What has happened is entirely legal and above board and was unanimously agreed by the Centurion board, gentlemen," said Sol, "Fate has now brought us new partners and new challenges. We also agreed that Harold would be the acting Centurion CEO and chairman should I die or become incapacitated. It therefore seems unrealistic for that reason alone to deny him a vote. But since there may be disagreement and/or misunderstandings among us, I suggest that this issue be temporarily tabled until the Centurion board can meet in private."

"I agree with el senor Weinberg," said Ramon Salva. "This vote can be held later. We should go on to new business."

Keith Bates was not to be sidetracked.

"That's not good enough for me," he persisted. "My daughter's interests in her deceased husband's estate must be protected."

Harold laughed with glee.

"Not a problem, Keith," he replied. "Danielle can see me anytime. But right now, the Greenwich police want to speak with her about Victor."

"She has an alibi," said Emilio.

"I'm sure," said Harold. "And Denise was probably not in San Juan when the menorah was stolen."

Emilio squirmed uncomfortably in his chair.

"We were together here in Fort Lauderdale. We have witnesses."

"Harold looked at Amison.

"How about that, Jonesey? They have witnesses. I imagine the police in San Juan would like to interview those witnesses." He turned to Leroux. "Europol too would probably like to see those witnesses. Am I right, Jacques?"

Leroux smiled and nodded agreeably.

"That is uppermost in my mind," he said.

Keith Bates lost his temper and stood up, declaring, "I won't sit here to hear my daughters are vilified. This is a vendetta against me and my family."

"Sit down, my friend," Ramon Salva broke in. "This is not the place to lose one's temper."

Keith Bates shook his head and reluctantly sat down.

In the meantime, Emilio banged the table with his gavel to bring the meeting to attention.

"I have something to say. Sid, will you assume the chair until I'm finished?" He looked around the table, asking, "are there any objections?"

Sid nodded and Emilio handed him the gavel.

"What do you want to say, Emilio?"

Emilio Gutierrez was short and slightly built and unaccustomed to the rough and tumble world he was inadvertently thrown into when he married Keith's daughter, Denise. He was uncomfortable at this meeting and was definitively relieved when Sid assumed the position of session chair. Looking at his son for a sign of approval, he began.

"I have been asked by Boucher & Salieri to ask Centurion when it plans to pay the billion dollar insurance claim for the menorah stolen in San Juan."

Sol fidgeted with his fingers and looked squarely at Emilio.

"Centurion will always satisfy legitimate client claims," he replied. "But it is premature to pay any claim before it has been fully investigated. We are still awaiting a report from the San Juan police and from Europol."

Felipe raised his hand and was acknowledged by Sid.

"I have been approached by a certain party," said Felipe. "This party might be willing to negotiate the return of the menorah if all persons connected with its theft are granted full immunity from prosecution in any country."

"What a fascinating proposition," broke in Leroux. "Tell us more."

"This certain party informs me that the menorah can be returned for a single payment of $500 million."

"That's blackmail," Sol Weinberg declared loudly.

"Who is that certain party?" Leroux asked.

"He will meet with a Centurion representative in Monte Fuego," said Felipe.

"Who will that representative be seeing?"

"He works here. His name is Jorge Ramirez."

Leroux threw Felipe a knowing smile.

"The thieves may need a new surrogate," he said. "Jorge Ramirez was found dead in St. Maarten on Wednesday with his throat cut."

Felipe was dumfounded and more loud gasps filled the room.

"The menorah robbery and Jorge's death are insurance and police matters," said Keith Bates impatiently. "We have more important things to review."

"Keith is right," said Max. "These matters should not be discussed here."

"I would say you are right," Leroux nodded. "However, his death does raise questions. For example, a knife traced to you was found with the body."

Felipe turned white, but he kept silent.

"I have never been to St. Maarten," said Max.

"We do not say you were, Max," continued Leroux. "Only the knife was. It was one of many produced by the Canaan Metal Works in Connecticut."

"Canaan can't be reached today," Harold said, throwing his newspaper on the table. "Their offices and plant were destroyed in a fire last night."

Max coughed and had to gulp down a glass of water.

It was at that point that Luis decided to speak up.

"We could discuss the diamond business," he suggested timidly to lower the heat of the discussion.

"It's your call," replied Keith who had calmed down. "Who's chairing this meeting now?"

Emilio put up his hands in disgust, saying, "Let Sid call the shots."

Sid shrugged and pointed to Keith.

"Your turn."

"Thanks. Gentlemen. I buy and sell high quality D-IF diamonds, minimum two carats each."

Luis Santiago's gold tooth reflected the light as Keith took a white table napkin lying in front of him, opened it, and spread in on the table. From his pocket he took a dozen diamonds and threw them on the napkin. He watched everyone's reaction as the stones sparkled brilliantly under the chandelier.

Keith had a self-satisfied look on his face.

"Right now, with what's going on in the world," he said, "I can walk out of here, sell this lot and put over $1.2 million in my pocket. That's the value of the diamonds you stole from me in Nassau. I want them back."

"That may be difficult, monsieur Bates," Leroux informed him. "They were confiscated and remanded to Europol as possible conflict diamonds. But I am sure we can come to an amicable solution."

"I don't know what this is about," said Keith. "But if you guys want a fight, you'll get it."

Sol Weinberg sighed and leaned his big frame forward.

"Keith. We're not here to fight but to discuss our differences and how they can be resolved."

While Sol was speaking, Amison beckoned to Jimmy Wales to come over and whispered into his ear. Jimmy nodded and left the room.

It was now Emilio's turn.

"I, for one, want to know who killed Jorge Ramirez."

Keith sneered.

"Who cares. I'm going to let the police decide who did what to whom," he said, taking a deep breath. "Right now, I want my diamonds back."

The verbal sparring continued until Jimmy Wales returned with the satchel Estrella had left with Amison. He gave Amison the bag and joined Virgil and Desmond Lyons near the open door with Jake Santana who had just dropped by to see how the meeting was progressing.

"Keith," said Amison. "To honor your engagement to Estrella Gomez, here is a million in cash. It will pay you for the diamonds."

Ramon Salva stood up. He was livid and shook his fist at Keith.

"Ladron!" he screamed. "Thief! I will see you dead before you steal my niece!"

"You've gone too far, Jones," Max broke in. "You'll pay for this."

Amison leaned back in mock surprise.

"Who! Me?"

Luis happened to look up at the air duct outlet on the ceiling to the side of the chandelier over the table where puffs of dust were falling out and quietly drew his gun. Bienvenido too went for his gun, staring at the same air duct while following a red dot on Amison's forehead momentarily blocked by Sol who leaned sideways to whisper to Sid. Jake Santana, who saw the same dot but knew it came from across the courtyard, yelled, "Chandelier!"

Jake swung around and fired through the open door at the window on the far side of the courtyard as Luis and Bienvenido emptied their weapons into the ceiling. Charlie Hand fell through the ceiling onto the chandelier which broke loose and crashed on top of the table.

Across the courtyard, a window shattered from Santana's shot and a body fell out. The meeting was over.

CHAPTER 16

▼

Recapitulation

It was a victory of sorts if scores can be counted in terms of dead bodies. Charlie Hand's bullet ridden body lay bleeding over the remains of the crystal chandelier on the table while on the other side of the courtyard, Al Garcia was sprawled face down among the flowering shrubs under the window. Sol had a slight shoulder wound but was otherwise unscathed. Most distressed was Sid Stone who ran around wringing his hands crying that he had the banquet hall booked that evening and was going to be out a lot of money if the place was unusable.

"At least," said Amison. "We know who's been bugging the hotel."

"Not funny," Sid grunted as he stalked away.

Whoever was the enemy, it was so far faring poorly. Sammy Luke and Jorge Ramirez were gone with Charlie Hand, Wayne Cabot, Al Garcia and Klondike Pete and nameless others. Felipe and Max were left but from whom were they getting their cues? Denise and Erica too knew more than they were letting on, and Danielle and Janice were also in the loop, but exactly how remained to be seen.

Police vehicles converged on the hotel from all directions, sirens blaring, and Jake Santana found himself in his element, barking commands, tossing cough drops into his mouth and pulling at his suspenders. Most of the hotel's lobby floor was taped off as a crime scene as Larry Goodman pulled up at the rear livery entrance in an EMS van to haul away the bodies of Charlie Hand and Al Garcia.

Sol Weinberg, slightly wounded, refused medical assistance until Sid agreed to accompany him. This left Amison, Frank and Luis to straighten things out.

Emilio Gutierrez and Felipe took advantage of the confusion and slipped away. Keith Bates and Ramon Salva were barely on speaking terms, but they stayed, sulking on opposite sides of the lobby, leaving Max Zimmer to wander about aimlessly with nothing useful to say or do.

However, Bienvenido and Luis had struck up a rapport and were joined by Ramon Salva and Jake Santana. Only Max had words for Amison when he showed up with a work crew to try getting the hall fixed up in time for Sid's evening function.

"You'll pay for this," Max threatened. "This was your doing."

Jacques Leroux came up behind them at that moment.

"Ah, Max. I was looking for you, my friend," he said, slapping Max's back.

"Did I hear you say that you were never in St. Maarten?"

"That's right," he snarled. "I've never been to the island."

"I believe you," said the Europol director. "But one M. Zimmer arrived by air from Miami this past Tuesday and checked in at the Grand Hotel. This M. Zimmer checked out on Wednesday, but there is no record of said individual ever having left the island. Most fascinating, would you not agree?"

"This is preposterous," Max sputtered.

"I am sure," said Leroux. "And I am sure an explanation exists for the knife found next to Jorge's body. We should discuss further in my office. Or, would you rather have an interview with Jake Santana?"

"Let's talk at your place," Max mumbled.

"A splendid idea," said Leroux. "Come to my office this afternoon and we'll talk."

Max was about to leave when Harold happened to catch a glimpse of a vest under his suit jacket. He reared up to his full height and bellowed down at the CIA operative.

"You mealy mouthed midget," he roared. "What's that you have on?"

Max shrunk back and Harold grabbed him by the throat and felt his chest with his free hand.

"What have we got here, man? A bullet proof vest?"

Max tried to squirm out of Harold's grip. But he was too weak. Harold ripped the vest off his chest and threw it at Luis.

"I want it analyzed," he yelled.

"That's government property," protested Max. "You can't take it."

Harold tightened his grip.

"Oh yeah? You're the CIA. Arrest me."

Amison jumped on Harold and pulled him off Max.

"Let it go, Harold," Amison implored. "We have one war on our hands; we don't need another."

Harold released his hold and Max, filled with indignation at being publically humiliated, straightened out his shirt and tie, and attempted a return comment.

"That was uncalled for, Harold. You're totally out of control. I'm going to recommend to Calvin Bard that we no longer use your services. Your people have too many enemies to be of use to us."

Harold eyed him with disdain.

"That's suits us fine, Maxwell. You don't have to recommend anything to anyone. We quit."

"You quit?"

"Right," said Harold. "Now, get the hell out of here."

Max mumbled a few words and slipped out of the hall. Keith Bates was still in the lobby and waited until Amison was alone to speak to him.

"A word, Jones." he requested.

But Amison seemed in no mood to talk.

"Take the money and run, Keith," he said. "It's the best deal you'll get."

"Keep it," he retorted. "I don't need it. And as for Estrella, it was a mere, innocent flirtation. I meant no harm and no insult to don Carlos. You can keep the diamonds too."

And to Ramon Salva, who was within hearing range, he offered a fig leaf.

"I trust you will accept my sincere apologies, sir."

Ramon Salva nodded his acceptance.

"We will meet again, I am sure," he said.

With nothing more to be said, Keith Bates went searching for Amison who was now busy in the courtyard getting the hotel's maintenance crew started.

Pulling Amison aside, he said, "I don't know what your angle is, Jones, but going after me isn't going to work. I have strong political convictions and you are making a big mistake if you think you'll succeed in attacking my Patriotic Front party or me. We are legitimate and duly registered."

Amison smiled blandly and pulled Keith to a corner of the courtyard.

"I have no quarrel with the Patriotic Front," he responded. "That's Leroux's bag. And I don't play in any political playground. But someone's after me and my guys, and I need to know who."

"I heard about Leroux's theory," said Keith, "and I know all about Europe's Patriotic Front. I like their ideas, but I'm not into world revolution. I'm an old man and I don't care much what happens to me. It's my damn kids that worry me. Their feet and quick but their minds are slow. I spent a lifetime trying to set them up and I don't want anything to happen to them. I want them kept out of your lousy witch hunt.".

"That may be too late, Keith. Your son, Quentin, is a killer. He took down Cecil and Chico."

"You're lying."

"I never lie," said Amison. "Frank and I were there when it happened and you know it's true. And one of your daughters killed Victor and the other stole the menorah in San Juan."

"They have alibis."

"Don't hold your breath, Keith. When we find out more about that scheme to return the menorah for a cool half billion, those alibis will fall apart. Let's face it, friend. You're on thin ice. That menorah heist, when it blows open, is going to expose that cozy, cat burglary operation you and the twins have going with Sol Weinberg. But that's our dirty little secret, Keith."

"So, what are you saying?"

"Listen, Keith. It won't take long for the cops to connect the dots. So even if we don't go after you, they will. However, we're well fixed with Europol and with the police here, in San Juan and in Connecticut, and may be able to help you out. It's your call, buddy. With whom would you rather deal, the police or us? We won't touch you and we'll keep the fuzz off you if you say to my face that you're not involved in any conspiracy to kill us."

"I'm not in any conspiracy and I'm not out to kill anyone," said Keith.

"Terrific. So tell me, who do you deal with at Kinshasa Export in Africa?"

The white haired diamond merchant fell deep in thought. Finally, rubbing his chin, he replied, "You know. I've never been to Africa and I've never met the people. I was introduced to Kinshasa by Max Zimmer years ago. He set up the deal with Africa and with Carib Financial that's kept me in business ever since. Felipe was an intermediary for Max. I gave him my purchase orders and he passed them to Max who sent them to Kinshasa who would ship the goods to my outfit, Black Star Trading. The financing came from Carib Financial, a bank owned by Ramon Salva."

"Is he part of the deal?"

Keith shook his head, replying, "No. His thing is money. Nothing more. But I will check my paperwork to see who's been authorizing the shipments from Africa."

"Great. How soon can you get back to me?"

"I have to attend several political rallies in Appalachia when I leave here.

Maybe in a week or so, I can give you some answers. But will you promise not to hurt my kids if I give you information about Kinshasa?"

"That's a tough one, Keith. Tell you what. I won't be the one to initiate any action against them."

"What about Quentin?"

"It's his White Knights I want. Try to get him to turn himself in and we'll make sure he's made comfortable in a padded cell for the rest of life. Is that fair enough?"

Fair enough."

Ramon Salva had momentarily forgotten about Keith. At the moment, he was more interested in reaching out to Bienvenido and in talking to Amison and his friends about the future of Sol's insurance company. He addressed his remarks specifically to Bienvenido. when Jake Santana left to supervise some police work.

"It is a new day for us," he started. "I trust we put the past behind us, senor de la Maza."

"If you are talking about the role your mercenary army played in destroying my movement, that will be hard to forget," answered Bienvenido. "But I have made my peace with el senor Jones and his friends, and I can make my peace with you, this time with money in my pockets. And for that reason, I do share your interest and that of my new friends."

"That is also my concern," said Salva. "So, should el senor Weinberg not recover from his wound, who will take over Centurion?"

"Your guess is my guess," replied Amison. "Harold may stay on for a while but his interests lie with Alliance. Centurion is your bailiwick and I don't see him challenging you leadership."

"Would a meeting with el senor Levy be in order?"

"Meetings are always good. wise. I can arrange one if you wish."

"Please do. I have a specific agenda. I want access to the treasure of Monte Fuego which I understand is buried in a cave under the mine. For that I am will-ing to give you information."

"You should listen to him, Jonesey," suggested Luis. "He makes sense."

"Is that why you are interested in Hernando's map?" Amison asked.

"Exactly."

"I too would like to see the document," said Bienvenido.

Amison burst out laughing.

"Virgil will give you the map before you leave, don Carlos, and we can have copies made for anyone. But take my word; the map is useless except for the letters written at the bottom. I've been unable to decipher them. What do they mean?"

"They describe the location of a passage to the mine from the streets of La Fortuna in the event the mine's main access ways are closed," replied Salva.

"Is that right?"

"Si. With the mine's entrances sealed, including a cave entrance from the sea, the mine must be reached directly from the city."

"How did you know about the entrance from the sea?" Frank asked.

"My men have been watching it from small boats for more than a year. We have also been shadowing a big white yacht that travels regularly from Europe to the Caribbean and discharges cargo in small boats that go directly into the cave. The yacht no longer makes that trip and has been replaced by private air charters flying into Monte Fuego. I am sure that treasure from Europe is flown into Monte Fuego and transported underground from the city to the mine for storage."

"If what you say is true," said Frank. "Then someone is already using that underground tunnel."

"Si. Our knowledge must be pooled to find out who and where."

And with those words he invited Bienvenido to join him for coffee at the hotel's sidewalk café.

Jake Santana returned as Raman Salva and Bienvenido were leaving.

"This is a den of thieves and traitors," he complained. "They get cornered, killed and don't talk. To Amison he said, "You must be worth a lot of money dead."

Virgil Holmes, who was helping the work crew and had overheard Jake, added, "The street says Jonesey has a million dollar bounty on his head."

"What about us?" Luis asked.

"You, Frank and Sid are each worth $500,000."

"I thought we'd be worth more," said Frank.

Amison sneered.

"We will be if they keep missing. And to make sure it stays that way, let's keep things pretty much to ourselves from now on."

"How about Harold and Sol?"

"We clue them in on a need-to-know basis."

Jake Santana scowled.

Clue me in, amigos. I can't help you if you don't help me. I need to know what's going on and you need to level with me."

Luis placed his arm around his cousin's shoulder.

"Let's go to the bar and I'll tell you a story about buried treasure."

Later that afternoon, Amison and Frank were relaxing, playing cards with Luis and Sid at Hamburger Haven when Harold dropped by the back room. The conversation eventually focused on the menorah robbery in Puerto Rico when Luis brokered the idea of having Amison and Frank go to San Juan.

"Gus Galindez is the detective in San Juan in charge of the menorah robbery investigation and Jake and I are friendly with him. What's more, Bienvenido has located Roberto de Silva for us. He lives near the sea at Punta Las Marias. Bienvenido wants to set up a meeting with him. He thinks Roberto might be able to decipher the letters for us."

Harold seemed enthused about the suggestion

"Do you have Hernando's map?"

"I gave the original to Salva and a copy to Bienvenido," replied Amison. "But we have many copies."

"Good. Take one to Puerto Rico. Matter of fact, we should probably hang out there until after the memorial luncheon and things cool down here. How soon can you start moving some of your guys to San Juan?"

Amison smiled.

"Today? Tomorrow? You set the time line, Harold."

It was agreed when Jacques Leroux stopped by briefly that Amison's men would be seeded gradually into the greater San Juan area over two weeks to avoid any undue suspicion. The Europol director also had a creative idea to finance their coming expenses.

"It is time to start pressuring Kinshasa Export," he said, his eyes lighting up. "I will arrange to have conflict diamonds fall into your hands. Their proceeds will amply cover your expenses and when Kinshasa finds out it is not being paid, its principals are bound to appear."

When Leroux was gone, Harold asked Luis if anything new had surfaced.

"It's an eye opener," said Luis. "Jake and I reviewed the barbershop tapes. They show Zimmer reading a paper with his back to the outside and Charlie Hand walking to the back room. Max raises his hand and two of the shooters waiting next to the car start walking to the revolving door and the third gets into the car. That's when Max dives under the table without bothering to look behind him and before a shot is fired."

Amison greeted the information with indifference.

"We kind of suspected that. Anything else?"

"Yes," replied Luis. "I ran a check of all the people at Centurion, Alliance, the Riverside and at other outfits that we work with. It turns out that Sol and his

Centurion staff are clean. So is the hotel at this moment with the exception of Felipe. But we do have a problem in Connecticut."

"I figured."

"Used-to-Be's is a White Knights watering hole and Tommy Hicks and Ray Booker pass intelligence to both the White Knights and the CIA."

"Are you sure?" Harold asked.

"Positive. Stan Mason did an IRS audit on their tax returns and they show income from both sources. They list themselves as consultants."

Harold turned to Sid Stone.

"Sid. Since you're now in our family, I need you to assemble a strike force against the White Knights in Connecticut. Virgil will help you. And Luis, you get rid of the Florida White Knights.

"Including Tommy and Ray and the guys at Used-to-Be's?" Sid asked.

"No. Just close the encampment down wherever it is. We'll take care of the rest later."

"I can find out through workers at the Delmar where the White Knights hang out," said Sid, "Connecticut is not a big state."

"Good," Harold agreed. "Anything else in your bag of tricks, Luis?"

"We've been tracking charter flights chartered by CIA front organizations under Zimmer's name going between Antwerp, Paris and the Caribbean," Luis replied. went on. "We plan to intercept one of those flights."

"Neat," exclaimed Harold. "I love action. It shows we're alive."

Amison put down his cards and got up to leave.

"Where are you going?" Frank asked.

"I'm packing for Puerto Rico. You coming, Frank?"

CHAPTER 17

▼

La Fuerte San Jeronimo

Amison and Frank were met by Gustavo Galindez on a hot and humid day under gray skies when their flight landed at the airport on Isla Verde serving the greater San Juan area.

"Good flight?"

The detective spoke English with no accent and easily guessed the question on their minds.

"My mother was a Wisconsin Swede who was seduced by a Puerto Rican fisherman," he explained. "Call me Gus. Any bags?"

"At the carousel, hopefully," answered Frank.

"Jake Santana and Luis Santiago called," said Gus. "They said you're here about that San Jeronimo robbery."

"That's correct," said Frank. "We have reservations at the Brittany."

"I'll drive you, and once you're settled in, I'll give you a tour of the fortress. Your friends are flying in for a police convention so they'll be joining us."

They collected their luggage and the detective took them to a waiting police car.

Gustavo Galindez was sandy haired, slightly built and a half head shorter than either Amison or Frank. The butt of a pistol butt peeked out of a shoulder holster inside his blazer and a badge pinned to his shirt pocket announced his livelihood.

Otherwise, he could have passed for a school teacher in his blue blazer, tan slacks and highly shined brown penny loafers.

"This is one of our more curious crimes in recent memory," he explained on the way to the hotel.

"Any clues?"

"A few. Like we found a man's school ring."

"How do you know it was a man's ring?" Amison asked.

"Size. It's a man's ring unless it belonged to a woman with big hands and fat fingers. I'll show it to you later."

The ride to the Brittany took less than a half hour and the sun poked its head out of the clouds when Gus let them out under the hotel canope.

"I'll catch you guys tomorrow morning and we'll visit the fortress."

A bellhop was on hand to greet them and bring their bags inside where they found Janice waiting for them at the reservations counter. She leaned over and let Frank give her a kiss.

"How are you doing, sugar," she said lightly. "Dinner tonight?"

"Sounds good to me. Can you fix Jonesey up?"

"Oh, I think Ruby's going to have to cope for himself. Erica's pretty pissed at him."

Amison discounted the comment.

"Count me out," he said. "I'm going to turn in early."

Janice suddenly remembered something.

"Oh, a gentleman came by earlier and left his business card. He wanted to see you and said he'd be back later."

"Do you recall the name?"

"Bienvenido de la Maza."

Amison took a deep breath.

"I'm going to the office to check the books and then to my room. He'll find me; he always manages to."

Amison's room was actually a suite facing the ocean and he had no reason to complain. The problem was that it had never been his idea to grow old in a hotel room staring at a light bulb. One thing he noticed, however; he had not smoked nor had a drink in days.

He was in the midst of another daydream, this time about his daughter and grand kids, when the phone rang. It was Erica.

"Janice said you were in town with Frank. Why didn't you call to say you were going to be in Puerto Rico?"

"Oh, I don't know, cookie. I thought you were pissed."

"That's ok. I should have expected it. But what's happened to my old, mean spirited Ruby?"

"Getting old, maybe?"

"Should I come over? I'm in town and Janice said you needed a date."

Amison paused before replying.

"I don't think so, Erica. I'm real tired and just want to get some sleep."

"Tomorrow then?"

"Maybe. I'll call you. Where are you staying?"

"At Janice's place."

He hung up and lay on the bed, staring at the ceiling until he fell asleep.

Gus Galindez called on Amison and Frank as they were finishing breakfast in the hotel restaurant to the left of the lobby's front street entrance.

"Too many exits," Amison was commenting when Gus barged in on them. "That creates a problem for the memorial luncheon."

"We'll deal with it," Frank noted, nodding to Gus. "How you doing, guy?"

"Your tour guide is ready," Gus said.

He led them out through the street exit and explained their itinerary.

"It's a short walk to the Caribe Hilton. You can see the hotel around the corner. A long driveway leads up to the front entrance. It's a big place and its back faces the beach and the sea."

"Where's the fortress?" Frank asked when they were in the open lobby.

"You can go through the hotel," he replied, pointing to a stone path that ran along an old sea wall. "Or it can be reached through a walkway from the road on the hotel side of the lagoon."

They followed him along the sea wall to a network of fortifications marked by ramparts and sentry boxes around a large compound that might once have been a troop mustering point.

"The El Morro castle was built in the early 1500's," Gus said. "Its role was to protect the harbor from a sea attack. The San Cristobal fortress lies between Old San Juan and the Hilton and was built to protect San Juan from a flanking sea assault. This one is smaller and was put up to stop an attack from the rear through the lagoon that you can see over the ramparts. On the far side of the lagoon is the Condado strip where the big hotels are."

"Where was the exhibit held?"

"Below us."

Amison and Frank followed Gus down a narrow flight of stone steps. The bright sun light above gave way to dull artificial light until they entered a big, dungeon like hall illuminated by electrified wall sconces where once torches did the job. Their voices and footsteps echoed in the vast space.

"This is the place," he said in a hushed tone.

"Yes, This is the place," echoed a fresh voice.

Out of the shadows emerged two human forms, one tall and rangy, the other shorter and huskier. The tall shadow belonged to Tom Clark, the big detective from Greenwich, Connecticut. Next to him stood Jake Santana.

"Ah," Gus exclaimed. "Our friends are here."

"With all this police brain power," Amison observed, "we should be able to solve every crime on this planet."

"Our goals are more limited," said Tom. "I have a murder on my turf; Gus has a robbery on his and you guys are giving Jake a big migraine. We believe Victor Duncan's murder, the menorah theft and Jake's headaches are part of a bigger picture."

"In what way?" Frank asked.

"Obvious," replied Jake. "The White Knights did the robbery, judging from the business card left at the crime scene. Keith Bates backs them through his Patriotic Front party, and his twin daughters are expert jewel thieves and cat burglars who steal for Keith. And besides, Denise Bates was identified as the woman in red here at San Jeronimo."

"Who identified her?"

"A sales assistant," answered Gus. "We interviewed him before he left San Juan and the police in Paris questioned him when he returned. He claims that it was the same woman who came to the Paris store a few years ago with her fiance to buy an engagement ring. The guy's name was Emilio Gutierrez. Does the name strike a bell?"

"Sure does," Frank nodded. "He's the new president of Las Olas University and Denise Bates is his wife."

Gus smirked.

"I thought so. But here's the hitch. We took a statement from Louis Salieri, and according to him, he never saw the woman in red before and has no idea who she is. He isn't even sure she stole anything. He would only say that she wasn't there when the lights went back on. This Salieri also said that Denise Bates works for him and that the woman in red was not her. The sales person was either confused, or else Salieri is lying.

"The French are stilling trying to sort it out, but there's more. It turns out that Centurion Insurance issued a billion dollar policy on the menorah. Your friend, Sol Weinberg, will have to pay up eventually and that will probably drive Centurion under. That brings me to Weinberg's deal with Keith and his daughters which Jake found out about. They steal Centurion insured stuff and then turn it over to dear old dad who has it certified by B&S and then sold to Emerald for resale at a high markup in the Caribbean. Centurion pays but Sol gets a kickback for looking the other way and everyone is happy.

"This time, a priceless menorah insured by Centurion was lifted. If I know crooks, it will be returned for the right price. What do you folks think?"

"You seem to have the case wrapped up," remarked Amison.

"Not so fast, Jonesey," said Jake. "It's not that simple. Denise is a suspect, but we have no proof beyond the sales person's statement that Salieri has all but refuted. The problem is that although she was seen here when the robbery was committed, she was also seen with Emilio in Florida. I'm sure he'd vouch for her and everyone else who saw them."

"It gets more complicated," added Tom Clark. "While Victor Duncan was being wasted in Greenwich, Danielle was in Washington with Juan Duarte Gutierrez of Monte Fuego even though she was seen shooting Victor."

"We have a dilemma," Jake concluded. "We have two alleged perpetrators of two seemingly unrelated crimes with rock solid alibis."

"I thought you might be able to help us, Jonesey," Gus went on, "especially since you once had an affair with Denise."

Amison gulped hard.

"I was one of many," he noted.

"Oh, we know all about the twins' affairs," said Tom Lyons. "We do our homework, you know. Love and lust make for rock solid alibis, so we always look behind them. Sometimes they hold and sometimes they don't."

"Talking about rock solid, how did the thieves leave the fortress?"

Gus laughed and pointed to a dirty rusted squarish metal plate under their feet that seemed to have been recently loosened.

"See here. We're standing on a centuries old manhole cover. There's a stone chute under it that empties into the lagoon. This place was a torture and death chamber in its day. The dead were thrown into burlap bags and tossed into the chute where they dropped into the lagoon. The chute was sealed at both ends when the United States took Puerto Rico from Spain in 1898. The two seals were pried loose weeks ago, suggesting that the thieves rehearsed their parts many times before pulling the job.

"My theory is that the robbers had an inside track from the day B&S made a commitment to run the show and immediately began planning the theft. I also truly believe that placing the menorah dining room exhibit directly over the manhole was not a coincidence."

His voice, slightly high pitched, echoed eerily in the large torture chamber.

"It's not that our security was blind sided," Gus went on in a monotone. "I mean it was, in a way. Museum security at this fortress was compromised at the very least, and I'm sure security at the Hilton and Brittany was likewise penetrated. The U.S. Coastguard and local police keep a watch in the lagoon and their surveillance was also breached. This robbery took a lot of planning and brass balls, I say.

"The chute was sealed at both ends with iron covers that were rusted. It had to take a long time to open them and whoever did it had good local knowledge of the fortress. The thief or thieves went down the chute with the menorah and left a go-fast boat in a matter of minutes. This job was done by a polished and professional team that went to great expense and had a lot of practice."

"How many on the team?" asked Frank. "Did you figure that out?"

"I don't think Denise physically moved the menorah. It's too heavy, maybe a hundred pounds or more," answered Gus. "She needed accomplices, two big guys, I guess. Two guys could have maneuvered the menorah down the chute with the rope and tackle we found. The thing is that there were no fingerprints and video cameras in the exhibit hall were turned off."

"Where do we fit in all this?" Amison asked.

"Law enforcement shares a mission in common with Europol and the CIA," replied Jake Santana, popping a hard candy into his mouth. "You, Frank and Luis are moving targets and we, the police, are stuck with this robbery and a bunch of killings. You help us do our work and we'll make sure you get the backup and cover you need with no questions asked. Deal?"

"If you're talking about working together to get back the menorah, I'd say that we can work together. But we're not into solving murders," said Amison.

"That works for us," agreed Tom Clark. "Solving murders is what we get paid for."

It was a deal, and as Frank observed later, "We could have done worse. One thing for sure, we don't need more enemies."

Amison nodded in agreement.

"I'd settle for a few clues."

Gus had his squad car waiting outside the fortress and dropped them off at the Brittany.

"We're going to a forensics seminar at the University of Puerto Rico but we'll be in touch. And don't forget to drop by my office," he reminded Frank. "I want you to look at that school ring."

"What about it?" Frank asked.

"It's from a private school, Cornwall Prep in Connecticut. You went there, Frank, didn't you?"

"Years ago. Me and many other kids."

"Well now, that narrows our list, doesn't it?"

Gus drove off, leaving them alone in front of the hotel under a burning sun.

"Wouldn't it be a fluke if that ring ended up being yours?" Amison joked.

"I've never been to San Jeronimo in my life," Frank insisted.

"Funny. That's what Zimmer said about never setting foot in St, Maarten and what Keith said about never having been to Africa."

CHAPTER 18

▼

La Cocina del Mar

A loud whistle from under a palm tree at the edge of a small park across the street from the Brittany interrupted their conversation.

Amison squinted in the strong sunlight. It was Bienvenido de la Maza who was motioning to them to come over, apparently being reluctant to cross the street.

"Amigos," he said, giving them each a hearty handshake. "It is good to see you again. I hear things went well in St. Martens."

"Well enough. And we owe you one for that. But why didn't you come to the hotel?" asked Amison. "It's hot out here."

Bienvneido shrugged.

"Too many eyes fill the Brittany," he said simply.

"Why? Sid Stone owns the hotel."

"Si. And so it must be as safe as the Riverside."

"Well," said Frank, looking around. "We can't stand here. Where should we go?"

"We go have lunch at La Cocina del Mar. The food is not very good but it will not poison you. I will take you in my car to meet a very special person." "Who is that?"

"Roberto de Silva. He owns the restaurant. Do you have the map?"

Amison smiled.

"It just so happens that I have it in my pocket," he said.

"Bueno," said Bienvenido. "Roberto has told me that he and Hernando drew the map and will explain the letters on it."

"Why the generosity?"

"He is old and wants me to buy his restaurant. I agreed to do so on condition that he tell us about the map."

"Then, why are you being so generous with us?"

"I am not being generous, amigo. We are in a forced marriage," Bienvenido replied in his husky guttural voice. "You saved my life and I did you a favor in return. Now, I have a favor to ask of you and your friends."

Amison's eyes narrowed.

"What kind of favor?"

"I want Max Zimmer and Felipe Gutierrez dead."

Amison and Frank looked at each other. Finally, Amison said, "We can do that, but not today."

Bienvenido smiled.

"I understand. However, you must promise that they will be dead soon."

Amison looked at Frank again who nodded.

"We can promise that," he said.

The drive to the restaurant took twenty minutes from the Condado's urban neighborhoods to the more sparsely populated Punta del Marias that stuck out into the sea about halfway between San Juan and Isla Verde. The car stopped in front of a ramshackle eatery with a bar and sidewalk café that stood alone across the road from the tall dunes which at that point hid the beach and the sea from view. A faded hand painted sign over the roof announced that this was La Cocina del Mar.

They parked and walked up to the rundown restaurant.

"Are you sure you want to buy this place?" Frank asked.

"The price is right," said Bienvenido.

"Why would you want a restaurant on top of your businesses?"

"Ask your friend, el senor Jones, amigo. He likes Hamburger Haven. Every working class neighborhood has a bar and grill like La Cocina. In English it would be called a seafood shack. It is a good place to meet and hire people for my business. It is a very popular place."

Indeed, La Cocina was a bare bones affair that never closed. Three walls and a heavy grate in the front that occasionally slid down during storms did little to distinguish it from any other store front on the strip. There was, however, a wide variety of liquor bottles on wooden shelves over the counter behind the long mahogany outdoor bar. Bienvenido had obviously been there before as he bragged proudly to Amison and Frank that La Cocina had over a hundred different brands of hard liquor, a wine collection that was the envy of five star restaurants and tap and bottled beer from countries all over the world.

The restaurant catered mainly to locals. Fishermen came at dawn for coffee on the way to their boats. Hotel workers, government employees, teachers, off duty policemen, airport personnel, merchants and day laborers came later on the way to work. From mid to late morning, the fisherman were back for a snack, having sold their catch to buyers waiting with refrigerator trucks and who filled La Cocina's indoor and outdoor for an early lunch. By noon, the fishermen and their customers were gone and were replaced by the regular lunch crowd which in turn gave way in the early afternoon to tourists, sun worshipers and beach bums. By late afternoon the flow of workers returning from their jobs filled the place for happy hour and early bird specials followed by couples and families who settled down much later for their long dinners. After midnight came the hotel and airport workers who had finished their shifts and later still arrived all the casino and hotel restaurant employees, stopping for a drink and a fast meal on their way home. And then the day started all over again.

"Come with me," said Bienvenido.

Amison and Frank followed him to the back where they entered through the kitchen where a parade of waiters marched with food trays on their shoulders through one of two batwing doors into the crowded eating area. Another line of waiters with empty trays and busboys carrying dirty dishes raced by in the opposite direction through the other batwing door.

Bienvenido stopped briefly to chat with the kitchen workers and then guided his guests through a side door into the dining area where three men behind the bar were feverishly filling drink orders for servers waiting on tables cooled by ceiling fans circulating air drawn from the sea.

A heavyset man with close cropped hair, wearing a gray sport coat, stood at the maitre 'd's station outside with a clipboard, tending to customers waiting to be seated by hostesses who flanked him with menus in hands. Making eye contact with Bienvenido, he handed the clipboard to a hostess and came over.

"Your friends are with Roberto at his usual table outside," he said in fluent English, nodding to a table near the street where Virgil Holmes and Desmond Lyons were seated and talking with a wizened old man. "I tried to tell him that he should change to an inside table to escape the draft from the sea but he has refused.'

"Gracias, Oswaldo," said Bienvenido. As an aside to Amison and Frank, he added, "Oswaldo is Rosina's brother and has been in the restaurant business all his life. He needed a job, and so I introduced him to Roberto a few weeks ago. He is now La Cocina's general manager. He will remain when I buy the restaurant."

Oswaldo left them at Roberto's table and returned to his station in the front of the restaurant. They shook hands with Roberto and sat down as Bienvenido introduced them.

"Mucho gusto," said Roberto. "A pleasure. You and Bienvenido bring many fond memories of the good old days in the Dominican Republic."

"Memory stretches the truth, senor de Silva," countered Amison. "The old days were sometimes not so good."

"Si," said Roberto. "More or less. Some were bad but many days were good. And I do remember how well you and senor Hoffman took care of my brother and his wife when they were alive. Bienvenido here has been very helpful and has helped me hire a good manager. I hear that you are also in the restaurant business, senor Jones."

Amison felt slightly embarrassed.

"I know something about food," he replied.

"Claro," said Roberto. "I understand."

A waitress came over for their food orders.

Bienvenido waited until the waitress was gone before coughing politely to draw everyone's attention.

"I informed Roberto that we wished to talk about West Indian Mines and he agreed to tell us what he knows. Do you wish to start, senor Jones?"

Amison nodded and began.

"Here's the problem, Roberto. Your friend Hernando's house was built over a cave facing the sea under La Fortaleza. Unfortunately, a recent earthquake destroyed the house and collapsed the cave."

"Si. I heard."

"Now, Hernando told us before he died that there was a way into the mine through the cave. Is that true?"

"Si. One can get in with a small boat at low tide when the water is only a few feet deep. The cave is about ten meters wide, three meters high and two hundred meters deep. At the far end of the cave is a large hole near the ceiling that opens into a huge cavern thirty five meters below. The cave is flooded at high tide and sea water cascades down the opening into an underground river that runs along the floor of the cavern.

"Hernando and I learned about it years ago when we saw small boats from a large yacht enter and leave the cave at low tide. We heard they were carrying valuables like jewelry, diamonds and gold and wanted to see for ourselves. So we built a trapdoor in Hernando's kitchen and slowly dug a secret passageway into the cave. Eventually, we were able to find our way into the cavern by climbing down a rope ladder alongside a motor driven lift that must have been installed by the miners. That is when we made a decision to steal some of that treasure for ourselves."

"Did you?" asked Frank.

"Si. But we took very little compared to what was in the mine. However, it was enough to make us comfortable."

"I have a map," Amison said, pulling a copy of Hernando's map from his pocket and showing it to Roberto.

"We don't understand the map's significance," Amison elaborated. "Can you help us out, senor de Silva?"

The old man eagerly seized the document and began examining it.

"I was a mining engineer and cartographer," he said. "This is a copy of an old street map of La Fortuna in Monte Fuego that we drew."

"Why draw this map, Roberto?"

The old man looked down at his gnarled hands before giving an answer.

"We knew of a vein of gold in the mine near the north wall of the mine and wanted to tap it."

"With this map as a guide?"

"Si. Yo me recuerdo bien," replied Roberto, searching his memory for the right answer. "I remember well. Hernando and I once attended a West Indian stock holders' dinner with Armando, Emilio Gutierrez and Victor Duncan and brought a hand made copy of the map with us to sell."

"Did you?"

"Si. For a $100,000."

A long moment of silence followed that was finally broken by Bienvenido who asked him in Spanish and then translated into English.

"What does the map tell us, Roberto?"

"The map tells us nothing. But we know the location of those veins of gold on the north wall, the location of the main cavern and the location of another vein of gold on the south wall that supports La Fortaleza. And of course, there was that huge mountain of treasure in the center of the cavern."

Eyes opened wide around the table as Roberto passed the map around while two servers appeared with their lunch orders.

"A mountain of gold!" Frank repeated to make sure he heard right.

"Did you say a mountain of gold, senor de Silva?" Bienvenido asked.

"Si. Gold, silver and diamonds. A giant underground mountain of gold."

"Can he describe the cavern and that mountain of gold on the map?" Frank asked.

Bienvenido translated.

Roberto smiled.

"Si. It is high like a subterranean cathedral. The mountain rises from the floor of the cathedral near the underground river and is built of gold. I saw it with Hernando."

"How did the mountain get there?"

"The conquistadores built it and over the years hundreds of Spanish galleons sailed into La Fortuna. They hid gold bullion and jewelry stolen in Mexico and gold coins robbed from merchant ships in the cave which then had an opening into the harbor. Unfortunately, an earthquake two hundred years ago sealed the the cave's entrance from the harbor.

"I hear that people from West Indian have dug new shafts into the mine from the surface but they have never gone into the north and south walls. If the gold is real, it is still there. But we found over the years new treasure being added in piles around the mountain of gold. More was added last year when we snuck in to have a look."

"What kind of treasure are we talking about?"

"Gold objects like wedding bands, necklaces, bracelets, even diamond rings, solid silver objects and even paintings and works of art. Almost the entire floor of the cave is now covered by this new treasure."

"How did you get to the cave last year?" Bienvenido asked him in Spanish and then translated for the rest of the table.

Roberto gesticulated with his hands.

"Through the cave by the sea. What a shame it is no longer there."

It was clear that Roberto was not lying. His eyes widened suddenly.

"The cave is cursed," he said. "It belongs to the devil."

Frank furrowed his brow.

"Why do you say that, Roberto?"

"People enter the cave but they never come out."

Amison wanted more information about the map.

"The map is unimportant," said Roberto finally.

"Why is that, Roberto?"

Again, Bienvenindo provided a translation.

"The letters at the bottom of the map are important. They point the way to a way into the mine from the city and also show where Hernando's original land deed, the grant of land to Hernando's family that was sworn to by Juan Duarte Gutierrez as being true and correct, is hidden."

"Can you show us how to read the letters?"

"Si. Each letter represents…"

Roberto de Silva never ended his sentence. His hand dropped to the table and his head fell back as if he had fallen into a trance. His mouth was still open and blood began oozing from his forehead while from the dunes, a stiff wind blew sand into the road.

CHAPTER 19

▼

The Ring

Fights at La Cocina del Mar were not infrequent, and some fights were fatal. But this was the first drive-by shooting that looked very much like a murder. At least, that was Gus Galindez's opinion when he arrived with the San Juan police. He became even more aggravated when he learned that when Roberto was shot, he was with Amison, Frank and Bienvenido, a former drug dealer.

"So, why this meeting?" Gus asked.

Amison thought it best to tell the truth.

"We wanted Roberto to tell us about a map giving the location of buried treasure in Monte Fuego."

He took the map off the table and gave it to the detective.

"Keep it," he insisted. "I have copies."

Looking at it suspiciously, Gus took it and passed it to one of his men. He then went about taking the usual statements from would-be witnesses, learning nothing. When the unhappy task of taking Roberto's body away he was forced to ask, "Does Roberto have any next of kin?"

Amison explained that Roberto was his uncle-in-law and that since he died an old bachelor and if blood lines were to be considered, he and his children, Gordon and Deborah, would be in line to inherit whatever Roberto left.

"Roberto owns this restaurant and a small house not far from here," Gus told him. "You might want to see if you can be assigned estate executor. You might even end up with both, including back taxes if he owns any."

Amison shook his head.

"I have enough headaches," he replied. "I don't need to go after Roberto's estate, whatever it's worth. It would only make me a suspect."

Gus laughed.

"Citizen," he said. "The world is a suspect unless proven innocent. Even my wife is a suspect. But I'm going to leave you alone right now. You have some new problems."

"New problems?"

"Yes. Your boss, Sol Weinberg had a heart attack. And don't forget. I need Frank to come by my office to look at that ring left at San Jeronimo."

The police left and the restaurant returned to its usual routine. Amison and Frank walked out to the street and called Fort Lauderdale on their cell phones to confirm Gus's story while the others waited at the bar.

Sol had indeed suffered a slight heart attack and needed a medical procedure followed by a period of rest and rehabilitation. Harold Levy took over for him at Centurion, insisting that he would serve not longer than a month.

Amison had been right. Centurion was never on Harold's radar. His interests lay with Alliance where he believed his Reel power base rested. Moreover, he hated hot weather and loved the Northeast with its four seasons.

On the flip side, Harold was not about to have his new authority challenged at Centurion. His orders to the company's large sales and underwriting staff were to aggressively develop new business, and he adopted a policy of total non-confrontation with the Centurion board directors by making sure that they received their expected dividends.

He courted the Centurion board members, the West Indian, Emerald and the B& S stockholders, making sure to wine and dine each one lavishly. He was especially differential to Ramon Salva who he treated as a senior partner.

"He's been keeping busy," Luis concluded. "What's going on in San Juan?"

"A sniper got Roberto," answered Amison.

There was little more to say.

When they had finished with Luis, Bienvenido invited Amison and Frank to join him at the bar.

Bienvenido folded his arms contemplated the drink in front of him.

"Tell me, my fine friends. I was invited to your meeting in Fort Lauderdale and two men are killed in front of my eyes and Sol Weinberg was wounded. I am asked by your Harold Levy to arrange for you to see Roberto and I tried to negotiate for the purchase of his restaurant. I do that and Roberto is killed. What am I doing? What are you doing?"

"The killings are not our doing," answered Amison. "And you are involved whether you like it or not. Besides, I'm not interested in La Cocina and am willing to sell it to you at Roberto's price if the place is mine to sell."

"That is good," said Bienvenido. "But it does not explain what is going on."

"Roberto's story fits with a Europol theory about gold, diamonds and other expensive household effects are being stolen and hidden away until they can be used to fund right wing militias like the White Knights. Monte Fuego may be the place where the stuff is kept. That's the reason why we are marked for termination."

"And so I should help my enemies who once tried to destroy me?"

Frank smiled sadly at Bienvenido and shook his head.

"We can curse the darkness or light a candle," he said. "Enemies live in the darkness; friends live in light."

Bienvenido unfolded his arms.

"Bueno. Good enough. I am not about to die over this, amigos. And neither should any of you. Have you and your friends any designs on the gold?"

Amison smiled.

"That depends which gold you're talking about," he answered. "We need to find and destroy the White Knights and its leaders before they get to us. Any treasure stored under La Fortaleza that was stolen must be returned. The rest is ours."

Bienvenido nodded. A glint flashed in his dark eyes.

"Spanish galleons filled with gold. And maybe a gold mine to boot. That is. what el senor Levy tells me as well. But what he could not solve for me is my problem with el senor Zimmer of the CIA who has me classified as a terrorist. He is beginning to cost me money and time for expensive lawyers and court appearances. If I lose, I will broke and deported to the Dominican Republic. You must kill him for me."

"Max Zimmer is no friend of ours," said Frank. "We'll be able to help you if we know that you'll be working with us."

"Ah. What is at stake for the CIA in this Europol matter?"

"The CIA subscribes to Europol's claim that an ultra-right wing transatlantic conspiracy is afoot. White Knight cells may already be operating in Caribbean and Central American staging areas. Pretty much the same situation exists in the States. The White Knights are in Florida and Connecticut and have become very aggressive. We believe that Max is a renegade CIA agent with an agenda different from that of our government."

"We do have mutual interests," Bienvenido agreed. "This is why we torched that munitions plant in Connecticut. We even took the files."

"Did the files tell you anything?"

Bienvenido nodded affirmatively.

"Si. The factory produces arms on special orders, authorized by the CIA, for a company in Africa."

"Africa?

"Si. Kinsasha Export. I do not know the company. Do you?"

"We heard about it," said Amison. "Can we see the documentation?"

"Si. But I can say that the authorizing signature to pay for the transactions is that of senor Zimmer. However, although Kinsasha Export may be the ultimate consignee, it is not the buyer. What I mean is that it is not the party who placed the order."

"Who placed the order?"

"A company in Monte Fuego called Carib Financial."

Bienvenido smiled.

"It seems that many things are in Monte Fuego." He took a deep breath. "I do not know much about that island but I know a little about Carib Financial."

"You do?"

"Si. My bank, Madsen-Umberto, is a regional foreign currency exchange clearing house for the Bank for International Settlements in Switzerland. It seems that a Carib Financial branch in Paris periodically deposits quantities of Euros at our bank for the account of Carib Financial to be denominated in East Caribbean dollars. This is how Carib Financial pays for the arms bought from the New Canaan Metal Works. The moment that proof of shipment to Kinsasha Export is received by our bank, it converts the East Caribbean dollars into U.S. dollars for remittance to the arms factory.

"I found something else out. The big white yacht that Luis Santiago has been tracking is an old de-commissioned cutter from the British navy that was sold to Carib Financial and leased to Kinsasha Export who gave it a refit two years ago in South Africa. I know because Madsen-Umberto financed the purchase and the lease. Our mutual friend, Max Zimmer, does not appear to have been involved in that transaction."

"What are you suggesting?" Frank asked.

"I am suggesting that while Max Zimmer is my personal enemy, he is not the keeper of the treasure of Monte Fuego and the source of your real problem."

He raised his glass in a toast.

"To the treasure of Monte Fuego!"

Amison and Frank returned to the Brittany and from there hailed a cab to Gus Galindez's office in Old San Juan where they found the detective ready to leave for the evening. He seemed glad to see them. He dug a hand into a desk drawer and pulled out a small plastic evidence bag. In it was a ring.

"It has the initials, F.A.H. Anyone we know?

He passed the bag to Frank.

"Frank Albert Hoffman," confirmed Frank. "It's my ring."

Amison could not resist saying, "You never told me Albert was your middle name."

"It's my ring," Frank repeated. "I gave it to Danielle several years ago when we were having a thing."

"A thing?"

Amison defined the term.

"They shacked up for a while like they thought they were in love."

"Damn," cried Frank. "So did half the world. You were doing Denise also."

Gil Galindez threw up his arms in despair.

"What is this? A Frick and Frack show? Maybe you can answer me this. If this is your ring, where were you two jokers when the woman in red stole the menorah?"

Amison's answer was too quick and glib for Gil's satisfaction.

"Sailing my catamaran from the Biminis to Florida,"

Realizing that he had been temporarily stumped, Gil allowed himself to smile and cooled down.

"On a boat, sailing. How convenient. So, how do you suppose the ring ended up at the robbery scene?"

"I'd say that if Danielle was wearing it around her neck as a keepsake, it may have dropped accidentally."

"That's assuming she was there," said Gil.

"Naturally," agreed Frank. "But if she wasn't there, who was?"

"Let me try something else since you seem to have answers for everything. Where do you think that menorah is headed?"

"It's headed for Monte Fuego?"

"Headed for where?"

This was the moment to come clean and to tell Gus Galindez exactly what they were doing in Puerto Rico. They took him inside to a bar near the police station, sat him in a corner and fed him the details of the events leading to their arrival in San Juan.

"Like you said at San Jeronimo," said Frank. "You back us up and we'll work with you and get that menorah back."

It was easier said than done. An invisible enemy surrounded Amison and his cronies and it was commanded by a ghost. It was true. the world was a suspect.

In the meantime, Gus Galindez had a high profile robbery and a cold blooded murder on his hands. Jake Santana had killings on his turf that were solved but he had no motives with which to satisfy his bosses in Broward County. Tom Clark was pretty much in the same boat. He had Victor Duncan's murder on his hands and no one to arrest.

Gus Galindez drove them back to the Brittany and was more worried than reassured when he left them,

"The problem," Amison told Frank once inside the hotel, "is that we have no strategy. We need to go to Monte Fuego and see that cave."

Frank shrugged off the suggestion.

"Let's go to the bar and talk about it."

At the bar, Amison ordered a coffee while Frank ordered a whiskey.

"I notice you haven't been drinking," Frank remarked. "You didn't order a drink when we met with Gus. Matter of fact, you haven't had a drink since we got to Puerto Rico."

"Not in the mood."

"You haven't been smoking either."

"Lost my taste."

Amison happened to look at the bartender who he had never seen before.

"Are you new?"

The bartender nodded.

I started yesterday," he said.

"I'm Ben Olsen. I worked at Used-to-Be's in Greenwich, Connecticut, until last week. Harold Levy owns the place now and asked Toby Sands to send a bartender to work here for a few weeks. Who are you?"

"I'm Amison Jones; I manage this place for Sid Stone."

"The guy who owns the Delmar in Connecticut and the Riverside in Fort Lauderdale?"

"That's him. And this is my friend, Frank Hoffman."

A call came into Amison's cell phone at that moment. It was Luis Santiago, calling to give him an update.

"We had a great trip fishing in the Everglades and Connecticut," he said.

A genuine smile of joy filled Amison's face when he heard the news.

"Everyone liked it?"

"Except the fish. The big one got away, but we did get a free meal."

"That's good. Now, tell me, I've been watching bird migrations from the north. Is Puerto Rico one of their stops?"

A short pause.

"It is for some. Oh. I almost forgot. Big Bird has a restaurant in Darien north of Hartford. I guess everyone's in the restaurant business. Must be good."

The conversation was over.

"What's up?" Frank asked.

"Let's go to a table," suggested Amison.

They took their beverages to a table out of the bartender's earshot.

"The White Knights have been neutralized," said Amison. "But Quentin got away."

Frank grimaced.

"Slippery bastard. What's this about a free meal?"

"Leroux is beginning to milk Kinshasa Export through Sid's hotel supply office here at the Brittany. It is buying diamonds from Africa paid for with a fake letter-of-credit issued by a dummy bank. Let's hope it keeps working."

"And this thing about bird watching."

Amison made sure his back was to the bartender.

"That dude behind the counter. Harold shipped him down. We need to take him down."

"When?"

"After the memorial luncheon next Friday."

"Who's going to do the hit?"

"You can, or I will. It doesn't matter."

Amison had no idea why Ben Olsen was the target of a contract. He seemed personable enough. He could only guess that the bartender was a member of the White Knights who may have been using the Connecticut restaurant as a hangout. Something must have aroused Harold's suspicions and he may have decided to start cleaning house early.

The rain that started falling earlier picked up. It grew dark outside and the atmosphere inside the bar was somber. Amison was usually talkative around Frank, but this time he was strangely silent.

"We seem to be doing well, but we're still in someone's cross hairs and we don't know who that someone is," said Amison after a while.

"You're talking about the bullet that got Roberto?"

"Right. It was intended for him, but whoever called the hit knew that he had something important to say and that we were going to meet him at La Cocina.

We're winning, Frank, but at the same time we're losing."

"So, what's our next move?"

"We keep dodging bullets until we either get smart or lucky."

CHAPTER 20

▼

The Memorial Luncheon

Amison hibernated in his room at the Brittany and rarely ventured out until the day of the memorial luncheon. He was getting used to it. Every morning, a serving table with hot plates covering a complete breakfast arrived at his door.

And when evening came, dinner was delivered. The routine was comfortable and nonthreatening. Breakfast, lunch and dinner, interrupted by short intervals of work. One small matter kept probing his mind: Sol Weinberg's restaurant. It was out of character for him and made no sense. As Harold hated hot weather, Sol detested the cold and was not known to venture often north of Washington. True, many aging executives dreamed of owning great restaurants and maybe this was one of those instances.

Tucker Andersen and Mike Quinn showed up after having taken rooms at El Canario, a small residential hotel in the Condado tourist area. Frank gave them the job of helping Virgil keep tabs on the hotel's security system.

There were tedious preparatory chores to complete and Amison left them to his associates. Sid Stone and Jacques Leroux were already at the hotel. Leroux worked on the guest list while Sid dealt with the caterer. He even went to the extent of having Gus Galindez recommend the caterers who were to augment the Brittany's staff for the function. The police detective had his office check the catering company's record and nothing irregular was uncovered.

Charlotte Fergueson showed up and was lodged by Sid in one of the hotel's suites. Estrella Gomez also arrived with Julio Maldonado and Ramon Salva, but they took a suite at the Caribe Hilton. Estrella was especially happy and Salva too was in excellent spirits. Charlie Hand's death had left his barbershop empty and Estrella's uncle took that opportunity to buy up the building it was in, allowing her to convert the premises into a unisex beauty parlor.

Leroux, however, was suspicious.

"We must watch Salva closely," he confided to Amison when they had a chance to meet. "I feel there is much more to him than meets the eye."

"Why do you say that, director?"

"It goes back to Hernando Gomez's death in Monte Fuego. Is it not odd that his daughter should fly away the very next day with Paul Boucher and her ex-husband, Julio, in Ramon Salva's private jet? I realize that you and Estrella share a special relationship, but let us not forget that she, along with Julio and Paul are persons of interest if not suspects. And remember, Julio and Estrella are Ramon's eyes and ears."

Amison could not disagree, but he preferred to be in denial when it came to Estrella. Harold Levy viewed Leroux's comments more objectively.

"We're all thieves and thugs," he said. "We move around and do things for our own gain which may have nothing to do with the big picture. We'll figure it all out in time."

"Have you had Hernando's map examined?" Amison asked.

Harold nodded.

"By the best, and they can't decipher the letter code. Salva is upset because he and his people can't figure it out either. One thing's for sure. The only way into the mine right now is through the city."

Luis Santiago flew in and was given a suite at the Brittany. Bienvenido de la Maza and Rosina Alvarez, Chico Alvarez's widow, were staying at the Hyatt in Dorado Beach and called to say they would be at the memorial luncheon on time after finalizing arrangements for Roberto's funeral with Oslwaldo.

Bob Byrne, the former coast guard officer who had helped Amison obtain gun boats for a previous mission, appeared at the Brittany's registration desk on Thursday and was greeted by Amison and Luis. He was slightly stouter and grayer now and walked with a slight limp. Otherwise he seemed spry and well. He looked around, waving at Virgil Holmes and a few of the others who he recognized.

"Is this a wake or a party?"

"A little of both," said Amison. "We may need some boats soon."

Bob Byrne replied with a broad smile.

"Boats, I have. Money, I don't."

"That can be arranged," said Luis.

"Where are we going?"

"Monte Fuego."

Bob Byrne grunted and said, "That's interesting. That big white yacht you guys asked me to track. It's been traveling to Monte Fuego and St. Thomas regularly."

Frank was nearby and overheard the conversation.

"What makes you say that?"

"It stops for maintenance at a British naval base in Antigua that's off limits to civilian craft. That's where we found out about its pedigree."

Amison rose early Friday morning, dressed, had breakfast, put on a white dinner jacket and raced down the stairs outside his suite as he had been doing for the past week. This time he came to a dead stop at the bottom when he was seized by a cramp in his groin and another in his left arm that made him wince. It was gone in seconds. He cursed silently and continued on his way.

The Brittany's staff, augmented by imports from the Riverside, was rushing to address the usual petty crises that always crop up at the last minute when Amison appeared. He saw Virgil at the livery entrance, ushering guests in from their limos, and walked over to his side.

"Everything good?"

Virgil whispered into Amison's ear.

"The jewelry in that bag, Jonesey. the bag you gave me for safekeeping at the Riverside? It's not old pirate stuff, but it's priceless. It's worth over $1million. I put it in with the cash."

"What kind of jewelry are we talking about?"

"It's European, less than a hundred years old."

Their conversation was interrupted by Frank, Luis, Sid and Bob Byrne who crept up behind him, also in dress whites, and tapped his shoulder.

"An old friend I haven't seen in years is here, Jonesey," said Bob

He pointed to an older, portly man sporting a full Santa Claus beard who was resting in a rattan armchair near the sliding doors to the banquet hall where the waiters were scurrying around with last minute table preparations.

They crept up to the armchair and left it to Bob Byrne to spring the surprise in a fake English accent.

"Dr. Henry Alstrum, I presume."

The old physician rose to his feet when he saw Bob. Tears rolled down their cheeks as they embraced.

"Where have you been hiding these past couple of years?" Bob Byrne asked.

"I was forced slow down after my heart attack," the doctor replied. "I'm fine now but I've reduced my patient load."

"Well, you look terrific."

"Yes. And I'm getting younger, like you guys. But to tell you the truth, I'm a walking pharmacy. I need a slew of drugs to stay alive. I have a bit of diabetes, high blood pressure and colitis, and now this a bum ticker. Other than that I'm good as new."

"Are you exercising and keeping to a diet?"

"You bet. I get out of bed every day and make sure I consume all major food groups," said Henry with a big grin. "I take my pills in the morning with a tall glass of low-sodium tomato juice to keep my potassium level up. I lace it with vodka for my sugar. Then I have a light lunch and wash it down with a banana daiquiri. That gives me my fruit and more potassium. For dinner, it's fish and a glass of red wine, for my blood. Finally, before I turn in, I'll have a cigar with a shot of whiskey. That keeps the blood flowing and my arteries open. That's the end of my day. How does yours go?"

He looked at the astonished faces around him and smiled.

Frank scratched his head, saying, "I don't know, Henry. I'll spring for maybe one martini if I'm close enough to a bed, but that's about it. I'm not sure about my friend here."

Sid grinned.

"I'm good for a shot of rum. Otherwise, I stick to prune juice and lime."

Just then, another pang briefly gripped Amison's groin.

Henry glanced around the lobby where the invited guests were beginning to assemble.

"Who is delivering Hank's eulogy?"

"I figured Jonesey would."

Amison knew he was on losing ground and tried once more to bow out.

"What do I care about eulogies? Why say nice things about the dead when there's nothing nice to say? And when there are good things, will words alone restore the dead to life? Hank is the reason why so many of us are no longer here. He was a double agent and a double crosser."

They listened quietly to Amison's tirade and when he was through, Frank yawned.

"So, Jonesey, you'll do the eulogy?"

Amison was barely listening. His eyes were on Felipe who was speaking to Jacques Leroux and Harold Levy. Sol Weinberg stood in the hallway off the lobby a few yards away chatting with Keith Bates, Ramon Salva, Estrella and Jose Maldonado. Felipe! What was he doing here?

Sol broke away from the others and joined the group.

"I hear you're doing the eulogy," said Sol. He had apparently sufficiently recovered so that he could attend the memorial luncheon.

Amison threw up his arms and caved in.

"Okay. Okay. I'll do the eulogy."

The nagging, stabbing pain in his groin returned, this time spreading to his upper chest and left arm.

"Are you ok?" Luis asked.

Amison recovered his composure and replied, "I'm fine," he said.

A line formed in front of the ballroom which was spacious enough to hold a hundred people at round tables. It had been recently redone in a style similar to the Riverside's ballroom, with chandeliers and mirrored walls in between the serving wings to make it appear larger and grander than it actually was.

Jake Santana and Tom Clark showed up at the last minute and were seated by Virgil with Harold and Sol just as the servers and headwaiter headed for their stations in the wings.

Henry Alstrum and Amison were among the last to leave the lobby.

"You're an old island rat, Henry. What can you tell me about Monte Fuego?"

"Does the name Monte del Fuego tell you anything?"

"Mountain of Fire?"

"Right. The brother of Christopher Columbus found the place and called it Mountain of Fire when the island erupted before a landing could be made. It took another century before the Spanish mustered enough guts to settle it. I don't trust the place."

"Why is that?"

"That volcano is waking up. One of these days it's going to blow."

Amison arched his eyebrows.

"That's neat, Henry. Now, what about Hernando? How did he really die?"

"Cardiac arrest from a diabetic seizure caused by bad pills. I hear that his buddy, Roberto de Silva, also bought the course."

"Shot," said Amison. "Shall we go in? Who are you sitting with?"

"With Quinn, Andersen, Bob Byrne and Felipe." Henry made a face, asking, "How come Felipe's here?"

"Beats me. He split after the Riverside shootout."

"Did he make the sitting arrangements?"

"No. Janice did."

Henry drew closer to Amison and asked, "Are you carrying a piece?"

"Not on me."

The physician opened his sport coat slightly and took out a small pistol. He shoved it into Amison's hand, saying, "Take this one. I have another."

Amison pocketed the piece, knowing better than to doubt the senior agent.

The biggest surprise for Amison was Emilio Gutierrez who showed up at the last minute with a high heeled, blonde woman in a black cocktail dress on his arm who he assumed was Denise. He was about to greet them when Harold Levy came over to ask him if he had spoken to Henry.

"You bet," answered Amison. "He gave me a gun. What's up?"

"Don't know. He spoke to Frank and Luis too. They're carrying pieces. So, keep your eyes open and your trigger finger ready. And keep your eyes on the broad. I'm not sure if it's Danielle or Denise."

Amison smiled and looked over at Frank and Luis who were wandering from table to table, watching and listening for strange noises and movements. But except for the clatter of dishes and silverware as waiters began serving the soup and salad appetizers, everything seemed normal. Luis thought it unusual for the wait staff, having finished serving the appetizer, to return immediately with the chicken entree, but he assumed that the plan was to get all the food passed around before the eulogies.

The place was full. Harold Levy strode up to the podium and knocked his fingers on the microphone while servers milled about the service corridors. The hall fell silent as he began, saying, "It is a difficult time when we must say farewell to those who have been a part of us for so long. I never knew Hank Lawrence and his friends personally, but many here were their close associates and would like to say a few words."

Sol Weinberg, as Centurion chief, was the first to speak. He made his way to the podium where he called Hank Lawrence's death an unfortunate loss. Sid Stone extolled Hank's virtues as a generous person who took care of everyone before taking care of himself.

This left much of the audience wondering if Sid was not eulogizing someone else until they grasped the hidden meaning behind the term "taking care of."

Mike Quinn and Tucker Anderson stepped up to honor Hank, Chico and Cecil and other companions who had died in past missions.

Finally, Luis Santiago stepped to the podium. With a Cheshire smile fixed to his lips, he flicked an imaginary spec from his moustache with his little finger and tapped the microphone with his pinky ring.

"Let us honor our friends who died that we may live. Let us greet the angels in the wings who have come to take them home. May we wish them Godspeed on their final journey and be not quick to invite the angels back for us. I will now ask Jonesey to say a few words. Jonesey?"

Amison rose as Luis stepped down and passed him on the way back to his table. "Avenging angels," Luis whispered.

Amison stepped up to the podium. His eyes were fixed on the waiters and then settled on Estrella Gomez who was sitting next to Julio. She blew him a kiss as the sharp pain in his body returned.

Suddenly, out of the corner of his eye, he saw Quentin Bates, standing in one of the service areas with arms crossed and legs apart, in a canary leather riding outfit and a joker's grin pasted to his thick lips.

With one hand resting inside his blazer, Amison gripped the podium's side with the other, took a deep breath, and began.

"Hank and his friends did not call the cards they got. But they played them well. They lived well and died with honor. May they now find the peace that eluded them in life. They were my friends too and will be my friends forever." Now he saw what else was wrong. The waiters should have been standing by with trays. But now they carried no trays. He quietly drew Henry's gun.

From where he stood he saw Frank, Harold and Sol. They had drawn their own weapons. Jake Santana, at a table with Tom Clark and Luis, frantically working his cell phone in an effort to call Gus Galindez. for backup.

Suddenly, Estrella screamed.

"Ruby! The waiters!"

And the world around Amison began turning in a slow motion blur.

Light reflected off gun barrels that appeared out of nowhere followed by the the staccato crackle of weapons and the blinding flash of gunfire. Estrella was caught in the first salvo and crumbled to the floor. Tucker Andersen and Mike Quinn caught bullets in the head and died on the spot. Oswaldo, who was at the affair at Bienvrenido's invitation, was hit squarely in the chest and bled to death from a ruptured artery. Sol Weinberg was shot drawing his own gun and fell under a table while Sid Stone fainted dead away.

Julio Maldonado rushed Ramon Salva into the lobby out of the line of fire and beckoned to Keith Bates to join them, but he was too late. His exit was blocked by Bienvenido who had thrown himself to the ground over Rosina. All Keith could do was to stand and stare at his son's unblinking eyes.

The cowboy clown sprang into action. With two long nosed revolvers in his hands, he began firing into the hall. Bienvenido drew a pistol and tried to take him down but the bullets scarcely fazed Quentin. Out of options, Keith Bates jumped on a table and tried to face Quentin down. The cowboy clown snarled and took careful aim at his father and squeezed the triggers of both revolvers together. Keith ducked and a round nicked Henry Alstrum's ear instead.

Virgil, Jimmy Wales and Desmond Lyons kicked over their tables and took shots at the rampaging wait staff, covering Harold, Frank and Luis who waded through a tangle of tables and chairs and guests, targeting every server in sight. Indeed, some guests, like Bob Byrne, were armed and their own withering fire proved deadly.

Denise and Emilio dove under a table as pandemonium filled the hall. Food spilled, silverware flew through the air, china and mirrors shattered while the unarmed guests screamed and scrambled to escape from the barrage from all sides. Amison crouched behind the podium, taking careful aim at the cowboy. He squeezed off a round, hitting him directly in the chest.

Nearby, Frank and Luis, having re-loaded, fired into the cowboy clown point blank, emptying their guns. Quentin fell back against the wall. He howled and brayed like a mule but he never fell. By the time they re-loaded again, he had released a gas grenade that covered him in a thick green cloud and made his escape with Keith Bates chasing after him.

Amison crouched behind the podium and took aim again but the cowboy was gone. Off in a corner, he saw Felipe cowering under a table and Sol lying on the floor. A few yards away lay the bleeding bodies of Tucker Andersen and Mike Quinn. Zeroing in on the maitre d' who was about to pump good luck shots into them, he fired.

The maitre d' fell twisting to the floor. The headwaiter ran for an exit but was dropped by a bullet from Harold.

Jake Santana and Tom Clark were also moving fast. They barreled down one side of the hall, guns blazing. The attackers fared poorly and most were killed. Those left alive fled followed by a hail of bullets.

It was over quickly and an eerie silence fell over the wrecked banquet hall. In the distance, Amison could hear the sound of choppers and police sirens. He started to move when the pain he felt earlier returned like a body punch. Again, it was gone in an instant.

CHAPTER 21

▼

The Tally

Gus Galindez was not a happy camper when he pulled up at the Brittany. He scowled at Jake Santana who tugged at his suspenders and tossed hard candy into his mouth, chewing hard and constantly.

"Who does San Juan have to thank for this?"

Jake had no answer. Instead he turned to Luis who had come up behind him. "What happened, cousin?"

"Whatever this is, cousin, we didn't start it," replied Luis. "You know what we know. We were bush wacked."

Gus tried to keep calm.

"Whatever it is that you didn't start, you need to finish it outside my turf," he declared. "This is not good for business, for tourism and for me."

Amison caught up with Frank and Harold as they joined Luis.

"Anyone see the cowboy leave?"

Frank looked over at the exit where the cowboy had stood. The smoke had cleared and the entryway was empty.

"The guy with the animal laugh?" he replied. "He's gone."

"He was hit him in the chest many times," Harold noted. "He must have had on a bullet proof vest."

Luis shook his head in amazement.

"If he was wearing one, it had to made of steel."

"No vest could have stopped that shot," remarked Amison. "You're a cop, Luis. Find Quentin Bates. He's our man."

"Former cop, amigo. So don't tell my what to do. I'll do my job and you do yours."

His voice was becoming testy and Frank had to step between them.

"Guys, guys. Not now. We have problems."

"Those waiters were assassins," said Harold. "The entire catering gang set us up. Who the hell checked them out?"

Gus Galindez coughed.

"My office did that," he confessed. "I guess we got blind sided."

"And we got sandbagged," howled Harold. "Is that great police protection or what!"

There was in fact little to argue about as they rummaged through the ruined banquet facilities wandered about the fallen bodies. Those who had survived the firefight had fled the hotel and milled about outside, leaving the ballroom to the police and EMS workers who were frantically working the floor trying to sort the dead out from the wounded with their life support equipment and stretchers.

Gus took a deep breath and recovered his cool.

"Problems like this can cost me my job," he mumbled. "Well, this is my turf and this is a catastrophe. So, you must help me sort this thing out. What's my first move?"

Jake Santana smiled.

"No problem. I'll tell you how we do it in south Florida. First. Muzzle the media when it shows up. Say that this was a terrorist attack by some extremist group and that the FBI should be called in. Whether we like it or not, the FBI is going to get itself involved anyway."

Gus looked at him sarcastically.

"Are you dragging me into your world of intrigue, murder and mayhem?"

Jake shrugged.

"No. You were dragged in the moment that menorah was stolen."

Tom Clark had to agree.

"We're all in the game," he said to Gus. "I got in when Victor Duncan was murdered."

A weary smile crossed the San Juan detective's lips.

"You hold things together here," he requested, "while I go arrange for more body bags. Anything else?"

"Yes," said Luis. "Less said, the better."

Gus barked some orders to his officers before leaving.

"No one leaves and no one enters unless on hotel business. I want ID' s on everyone and statements from everyone. Understood?"

A police officer saluted.

"Yes, sir," he said.

"Okay. Let's move it."

"You like that?" Gus asked Jake Santana.

"That's the way, Chief. Just put a little more authority in your voice."

Gus's confidence grew and he marshaled his forces together like a general on a battlefield, issuing commands as more police and EMS people filtered in and glided about with stretchers and body bags.

The hall was still now, but its acoustics were sensitive enough to catch the monotone voices of the medics who carefully poked around the wrecked hall, tending to the wounded and beginning the gruesome work of taking inventory of the carnage.

Gus returned after a few minutes, looked around and grimaced.

"How did this happen anyway. I thought you guys had good security."

"I thought so, too," replied Amison grimly.

Jake added.

"This was supposed to be a friendly memorial to praise departed friends."

Gus fell in behind them and followed as they moved slowly through the hall. They stopped at an overturned table where two EMS workers had just finished placing a filled body bag on a gurney.

"Whom do we have here?" Luis asked.

Frank unzipped the bag. It was Oswaldo. His eyes and mouth were open, as if he was speaking. He looked alive, but a small, bloody hole in the middle of his forehead told the story.

Amison shook his head sadly.

"Poor guy. He never had a chance."

Bienvenido, who was standing nearby, snarled.

"I want payback," he said.

"Does Rosina know?" Amison asked.

Bienvenido shook his head and replied. "She is outside waiting for me. I will have to tell her later." His voice choked and he had to excuse himself.

An officer came over, whispered something into Gus's ear and then spirited him away while the rest went to an open area where Felipe and Emilio's wife were huddled over a body surrounded by several officers and EMS workers.

It was Emilio Gutierrez. He had been shot in the chest and Felipe and Denise were on the floor, cradling his body.

Blood was dripping from a wound on Felipe's ear where a passing bullet had nicked him but Denise was unharmed. In her left hand was a small pistol she seemed to have removed from Emilio's pocket.

Felipe looked up tearfully at the group hovering over him.

"He's not dead!" he cried. "He's not dead. He's going to be fine."

The EMS people made an attempt to ease the university president on to the wheeled stretcher that had been collapsed to the floor.

"Don't touch him!" Felipe screamed. "My father is fine. He's fine!"

Luis placed a comforting hand on his shoulder.

"Of course, Felipe. You decide what we should do."

He winked at Denise and gently relieved her of the pistol with his hand in a handkerchief. He smelled it before giving it to Gus Galindez. It had been fired.

"You take care of Felipe, you hear?"

To the others he commanded.

"Let's move on and leave him alone for a while."

Amison and Frank helped Denise to her feet. Speechless, and not wishing to revive old memories, he was about to leave when Denise blurted out.

"I need your help, Ruby."

Amison drew back. He was surprised she had called him by that nickname.

"What for?"

"I want to find out who shot my husband and why?"

"Why don't you ask your brother, Quentin? He was here."

"Don't be stupid," she replied. "Sure he was here. He's just a big crazy kid along for the ride. He doesn't have the brains to pull this off. Someone put him up to this."

"I hope the police buys that story, Denise," he replied. "Where's Danielle?"

"You leave her out of this. She's scared. People think she shot Victor. She's in Monte Fuego at dad's place and she's not returning until the air clears."

"Well, that leaves us now with two totally innocent grieving widows, doesn't it?"

Denise sneered.

"What are you? Mr. Clean? I'm asking you again. Will you help me find Emilio and Victor's killers?"

"No, Denise. The police can do that. I need the dudes who want to kill us."

He walked away and caught up with the others who were gathered around Henry Alstrum who was sitting quietly at a table, staring into space, holding a smoking revolver limply on his lap. His beard was bloody from a shot that had grazed a cheek, but appeared fine otherwise. Leroux stood over him, pressing a table napkin against his face to stop the bleeding.

"We need assistance here, monsieur Jones," he said when he saw Amison.

Sprawled on the floor nearby was Angelo with a shoulder wound. Frank shook his head at the sight.

"We can't afford these hits," he lamented.

"Fascinating," remarked Leroux. "The shooters knew who to hit and how to hit. They zeroed in on our people."

A table away were two dead waiters, shot by Henry who sat quietly, letting Leroux nurse his wound.

"Are you all right?" Frank asked the doctor.

"Not too bad," Henry blinked and answered slowly.

Several EMS workers came over.

"Take care of the other wounded," said the physician. "I'm ok."

He waited until Frank and Luis had drifted off with Leroux to help with the other guests before turning to Amison.

"I told you were going to need a piece."

"How did you know?"

"A hunch, Jonesey. I arrived early and took a walk around the hotel. The ballroom kitchen was closed. That means the affair was being catered. I saw some white vans but I didn't see any catering trucks."

A faint smile crossed Amison's lips and he patted Henry's shoulder. "Thanks, doctor," he said. "Don't go away. We're going to need you."

Henry nodded.

"This gig you're in is bigger than you think," he said. "We need to talk."

"You think?"

"Si, my friend. The good doctor is right. We must talk."

It was Bienvenido who came over to help Henry Alstrum.

"Right, Jonesey," said Henry. "It's important."

Bienvenido helped Henry to his feet and led him away, leaving Amison to wander over to several EMS workers carrying a stretcher with Sid Stone and Julio Maldonado following in its wake.

Sid was wringing his hands.

"This isn't good, Jonesey. Estrella got hit."

Amison's face turned to stone and his eyes were expressionless, almost dead.

"Ramon is going to want many pounds of flesh for this," Luis noted.

Frank shook his head regretfully.

"Two may enemies and too few friends. That's what we have."

Bob Byrne was more sanguine.

"Too many fucking clowns have it in for us," he said. "I want to know why." "I'm going to kill those bastards," Amison said in a low voice. "Every one of them."

Gus Galindez, who had returned, asked, "What did you say, Jonesey?"

"Nothing, Gus. Nothing at all."

Jake Santana and Tom Clark dropped by to say that an elderly man, sitting on a chair in the lobby, had been wounded.

They left the EMS people to continue their work and ran out to the lobby where Ramon Salva was seated in an armchair with Harold standing by.

Ramon Salva waved when Amison arrived. Noone had yet told him about Estrella and Amison did not wish to break the bad news.

"The flesh is broken, senor Jones, but I am all right. But I must say, I find your receptions always full of surprises."

Yards away, Sid Stone had come to and began crying. Virgil broke away from the group and led him shaking and sobbing to the privacy of the hotel office where Charlotte gave him a sedative to calm his nerves.

Felipe and Denise were of no help at all, insisting on staying with Emilio's body, giving the local police no choice but to try capturing evidence around them while it was fresh. The hotel was roped off and even registered guests were not allowed to enter and leave the premises. Special details from ballistics and forensics arrived and began their work and cleanup crews gathered outside waiting for a signal to enter after the police were done.

Later that afternoon, when the process of examining and removing bodies had been completed, Gus Galindez took a breather and stopped to speak with Amison who was chatting with Tom Clark and Jake Santana and others in the lobby.

Gus wanted to be friendly and tried to cheer them up.

"Some memorial luncheon, huh Jonesey?"

"We're going to try not to have too many more."

"Your gentlemen got nine of them," said Gus. "Seven waiters, the maitre d' and the head waiter. But they're dead. So they won't talk. Two got away with the cowboy. We did find two vans, though. They were left behind the hotel.

We also contacted the caterer. They never came, claiming that someone from the hotel called to cancel."

Amison sat down and rested his head on his hands.

"Big fucking deal! This hit has torn us apart."

Harold overheard him and in his own way he tried to comfort him.

"We don't get angry in our business," he said. "We get even. Isn't that what you always said."

Gus shook his head.

"Not here. I may lose my job over this and don't need more problems. You need to settle your scores elsewhere." He paused before continuing. "But I can tell you this. Two choppers lifted off the beach. We didn't see them come in, but we did see them leave."

Amison eye's widened.

"Choppers? So that's what I heard."

Amison closed his eyes.

"Those choppers need a place to take off and land," he thought aloud. "And there's nothing but water around us. A mother ship must be in the area. It may the same one that killed the two fisherman in Monte Fuego."

He called Bob Byrne over.

"Have Luis and Frank bring you up to date, and then have one of your boats track down that yacht. It's probably the same one you were talking about."

"You got it, boss."

"And oh, stay alive, Robert."

"Do we intercept the yacht?"

"No. Just have your men keep it in their sights."

From the lobby, they could look inside the banquet hall and see Denise and Felipe still there, fending off EMS people who were trying to convince them to go to the local clinic.

"It's a flesh wound," Felipe insisted. "I can have it taken care of here."

Gus went over to reason with Felipe.

"No you can't. Felipe," he said. "This entire hotel is a crime scene and off limits until we figure out what happened. Besides, you'll probably need some stitches and a tetanus shot."

A compromise was finally reached. It was agreed that Felipe and Denise would follow Emilio's body to the clinic's morgue where Felipe would get medical attention. From there the body would be flown to Monte Fuego where he was born for a funeral.

"If Sid stays sick, who is going to run his hotels?" Frank asked.

"Who the hell knows!" Harold glanced over at Amison. "You take over for Sid until he's better and I'll continue standing in for Sol at Centurion."

"Ok," agreed Amison. "And maybe Bienvenido and Virgil can hold the fort here and And Jimmy Wales and Desmond Lyons can go back to Florida. But what we need to do is close the book on Max Zimmer. He has to have been behind this mess. We need to put him away for good."

He was about to add something when he felt a jolt that radiated throughout his body like an electric shock. He doubled over in pain and passed out.

Part iii

▼

THE TREASURE OF MONTE FUEGO

CHAPTER 22

▼

Henry's Revelation

Everything was at a standstill. Amison was out of commission; Sid had a nervous breakdown and Sol was in poor health and had been wounded again. The three of them were taken to the medical center on Ashford Avenue to be examined by Henry Alstrum. Sid's condition was mental and he was left in the care of Charlotte Fergueson who flew him back to Fort Lauderdale. Sol was in worse shape was airlifted home in a hospital jet. Harold followed the jet back to the States.

Amison's condition defied diagnosis. He slipped into a coma, leaving Frank, Harold and Luis to make decisions for him. One was to have Luis accompany Amison on another hospital jet to Florida for tests and treatment. It would now be up to Luis to run the Riverside until Amison recovered. Frank also booked a flight with Bienvenido's help to send the bodies of Oswaldo, Tucker Andersen and Mike Quinn to Florida for burial. Bienvenido had the unenviable task of telling Rosina of Oswaldo's death and Frank handled the chore of contacting Tucker and Mike's next of kin with the sad news.

Gus Galindez drove over to La Cocina del Mar with a detail of men early in the evening of the Brittany debacle and boarded up the place. He agreed with Frank that Angelo of Hamburger Haven would reopen the restaurant and run it until Amison was back on his feet. Major changes continued in the coming days. Bienvenido volunteered to temporarily manage the Brittany and Harold decided to watch over the Delmar.

Estrella Gomez was all but forgotten. Her body was whisked away by Julio Maldonado and Ramon Salva in his jet without airport clearance much to the dismay of Gus Galindez who had wanted to question them. He subsequently suggested to Tom Clark and Jake Santana that they might as well pack up and go home. Further communications would be through their respective offices.

Denise and Felipe flew to Monte Fuego with Emilio's body and were met by Juan Duarte at the airport. Preparations for a formal funeral began but the body was cremated the next day, which Leroux found odd.

Virgil Holmes stayed at the Brittany for a few days and then returned to Fort Lauderdale with Bob Byrne after taking Ben Olsen, the hotel bartender, for a drive from which he never returned.

In Fort Lauderdale, Bob Byrne took over Mike Quinn's boatyard and Virgil Holmes assumed the Riverside's temporary management with Charlotte while Frank hired Teddy, Jake Santana's driver, as a part time pilot. It was amazing, but within days he had successfully redeployed his people and enlisted the help of Dimitri and his brothers at Hamburger Haven. Frank now ruefully admitted that having the memorial luncheon at the Brittany had been a tactical blunder. Sid never had full control over the hotel and the guests at the affair ended up sitting ducks. It was a wonder that not more were killed and Frank vowed that it would never happen again. But first things first.

It was at the hospital that Amison awoke a week later with tubes sticking out of his body. He turned his head to see Dimitri lying on the bed next to him, a pistol peeking out of his blue gown. A bouquet of flowers in a vase stood on the window sill and a sign over the TV set read, "Eat Healthy and Live Long."

"What are you doing here?"

Dimitri winked at Amison and smiled.

"All in a day's work."

"Where's Angelo?"

Dimitri's smile faded.

"He's keeping La Cocina del Mar open for you. You inherited the place."

"Who's at Hamburger Haven?"

"My other brother, Octavio. He came over from Greece to visit. I put him to work. My other brothers will come soon."

"How many brothers do you have anyway?"

Dimitri held up eight fingers.

The TV hanging from the wall in front of the room was on and a news brief flashed across the screen. It was a shot of Keith Bates making a midday speech outside a church in a gray Pennsylvania coal mining town. So that was where he had disappeared to after the Brittany firefight. This guy never missed a beat, Amison snickered to himself. He was back on the stump, doing his thing. And yet, he had to admire the old man's audacity and tenacity. He was sticking to his guns until the end. And yet Keith had tried to stop his son at the Brittany.

That was hard to understand.

The speech was one of those chest beating tirades to a small group of miners and factory workers who, by virtue of their being there in the middle of the week, were probably out of work. It was filled with rhetorical questions that required no answers, only applause and the compulsory amens.

"America is a land of values," Keith Bates was saying. "A nation of family values. A land of Christian values that shapes our great society."

Amison unfolded his arms and sat up, struggling against the tubes.

"What is the secret of the American village?" he asked.

He answered his own question.

"Happiness, I say. There is more happiness in the American village than in any other place on earth."

These words were nothing new, Amison reflected. They had been uttered a long time ago by a former presidential candidate, Warren Harding, who had used almost that exact phrase in his campaign stops. Elected president, he died in office in the middle of a corruption scandal.

"But the American village is being threatened," Keith Bates announced in a steadily rising voice. Moans from the crowd.

"Many of you have lost your jobs."

More cries.

"You may lose your homes."

The moans were louder.

"Your Christian values are under siege. America is under siege. Your very lives are in danger."

His voice was rising in a crescendo.

"We must fight and restore our American way of life."

A roar!

"If you believe we must do something, say Amen!"

A smattering of amens from the audience.

"If you believe in America, say Amen!"

Louder amens.

"If you believe in family values, say Amen. If you believe in Christian values, say Amen. If you believe that America is for Americans, say Amen!"

And on and on he went until Amison shut off the set.

A cell phone rang somewhere in the room. Dimitri picked it up and handed it to Amison. It was Erica Brown.

"Are you ok?" She asked.

Amison stared at the tubes keeping him immobilized.

"Good as new," he lied. "Where are you?"

"Not far. Do you want a visitor?"

Amison cursed under his breath.

"I need a nurse," he answered.

"How about a wife?"

"I don't need more wives," he snorted. "I need a new body. What the hell are you doing in town anyway? Are you following me?"

"I'm here on business with Janice. I want to talk to you."

Now fully awake and alert, Amison pulled himself up to a sitting position.

"Not now. How long have I been here," he asked Dimitri.

"One week."

Amison could hear Erica over the phone saying, "I called Luis and he said you're going to be fine. Who's at the hospital with you?"

"Dimitri."

Amison twisted over in his bed as well as he could and again asked Dimitri.

"What happened to me?"

Dimitri shrugged his shoulders.

"Ask the doctor."

"What about Sid? Where is he?"

"Back to his old self and at the hotel. Don't worry about him. Charlotte is taking care of him and Janice came to visit."

"A voice from the door interrupted.

"Are you making trouble again, brother-in-law?"

It was Luis Santiago who had come to visit with Frank Hoffman and Harold Levy. Henry Alstrum, admitted earlier at the hospital as Amison,'s doctor, was already on the floor and walked in behind them. They found extra chairs in the corridor, brought them into the semi-private room and sat down, waiting while Henry checked Amison's his pulse and his vital signs.

Amison asked Erica to call back, hung up and cursed at Henry who started poking about his body with a cold stethoscope.

"You should be more grateful, Jones," Henry commented. "You're lucky to be alive. The good news is that you can leave here tomorrow. The bad news is that someone out there is waiting to kill you when you get out."

"I'll worry about that tomorrow" said Amison. "Right now, I'm starved."

"You should be. Your stomach was pumped out and you spent a full week on feeding tubes. What the hell did you put in your coffee in San Juan? I know you don't drink or smoke anymore."

"What are you talking about?"

"You were poisoned," Henry said.

"How could that happen? I had my meals in my room at the Brittany."

A voice responded from the door. It was Jake Santana, tugging as usual at his suspenders.

"That was the problem, Jonesey," explained Jake. "Your food was laced with an arsenic based bug killer, the kind restaurants use. Gus Galindez checked out the Brittany and found the stuff in the hotel kitchen. Now, that's normal; the only thing not normal was that some of it was used on you. The other thing is that the shooters at the Brittany ended up being White Knight hit men. What's hard to figure out is that someone is spending a fortune and spilling a lot of blood to bring you guys down. Are you worth that kind of money?"

"It's all about the gold," said Henry.

Amison stared at the doctor, repeating, "The gold?"

Henry nodded.

"I told you at the Brittany that we needed to talk but we never had a chance. However, Bienvenido was getting nervous and so I had a long conversation with him about what's hidden away in Monte Fuego. The long and the short of it that Hernando and Roberto got me into the mine through an abandoned shaft under La Fortaleza's north wall. It was filled with gold bars and coins hidden by Spanish conquistadores. We took what we could carry and left the way we came. I think at least fifty tons of gold is warehoused in that cave. That comes to more than a billion dollars at current gold prices. We saw more caves filled with gold but we never had a chance to check them out. A few weeks later, a slight tremor destroyed the shaft. That's when Hernando said we could get in from the sea and through a secret tunnel from the city. We wanted to steal it all, but we lacked the financial and logistical resources. So we never followed through. Hernando told me later that he and Roberto tried to convince Emilio Gutierrez to support them and even showed him where to enter the tunnel from the city."

"Jesus, Henry. Why didn't you come forward and tell us?" Frank asked. "If nothing else, we might have saved Hernando's life and even Roberto's."

The doctor hung his head down.

"It was greed. Nothing but greed. I thought we could eventually pull it off and get away with it. I told Bienvenido what we tried to do because I wanted him to know what he was up against. I never imagined there would be all this killing."

"There's much more besides the gold," said Harold. "In a way, you're real lucky to have backed off, Henry, or you too might be dead. At least, we know now what the whole fuss about West Indian is about."

Jake Santana, finally grasping the overall situation, added, "That explains the Brittany firefight and everything else. It is all about the gold."

Amison shook his head.

"No. It's more than that. We're up against an unbalanced genius who kills to keep a deep secret. Any gold in the mine is only part of the story. If Leroux is right, this mastermind needs West Indian Mines to feed the global mission he's been talking about."

"I don't follow," said Henry.

"It's like Harold says. It's about gold and much more. Besides the mine and its contents, there's the cash generated by West Indian. Gold is good but cash provides immediate liquidity. Now, West Indian received until now 50% of all receipts generated by Emerald and Boucher & Salieri. That must have run into the billions over the years and the dividends issued by West Indian aren't high enough to account for all the money taken in. Where has the rest of it gone?"

"The I.R.S. was finally able to get West Indian's financials from the day they started," said Harold. "But they're confusing. It's going to take months for our accountants to decipher them."

"We don't have months," Amison warned. "The gold. money and everything else in the mine will be gone and we'll be dead if we wait that long."

"So? Do you have a suggestion?"

Amison laughed.

"You bet, man. I called Alex Plotnikoff and Vincent Romaine a couple of weeks ago. Alex was Francisco Barberi's accountant until Bienvenido took over the old man's businesses and Vincent was his corporate attorney. Both guys have inside knowledge of West Indian Mines and are willing to tell us what they know. They've already gone over West Indian's books with a fine tooth comb and have shared their information with Stan Mason from the IRS. Their next stop is here to meet with us."

"Why isn't Ramon Salva on your radar?" Luis asked.

"Oh, he's no angel, but he has no political interests, and he might be unaware of what his pilot, Julio, is doing on his dime behind his back. I also thought of Keith Bates and Max Zimmer. Keith is a racist but beyond that he's a diamond merchant and thief too involved with his kids to have global ambitions. I think he'd like to kill his lunatic son for the grief he's caused him.

"Now Max Zimmer is a piece of work, and if we don't have to kill him first, he could lead us to the person we're looking for. Felipe too. I'm sure that he's in bed with Max. Now that his father is dead, we can decide what to do about him."

Amison waved his sinewy arms over the bed, watching the intravenous tubes do a dance.

"Listen," he said. "I've been playing multi-level word and name association games while I'm stuck jumping rope with these tubes."

Everyone looked at him as if he had gone crazy.

"Hear me out, guys. We have three levels of operation," he maintained. "At Level One is our nemesis. I call that person, X who has an agenda excluding the new West Indian stockholders. X has one confederate at Level Two who is under-cutting us. Max Zimmer and Felipe are at Level Three with others acting as accomplices but working for their own account."

"Any suspicions?" Harold asked.

Amison nodded.

"Quentin Bates and his sisters are in Level Three with Max and Felipe. So are Erica and Janice and probably Estrella, I'm sorry to say. Of course, she's dead now."

"What about Level Two?"

"Sol Weinberg," said Amison.

Harold's mouth dropped.

"Sol? That doesn't make sense."

"It does when you consider that Sol is in deep with Keith and his daughters in a stolen goods scheme," explained Amison. "But maybe it doesn't go any further than that. What's gumming up the works is the stolen menorah and the jockey-ing over the gold and treasure in Monte Fuego and probably the fact that the girls are now probably striking out on their own."

"I wonder if they'll be at Emilio's funeral in Monte Fuego,." said Harold

"They'll be there, Harold. Everyone will be there, and so will we."

CHAPTER 23

▼

The Hospital Visit

Amison was tired and wanted to sleep but he came alive when Jake Santana asked, "So, what can you tell me about Quentin Bates?"

"He's been after us ever since we put away several years ago," said Amison. "And now he's finally found a cause that backs his motive for killing us."

Jake found a hard candy and popped it in his mouth.

"Figures," he said. "We have an APB out for him, but I'm not worried. If we don't get him, Europol will, and if Europol doesn't; you may get lucky. But if he gets to you first, we'll be waiting. One way or another, we'll get him."

Jake enjoyed watching the expressions on his listeners and kept on talking.

"You don't suppose that there's a connection between the hit at the Brittany and an abandoned camp site forest rangers found in the middle of the swamps west of here last week?"

Luis looked at Harold.

"We don't follow," said Harold.

Jake started sucking on the candy.

"It's probably nothing, but bits and pieces of human flesh were fished out of the swamps. It seems that the alligators had a picnic."

"They must have been hungry," Frank suggested.

"Must be," agreed Jake. "And that probably explains why the White Knights haven't been seen around these parts for a while."

"Must be," repeated Luis.

"The funny thing is that pieces of several bullet proof vests were found. We had them tested. They're made from a high tech mix of fabric and metal alloys we've never seen, like flexible armor that could stop a howitzer shell. What's more, they're military issue. Even the cops don't have them. But it turns out that when we had the vest Max was wearing at your council meeting tested, we found it was made of the same material. Incidentally, they were produced by that factory in Connecticut that burned down."

Jake Santana heaved a sigh and abruptly changed the subject.

"Gus, Tom and I have been thinking about that menorah robbery and about Victor Duncan's murder. We too have a theory, just like Jonesey."

"What's that?" Amison asked.

"Danielle and Denise are twins, right?"

"Yes."

"Let's assume for a moment that Denise, pretending to be Danielle, was the one who killed Victor. That would have allowed Danielle to be in Washington with Juan Duarte Gutierrez."

"But it was Danielle who was seen shooting Victor. Even Victor identified her as he was being shot," Frank reminded Jake.

"Not quite," corrected Jake. "We know exactly what Victor's dying words were. He said, 'No, no! It's not me you want.' Tom Lyons doesn't think Victor would have said that if the shooter was Danielle who he would have assumed was after him because of his affair with Janice.

"So we did some thinking. The one he identified as Danielle was left handed, and it happens that Danielle is right handed. However, Denise is left handed. It's rare among twins but not unusual."

"Is that the only fact driving your hypothesis?"

"No. The pistol left at the murder scene was designed for a lefty. We know that from the position of the safety on the trigger housing. Right handed people would have used a gun with a safety on the trigger housing's reverse side. Or, they could use a weapon with an ambidextrous safety. But why use one built only for a lefty unless the shooter is purely left handed? That's why we say the shooter was left handed and not Danielle."

"What would be the justification for the switch?"

"Simple. If Danielle is Victor's killer, she loses her claim to his estate. If her alibi holds, she gets it. That leaves us with Denise. If her Florida alibi holds, it clears her of the menorah robbery and Victor's murder. And now with Emilio gone, her alibi is stronger than ever since the police have his written statement about being with her at the time. And of course, she inherits Emilio's estate. That's smooth work for those sisters."

"Well, if she didn't steal the menorah, who did?"

Jake's face lit up.

"It wasn't Denise. It was a woman masquerading as her. Woman Number Three, I call her. That woman knew the San Jeronimo fortress cold. She stole the menorah. That left Denise free to kill Victor in Connecticut."

"And what about Denise's Florida alibi?"

"That was Woman Four pretending to be Denise who was with Emilio. But his death raises questions. The round that killed him wasn't from the shooters. It came from a small caliber pistol normally carried by a right handed person. That was the weapon Luis took from Denise at the luncheon and it had been fired. I'll bet you dollars to doughnuts that it was Danielle and not Denise at the luncheon and that Danielle turns out to be Emilio's killer. An interesting scenario, isn't it? Denise murders Victor and Danielle murders Emilio. Now, I call that neat thinking. If snagged, a smart lawyer will get them a few years on second or third degree murder and they save their inheritances. Anyway, Tom, Gus and I call this our five women theory. Cool, isn't it?"

"Five women?"

"Yes," Jake replied smugly, concluding his argument. "A woman who does hair and makeup, the fifth woman. It has to be Estrella Gomez."

"Are you saying Emilio set up his own murder?"

Jake shook his head vigorously.

"No. But you're right in a weird way. He was in on the menorah heist with the twins from the beginning. So was Victor. They never suspected that the twins' plan to pull off the robbery included their murders. Once Denise and her sister had two look-a-likes to establish solid alibis, they were road kill. Victor was murdered for his estate and Emilio was disposable once he gave us a sworn statement saying that Denise was with him. A woman was with him but it wasn't Denise. I'll tell you something else. Those two look-alike women had to know way ahead of time what was going to happen to the guys and what was going down at the luncheon. That means they're close to Quentin and the folks who want to take you all down."

Jake tugged at his suspenders and prepared to leave.

"Let me know when you get some bright ideas supporting our theory."

He looked directly into Frank's eyes.

"Tell me, amigo. Did you really give your school ring to Danielle?"

The dead silence that accompanied Jake's exit from the hospital room was broken by Amison.

"Frank. Were you stupid enough to give Danielle your school ring?"

"Frank swallowed hard.

"No," he replied. "I was stupid enough to give it to Janice."

Harold, who was listening attentively to Jake Santana's suspicions, was fit to be tied, and when the police inspector was out of earshot, his temper exploded. "This is sheer bullshit," he bellowed in a voice that could be heard outside the hospital room. "I want to know exactly what's been going on behind my back."

"Should I leave the room?" Dimitri asked timidly.

Harold was livid.

"I don't give a shit where you go."

"You should keep your voice down, Harold," said a female voice from the door. "This is a hospital."

Harold's voice rose in pitch.

"I don't give a...!"

He stopped when he saw Erica and Janice standing at the door.

Amison rolled his eyes and sank back into the bed as Dimitri hiked up his hospital gown and tiptoed out the room, winking at the girls as he left.

Henry Alstrum tried to come up with an excuse to follow Dimitri but his exit was blocked Harold who told him to stay put.

"I want to know what's going on," he barked. "And since you women are here, tell me that you're not sandbagging me and my men."

"I don't know what you're talking about," said Janice brazenly.

"We did nothing to hurt Frank and Ruby," Erica maintained stoutly.

"Then, what did you do?"

Janice looked at Frank who squirmed uncomfortably in his chair.

"The police found my school ring at the San Jeronimo fortress," he said. "It was the one I gave you when we started going out again."

Amison wanted to keep quiet but Henry Alstrum jumped into the discussion and told the women about Jake Santana's theory.

"The long and the short is that Jake doesn't believe Frank's story about his giving the ring to Danielle."

Frank was at a loss for words and Janice came over and placed her hands on his shoulders.

"Frank's right," she said. "He gave me the ring, and I was the one who stole the menorah.

Her announcement could have aroused the dead.

"How did you end up being a jewel thief?" Amison asked when he had fully digested her words.

"Danielle and Denise were our best friends," she replied. "We went to school together. We lost touch for a while. It was after they married Victor and Emilio that we met by coincidence through their husbands."

Harold was beginning to calm down.

"What kind of coincidence?"

Amison coughed and Erica laughed.

"When Frank and Ruby cut us loose a few years ago, we needed money. We attended a party in Monte Fuego put together by Keith Bates in honor of Juan Duarte Gutierrez's election, and that's where we met Emilio and Victor, two guys who we thought were rich and well connected. It was basically our fault. We needed two sugar daddies and they were it." She sighed. "It was only later we learned they were married to our best friends."

"Danielle and Denise found out but they went along," said Janice. "We had no idea that our affairs with their husbands worked into a solution to their own problems."

"What kind of problems?" Harold asked. "They're cat burglars protected by the CIA because they do jobs for the Agency."

"That was one problem," answered Erica. "Danielle was having an affair with Max Zimmer while she was married to Victor and I had a fling with him years ago."

Harold slapped his head.

"Damn! Everyone's been sleeping with Danielle. I thought I was special."

"The other problem is Denise's thing with Felipe, Emilio's son."

Luis, who could not believe his ears, expressed his reservations about the story being spun by the two women.

"Why not?" Erica shot back sharply. "Don't you like young stuff?"

"That's different," Luis protested.

Erica shook her head.

"You're such a hypocrite, Luis. Listen. Emilio's a nice guy, but he's old, older than you guys, and he's pretty slow in the sack, if you get my drift."

"How the hell would you know?" Luis fumed.

"Because I slept with him," said Erica, smiling. "He kept me, remember?"

Amison wanted to bury his head in the sheets but the tubes restrained him.

"Denise never loved Emilio," she elaborated. "She loved Felipe, his son from an earlier marriage, but Emilio had money and position and so she married him and saw Felipe on the sly.

"Our own troubles started when Denise had the idea of stealing the menorah that was going on exhibit at San Jeronimo. She offered us $100,000 apiece and promised to keep our trysts quiet if we would do the job. Janice, who knew the fortress would dress like Denise and lift the menorah while I would pretend to be her with Emilio in Florida. Estrella Gomez always did our hair, so we cut her in and used her to make us up to look like the twins."

Amison's eyes widened.

"Who else was in on the robbery?"

"Felipe. And he recruited Juan Maldonado and Toby Sands for their muscle. Janice provided the diversion; Estrella cut the power; Juan and Toby got the menorah down the chute where Felipe was waiting with a boat. He took it to an airport near the cruise ship terminal where Julio Maldonado flew it in Ramon Salva's jet to Monte Fuego."

"We never planned to keep the menorah," broke in Janice. "We wanted only to blackmail Centurion into paying us $500 million to return it."

Harold's interest was now.aroused.

"Was Sol Weinberg or Ramon Salva or anyone else involved in this?"

Erica shook her head.

"No. This was our own little piece of work. Quentin coordinated the robbery for us but his dad was never in on it. Neither was Salva. Julio and Felipe were in with us for the money as was Estrella and the others. It's just too bad that she got caught short. That was strictly a bad coincidence that she was caught in the cross-fire at the Brittany. Jorge Ramirez was going to be our go-between until you guys took him down. At least, the saving grace is that now the money doesn't have to be split with him."

"What money?" Amison asked.

"The $500 million you're going to give us if the world ever wants to see the Menorah in one piece again," said Janice.

Harold walked to the door and closed it.

"You can also forget about splitting the money with anyone else," he said.

"I'll take that deal," Janice responded happily.

"What I'm saying," continued Harold, "is that you're no going to get a penny until we found out exactly who's trying to take us down."

When no response came from the women, Frank said, "The cops are already connecting the dots and will be looking for you for answers in connection with the menorah robbery and Victor's murder."

"That's crap!" Erica snapped back. "If the cops come after us, that menorah will be melted down and the gold sold along with the diamonds. We'll also tell them about the twins' stolen jewelry deal with Sol and Keith Bates. They'll all be dead meat. So, you figure it out, guys."

"That's right," said Janice. "It's your call. Harold, you understand. Just think of your relationship with the Jewish community. How is it going to react."

Harold laughed so loudly that the women were caught off guard.

"I keep telling people that I'm not Jewish and noone believes me."

He dried the tears from his eyes and turned to Amison, saying, "It's time for you to turn on the charm, Jonesey. Explain to these fine ladies what we want and what this is about."

Amison propped himself up in bed, tubes and all, and threw the women his best smile.

"Listen," he said. "There's going to be a funeral in Monte Fuego in the near future and we want that menorah back by then. But we have another shopping list. We also need to know who's after us; we want Quentin Bates, Felipe, Max and their handlers and we want you to set them up for us. You can melt down the menorah if you're stupid enough, but we don't care either way. That's not our mission. It's that simple."

"And if we don't give you what you want?" Janice asked defiantly.

"We'll be very unhappy," replied Amison.

Janice looked at Erica,

"What do we do now?"

"For starters, I'm speaking for Sid Stone," said Amison. "You're fired from your job at the Brittany." He looked at Frank. "Is that ok, old buddy?"

Frank shrugged.

"You're the boss, Jonesey. I'll have to find someone else to wear my school ring, if I can ever get it back from the cops."

Before Erica and Janice could say anything more, Harold ordered Henry and Dimitri to escort them outside where Virgil and Bob Byrne were waiting in the corridor and to take them to the Riverside.

"Give them money; put them on a flight out of here to anywhere they want to go and don't let them out of your sight until they're gone."

"We can take care of ourselves," said Janice.

"I'm sure you can," Amison agreed. "And you will once you're out of here."

Erica tried to get back on his good side.

"Why can't I stay with you? You can take me to the airport tomorrow."

"What about our clothes? Janice added. "They're at the hotel."

"We'll take of all that for you," said Henry softly. "But now it's time to go."

There was nothing more to say. Erica and Janice left under the watchful eyes of Henry, Virgil and Bob Byrne, leaving Luis to summarize the situation.

"If I told you once, I told you many times, scorpions don't make good house pets."

"Oh, shut up, Luis."

CHAPTER 24

▼

Fatal Intervention

"I taped the conversation," Harold bragged to Amison, Frank and Luis when they were alone for a few minutes. He tapped his jacket pocket. "I'm going to give it Jake Santana and let him figure it out."

"What for?" Amison asked. "Do you want the menorah back or do you want to end up with a pot of melted gold and loose diamonds that's going to create an international incident and cost Centurion a cool billion?"

"I'm not going to pay to get the menorah back," Harold shot back.

"We're not going to pay diddle," Amison assured him softly. "And the girls aren't going to break down the menorah either. It's a case where the whole is worth much more than the sum of its parts. They'll wait, just like we'll wait. If the menorah is in Monte Fuego, we'll find it when we get there."

Still, Harold had reservations.

"Oh, yeah? Where in Monte Fuego?"

Amison smiled and replied, "You'll see. In the meantime, keep the tape in your pocket until we need it. These women will unintentionally point us in the right direction."

Evening was approaching. Not wishing to leave Amison alone, they waited until Desmond Lyons and Jimmy Wales showed up before heading out. The nursing staff arrived minutes later to remove his feeding tubes, followed by a kitchen worker pushing a dinner cart of watery soup, crumbly crackers, and a hamburger platter that came with an unnecessary serrated knife.

"This mission sucks," Amison blurted out. "I should never have gone along with it and I should never have allowed you guys to get involved."

"You didn't get us into this, Jonesey," Jimmy assured him. "We got into this ourselves."

"That's right," said Desmond. "That's what we do for a living. We work for you. It's part greed and part loyalty. You need to relax, Jonesey. Don't be so hard on yourself. I think you need a new woman in your life."

Amison shook his head.

"I'm no good for women. They die when I'm around."

"That's not so," said Jimmy Wales. "Those things happen."

Amison threw his legs over the bed and sat up.

"Are you guys trying to tell me something?"

"No Jonesey. You know what you're doing even when you don't know it. That's why we'd follow you to hell and back."

Desmond nodded.

"You're the best, Jonesey. But we're in a funny business. We leave bodies, and some of them belong to friends and loved ones. But you can't use that as an excuse to steer clear of relationships. Look at Cecil Fergueson. He had a wife and raised a family all these years and no harm came to them. And there's your brother-in-law, Luis. He also raised a family, and they're fine."

"I...I don't know," Amison stammered. "I have bad memories. I was married twice and both women died."

"Damn it, Jonesey. Your first wife, Dolores, Luis' sister, died at childbirth, and your second wife, Bernice, was killed by Max Zimmer's old mentor, Jack O'Brien. Look at Sol and Harold. They too raised families. And look at you. "You have kids and grand kids. That's not too shabby."

Amison grinned sheepishly.

"You think?"

"We know. We're taking losses, but the bad guys are losing more."

Amison felt much better and felt better still when he put on his street clothes.

In the back of his mind, he thought he might not wait for morning to check out of the hospital. Much later that evening, Jimmy Wales accepted delivery of a fruit basket for Amison. He looked for a card and when it could not be found, he set in on the window sill next to the flower bouquet just as the room phone began ringing.

Desmond Lyons, who was about to go out for pizza, took the call.

"It's a woman, boss," he informed Amison.

He passed the phone to Amison. It was Denise.

"Are you having your period, Ruby, or may I come up?"

Amison whispered something to Desmond who beckoned who beckoned to Jimmy Wales to follow him.

In the meantime, Denise was not waiting for an answer. She hung up and appeared moments later at his hospital room door in form fitting slacks and a revealing blouse. She found him alone, lying in bed.

Sitting down on the bed, Denise gave Amison an amorous hug.

"The whole world is looking for you, woman." he said. "What the hell are you doing here?"

She smiled wickedly.

"Are there warrants for my arrest?"

"Not yet. But don't push your luck."

"Then, what's the problem? Are you going to snitch on me?"

Amison gulped hard and shook his head, but he took great care not to even hint that Erica and Janice had paid him a visit a few hours earlier and spilled the beans about the menorah heist.

Why Denise was at the hospital, he had no idea, and he was understandably cautious.

"How did you know I was here?"

"I try to stay connected," she replied evasively. "I made a couple of phone calls. You're easy to find."

"Did you send the flowers on the window?" he asked, trying to be casually social.

"Do you like them?"

"Thanks. They're nice."

"You couldn't care less about flowers unless they're plastic," she said. "I just wanted this place to look cheery when I got here. That's why I also brought the fruit."

"I appreciate that, Denise. But if I'm so dull to be with, why bother visiting?

"I told you. I want to find out who shot Emilio, and I want to make sure I'm not going to be cheated out of my inheritance."

"Where are you staying in town?"

"It doesn't matter. But say, how come you're alone here with only a couple of goons to watch over you." Who looks after you?"

"The goons are gone for the night. But I'm surrounded by women."

"Oh yeah? Where are they tonight?"

"Shopping," lied Amison.

"Oh, Ruby. Don't play martyr with me. I know you too well. Where are your other girlfriends?"

"Gone."

"Good. You deserve it."

"Aw, come on, Denise. I'm a sick man."

"Bull shit! A wooden stake through the heart can't stop you. You're healthy, and I need you to help me out of the mess we're in."

"What mess are we in, Denise?"

"The police is asking too many questions about Victor and Emilio," she said.

"Isn't that what they're paid to do?"

"My sister and I are clean. We have alibis."

"That's good news. That means you'll get Emilio's estate and Danielle will get Victor's fortune."

Denise laughed.

"Harold grabbed whatever Victor owned and Emilio's estate goes to his son, Felipe," she answered.

"Maybe you should marry Felipe?"

"He'd like that, Ruby. But I can't do that. I'm sure he was the one who shot Emilio and what's more, I think Harold put him up to it. They're both guilty as hell."

A vacant smile appeared on Amison's face.

"I'm curious, Denise. How come you picked Emilio over me?"

"You mean we should have gone romantic?"

"Something like that."

"You're lots of fun, Ruby, especially in the sack. At one time I was really hot to trot for you. I told you that in Paris and again in San Juan. But I learned a lot about you since we met. You're dangerous. You have no purpose in life except to make trouble and kill people. You're not the husband type. A woman needs peace and security and a good cash flow."

"And Emilio filled the bill?"

Denise went to the windowsill and poked about the flower bouquet. Amison could see her face in the reflection from the window. He watched the smile on her face change into a disdainful sneer.

"Life's a trade off. Gold or copper. Copper tarnishes and gold doesn't, I went for the gold. Let's face it, Ruby. I'm a gold digger because that's what life's all about. It's about the money and the power it buys. Anyone thinking different is not long for this world. Danielle is like me, and so are Erica and Janice, in case you and Frank are thinking of getting serious with them. Emilio and Victor are scum bags; they always were. They couldn't support us in style without dad's help; and they couldn't even take care of their mistresses."

That sweet smile was back on her face and she turned around.

"But you're different and I need you, Ruby," she pleaded. "We can make great music together."

Denise walked over to Amison and sat down on the bed next to him.

"I'm a widow now and you and I can make a fresh start. We'll be rich once you take over your inheritance of the West Indian Mines property."

Amison felt her hand on his thigh.

"You mean the land that Hernando says is his?"

"Yes," answered Denise softly. I know where his deed is hidden."

"I'm not sure that I'm interested in owning anything," said Amison. "I might do a good deed and give the whole thing away for tourist development."

"Damn it, Ruby. I need you. I need you to be my lover and my partner. We'll grow old and rich together. You can't afford to be that generous."

Denise leaned over and gave Amison a more passionate kiss.

"I'll have to think about that, Denise. We're going to make some people unhappy."

"Like Harold? We can kill him."

"What about Felipe?"

"We don't need him or anyone. We'll kill them all and keep everything for ourselves."

"How about Erica and Janice?"

"You figure it out, Ruby. How many women do you want to keep?"

She began rubbing his thigh.

"That's a good point, Denise. So, what's our next move? Do we also take care of Max Zimmer?"

"That's no problem, sweetie. Sol Weinberg owns a restaurant in Connecticut and Max uses it as a safe house."

"I'm going to think about your offer overnight," said Amison.

"It's your call, Sweetie. Now, do I go home alone or do you get rid of your goon and help me water my flower bouquet?"

They stayed together for about an hour until Denise noticed that Amison had dozed off. She dressed without disturbing him, rearranged the flowers on the window sill and placed the fruit basket on a tray table on her way out into the corridor.

At the end of the corridor was the duty desk, directly across from an elevator and flight of stairs. A nurse was alone, working behind the counter when a tall shadow ducked into closet. A red light from a patient's bed in another corridor lit up the monitor behind the desk and the nurse went off to investigate.

The shadowy shape emerged from the closet and floated past the duty desk and Amison's room. The shadow belonged to Quentin Bates.

He stopped briefly by the chair in front of the door. It was empty. He slowly opened the door, let himself in and closed it without making a sound, moving like a big cat to the bed in which Amison was asleep under a blanket with his hospital gown sticking out from under the sheets. The fruit basket was still on the table but the flowers on the window were gone.

Quentin pulled out a silencer-equipped pistol and fired into what he thought was Amison's head. He need not have bothered. A grim faced Amison sprang up from under the bed and with the serrated dinner knife in his hand, he drew it across Quentin's neck and slit his throat.

The cowboy clown stepped back, held his throat with one hand and tried to get off another shot. But the bathroom door opened and Luis Santiago jumped out with a machine pistol, discharging it into Quentin's body and head.

The cowboy clown turned and staggered to the door where Frank Hoffman stood with a shotgun blasting away. Quentin's knees buckled and Frank fired again.

This time, Quentin crashed to the floor with the tray table and fruit basket tumbling down over him.

Amison turned on the lights.

"We have to win one eventually," he said.

CHAPTER 25

▼

Aftermath

Quentin Bates was dead at last and the happiest people in the world would undoubtedly be Charlotte Fergueson and Rosina Alvarez. Amison felt good now and it made no sense to stay in the hospital. Once the police inquiry was completed, Amison returned to the Riverside and went to Hamburger Haven for his first full meal in many days.

"It wasn't a social call and I figured that Quentin was not far behind. Denise came for a deal," Amison explained to his friends and to Jake who had come to join them. "The sex was a bonus, and when she concluded that I wasn't biting, she threw it in gratis before signaling her kid brother.

"Meanwhile, I had Desmond Lyons and Jimmy Wales get Frank and Luis for backup. The flower bouquet had tiny canisters of sleeping gas in it that Denise released when she was toying with the bouquet. The fruit bowl on the window was a signal to Quentin that she was in the room, and when she removed it, it was a sign that she was leaving and that I was alone. The gas was supposed to make me fall asleep, but Luis is allergic to just about anything. He found the canisters and put the flowers in the bathroom. That's about it, folks."

"We had no choice," said Luis. "It was self defense."

"The problem with these self defense killings is that they look too much like a gang war and make me look bad," said Jake. "They also make Gus and Tom look bad. We need some sort of closure, or at least, we need to show that we're making progress."

Amison sighed and nodded in Harold's direction.

"Harold recorded a conversation we had with Erica and Janice when they showed up at the hospital. I didn't want to let it go at first but maybe now you should listen to it."

A look of relief passed over Harold when Amison gave the word. He smiled and placed the small tape player on the desk and turned it on.

Jake listened, riveted to the inadvertent confessions being made by Erica and Janice, and when it was over, he shook his head, saying, "I can't believe what I'm hearing. Those broads just about laid the whole thing out for us."

Frank shook his head.

"Not entirely," he cautioned. "This solves the menorah robbery in a way, but it doesn't solve the murders of Victor and Emilio and it doesn't tell us how and where to find the menorah in Monte Fuego. It also doesn't give us much of a leg up on Leroux's larger right wing conspiracy."

"Well, what do I tell Gus Galindez and Tom Clark?"

"Tell them what we know and play the tape," said Harold. "Just don't go off half-cocked arresting anyone yet. Let us do our thing and you'll soon be able to finish your business in a blaze of glory."

While Harold was talking, Amison took a call.

"Who's that?" Harold asked when he had finished speaking with Jake.

"Alex Plotnikoff and Vince Romaine," replied Amison. "They're coming in next week. We'll need to have them picked up at the airport."

Jake Santana got up and prepared to leave.

"Let us know when you have something," he said. "But right now, try to stay out of trouble as a personal favor to me."

He left as Dimitri walked in with the morning papers to say that Erica and Janice were placed on a flight to Monte Fuego without incident and Denise had disappeared from sight. He tossed the papers on the table and pointed to a short article under a bold headline that read, "University Seeks New Prez."

The article chronicled Emilio Gutierrez's life up to the time of his death from a heart attack at the age of sixty. It also quoted Sol Weinberg, chairperson of Las Olas University's board of trustees, as saying that an interim president was to be appointed pending the creation of a search and screen committee to find a new chief executive.

Also in the local news was, strangely enough, was a piece on the accidental shooting death of Estrella Gomez in Puerto Rico, a West Indian Mines heiress whose estate was being contested by Juan Duarte Gutierrez, president of the Republic of Monte Fuego. It named the estate's executor as one Amison Rubin

Jones and went on to indicate that although no recorded will was found, a hand written one was found among her personal belongings that seemed to leave the disposition of her assets, including her stake in West Indian to Amison Jones and to a Carlos Ramon Salva, her paternal uncle.

The article quoted Juan Duarte as suggesting the document to be a fake that would be contested in a court of law. Lawsuit! Amison thought of how Ramon Salva was going to react to the unfolding legal machinations. He was not one prone to solving problems in court. To him, his niece had been murdered and before showing up in any court, Amison was sure he would come hunting for his pound of flesh.

Amison felt the same way. Estrella's major sin was to take care of herself as best as she could and could not be faulted for being in complicity with a plot to steal the menorah and certainly did not deserve to die over it. He set the blame for her death squarely on the cowboy clown and the gang he worked for. Now that the clown was dead, someone higher up would have to pay.

"My question is," said Amison. "Assuming that the only way in and out of the mine right now is through the tunnel, and assuming that tons and tons of good stuff lies inside the mine, how is anyone going to get it out?"

"You mean, how are we going to get it out?" Luis clarified.

"We're going to dig our way in when we take physical control of the mine and once we get through the lawsuits and restraining orders," said Harold.

Amison was about to comment when his cell phone rang. It was Jacques Leroux calling from Paris inquiring about his health.

"Back on my feet, director."

"I heard from monsieur Santana earlier and he entertained me with the story about your encounter with the cowboy clown."

"That's good, director. Is there anything else you wish to talk about?"

"Yes. My associate at the CIA, monsieur Calvin Bard, sends his best wishes and his congratulations for the termination of Quentin Bates. But on another note, monsieur Bard has informed me that our mutual friend, Max Zimmer, has been retired from the agency."

"Excuse me, director. Frank, Luis and Harold are in the office with me. May I put this call on the speaker?"

"Yes, of course."

"What precipitated his retirement?"

"Calvin Bard is revamping his department and Max did not fit in his plans.

Besides, Max was up for retirement. He leaves with a pension and full benefits. I don't want to bore you with details, monsieur Jones, but Max is a free agent and monsieur Bard has given us the green light to deal directly with him."

Leroux could not have been more explicit and the expressions of joy flashing across the faces of his listeners were quite obvious. Calvin Bard had strung his agent out to dry. Here was the go-ahead they needed.

But Amison was a realist. Max would not have allowed himself to be pushed out of the CIA for retirement and reorganization reasons alone. Something else was afoot.

The Europol director must have been reading his mind.

"You are aware, my friend," he said, "that Jorge Ramirez's death in is still an on-going investigation. Europol and Dutch authorities, on behalf of the police in St. Maarten, wish to interview Max about that unfortunate affair."

So that was the deal. The CIA was not about to be dragged into a murder in which one of its own agents was a suspect. Calvin Bard wanted Max out and dead.

"I hear that hunting season is starting in some areas of the world," Leroux was saying. "I trust you will be soon be hunting."

"Soon," said Amison.

"Splendid, monsieur Jones. Now, you do remember our poor fugitive, Paul Boucher, do you not?"

"Has he finally been arrested?"

"I am afraid not," answered Leroux. "He and Louis Salieri died in a murder and suicide pact in Paris a few days ago."

"Indeed. Exactly how did they die?"

"Paul shot Louis and then shot himself. It was a bullet to the right temple."

Amison sneered.

"That would have been difficult, director. Frank and I met Paul Boucher in Monte Fuego at Hernando's bedside. He was left handed."

"Are you sure?"

"Positive. You better have the Paris police check its facts."

"A double murder, then?"

"Seems that way. Two witnesses wiped away in one stroke, one a witness to Hernando's killing and another to the menorah robbery."

"That is too bad," Leroux went on. "But a good reason to move faster. Have you been giving thought to a proactive strategy?"

"We were in the process of discussing the issue when you called."

"Well, I have one more news item for you. I asked Bienvenido de la Maza to have his bank inquire about Kinshasa Trading with the Bank for International Settlements in Switzerland.

"The BIC?"

"Yes, the clearing house for cross border banking transactions. It documents a link Carib Financial, Black Star Trading, Boucher & Salieri, Emerald House and Kinshasa Export."

"We know all that, director," Amison reminded him.

"Yes, but we now have two signatures on the paper trail. One belongs to the son of Emilio Gutierrez who appears on Carib Financial's documentation."

"Felipe?"

"Yes. But he is only a surrogate, I am sure. Carib Financial itself is owned by Kinshasa Export who underwrites its shipments to Emerald and B&S through Carib Financial which backs Keith Bates and his customer network. The name that keeps showing up on Kinshasa Export's documentation belongs to Charles Underwood Lawrence."

"That's Hank Lawrence's father," said Amison sarcastically. "He died in a fire years ago. He would be almost a hundred years old today if he were alive."

"The signature might be that of his son, Edward Lawrence, current identity and whereabouts unknown, assuming he is still living," Leroux said. "Europol did a background check on monsieur Lawrence senior. He was quite a guy, as you would put it in America. He was a grand dragon in the Connecticut KKK."

"The Ku Klux Klan? How does that affect his son?"

"Simple. Hatred of specific people and individuals is much like the love of a fine champagne, my friend. It is an acquired taste. It could be that son Edward has borrowed his father's name and acquired his rabid hatred of the non-white and non-Christian world."

"Why would he be after us?"

"He could be seeking revenge for brother Lawrence's death. It could be that he has amassed a great fortune in the African diamond trade, enough to wreak havoc in the world. Big money buys mercenary armies, navies and any number of killers for hire, as you well know."

"Are you sure your imagination is not working overtime, director?"

"No. Would you care to place a small wager on my assertion that Edward Lawrence is our man?"

Amison laughed.

"Where do we find this Edward Lawrence of yours? In Africa?"

"If I knew, I would not need you. That is for you to find out."

"Have you spoken to Sid Stone about your theory?"

"No. You and your friends can do that when he is feeling better. And you should also watch your back more carefully. Your popularity has become legendary. Even the president of Monte Fuego is one of your fans."

"Juan Duarte Gutierrez?"

"Yes, but he will use the judicial system first to challenge Estrella's will."

"I have no problem facing him in court," said Amison.

"In your country?"

"In any country, director. But I'll see him in Monte Fuego. Everything will be settled there."

"Wonderful," said Leroux. "I too will be there."

CHAPTER 26

▼

Mixed Signals

Things were slowly getting back to normal at the Riverside. Sid Stone took a week's vacation and when he returned he was tan and relaxed. Amison found him in his office relaxing with Henry Alstrum who had just returned from the Caribbean to make the rounds of his patients.

"Good trip?" Amison asked.

"Not bad," replied the physician. "I made a pit stop in Monte Fuego along the way and saw the volcano acting up a bit."

"Is that thing going to erupt?"

"It's always making noises," said Frank who happened to walk in with Luis.

But Sid was excited about something else.

"Remember that private eye I hired to find out what happened to my mother? Well, he found her grave."

Amison was all ears.

"Where is she buried?"

"At the Forest Hills cemetery near Westport in Connecticut. She lived in the town for ten years and spent her last year at Sunrise Manor, a nursing home in Norwalk. She died two years ago. The private eye said all her bills were paid ever since she was in Connecticut by her son, Edward Lawrence. That would be Hank Lawrence's brother and also my half brother. My next challenge is to find him."

Sid looked up hopefully at Amison.

"That shouldn't be too hard, should it, Jonesey?"

Amison slapped Sid on the back.

"It may be easier than you think, Sid. How about lunch? Is Harold back from Connecticut?"

"He's with Bienvenido at his warehouse in North Miami."

"Tell them we want to have lunch at the Palm in Bal Harbor. It's important." Just then, Amison happened to look down at his wrist. Feeling his left wrist, he knew something was missing.

"My watch," he cried. "Where's my watch? I had it at the hospital."

"You had it on in the car when we drove here," Frank said. "You may have dropped it. I'll look later; it won't go anywhere."

An hour later, they were in Bal Harbor seated at a long table where Harold and Bienvenido de la Maza were waiting.

"Is this our new conference room?" Bienvenido inquired.

They buried their noses into menus as waiters came by to take their lunch order.

"It's not a bad place," answered Amison, giving the wait staff time to work its way around the table. "The food is good, and we have much to be thankful for. I'm back on my feet and Sid is feeling better."

"I'm back to normal, Jonesey. And I'm sorry. I don't know what came over me at the Brittany."

"Well, I wouldn't have been happy either if I owned the hotel."

"That's what we need to talk about, Jonesey," said Sid. "Frank and Luis are right. We need younger folks to do the grunt work we once did."

"Amen to that," said Harold. "But that depends on the grunt work we have in mind. Sol has me making funeral arrangements for the people we lost. They'll be small, intimate affairs, nothing fancy, and any life insurance policies they had held through Centurion are being paid out as we speak so we don't have to worry about turning beggars out into the street. Our need now is people to run Sid's hotels."

Sid looked at Bienvenido.

"You mentioned that Rosina wants to get into hotel work. She helps run the Brittany's front office. Maybe she can keep the books."

"That would be good," Bienvenido noted. "The Brittany could use a loyal employee. It would be good for me too. Rosina needs to be busy now that her children are in school."

"What about the Delmar?" Amison asked.

"Charlotte Furgueson could use a change," said Frank. "She's smart and may do well at the Delmar in Greenwich. What do you think, Sid?"

"That could work," he replied. "Is that ok, Jonesey?"

Amison nodded, adding, "We'll keep Angelo at La Cocina in Puerto Rico. I seem to own the place now and we should probably keep it. Dimitri is looking to expand Hamburger Haven and says he'd like a place in the islands. I'll give him a good price if he goes for it."

"Now, what about the Riverside? It's our weak spot," said Luis.

"Desmond Lyons can take the assistant manager's slot and replace Felipe," Amison suggested.

This last statement was met with a stony silence.

"Well, that's that," said Harold at last, looking around the table as waiters began serving lunch. He sat back in his chair with a knowing smile on his face and focused on Frank.

"Now to other business. Sol wants to appoint you as Las Olas University's interim president."

Frank was stunned.

"Why me?"

"Because the university needs a leader and you were once its president. It also fits into Sol's goal of expanding the institution's hotel/restaurant program into Monte Fuego to coincide with Sid's plans to build a major resort on the West Indian Mines property."

Amison was as surprised as Frank.

"When did this come about?"

"Sol and I talked while I was on vacation," answered Sid. "He likes the idea, and I think Leroux is interested."

"Is there a time line on this project?" Amison asked.

"Initial meetings to work out a protocol agreement with the government are supposed to take place in La Fortuna at the time of the funeral, according to Sol," replied Harold. "And that's fine with me, but I'm keeping Alliance out of that scene. So while the meetings are going on, you and your team will do your bit. Everything in that underground cavern must be removed. We should be able to penetrate the mine by then."

"It would be funny if I or Ramon Salva ended up legally owning all the land under West Indian Mines," commented Amison half in jest. "We could end up charging rent."

A voice behind Amison broke out laughing.

"It's your right, Jonesey. But let's face it. Your claim hasn't a snowball's chance in hell of getting a hearing in Monte Fuego. Juan Duarte has the legal system sewed up. But tell you what, I'll buy your claim for the nice tidy sum of, say, one dollar."

Amison turned and found himself looking up at Sol Weinberg.

Everyone guffawed and Amison felt he should go with the flow and join in the joke. Bienvenido waited for the laughter to die down to voice his opinion, "I hear too that the land may belong to el senor Jones or to don Carlos or to both of them. I have met with don Carlos. He will back senor Jones in court in return for senor Jones' help in finding the people who murdered his niece. I am myself indebted to senor Jones for saving my life and will support his claim if he intends to press it. I am sure el senor Levy will support him as well."

Harold backpedaled quickly and agreed with Bienvenido and Sol was forced to concede that of course he was joking and that Amison's land claim should be backed. But it was clear that the dynamics of the relationships at the table had changed. Sol Weinberg had an agenda of his own that included Sid Stone. Nor did the new dynamics escape Frank, Henry and Luis. Decisions had been made behind their backs, but they resisted the temptation to argue. Only Frank had something to say.

"I don't think I'll be well received at the university," said Frank.

"They'll love you," Sol assured him. "You left a hero and you're returning a hero. You start next week. I'm also funding the opening of an outward bound camp in Culebra, that island off Puerto Rico where you had your last mission. It's part of our country and will make an excellent training ground for young people interested in things like marine biology and tropical land conservation, and maybe counter terrorism. I met with Max Zimmer and actually that was his idea."

He looked at Frank's less than grateful expression and added by way of an afterthought, "But if you don't want the job, it can go to Henry Alstrum."

Frank was perplexed.

"How did all this come about?"

Amison threw him a knowing smile.

"If you're talking about that land in Culebra, Bienvenido owns it now. He's going to collect the rent, so he's in a win-win position."

"Does that mean that we're going to work again with our Latin American compadres?" Luis asked.

"Yes," replied Amison. "It seems that way."

Frank looked wide eyed at his old friend.

"Where are we going to get the recruits, Jonesey?"

"As president of the university, Frank. You'll work it out. Just make sure they're good old boys, red necks born and bred in the backwoods of our great country like fine whiskey and beer. We want them to be more American than Quentin's White Knights, and of course we don't want Hispanics."

"Bienvenido is not going to like that."

Bienvenido threw down his napkin.

"In fact, I am going to hate that," he announced.

"Jonesey is over reacting," said Sol. "Furthermore, I want you all to know that I'm feeling fine now and I'm still in charge here."

Sol Weinberg lumbered over to an empty chair at the next table, pulled it over and sat down."

"It's not that simple, Sol," said Amison. "Frank, Luis and I work for Alliance and not for Centurion, and you don't own close to half of Alliance. You can't take any unilateral action without a stockholder vote and consulting with us, Sol."

Sol was speechless and stared openmouthed at Amison.

"This stuff you want to do is a side show," went on Amison. "So is my claim or anyone else's. Everything has to wait until our mission is completed. Now, I want you to listen to something, Sol. Erica and Janice came to see us when I was in the hospital and Harold recorded the conversation. I made another copy of the tape," he continued, brandishing a pocket recorder in the air like a battle sword. "Jake Santana knows about it so it's not much of a secret anymore."

He flipped the 'on' switch for Sol.

They listened to the conversation between Amison and Denise in a hypnotic trance. Bienvenido's mouth dropped in amazement but Sol began sweating at the part of Max using his restaurant for a safehouse.

By way of a concluding statement, Amison said, "We have issues to address before we run off half cocked to seek our fortunes in Monte Fuego, Sol. One is our mutual buddy, Max Zimmer. If you see him, you can tell him that he's on my short list. Another issue is Sid's half brother. Leroux called this morning to say that his name comes up at Kinshasa Export. He may be the one trying to take us down all these months. We can't allow this bullshit to continue. We've been on the run long enough."

"Jonesey is right," said Harold. "It's time to move forward and to settle old scores." He went on to explain the details of Leroux's earlier phone call.

Sol Weinberg was totally taken aback. He looked at Sid Stone who hung his head down. It was clear that he felt crushed by what he was hearing.

"Do you mean to say that my long lost bother, Edward, is out to kill us?"

Amison shrugged.

"You tell me. What the hell is he doing in Africa with Kinshasa Trading?""

Frank tried to set the discussion back on a more congenial track.

"Jonesey has a point. We have a mission to execute and our lives to protect, Sol. I think under those circumstances that I must decline your offer of interim president at Las Olas University in favor of Henry Alstrum. He's a good man, and that would be a crowning capstone to his long and illustrious career."

Sol Weinberg crossed his arms, his eyes wandering around the table.

"You guys are right," he conceded. "Henry will be my man at the university. And this tape. It changes things. How about it, Henry?"

Henry looked around the table which has fallen silent and sighed.

"I'll do it for one year, Sol. One year, and then I'm out of here."

Sol mopped his brow and rose to his feet.

"I think you guys have things pretty much under control. I'm going back to the office. Just let me know what you decide. But whatever you do, let's not do it for revenge. You coming, Sid? I'll drive you back to the hotel."

But Harold was fixated on revenge and was much less subtle. The moment they were out of earshot he bellowed.

"Those fucking bastards. We need to get them before they get us."

Luis spoke up for the first time.

"Do you remember our conversation about moles in our midst?"

"What about it?"

"Those military flights chartered by Max Zimmer. We finally intercepted one and found out that its flight plan was issued electronically from an operations center in Connecticut and the flight itself was monitored by that same center."

"So?"

"The signals came from your office, Harold, and that made me curious. So I asked Tom Clark to do some checking. It turned out that the signals originated in the office where your guy, Ray Booker, works. He also found that Ray and your driver, Tommy Hicks, belong to the White Knight members and besides running Zimmer's airlift business, they've been keeping tabs on you. You're being blind sided, Harold. We've got to finish the housecleaning you started."

Frank urged a more cautious approach.

"We should wait," he said. "We know what they're up to. It might be better to just keep our eyes on them now that we know what they're up to."

It was not a response that Harold wanted.

"I'm tired of waiting," he growled. "I trusted Booker and Hicks and how did they repay me? They betrayed me. I want them killed."

Amison jumped in to support Frank.

"He's right. Killing them gives us nothing right now and removes a line of communication with our enemies. Let's compromise."

"What do you propose?" Harold asked.

"Make Ray Alliance's executive vice president for communications. We can then use him to feed disinformation up the line to his big boss who I guess is most likely Sid's half brother."

"What about Tommy Hicks?"

"He goes," said Amison.

"And the gang at Used-to-Be's?"

"They go. The jobs will be done at sea to avoid publicity and Bob Byrne will help us out. The housecleaning must be completed before we go to Monte Fuego…"

He was about to say something else when a call came in on his cell phone.

Looking up with a broad smile, he announced, "Boris Plotnikoff just landed in Miami and Vincent Romaine is waiting at the West Palm Beach airport."

CHAPTER 27

▼

Snow Geese

Boris was met up by Luis and Bienvenido in his limo a half hour later and whisked north to Fort Lauderdale. Vincent was picked up by Frank in his car and headed south. He found Amison's gold watch on the seat and threw it in his pocket.

An unforseen traffic jam on the interstate resulting from an accident created a ten mile two-way backup, forcing both vehicles off the highway at the nearest exits where they proceeded on back roads through more rural areas to converge on the Riverside. They were less than ten miles away from the Riverside when the two vehicles, still miles away from each other, fell under what seemed to be missile attacks from above.

The limo was armor plated and managed to limp away with flat tires. Frank and the attorney were not so lucky. They dove out of their car as it was on fire and had to hitchhike to a main road where they found a cab. By coincidence, they all reached the Riverside, shaken but unharmed, minutes apart.

They were greeted by Amison and taken directly to Hamburger Haven where Harold and Sid Stone were waiting. The general mood was subdued and few words were exchanged.

"Some welcoming committee you have, Jonesey," remarked Boris in a thick Russian accent after all the introductions had been made.

"I charge double for hazardous duty," said Vincent.

Boris Plotnikoff was a big barrel chested man with wide shoulders, a thick neck and a bullet shaped head. Thin flaxen hair, a snout shaped nose, small round ears and beady eyes defined his face. His words came out slowly, in a monochromatic tone that could put his listeners to sleep. By contrast, Vincent had the head of a snake, a long neck and was short and skinny, his clothes too big for his body.

"Did anyone call the police?" Vince Romaine asked.

Sid nodded.

"Witnesses who saw the choppers called the police and Jake Santana called us. The only thing known for sure is that the choppers headed out over open water and disappeared over the horizon before they could be chased down and apprehended."

"That's not good, Sid. Those choppers knew when and where to strike."

"That's been the problem, Vince," said Amison. We're sitting ducks."

A long moment of silence followed. In the background, Amison could hear dishes and silverware clattering and pots and pans banging as Dimitri and his brothers yelled and hustled between the kitchen and the front taking care of customers.

Well anyway," said Boris, breaking the silence. "It has been a long time and we sure are glad to see you again."

"This is great, Boris. The last time we got together, we had an assignment in Rio. When we finished, we hit every bar along the beach and got smashed. The local cops hauled us in and Vince here had to come get us out."

"That was the old days, Jonesey."

"What have you been doing with yourself?"

Boris looked at Vince and winked.

"Keeping out of trouble. Vince got me hooked up with old man Barberi and I kept his books for a few years."

"Bookkeeping?" Luis asked.

The Russian nodded, explaining, "Yes. The same thing Jonesey does. I quit when the old man died."

"I own his businesses now," said Bienvenido.

"Yes, I heard. That is why I quit. I thought you would be replacing the staff."

Luis understood and Boris went on.

"I have been retired until you called, Jonesey."

"What about you, Vincent?" Frank asked.

"No change. I work out of Washington on title insurance cases dealing with cross border mergers and estate settlements. I can't afford to retire like Boris."

Harold interrupted them.

"Do you guys want lunch?"

He motioned to Dimitri who brought over several platters of hamburgers and several cups of coffee.

"Why are we meeting here, Jonesey?" Boris asked.

"We're in trouble," replied Amison. "That's why I called you. We need your help."

Boris lit a cigar and offered one to Amison who declined.

"Don't smoke anymore?"

"Jonesey is turning chaste in his old age," said Luis. "He doesn't drink and smoke anymore. Besides, this is a no-smoking area."

"Sorry." Boris extinguished his cigar and shoved the unused portion into his jacket pocket. "But getting back to retirement, I have been keeping busy with my new hobby, bird watching."

"Bird watching?"

"Bird watching. That is my new hobby. We see many birds, small birds and big birds. I like birds. Even big ones, but I cannot tell the difference between birds. Like owls, falcons, hawks and eagles. They look the same to me. But I like them anyway. They are peaceful. Not like us. They only kill to eat. We kill for fun, sport or business. I saw an eagle once and my friend said it was a bald eagle. But he was wrong. That bird was blue. A blue eagle, and it was fighting a bunch of snow geese. What about you, Jonesey? Have you ever seen a blue eagle or a snow goose?"

"I'm no bird watcher," answered Amison, catching on. "What can you tell me about blue eagles and snow geese?"

"I have an old ham radio. I can tune in on conversations anywhere."

His eyes narrowed to slits and he looked carefully at Virgil who was playing cards with Dimitri at a small table near the rear exit.

"You can relax, Boris. They're family. They're in our boat."

"Thanks, Jonesey. It is good to work with trustworthy people. Blue Eagles fly alone," he explained. "Snow geese fly in a flock. Snow geese is the label given to mercenary armies. Your code name is Blue Eagle and the snow goose leader operates under the moniker, White Goose. That is what I learned on my ham radio."

"I thought ham radios are obsolete," said Frank.

Boris smiled.

"They are. Obsolete but useful. Do you know where to find White Goose?"

"They shook their heads.

"In a place called Darien, in Connecticut. I believe it is near Stamford. Now, you must tell us more about your problems."

Boris sat back in his chair and began working on his hamburger while Luis explained in painstaking detail the history of their circumstances.

"There's a footnote to all this," said Amison when Luis was finished. "I have a piece of paper with a bunch of letters and numbers written on it. It's the map we were talking about."

He pulled a copy of Hernando's map out of his pocket and gave it to Boris.

"See if you can decipher it. We're in a bit of a rush."

"What about your title claim to the land?" Vincent asked.

Amison shook his head.

"That's a separate issue for the courts to decide," he replied. "The main thing to bear in mind is that our snow geese, as you call them, are being paid to make sure we fail. But they too need to get into the mine and remove whatever is in it before the deadline."

"I thought so," he commented when Amison finished. "You want to catch the snow geese and find the gold. Now, where am I staying?"

"Right here at the hotel," Sid answered.

"That is fine, Sidney. I heard much about you on my radio," said Boris. "I hear you are very smart and also very gullible. I would move very carefully on that hotel project in Monte Fuego. It is a trap."

Sid looked at him incredulously.

"A trap?"

"Yes. For you and your friends. You will be killed in Monte Fuego after you have been parted from your money."

Sid did not know what to say.

"Is that a prediction or a prophesy?" He asked finally.

Boris smiled.

"I have no intention in meddling in your personal plans, Sidney. I am telling you what I have heard."

He turned to the others.

"Now, what do you want me to do?"

"Find and kill White Goose," said Luis, munching on a sandwich.

"Good. I like that. I hope I can be helpful."

"And I assume Jonesey's land claim is also at stake," said Vincent.

"It is," Frank said. "We also have issues arising from the deaths of Victor Duncan and Emilio Gutierrez. The problem is that we don't know where to start without stepping on the wrong feet."

Vincent Romaine smiled.

"We start small and end big," he said. "But we have a head start. We already met with Jacques Leroux and Stanley Mason. And well meet with them again if it's ok with you. But right now, quite frankly, we're concerned for our lives.

Those missiles that were aimed at us on the way from two sources and had to be guided by a homing device triggered by a sensor. Were the shooters after us or after you?"

Boris held out a huge paw and pointed to Frank and Luis.

"Not after us, Vincent. After them."

"Why would they not be after me?" Bienvenido asked

Boris looked at the gold watch on Luis's wrist.

"Nice watch," he noted. "I see that Frank is wearing the same timepiece."

Frank stared at the gold watch on his wrist and exclaimed, "Damn! I have Jonesey's watch in my pocket. He left it in the car earlier. Pulling the watch out of his pocket, he returned it to Amison.

Boris held out a hand.

"May I see the three watches?"

They handed them to Boris who showed them his own. It was identical to theirs.

"Not many of them were made. They're solid gold and custom made. Mine was made by Louis Salieri of Boucher & Salieri, the Paris jewelers. He's their watch and clock man. A true specialist."

He fingered his watch lovingly.

"It originally contained a tiny sensor. It worked off a spy satellite equipped with a tracking device that was able to monitor the wearer's movements. The CIA gave it to me a few years ago to for a job I had to do. When the job was done, I kept the watch as a keepsake and had the sensor removed. I bet your time-pieces have sensors their works. Whoever ordered them wants to kill you. This is why Sammy Luke was shot, Jonesey. He was wearing your watch."

Boris slowly passed the watches back to his hosts who this time did not put them back on.

Amison said, "I think you just gave us the missing piece to our puzzle. Does the name Carlos Ramon Salva strike a bell? He gave us the watches as gifts." Boris smiled and looked at Vincent.

"We have a file on him in connection with that larger problem you asked us to investigate. But you have something else, Vincent, don't you?"

"I know the name," recalled the attorney. "He contacted my office a year ago to inquire about making a land claim in Monte Fuego on behalf of his niece. I said I couldn't help him and that his niece, if she was an adult, had to press her own claim. I never met the man, but from our phone conversation, I felt he was trying to bypass his niece. It was the first and last time we had any contact but we have lots more on him.

"My IRS contacts say he has been under surveillance by the CIA and FBI for a long time. He finances mercenary armies and deals in anything that makes a buck but he tends to stay in the background and never takes a position. But he could never have had those particular watches without government sanction."

"Vince is right," added Boris. "Salva may have given you the watches, but he could not have had them made. They are classified government issue and are made to order on special requisitions by authorized intelligence personnel. The watches had to have ordered from B&S by the CIA. Salva was a messenger of death only and may be unaware that the watches were rigged."

"Perhaps we should back up and tell you what we found out since you called us," Vincent suggested.

"Please do," said Harold.

"Well, here's how it goes," Vincent started. "It starts with the looting of the Holocaust warehouses by the European White Knights. High priced, heirloom treasures are sold by B&S to their better customers throughout the world. The rest, expensive but not so rare, is shipped to Caribbean distribution points for sale through Emerald House outlets at fancy markups to unsuspecting tourists and locals. Part of the proceeds from these sales are used to buy high quality diamonds from Kinshasa Export which are also sold by Emerald; the balance, about 50% of gross revenues, is remitted to West Indian Mines. That's what Stan Mason of the IRS explained to us." He took a deep breath. "You know that part, but now it gets interesting.

"B&S and Emerald are always on the verge of bankruptcy due to the high management fees they pay West Indian who is flush with cash. West Indian in turn funnels the cash to Kinshasa Export who uses it to buy military equipment and weapons, much of it from U.S. vendors like Canaan Metal Works…"

"What kind of equipment and weapons?" Harold asked.

"Small arms, state-of-the-art anti-personnel systems, missile systems, even aircraft, shoppers and a few ships…"

Amison's eyebrows arched.

"Ships?"

Boris laughed.

"Not battleships," Jonesey. "Smaller boats like chasers and cutters; too small for naval warfare but large enough to disguise as large, luxury yachts armed to the teeth."

"Like the one you talked about; the one that attacked those two fisherman in Monte Fuego," said Vincent. "We confirmed the reports your people gave us about the chopper attack over Bimini; those choppers came from the very same vessel."

"But who called the hits on us?"

"And senor Romaine," Bienvenido added, "You must tell us how my bank dovetails with Carib Financial and Black Star Trading."

"Boris can help you with that." Vincent answered.

Boris finished his coffee and asked for another cup. He spoke slowly, taking sips of coffee as he went along.

"To round out the big picture," he said. "Luis gave us a very good lead when his people intercepted a charter flight filled with Holocaust goodies. We found out that this is the way the stuff has been making its way to Monte Fuego for a good many years. It also turns out these flights are booked through the military attache's office at our embassy in Brazzaville, the capital of the Congo which happens to be across the river from Kinshasa, the capital of the Democratic Republic of Congo. What's more, the embassy is on one side of the bridge over the Congo river and Kinshasa Export is on the other."

Alex moved his eyes soulfully around the table.

"Am I helping you with the picture?" He asked in his thick Russian accent.

Harold folded his arms and leaned back in his chair.

"Any names?"

"This is the strange part," answered Boris, plodding ahead methodically. "I obtained copies of the charter contracts and they indicate that the authorizing signatures are those of one Edward Lawrence in Brazzaville which is similar to the name of the president of Kinshasa Trading, Edward Underwood Lawrence. I am not sure, but I think the two names may belong to the same person. If so, we have that person authorizing charters between Europe and Africa that drop off Holocaust cargo in Monte Fuego and continue on to Africa where they pick up diamonds from Kinshasa Export for delivery to Emerald outlets throughout the Caribbean on their way back to Europe where the cycle begins again. I am personally very impressed. That Lawrence person is a very active dude."

Sid Stone coughed and suppressed a smile.

"He's my half brother," he said, almost proudly. "Edward Underwood is his father's name, but he's dead."

Boris nodded.

"You seem very smart too. I hear you own hotels and things."

"I do, but getting back to Edward Lawrence. How does he get away with a double identity and life?"

"Easy," said Vincent Romaine. "He commutes between two countries whose capitals happen to face each other on the river. You see, the American embassy is a five minute walk over the bridge from Kinshasa Export's office."

"But what about the money and paper trail?" Bienvenido persisted.

"When I worked for your late father-in-law," replied Boris, after downing his second cup of coffee. "I made sure that his West Indian dividends transferred from Carib Financial over to his private bank, the one you own now. However, I was friendly with a woman who worked for Carib Financial. She told me that all financial decisions for West Indian and its affiliates were made at monthly meetings of the bank's directors. That meant nothing to me then since my boss was not a director. He was merely an investor looking for a high, guaranteed rate of return. He asked no questions and was happy so long as he received his piece of the action. So, when I reviewed New Canaan Metal's records that Mr. de la Maza left with me and did an audit of West Indian's financials for as long as I could go back in time, I tried to match everything with information that Europol and the IRS had on West Indian's affiliates. I found that what she said was true. All monies made by Emerald, B&S, West Indian, Black Star Trading and Kinshasa Export goes through Carib Financial as do payments to suppliers like New Canaan Metal Works."

"That's what we suspected," noted Amison. "But who runs the show?"

Boris seemed puzzled and looked at Vincent Romaine.

"What does he mean? I thought it was obvious."

The attorney turned to Amison.

"We thought that you knew, Jonesey" he said. "Juan Duarte Gutierrez is the bank's executive director with 25% of its stock. Edward Lawrence has 25%."

"What about the rest?"

"The rest is owned by Centurion Insurance."

CHAPTER 28

▼

The Mystery of the Gold Watches

"Centurion Insurance. You mean, Sol Weinberg?"

"That's right," said Vincent. "Ed Lawrence, Juan Duarte Gutierrez, Ramon Salva and Sol Weinberg run the show, as you say. Maybe one of them is after you, or maybe all of them."

Amison banged on the table with his fist.

"Damn," he cried out. "We were being conned from the beginning. Why were we blind to the obvious for so long? Were we all in denial?"

Bienvenido rose, went over to Amison and placed a hand on his shoulder. "It happens with friends," he said. Doing business with enemies is much better. There is more honesty among thieves."

Bienvenido picked up the watches and examined them closely.

"Our mutual friend, el senor Max Zimmer. He was with the CIA and must be the person who requisitioned these time pieces."

"Calvin Bard must have discovered that Max was a rogue agent. That's why he let him go," Frank said. "I wonder if Bard ever knew about the watches."

Harold asked for the watches and Bienvenido handed them to him. Holding them up to the light carefully, he grunted several times and placed them back on the table.

"Military issue," he said. "Boris is right. These are the kind that are usually tracked by satellites. The CIA is the only intelligence agency in the world that has this type of technology. The satellite relays signals from the watches to a land base that can instantly transmit the target watch's position to a shooter. Isn't that the way it works, Boris?"

Boris grinned boyishly.

"I'd wear one if it wouldn't kill me."

Then his smile went away.

"But seriously. This is not new technology anymore. It works like a satellite based GPS system. We have it on cars, boats, big ships, airlines, everywhere, and on weapons guidance systems. Law enforcement uses the technology on ankle collars and wrist bands to keep track of potential parole and probation violators, and it is in common use by the world's intelligence communities if they have access to our satellite systems or if they have their own pots in the sky. Don't you guys use tracking systems in your line of work?"

"We do when necessary," answered Amison. "But we got fooled here."

Sid Stone, clearly distressed about Boris's expose linking Kinshasa Export to West Indian Mines and its affiliates, felt compelled to argue on behalf of his half-brother.

"We shouldn't run off half-cocked, you know. We should contact Edward and ask him if these things we're hearing are true. There might be a reasonable explanation for what's going on and he may be totally innocent."

"We're not saying he's guilty of anything, Sid" said Amison. "Leroux and Boris gave us a name; that's all. It could be that some lousy imposter is using his name and that your brother is dead. In any case, we need to find out. Why don't you communicate with him? If he's at Kinshasa Export in Africa, he's easy to reach. He and the company must have an address and an e-mail. Give it a shot, Sid. You can contact him as his brother. We can't, especially if he's not clean."

"You wouldn't mind?"

"No, Sid. None of us will mind. You're family and we trust you."

"In the meantime," Harold asked. "What do we do now?"

"Don't wear the watches?" Frank suggested by way of a weak joke.

But Luis took his suggestion seriously and shook his head.

"No. The targets will become stationary and warn our unknown enemy that we're on to his game. I have another idea. We can re-program their insides to create false targets at different locations where no people can be harmed. The CIA shares a new lab with the FBI outside Miami that does this kind of work. What do you think, Jonesey?"

Amison yawned and stretched his arms.

"I want to mull that idea over first. Let's hold off for a while."

Bienvenido scratched his head.

"Why?"

Amison ignored him and looked at Harold.

"Do you have anything that floats up in Connecticut?"

Harold smiled.

"Sure do. I just bought an old yacht at salvage and was going to have it fixed and up-dated. It's name is Reel Deal. You want to go fishing?"

"You got it," replied Amison. "We could use the R&R."

They finished lunch, ducked out the back of the restaurant and walked back to the hotel through the rear livery entrance. The attorney went directly to his room. Amison and the others stopped at his office to discuss their moves for the rest of the week. They were surprised to see Felipe making himself at home behind Amison's desk. He was on the phone and hung up quickly when they barged in.

If they were surprised, Felipe jumped as if he had seen a ghost. Not that it was unusual for him to occupy the dark green leather armchair behind the big desk as the hotel's manager when either Sid or Amison were away. It was his demeanor, especially his reaction to their unannounced presence, that bothered them. Something about Felipe did not resonate well with Amison and Frank.

"What are you doing here?" Felipe shrieked. "You're supposed to be dead."

"Why should we be dead, Felipe?"

"That's what I heard. There were some horrible accidents."

"Who were you talking to, Felipe?"

Felipe knew he was cornered, but instead of cowering, he leaned back in the armchair and smiled defiantly.

"None of your damn business," he replied.

Luis was more direct. In an accusatory tone, he said, "You set us up to be killed today, didn't you, Felipe?"

Felipe looked directly into his eyes and said, "I don't have to answer your questions. We have Charlotte Fergueson."

Sid suddenly sprang across the desk, grabbed Felipe by the neck and began strangling him.

"Where's Charlotte?"

Amison and Frank jumped on top of Sid and pulled him off.

"Not here, Sid. We need to find out what happened to Charlotte first."

Felipe's smile widened.

"On the way to Monte Fuego," he said. "She dies if you don't play ball."

Boris Plotnikoff listened to the war of words that was slowly shaping the standoff emerging between Felipe and the others.

"Whatever you do, you can't touch me," Felipe went on. "I have diplomatic immunity."

"You have what?"

He pulled a passport and some papers out of his pocket and waved them in front of everyone's noses.

"I am a citizen of Monte Fuego and have just been appointed consul general of Monte Fuego. I have diplomatic immunity."

"I thought you were an American citizen," said Sid.

Felipe shook his head.

"You never did your homework, Mr. Stone. "I was born out of wedlock. My blood father is Juan Duarte Gutierrez. Emilio adopted me to help Juan Duarte avoid a scandal that would have been bad for his political career. Recent events have brought us closer and my father thought it would be good for me to enter the diplomatic service of Monte Fuego. I have full diplomatic immunity."

Sid was not about to be outdone.

"Where is your consul general's office? In Florida or in Washington?"

"I'm counting on using this office," Felipe said.

Sid nodded.

"What a great idea, Felipe. I'm not even going to question your documents. I believe in your basic human honesty. A diplomatic office in our hotel would be good for us. Our rental price is $2million a month on a five year lease with one year security, effective immediately."

He went to a side paper cabinet and took out a blank lease and shoved it in front of Felipe.

"Sign and date it," he demanded.

All in a single second, Felipe's bravado and nerve were gone.

"I don't have to do anything. I have diplomatic immunity." he kept repeating like a broken record.

"Sign it, fuck face, or you'll never leave this room alive," said Amison.

"Charlotte has been kidnaped and will be killed if anything happens to me," he told Sid in a cracking voice.

Amison shook his head.

"Let's see exactly how much Juan Duarte loves his bastard son. Sign!"

Drained of courage and sweating like a pig, Felipe never bothered to read the document. He signed the bottom and dated it.

"It's terms will have to be ratified by the government of Monte Fuego," he argued weakly.

"I'm sure," said Amison.

He walked behind the desk and gave Felipe a wack with the back of his hand that knocked him out. Grabbing the lease document from Felipe's limp hands, he shook it at Sid.

"I hope you live to collect the rent, Sid."

"So, it's signed. Big fucking deal! What do we do with it?"

"We give it to our high priced lawyer and let him work it out," said Amison.

"I'm going to be blackmailed into giving up everything," Sid complained.

"That's what you get for over reaching, Sid. In the meantime, we put Felipe on ice and try to figure out what to do next?"

"Can I help?" Boris asked.

Boris Plotnikoff's monotone voice reminded them that something had to be done with Felipe. Boris lifted him up in his arms and laid him down gently on the couch.

"Asleep," he said. "But I do not think we want to waste him here. We must find a better place, and he must first tell how to find your lady."

Sid agreed.

"We'll keep Felipe in the boiler room until tonight."

He nodded towards a small corner door behind the desk.

Amison nodded, adding, "Later, we'll take him to the boatyard and hide him on Red Fish. The guys can work on him until he talks."

Felipe for sure had overplayed his hand but he needed to be handled with kid gloves and his claim of diplomatic immunity had to be taken seriously in order to avoid a diplomatic conflict between Monte Fuego and Washington.

This was where Boris and Vincent were very well suited for the work cut out for them. Boris took care of Felipe's creature comforts aboard Red Fish and convinced him that he would be released soon to take over his new consular office being prepared for him at the Riverside. It happened that Felipe carried a weapon, a small pistol registered in Florida. It was the same as the one Amison took from him at the ill fated Brittany affair and later returned. Boris removed it from Felipe and gave to Amison for his trip to Connecticut.

Vincent was equally busy in the next few days. With well placed phone calls, the attorney confirmed that Juan Duarte had indeed appointed Felipe Gutierrez as Monte Fuego's consul general. Acting for Felipe who he said was away on a vacation, he arranged for a number of blank visas to be prepared and delivered to Felipe Gutierrez at the new Monte Fuegan consul in Fort Lauderdale.

The attorney also came up with a startling bit of news. Juan Duarte Gutierrez once had a girlfriend who happened to be Sol Weinberg's sister who had long since died. This girlfriend had given birth to Felipe, not in Monte Fuego but in Miami. It all made sense to Amison now. At the very least, it explained the tie between Juan Duarte and Sol.

In the meantime, the names White Goose and Darien kept clicking on and off in Amison's mind although Sid Stone was more preoccupied with the goal of securing Charlotte's release who was most likely being kept at Juan Duarte's Fortaleza residence. Amison nixed the idea of mounting an immediate rescue operation when he had dinner with him, Frank and Luis after Harold had gone north to Stamford to make sure his yacht was ready for their fishing trip.

"If we charge into Monte Fuego, we'll be killed," he warned.

"Ok, wise leader," said Sid. "What are we supposed to do?"

"We don't get mad," Amison answered quietly. "We get even. They're going to use Charlotte to make us back off, but they never counted on Felipe being stupid. He's also making it with Denise who I'm sure has Juan Duarte's ear since she's his sister-in-law. So long as we have Felipe, Charlotte will be safe."

"Can't we be accused of kidnaping a foreign diplomat?"

"Not unless there's a kidnaping. Let Boris and Vincent work this out for us. That's why they're getting big bucks. They'll take care of things here while we take care of things in Connecticut."

They knew that Amison was ready to roll and that it was futile to argue.

"What's the game plan, brother-in-law?" Luis asked.

"We're going fishing on Reel Deal," said Amison told them. "Harold will set things up for us. Virgil, Desi, Jimmy and Bob Byrne are going up tonight and are going to hole up at the Delmar. Catch up with them tomorrow and check in with Harold. He'll have your marching orders."

"I don't do guns," said Sid.

"That's ok," Amison's responded. "You're staying here."

"What about you?" Frank asked.

"I'm going to Darien to find a snow goose," he replied.

"Where are you going to find a snow goose in Darien?"

"It's a restaurant called the Wild Turkey in an alley in the center of town off the Boston Post Road. It used to be called the Snow Goose."

Amison went to a drawer in the kitchen and pulled out four gold watches.

"Boris gave them to me today. They're similar to the ones we used to wear."

He put one on and gave the others to Frank, Luis and Sid.

"They work fine. They have sensors that will help us keep track of where we are."

CHAPTER 29

▼

House Cleaning

It was a cold clear day in Stamford, Connecticut, when Harold Levy, at the request of Calvin Bard and Sol Weinberg who wanted to be briefed as to the latest developments in Monte Fuego, had breakfast with them and Stan Mason at the local Marriott hotel. He explained that he was going on a brief hunting trip with Amison, Frank and Luis to Maine before flying to Monte Fuego to settle things once and for all.

Afterwards, he met privately with Ray Booker. When it was over, Harold called his employees to the company cafeteria to announce that Ray would be Alliance's next CEO upon returning from a well earned trip to the Bahamas on a party boat with the Used-to-Be's staff. Ray was pleased to hear of this added bonus and thanked Harold profusely.

Meanwhile, back in Florida, Amison borrowed Teddy from Jake for a few days to fly Bienvenido's jet.

Tommy Hicks was another matter. Harold invited him out to lunch on the day the party boat was to leave for the islands.

"I have something for you," Harold explained down in the garage where his limo was kept.

Tommy smiled with anticipation when Harold introduced him to Virgil and Jimmy Wales.

"I'm promoting you, Thomas," said Harold. "You're replacing Ray Booker in communications. And since you're moving up, I hired a new chauffeur and a body guard. They're going to report directly to you."

"Aw, that's great boss. I don't know how to thank you."

"No thanks necessary."

Tommy instinctively headed for the limo's driver side.

"You don't have to drive," said Harold. "Jimmy's the new driver."

Tommy nodded.

"Oh, let me drive one more time. Jimmy can sit next to me and pick up some pointers."

Harold shrugged.

"Suit yourself,"

They piled into the limo with Harold sitting behind Tommy, Virgil sitting next to Harold, and Jimmy seated next to Tommy in the front seat. They drove out into the street where Tommy asked, "Where to?"

"East Stamford Yards. You know the way."

They drove through the city of Stamford until they reached a large marina on a lagoon separated from Long Island Sound by a breakwater. Harold's yacht, a sleek ocean cruiser named Escapade, was tied on one side of a long dock at the end of the marina. Its neighbor on the other side of the dock was an aging party boat that had seen better days. The name on the transom with the peeling paint read, "Reel Deal." Harold saw Bob Byrne waving from the bridge.

Tommy Hicks parked the limo in its usual spot and was about to turn off the ignition but he never had the chance. Harold leaned forward and placed both of his large hands around his throat and strangled him. Virgil and Jimmy removed the body and dumped into the trunk as Harold took the driver's seat and waved to Desmond Lyons on Escapade's hull side cargo companion way hatch.

With a signal from Virgil, Desmond pulled a lever and a ramp slid out of the cargo hold. Harold drove up the ramp, parked the limo inside and checked the time on his watch. It was noon.

"Everything on board?" Harold asked Virgil when he met him on the bridge.

"Yes," answered Virgil, and Harold have the order to cast off.

The gangplank was pulled up, the cargo hatch shut tight and within minutes Escapade had slipped its dock lines and was headed up the Sound bound for the Twin Forks of Long Island. Meanwhile, Luis and Bienvenido were trolling in the Sound on Triple Play, Frank's sports fishing yacht, waiting for a signal from Bob Byrne on Reel Deal that it was leaving port.

They did not have to wait long. Escapade was gone less than an hour when limos pulled up at the dock near Reel Deal with Ray Booker, Jack Stewart and other selected employees from Alliance and Used-to-Be's who were had been invited by Harold for a two week cruising vacation of the Bahamas.

Bob Byrne, in a white captain's uniform complete with epaulettes, personally welcomed each guest in the lounge over drinks, leaving Dimitri, Angelo and three more of their brothers to bring their bags to designated staterooms. Once done, they rushed to the lounge to relieve Bob Byrne who left for the bridge to get Reel Deal underway. On the consol next to him lay the three gold watches that once adorned the wrists of Amison, Frank and Luis.

It was mid-afternoon and Amison was chatting with Frank, Boris Plotnikoff and Vince Romaine in Hamburger Haven's back room when Boris took a call from Reel Deal on his cell phone.

"It is in the Sound," he said, hanging up.

Amison nodded and they continued making small talk for a half hour until Vincent fished his cell phone out and dialed Luis on Triple Play who relayed the word forty five minutes later to Harold on Escapade.

Frank glanced at his watch.

"Where do you think they are?" he asked Amison.

"Rounding Plum Island with Escapade in front, Reel Deal in the cradle, and Triple Play in back. They'll pass Montauk by dinner time and be out at sea by sundown. We should get another message in a day or so when they're south of Bermuda."

"In the Bermuda Triangle?"

"Is that's what it's called?"

They waited. Night fell. Boris and Vincent left for some shuteye at the hotel while Amison and Frank took turns sleeping in shifts on Phoenix.

At dawn, they went to Hamburger Haven for coffee.

"Anything?"

Amison shook his head.

"No news is good news."

Frank understood.

The sun never came out that day. Clouds rolled in followed by a pouring rain that lasted late into the evening. Then a little past midnight, when Amison and Frank were having a late dinner at Hamburger Haven, Frank felt a vibration on the cell phone nestled in his belt holster.

He grabbed the phone nervously and listened. Hanging up seconds later, he turned to Amison.

"It's done," he said. "So is the great white yacht."

Amison sighed. He was not surprised. They had almost been betrayed.

Frank tried to change the subject, asking, "How do we deal with Erica and Janice when we get to Monte Fuego?"

"Your guess is as good as mine," answered Amison. They're mixed up with the people who are trying to kill us. What would you do?"

Frank furrowed his brow and buried his head in his hands.

"That's a hard call, Jonesey."

"Well, we time to think about it. Meanwhile, I'm paing the Wild Turkey a visit."

"Sol's restaurant in Darien?"

"That's right. He's waiting for me."

"How do you know that?"

"It's a feeling."

"Does he know what you're coming to do?"

"He knows without knowing," replied Amison. "Are you going to see Sid?"

"Do you have a better idea? I'm sure he called Sol who contacted the yacht."

"It probably has to be done. But wait to hear from me or Sol before you see him. And if it has to be, do it quick and keep it simple."

"Do we still spring Charlotte?"

"Of course. We owe it to Cecil and his kids, and we owe it to Sid."

Teddy was ready with Bienvenido' jet when Amison called, and early the next day, the private jet took off for Westchester County where a rented car took them the rest of the way to Darien.

The sun was still high in the sky and he began walking Darien's main street that straddled the Boston Post Road. The Wild Turkey restaurant was one of its more exclusive dining establishments, a reservations-only restaurant catering to an executive dinner-only clientele. It was pricey and never crowded.

The entrance to the Wild Turkey was through a door in an alley although the restaurant faced the Boston Post Road, a major truck route. The bar and dining room were on the street level. The offices and a private party room were on the second floor.

Amison guessed that Sol Weinberg would be in his private office going over the day's receipts once the restaurant closed. There was a possibility that Max Zimmer could also be around, but with Europol and the police looking for him, it was more probable that he had run off to Monte Fuego.

Hour after hour passed and Amison kept walking, sometimes sunk in thought and sometimes his mind totally blank. At long last, the sun went down and the restaurant opened for business. Shortly after midnight, the restaurant's lights began to dim and Amison made his move.

He put on a pair of surgical gloves and found the back service door facing a darkened parking lot. He walked past two workers sorting bags of garbage and nonchalantly entered the kitchen. It was empty. He peeked into the restaurant and bar area. Only the bartender was left. He was closing for the night and on the phone, asking Sol upstairs if he needed anything.

"No. And don't lock up," was the reply. "I'll do that on the way out."

Amison waited in the shadows until the bartender left and then tiptoed up the stairs to the dimly lit party room. Beyond the room, an office door was ajar and a soft amber light poured out. He walked over to the door, opened it wide and found himself face to face with Sol Weinberg who was sitting behind his desk. Behind his desk was a wooden crate. Sol seemed to be expecting Amison and appeared amiable enough. Speaking in a low voice, he said, "So you're alive and found me Jonesey, I always thought you were the one with brains. How about Frank and Luis? Are they ok?"

"Thanks for the compliment, Sol. It means a lot, coming from you. Luis is ok and Frank is waiting to see Sid."

"I was hoping everything would work out," said Sol, watching Amison very carefully. "When Sid called to say that you were going fishing and Harold told me you were going hunting, I knew something was up but I went along and passed the word."

"I thought you would," said Amison.

"Somehow I knew you had found out about the watches and that you were going to put them on Reel Deal. But what about Reel Deal's crew?"

"They're fine, Sol. The jumped ship long before the choppers blew up the ship. Now why don't you tell me to whom you passed the word."

"Ed Lawrence, Sid's half brother. I called him in Africa."

"No you didn't, Sol," Amison corrected him. "Ed Lawrence and Calvin Bard are the same person. You were with him at the Stamford Marriott the other day when you met with Harold."

Sol slowly drew a snub nosed revolver from his jacket pocket and laid it on the desk.

"Is that the gun you used on Paul Boucher?" Amison asked.

Sol grinned.

"It is. On Louis Salieri too. It has a few bullets left."

"I have a gun also," said Amison. "It too has a few bullets left and I'm faster than you. Do you aim to out draw me?"

Sol moved his hand away from the revolver and looked into Amison's eyes.

"Can you cut me some slack?" he asked.

Amison shook his head.

"It's kind of late for that, Sol. Too bad you threw your chips behind Zimmer, Salva and Bates."

"You're right about Zimmer, but wrong about Bates and Salva," said Sol. "They never knew how the watches were made. Zimmer did. He was the only one who had access to that kind of technology. Salva was in for money, that's all. I wanted him killed because I was greedy, but you never took the bait."

"What about Bates?"

"He's a thief and I was in with him, but he's no killer."

"Lawrence wanted you, Frank and Luis dead from the moment you guys had a piece of West Indian's action. He was afraid that you'd find out what was up in Monte Fuego and try to grab everything for yourselves. Zimmer worked for Lawrence."

"You mean the Holocaust treasure?"

"That and everything else stolen and hidden in the mine."

"Is that how the White Knights and the Patriotic Front were financed?"

"You got that right."

"That's what confuses me, Sol. I don't see you in the cross burning business and Zimmer is too stupid. Is Lawrence behind this horror show?"

Sol stared sadly at Amison.

"I was never in any right wing movement, Jonesey," he replied. "Unclaimed Holocaust treasure was up for grabs insofar as I was concerned and I wanted a piece of it. It made money for me and covered those Horizon operations that never paid a return. And Ed Lawrence? I never met the guy and I never dealt directly with him. Max set up the deal years ago and I went along. The whole scheme began unraveling when Europol and the IRS wised up to us. And now with the volcano acting up in Monte Fuego, everyone is panicking."

"What about Quentin Bates?"

"He got his orders from Max. Keith Bates never could control the kid."

"And the twin sisters?"

"Vipers, Jonesey. But good jewel thieves who can also kill on a whim or on command if they're paid enough. They orchestrated the menorah heist for us with Erica and Janice…"

"Us, being who?"

"My personal little gang, the four women, Estrella, Felipe, Julio and Quentin. The idea was to grab the menorah, hide it in the mine and extort $500 million from Centurion for its safe return. The problem is that only Emilio knew of the back way into the mine and he wouldn't tell us unless he was cut in. I'm sure Victor was killed for his estate and for personal reasons, but Emilio was killed for refusing to tell them about the tunnel from La Fortuna."

"Did Zimmer organize the Brittany hit?"

Sol nodded and looked at Amison through his sad hound dog eyes.

"It's over," he said. "It's over."

Amison sighed.

"But it was good while it lasted, wasn't it, Sol?

"It was, but listen. It's not over yet. I know where to find Ed Lawrence."

"That's interesting stuff, Sol."

"Does that mean we can deal?"

"Doubtful, Sol. It's not your thieving deals that get me, it's all that useless killing. Besides I know where to find Ed Lawrence and Max Zimmer. Calvin Bard and Ed lawrence are the same person and Zimmer is in Monte Fuego."

Sol anxiously eyed the revolver on his desk.

"You're going to waste Sid, aren't you?"

Amison squinted slightly.

"Frank is going to do that, Sol."

Sol began sobbing.

"It's my fault, Jonesey. Sid doesn't deserve to die. Ed Lawrence is his only surviving brother. He doesn't talk much, but the death of Hank Lawrence got to him more than the death of Mark Stone years earlier. He told me what you guys were cooking up because he thought Ed Lawrence's life was in danger, and he wanted to see him at least once before you killed him.

"That's why I tipped off Calvin Bard, so he could get away, but I never told him about Reel Deal. His yacht simply followed the signals from the watches you must have placed on board. I also called Leroux and explained everything. It's over for me and you can kill me, Jonesey, but Sid doesn't have to die over this."

Amison watched the tears flow down Sol's heavy cheeks and called Frank in Fort Lauderdale from the office phone, saying, "Wait for Sol's call."

He hung up the phone and turned to Sol.

"Tell you what, old buddy. I'll cut you a deal anyway. I'm going downstairs. You have one gun and I'm leaving you another. It's Felipe's. Call Frank and tell him what you told me. Maybe you can save Sid's life."

He pulled Felipe's weapon out of his boot and placed it on Sol's desk.

"The rest is up to you, Sol. I know you'll do the right thing."

Amison walked out of the office and went downstairs where he waited by the phone at the bar. The red light was on, indicating that the phone was in use. He watched trucks race by the front window while he waited. The red light finally went out as several eighteen wheelers roared by. Their sound of their engines drowned out two gunshots that echoed down the stairs.

CHAPTER 30

▼

Mounting Evidence

The ruse had worked and details began pouring in by the time that Amison was back at the Riverside. Escapade had picked up a blip on its radar in the middle of the night south of Bermuda that another vessel was lurking north of the Sargasso Sea and heading swiftly in their direction. That same blip was picked up by Triple Play who signaled Reel Deal.

Bob Byrne put Reel Deal on autopilot and jumped ship with his crew in a lifeboat during a drinking party in the middle of the night. They were picked up by Triple Play which continued tailing Reel Deal while Escapade placed itself well to the east of the course being followed by the blip.

Shortly after dawn, in the middle of a pea soup fog, two smaller radar blips were caught leaving the big blip in the direction of Reel Deal. Escapade and Triple Play idled their engines and waited.

The two small blips converged on the slightly larger blip that was Reel Deal and it soon disappeared from their radar screens. The crew aboard Triple Play saw nothing, but could nevertheless hear an explosion. Its more distant sound reached Escapade and Harold, standing on the bridge, smacked his lips and ordered Virgil to fire the rockets. One rocket found the big blip and two more rockets found the small air bourne blips. Only Escapade and Triple Play were left as solitary blips on their respective screens.

With the exception of Tommy Hicks's body in the trunk of Harold's limo, there were no bodies to worry about. Reel Deal had sunk with the choppers and the great white yacht and Harold solved his own problem by having his limo dropped overboard with its windows open. It sank like a rock, and the saga of the White Knights and the Patriotic Front in America was over.

Once Amison received word that Escapade and Triple Play were putting into the Turks and Caicos for a few days to refuel, he passed the word to Boris and Vincent to turn Felipe loose on foot in the outskirts of Fort Lauderdale. He and Frank also made their peace with Sid Stone.

"What the hell possessed you to blow the whistle on us?" Amison asked.

Sid hung his head down in shame.

"I thought you were going to kill my brother. That's why I called Sol."

"Well, you almost got us killed. Your half brother was with Sol," said Frank.

"Edward in Connecticut? Why would he be there? He was supposed to be in Africa."

Amison shook his head.

"No way. Harold met him with Stan Mason and Sol Weinberg at the Marriott in Stamford. You told Sol we were going fishing but Harold said that we went hunting. The whole thing had a happy ending anyway. Your brother believed Sol's story and went for Reel Deal where we planted the gold watches. That's what we counted on. So, in a way you did us a big favor, Sid. The long and the short is that we're alive and you're alive and that's good."

"What was my brother doing in Stamford?"

"Because your brother is Calvin Bard. They're both the same person. Your brother was leading a double life."

"They're right, Sid."

Jake Santana stood smiling at the office door.

"We're ahead of you guys. Tom Clark went over to the Marriott and checked the hotel bookings that showed an Edward Lawrence but no Calvin Bard. And yet, we know that Bard met with Harold because Tom was hanging around at Harold's invitation and he recognized the CIA man as the one he had seen at Used-to-Be's with Harold on the day Victor was murdered."

Jake walked into the office and sat down on the sofa.

"It was Tom Clark and Gus Galindez who put everything together with the help of Europol. At first we thought that Max Zimmer was pulling the strings but when I looked at his CIA record and had him tailed, it didn't make sense.

He wasn't high enough in the CIA to make big discretionary decisions on his own like buying entire weapons systems. He didn't have access to big money and lacked authority to approve transactions between that Canaan Metal Works outfit and Kinshasa Export without Bard's written approval. And he never did much traveling. But Ed Lawrence, aka, Calvin Bard, did, and what's more, we found out from Jacques Leroux that the commercial attache in Brazzaville and the president of Kinshasa Export were the same man, but you already knew all that."

Jake took pleasure in seeing the looks of surprise in the faces around him.

"One person I haven't seen in a while is Felipe Gutierrez. Any idea where he might be?"

Amison indicated that he had not seen him since learning he had been been given a diplomatic appointment by the government of Monte Fuego.

"I know that," said Jake, tugging as usual on his suspenders. "He went north to Connecticut and killed Sol Weinberg. The Darien police found Sol's body at the Wild Turkey restaurant. Tom Clark got the news and called me. There's an APB out for Felipe."

"That's great for Monte Fuego's international relations. What happened?"

"Apparently, he waited until the restaurant closed before barging in on Sol who was sitting at his desk upstairs. Both had guns. They must have argued about something, according to the cops up there. The way the crime scene was reconstructed, Sol fired his weapon, but the shot went wild. Then Felipe fired. The shot entered Sol's mouth and blew out his brains. He never knew what hit him. That Felipe must be some shot."

Amison agreed.

"Something else was strange," said Jake.

"What's that?"

"Tom Clark went to have his usual lunch at Used-to-Be's and found it closed with an IRS lock on it. He went next door to Emerald House and it too had an IRS lock on the door. Why is the government closing down those businesses?"

"Beats me," answered Amison. "Maybe tax evasion?"

"Could be."

They chatted a few minutes longer.

"Make sure you call me when you see Felipe," Jake reminded them as he left.

There was little more to say. Jake had summed up the situation in Connecticut well. After he left, Vincent and Boris dropped by to explain why Used-to-Be's and Emerald House in Greenwich were shuttered.

"We made a few arrangements while you were gone, Jonesey." said Vincent. "I spoke to Stan Mason from the IRS and agreed to freeze the stateside assets of Boucher & Salieri, Emerald House and West Indian Mines for tax evasion. Leroux took care of closing down Boucher & Salieri in Paris, including what they have elsewhere in the world. Victor Duncan's assets are also frozen until his murder is solved. That goes for Emilio Gutierrez as well. Incidentally, Stan thinks that his tax evasion case is now much broader than he envisioned and that it might involve Centurion, top CIA people and the government of Monte Fuego."

Amison had a broad smile on his face.

"You did well, Vincent. The question is: how did you do it?"

Vincent pointed to the computer planted on the credenza behind the desk.

"Legal research is a wonderful thing, Jonesey, and we attorneys have access electronically to anything on this planet with political and legal ramifications that can be plugged into the latest computer models and games. Based on what you told us, Boris and I played some of those games and showed Stan Mason the results. They proved Leroux's conspiracy theory to Stan, at least from a tax evasion angle. They also prove out his larger conspiracy theory."

"What have you been doing these days, Jonesey?" Boris asked.

Amison coughed and pointed to Sid.

"We almost cashiered Sid," he replied. "Let him tell you."

Sid laughed and explained what had transpired since Harold's meeting with Calvin Bard and Stan Mason in Connecticut.

"You are a very lucky man," said Boris slowly in his thick accent. "My good friends here rarely hesitate when their minds are made up. I hope you and they stay lucky when you are in Monte Fuego."

"Yes," agreed Vincent. "You will find few friends on the island. I received a call from Jacques Leroux who indicated that all your admirers, including Max Zimmer, are gathering on the island."

"Will Juan Duarte be a problem?" Amison asked.

"Well, he does have Charlotte," Boris pointed out. "But Calvin Bard will be more of a problem."

"I think we can count on finding him in La Fortuna now that his cover has been blown," said Vincent. "The saving grace is that he may not yet know that you're still alive."

Vincent raised his hands for effect.

"I do call that murderous luck."

"Does Leroux think we're alive?" Frank asked.

Vincent broke out laughing.

"Good question. His line went dead as we were talking."

"You lost telephone contact?"

"Service is intermittent," Vince replied. "I think it has to do with that volcano on the island. You better get there fast if you expect to finish whatever you set out to do."

Boris reminded Vincent of something they had talked about earlier.

"You said three things did not add up," Boris repeated to refresh Vincent's memory.

The attorney's face lit up.

"Oh yes," he recalled. "We discovered that Keith Bates's kids have accounts with Caribbean Financial. Two days after Victor died, Denise's account went up by $200,000. The same thing happened to Danielle's account when Emilio died."

"What about Quentin Bates?"

"That gets more interesting. His account swelled by $500,000 when Cecil Furgueson and Chico Alvarez were killed. Now, don't get me wrong. I'm sure they were great guys but were they worth that kind of money? I'd rather think that you and Frank were the intended targets."

Amison nodded.

"We already figured that out, Vince. Do you know who put up the money?"

"Max paid it out from his Caribbean Financial account which was kept flush by deposits made by Kinshasa Export. That's how Calvin Bard, a.k.a. Edward Lawrence, took care of his operatives' expenses. But Max is cut off now."

"Cal isn't stupid," said Amison. "Cal shit canned Max to deflect the heat off himself. But it won't work. By the way, is Felipe free?"

"He's gone," replied Vincent. "We drugged him, gave him a few drinks and cut him loose."

"Good," said Amison. "He'll be picked up by the cops."

"Supposing he says something about Red Fish?"

"Let him. Red Fish will be gone tomorrow."

Amison went on to add, "When the police interview him, he may need an attorney. You might want to recommend one."

"It's an idea," said Vincent. "I'll wait until he's arrested."

"I'm going to Monte Fuego with you guys," declared Sid suddenly.

"What for, Sid," said Frank. "This isn't your fight."

"It is my fight," Sid insisted. "It almost got me killed. I want to see Charlotte and I want to see my brother up close and personal."

"Who's going to take care of things here?" asked Amison.

"Who the hell cares," said Sid, beginning to raise his voice. "I'm selling this place and my other hotels. No one will miss me. The regular staff can take care of things. They'll just steal more. I'm going to Monte Fuego, and that's that."

Sid was understandably in a foul mood. His mind was made up and it made no sense to argue. He had his own jet, plenty of money and could obviously go wherever he wanted. He left the office in a huff, leaving the others to ponder their next move.

Amison wasted little time and got busy working the phone. His first call was to Tom Clark in Connecticut.

"Would you like to catch Victor Duncan's killer?"

"Sure would, Jonesey," replied the John Wayne type voice. "Any ideas?"

"You might be able to do that if you can find your way to Monte Fuego."

"I don't travel in those circles," Tom said. My department is broke."

"Your killer is Denise Bates."

There was a pause.

"I know that. Can you prove it beyond that left handed-right handed crap?"

"Yep. In Monte Fuego. Are you due for a vacation?"

"I have a bunch of vacation time. Where are you staying on the island?"

"At the Excelsior hotel in La Fortuna. I'll be there in a week."

Amison's second call was to Gus Galindez in San Juan.

"How would you like to solve that menorah robbery?" he asked.

He could hear Gus laughing over the phone.

"I've got Tom Clark on the other line," he said. "That's why I'm laughing. Don't tell me you need me in Monte Fuego too."

Amison smiled.

"Only if you want to solve a murders and the menorah heist."

"You're talking about Emilio Gutierrez?"

"You got it, Gus. Danielle will be there and I think she was the shooter."

"Can you prove it?"

"Positive."

"And you'll be at the Excelsior, right?"

"You got it."

Amison waited ten minutes before making his third call which was to Jake Santana.

"I heard," said Jake. "You want me to fly to Monte Fuego. What's in Monte Fuego besides trouble?"

"Great weather and answers to a lot of questions. You'll be able to close the book on all those nasty things that have been happening on your turf.".

"Will this trip help me keep my job?"

"I guarantee it, Jake. For starters, you'll soon be arresting Felipe Gutierrez who happens to be the bastard son of Juan Duarte Gutierrez."

Jake was becoming suspicious.

"Are you hiding the guy?"

"Of course not. But unless you're blind, you'll be picking him up in a day or so. But his old man will demand that you cut him loose."

"I'm sure he will," said the police inspector. "But that's not going to happen any time soon if he's charged with murder. He'll go back to Connecticut first. By the way, why would Felipe want to kill Sol Weinberg in the first place?"

Amison attempted an answer by explaining the relationship between Felipe, Juan Duarte, his sister and Sol Weinberg, but Santana refused to bite.

"That still doesn't give us a motive," he remarked.

"Forget motive," said Amison. "Felipe has diplomatic immunity. If word of his involvement in Sol's murder and of Charlotte's kidnaping leaks out, we'll get a nasty international incident ruining everything for everyone. I'm hoping Juan Duarte will see the light and release Charlotte Furgueson in exchange for Felipe going free. But to spring Charlotte in Monte Fuego, Felipe needs to be there too. And I'm sure you'll want to be the one making the exchange."

"I guess the publicity might be helpful," said Jake upon thinking it over.

"Great! Now, I could use a favor."

"What?" Do you think Juan Duarte put him up to murdering Sol?"

"I need to borrow Teddy again for a few days. I need him to…"

"I don't want to know," snapped Jake, hanging up.

Amison smiled. Over lunch finalized his arrangements with Vince Romaine and Boris Plotnikoff.

"Here's the pitch," he began. "The funeral for Emilio Gutierrez and Victor Duncan was scheduled a week and half from now and was timed to coincide with West Indian Mines's annual board meeting. We're going to be there and we'll need you there as well with Jake Santana to coordinate the exchange of Felipe for Charlotte."

Vincent coughed delicately, asking, "Dare we mention money?"

"Not a problem. I have a million dollars in cash reserved for you and Boris when we get back from Monte Fuego. Fair enough?"

Rosina Alvarez was waiting with a dozen men standing around their gear at the dock behind the hotel when Amison and Frank showed up that evening.

"These are Bienvenido's men," she said. "They are well trained and will go with you to Monte Fuego. Please bring my Bienvenido home safely."

Amison noticed that some of the men carried the blue and white insignia of the United Nations peace keeping force.

"What is this about?"

"The U.N. may have to help evacuate Monte Fuego," she replied.

Amison ordered half of the men to follow Frank to Red Fish and the rest to board Phoenix.

CHAPTER 31

▼

Monte Fuego

Phoenix and Red Fish were underway by midnight and were soon threading a course through the Bahamian islands, passing Nassau at dawn. Their bearing was east southeast, keeping Cuba and the island of Hispaniola to the south and the Bahamas and Turks & Caicos to the north. That leg of the trip was totally uneventful, thanks to cooperating weather. It was dull enough so that Amison, who was sailing the catamaran singlehanded, was able to put it on autopilot and relax. The two vessels stopped in Cockburn Town on Grand Turk Island where they met up with Escapade and Triple Play.

There, they received a satellite transmitted news report about new tremors on Monte Fuego. A stateside TV network station had landed several helicopters complete with cameras and reporters on Antigua about a hundred miles away and sent one of the choppers to take pictures. It flew close to the volcano east of La Fortuna and began shooting and transmitting live images to the world of the crater belching smoke into the sky.

A stream of lava rimmed with a reddish glow doing a slow crawl down the mountain's western face to the Rio Blanco in the direction of La Fortuna was caught on camera and broadcast to the world.

"If that lava flow reaches the river, the city will be turned into a steam bath," Frank commented upon watching the television.

Amison was more sanguine.

"La Fortuna will be incinerated first." he said. "We'll need to move fast if we're ever going to make it to the mine."

Everyone was nervous and Bob Byrne even broached the idea of aborting the mission as Harold got into an argument with Amison over his catamaran.

"When the hell are you going to get rid of that derelict and start living like a human being?

"Phoenix is my home and Blue Eagle is my lucky bird," said Amison with a smile and a tone of voice that conveyed a feeling of feigned hurt and a measure of self pity. "I can't afford a real home."

His statement broke their preoccupation with the volcano.

What the hell are you doing with your money anyway?"

"The problem with Jonesey," Luis tried to explain, "is that his assets are tied up in cash."

"It's not that," chimed in Frank. "His pockets are so deep and his arms are so short."

"Perhaps," said Bienvenido, "el senor Jones would like to invest in my new venture."

"What's that?" Amison asked.

"A gold mine in Monte Fuego."

Everyone laughed.

"How about a funeral home and cemetery in Monte Fuego?" said Frank.

The laughter stopped.

Sid Stone, who had flown in an hour earlier in his jet on the way to Monte Fuego, raised his hand.

"There's potential in Monte Fuego," he said. "It's not the gold or whatever is buried on the land; it's the land itself."

Harold tried to pin him down.

"What's so great about the land, Sid?"

"It's that vision thing, Harold. It's called tourism. That's the real answer for Monte Fuego and for us. That's where the gold is. The mission itself is total bullshit because whatever we find in the mine that was stolen from Holocaust victims already cost millions of lives and it's not going to bring back the dead. What's more, it's going to cost us more lives and even that's not going to bring back the dead. We should try to work a deal with Juan Duarte. I don't want to lose Charlotte over this."

"What about that damn menorah? Harold reminded him. "Isn't that worth fighting for?"

"Fighting, but not dying. The menorah isn't damned, Harold. We are. The menorah, if it is what it's cracked up to be, it should be public property and in a museum, not decorating some rich shit's dining room. You know, there are courts of law where these disputes can be settled. We don't need a bloodbath," "Sid is right," announced a voice from the door.

It was Vince Romaine, on his way to St. Marten's, making a pit stop to drop off the tourist visas needed for entry into Monte Fuego.

"All disputes can be adjudicated in courts through legal process. The trouble is that most aren't. We fight, destroy and kill and when we're finished we see that nothing has been solved and then we hire the lawyers and the judges to see what they can do. Of course, I'm always willing to serve."

He smiled and threw the stack of visas on the table.

"Each one is signed by Felipe Gutierrez. It was his first and last official act as consul for the Republic of Monte Fuego. He was arrested a few hours ago for the murder of Sol Weinberg. And we aren't yet talking about his role in the kidnaping of Charlotte Furgueson. That comes later."

A gasp went around the table.

"Felipe's arrest is Charlotte's ticket out of Monte Fuego, Sid." Amison said quietly. "Felipe never saw Connecticut. Sol committed suicide with Felipe's gun. Vincent is going to represent Felipe to that effect in return for Charlotte's release, and he's going to win. If he wins, Charlotte wins, you win and we win. Juan Duarte will do nothing while we do our thing. You may even end up with your hotel project. Do you still want to abort the mission?"

Sid looked sheepishly around him.

"I don't want anything to happen to Charlotte," he said.

"Neither do we," Amison continued. "And I don't want anyone else to die. Sid's right. Too many people have died for nothing."

He turned to Harold, saying, "Each of us may have a different agenda that has been justified in one way or another. And that's fine with me. My agenda is different too. I want to do the mission we received from Europol and I want to see Max Zimmer and Calvin Bard dead or behind bars. That's all I want and that's all I'm interested in. There might be gold in untapped veins deep in the mine, and if it exists I won't stop anyone for going after it. I hear that Spanish conquistadores may have hidden treasure in the mine and it too can be up for grabs. I won't fight anyone for it even if I end up owning the land. But I think the pilfered Holocaust valuables and the menorah stolen in San Juan are worth fighting for even if there's no glory or money in it. It's just the satisfaction of doing the right thing. If we allow the volcano to spook us and it doesn't blow, we lose and stand a good chance of being killed one by one. In my mind, we can't back out.

"You may see things differently and I don't want to queer your thinking. As for me, once this is over and if I'm still alive, I'm retiring for good and I'm out of here. Phoenix will be my escape route and I hope you've planned yours. But if you're not in this with your hearts, back out and go home. I'd go home too if I had one."

Amison left and went back to his catamaran. By dawn, he and his crew were ready to set sail again. He was about to cast off the dock lines when he found Frank and Luis dockside with Bienvenido, Harold, and Sid standing behind them.

"We're staying the course, skipper," said Luis.

Amison's joy was obvious.

"We're all in," said Harold. "We're here for a plan. Do you have one?"

"I'm glad you asked. Keep each vessel three hours apart and maintain radio silence at sea," said Amison. "This way we'll enter La Fortuna harbor without raising eyebrows. If we average fifteen knots around the clock, with a fuel stop along the way, we'll pull into La Fortuna's harbor in less than five days."

"What are the way points?"

"I've plugged them into Phoenix's computer and copied them to CD's for the boats. When you get to La Fortuna, anchor in the harbor away from the docks. It'll be easier to leave quickly if necessary. I have a scheduled meeting set up with Juan Duarte so I'll be at the public dock which is a short walk from his office. I'm counting on him giving us what we want."

"How is that going to happen?" Sid asked.

"Juan Duarte is going to be my friend," replied Amison.

"You're joking," exclaimed Luis.

"I never joke, brother-in-law," Amison said. "Vincent Romaine and Henry Alstrum are going to convince him to be friendly and cooperative."

"What happens then?"

"Juan Duarte delivers Charlotte safe and sound and then, during the funeral we'll go take a look at the mine."

"How are we going to do that?" asked Harold. "We don't know the way in."

"I know the way," said Amison. "It will save us time and blood."

"What I want to know, Jonesey," said Harold, "is who goes after what once we're in?"

"That's your call, Harold, not mine. I say, play it by ear. The volcano may have other plans. If we do ever get to see the good stuff, I'd split everything down the middle if only to avoid a bloodbath."

"How about Sid's share and my share?"

"You're rich in your own right, Harold. And with Sol dead, you're ending up with Centurion, Alliance, West Indian Mines, Boucher & Salieri and Emerald. That's an empire, old buddy. And Sid, you'll have a shot at developing a resort on Monte Fuego. Best of all, you'll get Charlotte. Isn't that great reward for an old bachelor like you, especially if you end up marrying her?"

Sid gave Amison the international sign of ill repute.

Luis snickered.

"Am I glad I'm married all these years and don't have to be in love again."

Frank gave him a friendly punch on the shoulder.

"For that crack, you distribute the CD's."

Frank and Luis decided to sail with Amison and sent Bienvenido's men to Red Fish and Escapade. Red Fish and Triple Play were placed in the hands of Virgil and Bob Byrne, and Bienvenido transferred over to Escapade. Amison had wanted to ask him about the U.N. peace keeper bands some of his men had with their gear but by the time he remembered Bienvenido was gone.

Going below into the main cabin with Amison after Luis finished giving out the CD's, they turned the marine band radio in time to hear that Monte Fuego was jolted by an earthquake that registered 4.0 on the Richter scale.

"Ignorance is bliss," he joked.

The new course called for a southeasterly heading to the Mona Passage that separated the Dominican Republic from Puerto Rico and then due east under the belly of Puerto Rico with a more southerly east-southeast turn when they reached St. Croix. At that point, Monte Fuego would be less than one hundred miles away to the southeast.

Escapade stopped briefly to refuel in Ponce, Puerto Rico, Red Fish stopped in St. Croix. Triple Play raced on to St. Marten's where it met up with Teddy who flew Harold's jet in with Jake Santana, Boris Plotnikoff and Felipe. Vince Romaine was waiting to join them for the balance of the trip to Monte Fuego.

Phoenix, which was a fast, twin hulled sailboat with two diesel engines, did not require refueling and was the first to reach landfall outside Monte Fuego under a hazy sky in the middle of the afternoon.

Luis sniffed the acrid air, asking, "What's that I smell?"

Amison passed him the binoculars hanging on a strap from the wheel.

"It's called, 'rotten egg' gas. Hydrogen sulfide. Have a look."

Luis peered through the glasses. He could barely make out the outline of the island's western coast, but the volcano and the line of black smoke rising to meet an ugly black cloud above stood out clearly.

"Welcome to Monte Fuego," said Amison, "Your Caribbean Paradise."

He did not sail Phoenix directly into the harbor, suggesting to his two friends that they should hug the shore line first and get the lay of the land. He guided the catamaran up and down the coast to get a fuller view of the island and the spewing volcano. The sight of the smoking mountain and the rumbling sounds way above La Fortuna reminded Amison of the capriciousness of life and that in the end success and failure depended less on human effort and more on the whims of Nature.

"People plan and God laughs," Frank whispered.

Through the binoculars, they could see the rocky spit of land jutting out into the sea under La Fortaleza upon which Hernando's house once stood. The old fortress was intact and they guessed that Juan Duarte still used it as his abode and that Charlotte was sequestered within its walls.

They could also see the harbor. It was filled with ferries and skiffs of every size and description. Focusing the binoculars slightly to the right brought the Rio Blanco, winding its way into the harbor from the hills, into full view along with the narrow twisting streets leading inland from the Avenida Nacional.

The streets and bridges over the Rio Blanco teemed with people, jitney buses and cabs trying to leave the city one way or another. Most were headed for the docks, jamming ferries that would transport them to neighboring islands. But some were attempting to cross the island to the airport on the other side. Above the cloud cover all sorts of aircraft could be seen either leaving or else coming in for a landing with increased frequency while at sea, warships from several countries circled the horizon waiting to move in if called.

CHAPTER 32

▼

The Deal

Amison handed the wheel to Frank and went down below to see how Luis was doing. He found him in his small cabin in the starboard hull getting his gear ready. On top of the locker next to his berth was a small frame that held an old family photo of him, his wife and his children.

"The kids are very young in that picture," noted Amison. "And so were you and your wife. What happened?"

He could not see the tears in his brother-in-law's eyes until he turned. Luis was trembling.

"That was years ago, Jonesey. We were all young then."

Amison grabbed his arm.

"What's wrong, Luis?"

"I'm scared, Jonesey. I'm afraid I'll never see my family again."

"We're all scared, old buddy."

"I don't want to die."

"Neither do I, Luis. I like living. It's great. It's not that the world or that any-one in it needs me, or that I have much work left to do. The fact is that I never had much work to do and I don't care if the world needs me. I just don't want to die. I'm scared stiff of dying."

Luis opened his eyes wide.

"You are?"

"You're damn right. But I have to see this thing through. You don't."

"What do you mean?"

"This place is Hell waiting to blow. You have no personal stake here. I'd go home to your family if I were you."

"What about you and Frank?"

"We'll manage."

Luis stopped trembling. His mood turned from self pity to indignation.

"What do you mean, you'll manage, amigo. I thought we're a team."

"We are a team," Amison retorted angrily. "I just don't want us to be a dead team. Frank has no wife and kids to look after; neither do I. You do."

"I'm staying," said Luis. "You're not going to do this thing without me."

Amison shrugged his shoulders.

"Suit yourself. We're going ashore and joining the party."

With age comes an inevitable procession of death among contemporaries, a fact that suddenly struck Amison and forced him now to confront his mortality. The difficulty was that in his line of work, people rarely reached their natural, biological age potential. Those who had died since the day he had been rescued at sea months ago were young to middle aged. In that context, Sol Weinberg, in his early fifties, was old. So were Harold and Sid Stone. And Amison, Frank and Luis, well in their fifties, were probably considered ancient by the up and coming generation in the intelligence communities of the world. Herein lay the fickleness of life. One could be here one moment, gone in another. Death was an equal opportunity caller, and sooner or later, it called all. In some lines of work, it called earlier.

"It's a minefield out there. We must step with dainty feet."

Phoenix headed for the harbor and parked at the municipal docks along Avenida Nacional's embankment facing the presidential palace that housed the ministry of justice. Clearing customs was quick and incident free. Indeed, a local customs official wondered jokingly why they were trying to get into the country when so many people were trying to leave.

Amison explained that they were amateur geologists. The official laughed. He muttered something about someone being loco, and waved them through the customs barrier without further comment and without bothering to examine their bags.

Moments later, he and his companions were mingling in the blistering heat of the day with the crowds who jammed the kiosks and stores of the central bazaar on the square in front of the Spanish style government building.

"This is a jumping place," said Luis above the din of the crowd.

"They're stocking up with food, water and batteries," Frank noted. "People are expecting the volcano to blow and may be digging in."

"Maybe not," said Amison, pointing to the harbor. "They may be picking up last minue stuff for a long trip. We have company."

They looked out into the harbor where a destroyer, a hospital ship and troop carrier flying American and United Nations flags were anchoring.

"Looks like a rescue operation waiting to happen," observed Luis.

"Everyone's here for the party," said Frank.

Amison had reservations for the suite he and Frank had shared the last time at the Excelsior on Calle Uno around the corner from the presidential palace. It was agreed that he would use the room and take turns with Frank and Luis in keeping an eye on the comings and goings at Emerald House and Boucher & Salieri on the opposite side of the street. Whoever was not staying at the hotel would stay on Phoenix.

"What's out time line?" Luis asked.

"I have a morning meeting with Leroux and Juan Duarte at his office at the justice ministry. Vincent set it up with Henry. If we're lucky, Charlotte should be a free woman by within a day."

"What then?"

Amison grinned.

"The memorial dinner at the justice palace for Victor and Emilio is scheduled for Friday with their funerals to follow. We take Max and Cal down after the funeral. Then we take the mine, if the volcano doesn't blow."

"Well, if we have nothing doing tonight, I'm going to scrounge around," said Frank. "I'd like to see where Salva and Bates hang out."

"Suit yourself. Are you also going to see Janice?"

"She should be at Erica's place."

"Sounds good to me. Just watch your back. What's the address?"

"She lives over the clothing store that she owns at Number Ten, Calle Cinco, or Fifth Street. You could pay them a visit too, you know."

"I may just do that, Frank, even though I think they almost got us killed."

"What else were you thinking of doing?"

"I was going to try finding that back way into the mine."

The tremors that occasionally rocked the city came with increased frequency. They were stronger now and lasting longer as the sun began to sink over the busy harbor. Some were strong enough to loosen bricks and drop mortar onto the streets and entire families lugging their belongings began to jam the ferries for the neighboring Leeward Islands. The ferries filled up fast and those unable to board formed long lines at the embankment to await the next boat. Looking up into the darkening sky, Amison could see the lights of planes heading away from the island. The volcano was now invisible, but its rumbling and belching was now non-stop. The troop ship was also beginning to fill up.

At last, as the night wore on, the volcano fell silent and they were able to get some sleep. Morning brought foul weather and Frank was not yet back. Luis stayed aboard Phoenix to wait for him while Amison donned a pair of slickers and walked to the justice ministry across the square.

"Senor Jones?"

Amison was startled by the voice that stopped him in the courtyard inside the justice ministry compound. It was Rafael Perez, Leroux's assistant. He held a small leather portfolio under his arm.

"Rafael. I didn't see you in the shadows."

"Monsieur Leroux is expecting you," he said. "The director went me down to tell you that his excellency, Juan Duarte, is on his way."

"Who else is at the meeting?"

"Your friends, Dr. Alstrum, el senor Levy, el senor Romaine and el senor de la Maza are there."

"It should be a good meeting," said Amison.

Rafael smiled.

"I hope for you that it is, senor Jones. I coordinated it. It is my expression of gratitude for arranging that trip for me and my family to Disney World."

"Did you have a good time?"

"It was wonderful, senor Jones. I took pictures and even made a detailed map of all the sights I visited at Disney World."

Rafael gave the portfolio under his arm to Amison who in turn passed him a small envelope.

"What's my starting point?"

"The obelisk in the center of the square. The tunnel to the mine runs under it. But one cannot get to it from the obelisk. It is sealed. But there is way close by, under a house. Which house I do not know. The map will help. However, you should know that a tremor has re-opened one of the shafts above the mine. I discovered it yesterday and can take you and your friends there later."

Rafael pocketed Amison's envelop and looked around furtively.

"Shall we go upstairs?"

Leroux's second floor office, like most in the ministry, was filled with gold gilded furniture that could have jumped out of a museum catalogue. It was in keeping with the grand conceit that colonies developed in the heyday of the

Spanish Empire and heralded the importance of its occupant in the pecking order of the bureaucracy.

Much of the decor was in a Renaissance era motif that caught the natural light flowing in generously from the high windows facing the main square. A huge crystal chandelier hung from the ceiling over a generous bouquet of freshly cut flowers arranged on a round, gold leafed conference table. On the walls were electrified bronze sconces lighting works of period art. Upon closer inspection, the place looked strikingly familiar, reminding Amison very much of Leroux's Fort Lauderdale office. However, he did notice that cracks and fissures in the ceiling and walls were beginning to appear from the volcano's incessant tremors.

Rafael deposited Amison at the door of Leroux's office and left discreetly.

"So this is the seat of empire," said Amison as Leroux greeted him.

The Europol director smiled casually.

"My Caribbean empire," Leroux corrected.

He motioned Amison to a chair next to a coffee table around which Harold, Bienvneido, Henry and Vincent were already seated and sat down next to him. Anticipating the next question, Leroux explained the reason for the similarity between his two offices.

"As I explained to your friends, I detest change. This office and the one in Fort Lauderdale are replicas of my Paris office. The big difference is that Europol pays for Paris and Fort Lauderdale but this office is self-supporting."

"Oh?"

"Do not be surprised, my dear monsieur Jones. Europol is rich but not that rich. This facility is privately owned and is an independent agency functioning on behalf of Europol. I make money by servicing the Caribbean needs of many intelligence organizations, including your CIA, and pay Europol in Paris a ten percent royalty for the use of its name."

"Who owns this franchise?" Amison asked.

"I do."

"Why are you telling us this now?"

Harold chuckled.

"This guy is in business for himself," he whispered, "These fucking frogs are all the same. They're a bunch of snail eating, truffle sniffing cock suckers and can't be trusted."

"I want you to understand that my relationship with Monte Fuego is of most importance to me and to Juan Duarte. My ability to make investments hinges on my ability to generate income for Paris. I explained all that to your friends."

Amison was slow to understand what Leroux was getting at.

"Can you speak plainly, director? Does this have to do with our mission?"

Leroux shook his head emphatically.

"Oh no," he said. "The mission is almost completed and quite successful, I should add. I merely want you to appreciate where I stand."

"Exactly where do you stand, Jacques?" Harold asked.

Leroux smiled enigmatically.

"I stand for my future and for life after Monte Fuego," he replied. "I would like you to reveal to me the back way into the mine."

Leroux's office door opened and Juan Duarte Gutierrez walked in.

Everyone rose to their feet, but he waved at them to be at ease.

"It is much too late for politeness," he said, sitting himself down behind Leroux's desk. "By coming to Monte Fuego with your friends, senor Jones, you have placed la senora Charlotte Fergueson's life in danger. You can also be arrested for illegal entry into our country. But you can redeem yourselves."

"These gentlemen are in your country legally," said Henry Alstrum.

"Oh? How is that?"

"Their visas are signed by Felipe Gutierrez, Excellency," Vincent informed Juan Duarte. "In his capacity as your country's consul general."

Juan Duarte rose to his feet.

"That is preposterous. Felipe would never do that."

"You have time to ask him about that," said Vincent. "He has been arrested for the murder of Sol Weinberg."

"A lie!" Juan Duarte yelled. "Who are you to make such lies."

"The man isn't lying," said Henry softly. "Vincent Romaine is an attorney and is knowledgeable in such matters. I suggest giving him a hearing."

Juan Duarte was visibly agitated but he sat down again.

"I do not understand," he said.

"Monte Fuego has many challenges, Excellency," Vincent went on to explain. "Several businesses in your country are facing tax evasion charges in America and in France. Principals in these same enterprises are also being charged with international theft, smuggling and murder. To cap it all, your son, a consul of your country, stands accused of murder. As we speak, Excellency, agents from the IRS and CIA are in La Fortuna, and police officers are on their way from Fort Lauderdale, San Juan and Connecticut to further investigate these charges and people of interest who have been tracked to Monte Fuego. Finally, in the interest of justice, you should be interested to know that the accounts of all the businesses in question have been frozen in their major markets."

"Senor Zimmer is with the CIA," said Juan Duarte. "He is in Monte Fuego. I shall speak with him, He will take care of these matters as always."

Amison smiled.

"Ex-CIA, Excellency. He's wanted for murder. Is that not so, Jacques?"

Juan Duarte looked at Leroux who waved his hands helplessly.

"Well then, I shall personally consult with Calvin Bard."

"You mean Edward Lawrence of Kinshasa Export, don't you? Amison said.

"I do not follow," replied Juan Duarte.

"Ed Lawrence or Calvin Bard, Excellency. It doesn't matter. We need to find him."

Harold was more direct.

"It's time for you to consider your options," he said. "Sol Weinberg is dead and Centurion and Alliance are mine. Quentin Bates is dead and Keith and his daughters are on our short list. So is Ramon Salva. And With Victor Duncan dead, I get his action in every business in which he had an interest. Before the week is up, I can guarantee you that my friends and I will control West Indian Mines. However, you have a chance this into an opportunity."

There was a sudden tremor and a jolt that knocked them out of their chairs. More plaster from the ceiling fell to the floor as Amison helped Leroux to his feet, saying, "It's now or never if we're going to dance."

They dusted themselves off and retreated to Leroux's desk area.

"What do you propose?" Juan Duarte asked.

"Release Charlotte Furgueson in exchange for Felipe and stick to running your country," Harold said. "We'll make your problems disappear."

"What's more," added Amison. "I will renounce any claim I have to the land occupied by West Indian Mines in exchange for a long term lease on the West Indian Mines property that you will give to Sid Stone for resort development."

"What about Keith Bates, Ramon Salva and Max Zimmer?"

Leroux sighed.

"It may be time to cultivate new friendships, Excellency. I am saying this as Europol's member to the Court of Justice's search and screen committee for a director of their commission in charge of investigating corporate crimes. Your name has come up several times as a likely candidate by virtue of your long, unblemished record and dedicated service. You do not need your old friends to tarnish your illustrious past."

"You would nominate me?"

"Of course. Who else would I nominate?"

"But what can be done about Felipe? His arrest can destroy me."

"He does presents a problem," said Amison. You see, the police believe that Felipe shot Sol. That can't look good if word gets out that your blood son, who was recently appointed as Monte Fuego's consul by you, is a murderer."

Juan Duarte held his head in his hands and moaned.

"It could end up being a scandal of monumental proportions," Amison went on. "It may even bring down your government."

"A terminal career event," added Harold gleefully.

More moans and groans.

"But there's a way out, Excellency," said Amison.

Juan Duarte looked up.

"There is?"

"Yes. It can be proven that Sol committed suicide and with Felipe's gun. I even have an attorney who can clear his name."

"You can? Who?"

Amison pointed to Vincent.

"He's the man for you. I guarantee it. He will even negotiate a confidential deal to absolve you of all complicity with your former associates."

"You can end up being a hero," Vincent added.

"True, Excellency," agreed Leroux. Your cooperation with the United States and France will be duly noted. And your help in stopping renegade companies from taking advantage of Monte Fuego's very favorable investment climate for rob our countries of taxes and to create mayhem in the world will define you as one of our leading global statesmen."

Leroux never ceased to amaze Amison. He could sure pour it on.

"I no longer wish to be associated with those rascals," said Juan Duarte.

Vincent gave him the answer he was looking for.

"No need to if they are put out of business," he said. "Listen. All we want is Charlotte delivered to us by noon tomorrow at the Excelsior. It just so happens that we have Felipe here in La Fortuna. We will exchange him for Charlotte. It should be a mutually satisfactory arrangement."

"And we need the right to stay in Monte Fuego to do what we have to do on behalf of Europol," Harold said. "Anything else, Jonesey?"

"Yes. Two things, Excellency. Where do we find Max Zimmer and Edward Lawrence?"

A fresh tremor shook the chandelier above their heads and more plaster fell around them. Juan Duarte got up with a resigned expression on his face.

"I will have Charlotte released in exchange for Felipe. As for Max Zimmer, he often stays with his girlfriend, Erica Brown, in an apartment over her store. He should be there now and Edward Lawrence sometimes stays there as well. My brother owned the building and let Erica and Janice use it." He slapped his hands emphatically, adding, "They are all yours, amigo. But I need something in return now."

Amison was hardly listening as he replied, "What is that, Excellency?"

"Leroux and I want the location of the entrance to the tunnel that leads from the city to the mine and we do not want senor de la Maza and his men to stand in our way."

"Not a problem," said Amison. "It is under the obelisk in the square. It's all yours."

Juan Duarte's mouth dropped.

"Under the obelisk? It will take days to dig around it and we can't wait. The volcano is about to blow and we might even have to cancel our funeral plans."

Amison looked at Bienvenido.

"That's the best we can do, Excellency, but my friend here won't interfere." Bienvenido nodded.

"Senor Jones has taught me morality, Excellency. My men are contracted to the United Nations to help in a possible evacuation of the island. They do not seek to interfere in the country's affairs."

Harold was aghast.

"We're being sandbagged by a volcano," he whined loudly.

"No so," protested Leroux. "The fees for your services are guaranteed and so are those of monsieur de la Maza. Your services are needed to finish the house cleaning you have begun. But you can understand that whatever was stolen must be returned. It is only right. Besides, I personally receive ten percent of the value of returned inventory. That is my arrangement with Europol. Juan Duarte has asked to share my commission and I agreed. For that reason, we must make all efforts to penetrate the mine."

Amison turned to Harold and Bienvenido.

"We'll make do," he said.

"What do you mean, we'll make do?" Harold asked.

When the meting broke up, Amison informed Harold of his earlier encounter with Rafael Perez.

Somewhat mollified, Harold followed him outside with Bienvenido, Henry and Vincent where Rafael was waiting with a van. They jumped in and drove to the mine which they reached on the far side of La Fortaleza under falling volcano ash.

The old fortress cast a dark, cool shadow over the half open mine shaft that Rafael had discovered. One by one, they climbed the shaft until they reached a cave in which abandoned mining equipment lay about. Bienvenido pointed to a high mound from whose top streams of hot molten lava was creeping down to the floor of the mine. They made their way to a much larger cavern in which wavering lights were powered by a diesel generator that seemed about to die. The flickering lights threw an amber glow on countless rows of tables standing around steaming springs that periodically shot geysers into the air.

On some of the tables were jars filled with gold wedding bands. More jars were filled with gold filled human teeth and many jars contained only gold fillings. Then there were row after row of tables of large corked bottles filled with diamond rings of all sizes and descriptions, and bottles with thousands of big, loose diamonds.

Countless rubies, emeralds, aquamarines and pearls were stored separately in their own containers. Larger jewelry items like bracelets and necklaces were stacked on display poles anchored to the tables. But search as they might, they could not find the menorah.

The ground shook under them, a fissure opened in one of the walls and lava began seeping through. It was time to leave.

CHAPTER 33

▼

The Trade

Ordinarily, Amison would have been happier than the cat that swallowed the canary, but he and Luis were beginning to worry about Frank Hoffman who had still not returned. They wanted to search for him but had to put off the plan to attend a dinner party at the Excelsior hotel to honor Henry Alstrum and Juan Duarte Gutierrez. Henry was being honored for his recent appointment as Las Olas University's interim president and Juan Duarte for his nomination to the university trustees. It would not have looked right to refuse the invitation. Agreeing to wait one more day, they forced themselves to believe that he was lying low for a reason and that he would eventually show up.

Morning came. Still no Frank, and they had to be back at the hotel to insure that Charlotte's release went off without a hitch. Boris Plotnikoff and Victor Romaine, with Jake Santana's connivance and Europol's help, had apparently spirited Felipe Gutierrez out of Florida and into Monte Fuego via St. Maarten, the plan being to have him and Charlotte released at the same time.

The Excelsior hotel lobby buzzed with activity as the noon hour approached and Amison and Luis felt they had to be present to make sure the exchange of Charlotte for Felipe would go off without a hitch. One would have thought that it would be empty as word that the volcano might explode spread but the hotel was full and a festive holiday mood filled the air.

Many hotel guests were consular representatives of foreign governments in town to issue visas to residents wanting to leave. Others were wealthy locals who booked suites for their families, waiting for their yachts in the harbor to be cleared for departure. The general feeling was that the volcano's imminent eruption would be flashy and colorful but harmless. The evacuation was seen as a precaution and many planned to watch the fireworks offshore from their floating palaces.

Gus Galindez, Jake Santana and Tom Clark had made advance reservations at the hotel and were having lunch at the Crimson restaurant near the bar to the right of the registration counter with Felipe between them. Amison and Luis were trading jokes at the bar with Bienvenido, and Sid while Harold was chit chatting with Henry and Jacques Leroux nearby in the lobby.

The lobby itself was jam packed and resembled a refugee camp with guests trying to leave bumping elbows with arriving guests, mostly international Red Cross and relief workers, trying to register, There were also network televison crews who had converged on Monte Fuego to cover the volcano's anticipated eruption.

Sid Stone's attention was diverted by a loud argument that resonated from the registration counter that attracted Amison. Two men and a woman were engaged in a dispute with the registration clerk. One was short and fat; the other was tall and slim. The woman was Janice Ray. Harold also heard the noise and turned to look, doing a double take.

"Shit," he muttered, "Stan Mason. Calvin Bard and Janice."

"That's my brother," stammered Sid."

Harold put his hand on Sid's neck, saying in a low voice, "You stay cool and don't let on you know him, you hear, or else we're all dead."

He released his hold on Sid and went over to the bar. With his back to Calvin Bard, he covered Amison, Bienvneido and Luis with his wide frame.

"Don't look now, but that's Bard and Mason trying to check in. Hang loose."

Amison smiled amicably.

"We should help them get a room," he said. "That's what gentlemen are for."

He detached himself from the bar with Harold behind him and made his way through the crowd to the registration counter where Calvin Bard and Stanley Short were still locked in a verbal duel with the clerk. He gave Janice a casual greeting and a peck on the check and asked the clerk, "What's the problem?"

"We have no rooms," replied the clerk stiffly. "We are full."

"Does a Solomon Weinberg have a reservation?

The clerk stared at his computer.

"Si, senor. He reserved a suite."

"What about Emilio Gurierrez and Vincent Duncan? They are supposed to be here for a meeting."

The clerk checked his computer again and answered, "Si. They are here for a board of directors meeting. They have not yet arrived."

"They won't be checking in," said Harold.

"I do not understand."

"They're dead," Amison informed him in a low voice but loud enough for the CIA manager to hear.

The clerk stared at his computer and kept hitting buttons as Janice discreetly backed away and melted away in the crowd.

"The screen won't bring them here," Amison went on. "But these gentlemen are guests of Juan Duarte. Take our word for it."

"We'll take their rooms," said Harold. "And we'll pay cash."

The beleaguered clerk finally caved in and surrendered the rooms.

Stan Mason was overjoyed but Calvin Bard said nothing.

"This is great," Stan exclaimed. "I don't know how to thank you,"

"Don't thank me, Stan. Thank the dead. Their bad luck is your good fortune. You now have a front row seat to watch your tax problems being resolved."

Harold introduced them to Henry Alstrum who had joined them.

"Dr. Alstrum is the interim president at Las Olas University and he and our Vincent Romaine have been working around the clock with the government of Monte Fuego to find an amicable solution to the situation facing West Indian Mines and it's affiliates. Haven't you, Henry?"

The physician smiled through his Santa Claus beard.

"Yes," he said. "Your problems are not that taxing, if you pardon the pun. I assume that you've been in communication with Vincent Romaine?"

Stan Mason nodded.

"Many times. We discussed Juan Duarte's idea of folding West Indian Mines into a new business development corporation whose equity would be owned by the Monte Fuego government and outside investors. Our understanding is that Keith Bates, Ramon Salva and Max Zimmer would be excluded from this new company. Does that sound good to you, Cal?"

Calvin Bard squinted through his thick, horn rimmed glasses.

"Our interest has always been to remove West Indian and it's affiliates from engaging in political acts which threaten America's national security. This plan to neutralize West Indian meets our foreign policy goals and would compel me to consider this mission successfully completed," he said in robotic diplomatic tones, all the time searching for Janice with his eyes.

"That assumes we get our pound of flesh for back taxes," said Stanley. "We need about $500 million. Vince Romaine says it won't be a problem."

"It won't," Harold assured him. "Upon Sol's death, the management of his insurance company fell to me. Centurion has the liquid cash reserves to pay the IRS on demand. You can bank on it."

"What about Keith Bates and Ramon Salva?" Stanley asked. "They remain factors to consider."

Calvin Bard was growing restive and wanted to make a graceful exit.

"I'd assume Amison and his people will handle that problem and that Leroux gave them appropriate instructions."

He looked around cautiously.

"I was hoping to meet Amison Jones and his two friends. Are they here?"

Amison half-raised his hand.

"You're looking at him, Calvin. Luis is at the bar and Frank is probably with an old girlfriend."

The CIA man blanched but he quickly recovered his senses.

"What a pleasure," he said, giving Amison a limp handshake. "But I must go up to my room."

At that moment, Charlotte Furgueson suddenly appeared at the lobby door.

She looked none the worst for wear. In truth, to Amison, she looked radiant, almost as if she was better off now than when she was married to Cecil. She certainly did not look like a hostage. Nor did she look like a kidnap victim.

She was escorted by Juan Duarte Gutierrez, followed by Leroux, and his assistant, Rafael Perez, and delivered into the waiting arms of Sid Stone as Jake Santana, all smiles, escorted Felipe to the president's side.

Juan Duarte and Leroux beamed triumphantly like Roman conquerors. It was a spectacle designed for the TV crews and reporters who were present and had their cameras rolling.

Charlotte Furgueson and his son, Felipe Gutierrez, had been kidnaped, Juan Duarte declared in front of a microphone that had been thrust in front of his face, by terrorists bent on the destruction of the Free World. These were not run-of-the-mill terrorists with hoods over their faces, but corporate thugs who wanted to enslave the world and create an empire that would crush legitimate governments and create a global monopoly of global power based on Nazi power.

Why were they kidnaped? Because they threatened to blow the whistle on those evil doers. Thank God they were now free. Who rescued them? It was the government of Monte Fuego, with help from Europol, the American CIA and the IRS who unmasked the front organizations as tax frauds.

Amison did not know if he should laugh or cry as he witnessed a most tearful reunion scene between Charlotte and Sid dutifully recorded by the cameras. It was so staged that he found it embarrassing. Harold sensed his apprehension and whispered in his ear.

"It's a big game, Jonesey. Vince caught on when he met with Henry. But, let Sid enjoy himself. Who knows, he may even end up with this hotel before it's over."

Amison smiled benignly and went over to kiss Charlotte and congratulate Sid. They seemed glad to see him, but at the same time they were impatient. "Can this keep, Jonesey? We have to pose for pictures," said Sid, looking at his watch.

Amison was somewhat taken aback but he managed to stay agreeable.

"Not a problem."

Bienvenido and Luis came over to join him as he raised his head above the crowd to see if he recognized anyone else in the lobby. Out of a corner of his eye he saw Julio Maldonado, Salva's pilot, trying to leave the hotel undetected. "Julio," he called out. "Julio Maldonado."

It was too late for Julio to leave unnoticed. He turned around and Amison sent him a stupid hand wave. Julio tried to look surprised and acknowledged him with a weak smile.

"Jonesey. Great to see you. Haven't seen you in ages."

Amison stuck his hand out and grabbed Julio's in a handshake that made him wince. He found it odd because he had barely squeezed his hand.

The others too shook his hand, getting similar reactions.

Julio tried to conceal his pain, asking in breathless rapid fire order. "What are you all doing here? Are you staying at this hotel?"

"Yes. What about you?"

"No I had to see someone here. I'm staying at Salva's country house."

"Pleasure?"

Julio shook his head.

"Business. Salva is here for the board meeting."

A voice behind Amison called as Julio was talking.

"Senor Jones?"

It was Rafael Perez.

"Rafael. Have you met my good friends?"

"Yes. Once. At the meeting you had with my boss in Fort Lauderdale. And I have met el senor de la Maza several times."

"And have you met Julio Maldonado, Ramon Salva's pilot?"

"Yes," replied Rafael. "I flew back from Paris with Julio earlier this year to deliver the gold watches that were designed for you and your friends by Louis Salieri."

Amison grinned.

"They were fine watches," he said, holding up his hand. "That must have been in the Spring?"

Rafael shook his head.

"In March, actually. Isn't that so, Julio?"

"I do not remember."

"Yes. It was March. I remember because I was in Jacques Leroux's office with monsieur Bard gave me a box of special watch mechanisms he received from Africa to bring to Salieri. Less than a week later the watches were ready. It was definitely March."

At that moment Sid Stone walked by, overhearing the conversation. "Calvin Bard? Calvin Bard gave you the watches?"

"Of course," replied Rafael. "I have met him many times."

"Is he here at the hotel?"

"On your floor," said Amison.

Sid mumbled something inaudibly and left to rejoin Charlotte at the photo shoot.

Bienvenido recognized Julio and added.

"And you came to see me in Miami a few weeks ago to talk about Estrella Gomez."

"You must have me confused with someone else. The poor woman is dead."

"I am terribly sorry," said Bienvenido. "Please pardon my error."

"I must go," Julio said nervously.

"So must we," said Amison. He was about to say something more when a thundering crack broke the air. The earth shuddered for less than a second and then everything stood still. Frozen faces and bodies moved and life returned to normal, but with a greater sense of urgency.

Turning to Rafael who had a stricken expression on his face, he said, "You should consider moving from here, friend. The weather is better in the States."

Rafael broke down and began to sob.

"My wife and kids live here and have no visa. I cannot leave them. And then, how would I make a living?"

Harold and Vincent came up behind them.

"You'll come back with us," said Harold. "And Vincent here can take care of things in Florida."

"I'm sure we can find a way," agreed Vincent.

"I would listen to them," urged Bienvenido. They can help you leave Monte Fuego. Once you are in Florida, I can give you a job."

Amison was more direct.

"Go pack, Rafael. There's not much time,"

"What do I tell my boss?"

"Nothing," said Luis. "It's best to leave quietly."

Rafael thanked them and left.

"So, where does this leave us?" Bienvenido asked.

"Between a rock and a hard place," answered Henry who came to join them. Frank nodded in the direction of Sid who was still mugging for the cameras with Juan Juarte and Charlotte.

"What the hell is going on between them?"

"It's called a fix," said Henry. "Let's go to the English Pub next door. It's more private and we can talk."

They trooped out to the Tudor style restaurant that lay between the hotel and the justice ministry and settled around a large table in the back. Crowded as the hotel was, the English Pub was nearly empty. The Victorian style eatery dated back to the English colonial period of the nineteenth and twentieth centuries and catered to personnel from the English consulate and to English tourists. The British embassy had sent most of its people to Antigua and Jamaica and most of the English tourists were long gone. Indeed, even the Pub's staff was preparing to close down and leave. Leftover sandwiches, warm beer and chips were the only items left for consumption on the menu.

"Charlotte was never kidnaped," Henry announced. "Vincent figured it out."

"That's right," said Vincent. "It was a ruse. Juan Duarte saw his entire world folding and Calvin Bard wanted to stop Jonesey's juggernaut. They invited her to Monte Fuego on the pretext that she could surprise Sid with a deed to a big tract of land for hotel development. Charlotte went willingly."

"What do you mean?"

"Juan Duarte wanted to see hotel based tourism developed on his island and wanted to deal with Sid but he was in too deep with Ed Lawrence and his crazy right wing plan. Sid and Sol had money. Sid wanted to build a hotel and casino on West Indian land and Sol wanted to finance and insure the property."

"What about Charlotte?"

"She wanted something better to do than to play second fiddle as she did for years when she was married to Cecil and this gave her a step up. Juan Duarte took Felipe into their scheme by appointing him consul general since he was already spying on your operation for Max Zimmer and this new position might give him clout in Washington and therefore over you. He never suspected that Felipe was basically stupid, a coward and would get himself arrested.

"Juan Duarte and Cal wanted you to believe through Felipe that unless you canceled your mission, Charlotte would be killed. But that would have never happened. Juan Duarte is not a killer and he did want his son back.

"But stopping your mission cold was Cal's thing. He wanted West Indian and its affiliates to keep operating and buy time for the White Knights and the Patriotic Front to re-group. Sid would have his resort and you would be gone one by one. But Charlotte was clueless and so was Sid. The winner right now is Juan Duarte. Bard is a loser and that makes him more dangerous than ever."

"Bard has had in for us since Armando filed his will," said Amison." I don't know why he didn't give Bienvenido a gold watch."

"Because Barberi was still alive," said Harold, "But you, Frank and Luis were written off the moment Armando's will was written."

"It seems that way," continued Vincent. "Everything began to unravel when those hits against you failed and when the IRS launched its investigation. But what ruined it for West Indian was the brazenness of the Patriotic Front and White Knights. That woke up the CIA and Europol. Juan Duarte also woke up, realizing he was on the wrong side. Before Hernando's death, he was just the corrupt leader of a banana republic. After, he found himself boxed in by crimes beyond his control and by a conspiracy with this crazy Ed Lawrence character to create a new world order. He needed time to distance himself from Bard and his gang as you guys began closing in on Bates, Salva and Zimmer who was by then in Calvin Bard's sights. He thought Leroux would be flexible and that by working with him, Sol and Sid, and by sidelining you, he'd get himself out of trouble. It's worked so far. Juan Duarte has forged a partnership with Leroux. They'll get what they want and so will you."

"That brings us to the fix. You leave Juan Duarte alone. Felipe goes free and you don't touch him. But Bates and his daughters are yours along with Ramon Salva, Max Zimmer and Calvin Bard. You also get to decide about the other two broads. Frank may have to fight Calvin for Janice and you, Jonesey, may have to go through Zimmer for Erica."

Amison sighed.

"This place is history for me," he said. "I was wondering, Vincent. Do you know anything about the backgrounds of Calvin Bard and Max Zimmer?"

"Calvin Bard or Edward Lawrence is easy. His dad was a white supremacist and Edward took his ideas to a higher level, creating a double life for himself where he could maximize his power and influence. Max was his protégé. Does the name Arthur Zimmermann ring a bell?"

"The German ambassador to Washington in 1917?"

"Yes. Zimmermann plotted to have Mexico enter the war against America, but that's another story. Mexico stayed neutral. The name belongs to an old German family. For example, a distant cousin was a building engineer who designed the first prototype concentration camps. Max Zimmer was actually born Maximilian Zimmermann. He changed his name to Max Zimmer when he emigrated to the United States. He joined the CIA but maintained his neo Nazi connections and allied himself to Calvin Bard. You know the rest."

Bienvenido, who had said little up to now, felt constrained to return to the issue of Julio Maldonado.

"I remember Julio now. He wanted to work for me, saying that he had killed Chico Alvarez and that he knew where the menorah was hidden. He thought I might give him a job or reward for the information. I threw him out."

"Damn!" Amison exclaimed. "That explains Julio's sore shoulder. He was Quentin Bates's chopper pilot. He never shot anyone, but we did hit him with a lucky shot." And he went on to explain how Chico was killed.

Bienvenido pressed his point.

"It is possible that Julio did no killing, but his claim about the menorah may be important."

Bienvenido raised his hands about three feet apart.

"Consider the size of that candelabra," he said, demonstrating with his hands.

"I saw it many years ago in France. It is big and heavy. Solid gold impregnated with very large diamonds bolted on to a heavy brass or bronze coated cast iron pedestal base. How easy could it have been to lift, let alone carry it? The stolen menorah must be a fake."

The table fell quiet. At last, Amison broke the silence, saying, "We'll have to find out for ourselves, won't we?"

Vincent Romaine sighed, picked up the lunch tab and left some money on the table.

"Lunch is on me for that, and I do hope you're not spinning your wheels. Do let me know how things work out. But right now, Boris and I are leaving this place. You guys should do the same."

CHAPTER 34

▼

Final Confrontations

"Vincent is right," said Harold. "We can't do much more before this place blows up around us."

Bienvenido agreed with his assessment.

"This island has been cursed from the beginning. I'm pulling out also. How soon can we leave?"

"Our boats are in the harbor," replied Harold. "We're going to try to get out tonight."

"I'm staying," declared Amison. "I'm not finished yet."

"You're out of your mind," Harold responded, his voice rising. "It's over and this miss mission is done. Let someone else go for the gold. I don't intend to fry in this hell hole."

"Neither do I," said Amison calmly. "But I'm not leaving until I find Frank."

"I'm not leaving either," joined in Luis.

Harold calmed down.

"It's your call," he said. "You stay lucky, you hear?"

There was nothing much more to say. Harold left with Bienvenido and Henry to prepare for their departure and Amison and Luis returned to Phoenix under a cloudy sky. Volcanic ash began falling like snow flurries and they found the catamaran covered with a light gray coating. To their happy surprise, they also found

Frank, armed with a broom and a water hose, first sweeping and then hosing the ash off the boat.

"Damn you, Frank," yelled Amison. "Where the hell have you been?"

"Come down below and I'll tell you."

Frank explained that he had decided that it had made no sense to pay Janice a visit. He hired a car instead to drive to the estate area near the airport to see if Ramon Salva was at his vacation retreat. He planned later to see Keith Bates who had his own vacation home on the island's far side. His idea was to broker a truce between them and to solicit their support.

"I could have saved my time and energy," he confessed.

Ramon Salva, he was informed by a servant, had gone to the airport where he kept a Cessna, the type used for lessons, and took off to see Keith Bates who the servant said had his own landing strip.

"I drove to the airport to verify the story. People I spoke to said he lunched on French pate, cold vichy-souse soup, smoked salmon diced with kippers, a pitcher of Sangria, more canapes and an excellent bottle of vintage champagne capped off by creme brulee and cognac before taking off.

"I then called Keith Bates from the airport and was told by a servant there that he was on his patio having lunch and expecting company and could not be disturbed.

"I drove over anyway," said Frank. "When I arrived, firefighters and police were there. The house was burning and the wings and fuselage of a small plane stuck out of its side. It seems old man Bates was indeed on his patio when the Cessna dove down and broadsided him. The crash killed him and destroyed the house, setting it on fire."

"Was Salva in the plane?" Luis asked, already knowing the answer.

"Yes. Dead on impact."

He looked at his friends.

"So. What have you guys been doing?"

They briefed Frank on what had happened since he had gone off by himself and Luis suggested that perhaps they should leave Monte Fuego while there was still time. Amison nixed the idea, saying, "The hornet's nest may be gone but the hornets left alive will follow us home. The job must be finished here.

Besides, I know where Hernando's deed and the tunnel entrance is located."

That afternoon the volcanic eruptions subsided and they treated themselves to a late lunch at a café near the docks. When they were done, Amison looked at his watch and declared, "I'm going to find the tunnel entrance now." Amison informed his two friends.

"Are you sure you want to do this?" Frank asked. "The mine is dangerous."

"I'm not interested in the mine," Amison assured him. "It's the menorah."

"But didn't Bienvenido tell you it might be a fake?" Frank asked.

"He did. But fake or real, I'm betting that it's near the tunnel entrance right here in the middle of La Fortuna. So is Hernando's deed to the mine property."

"You're sure?"

"Positive."

"But where's the tunnel entrance?"

Amison took a calculator type object out of his pocket.

"This is my GPS," he said. "The display gives me navigational coordinates."

He turned it on and a series of numbers appeared on its digital screen.

"See? It tells us exactly where we are in within ten feet in degrees, minutes and seconds of latitude and longitude."

"Gee, Jonesey," said Frank. "We know all that. What are you telling us?"

"I finally deciphered the letters on Hernando's map," Jonesey declared. "He and Roberto knew nothing about code but they knew navigation since they did a lot of fishing and boating. All they did was transpose navigational points or coordinates into letters. It was too simple for us to figure out, but I now know where the tunnel entrance is even without the coordinates. Juan Duarte set it up for me. I'm also counting on Bard, Zimmer and anyone else left alive to follow us."

"What happens then?" Luis asked.

Amison grinned.

"We kill or be killed."

He looked at his friends and asked, "I'm staying here. You guys hang out at the cat and take turns on watch. Any of our people at the hotel?"

"Harold is probably gone by now with Bienvenido and his men, and Bob Byrne and his guys must also be on the boats," answered Luis. "That leaves us Virgil Holmes, Desmond Lyons and Jimmy Wales at the hotel. Calvin Bard and Stan Mason are down the hall from you. So is Gus Galindez, Tom Clark and Jake Santana. I don't know where Leroux is hanging out; he may have split. Sid too. Shouldn't we hit Calvin Bard now before he gets us?"

Amison shook his head.

"No. Let him come after us. He has no choice.""

He left the café and returned to the Excelsior and standing in the lobby when he found himself staring at a woman in spiked heels and a gray suit ensemble with long blond hair curled over her head. It was Denise.

In a way, Amison was not shocked. She was bound to surface sooner or later. But her presence now left him cold.

"It's good to see you, Denise. What brings you to Monte Fuego?"

He wondered if she had received the afternoon's news.

"You, Ruby."

"Me?"

"Can we talk, perhaps at the bar?"

"I would, Denise. But I'm tired and not in the mood for a drink."

"Can we talk in your suite, then?" She asked coyly.

Refusing her was pointless.

"Let's go," he said.

The elevator was small and a local family, laden with empty suitcases, filled the cavity. They wriggled into the narrow space where Denise tried to press her body against his without much success.

Was this a set up? Of course. An amorous encounter? Amison knew better. This was an act of desperation for her part that would end poorly one way or another. He was suddenly scared and he wondered if Virgil Holmes and his guard duty cohort were around.

The elevator moved slowly, agonizingly, groaning under the weight of the locals who could have used generous doses of deodorant, and deposited them mercifully after what seemed an eternity in front of Amison's suite.

The suite was actually a small apartment. The hallway door opened into a vestibule lit by a chandelier and furnished with a table and two arm chairs. It also featured a small closet where guests could hang their up outer garments without cluttering the suite.

A door to the left lead to a service corridor that circled an inner courtyard where room and linen service could be discreetly provided without using the guest hallways. Another door on the right lead to the living-bedroom suite that overlooked the street through a pair of french doors opening on to a balcony. Behind the living room was a two-room bathroom-vanity combination with a window whose glass was opaqued to block the view from the unsightly inner courtyard.

The suite was done in typical English style and the bed, a huge king sized affair, was flanked by an ornate wall mirror. Above an elegant sideboard facing the bed was another gilt framed mirror that reflected an unopened bottle of scotch, two glasses and a bucket of ice left earlier by the hotel.

Denise went over to the sideboard, threw some ice cubes into the glasses, opened the bottle and poured it over the ice. She gave Amison one glass and took another and loosened her hair, allowing it to fall smoothly around her shoulders.

"To us," she toasted. So far, not a word about her dead brother, Quentin.

"To us," said Amison, pretending to take a sip.

She was about to remove her jacket and skirt but Amison shook his head.

"I don't think so, Denise. I'm not interested."

She drew back with a pained expression on her face.

"Why, are you having your period?"

"That's a bad joke, woman."

"Then what is it? You never turned down a little pussy before."

Amison slapped her across the face and she fell on the bed, screaming.

"I could have you killed for this."

"Oh yeah? By whom?"

She regained her composure and pulled herself together.

"I like you and I think we can still make a great team."

"Is that why you're here?"

"You know where the menorah is," she said.

"I o? What about the secret way into the mine?"

"You know that too."

"Well, maybe we can deal. But besides that. Are you in for a screwing?"

"Boy. You do have a one track mind," she said, placing her arms around him.

"What the hell else do you want me to do with women, Denise? Throw rocks at them?"

"You're a good man anyway, Ruby. You know how to take care of things, and you know how to take care of women. I like that."

"I try, Denise."

"But you'll need my help and connections to steal the menorah and get it out of the island. I'm good friends with the guy who wants you dead."

Amison grinned.

"Is he being cut in on our take?"

"Of course not, sweetie," Denise answered, tweaking his chin. "We'll buy him off and then kill him. We're going to keep everything for ourselves. That's what love is all about."

Amison loosened her hold around his neck and refilled her glass. Going over to the french doors facing the balcony, he swung them open and looked out.

"That's Boucher & Salieri's store across the street," he said. "I wonder who is running the show these days."

Denise came over to draw him away from the window.

"Who cares. It's us that counts."

Amison was about to turn away when he detected a movement behind one of the windows in an apartment above the store.

"How did you know I was going to be at the hotel?"

"A lucky guess."

"Your luck is my luck. I say we have ourselves a deal. The tunnel entrance is under Erica's store. And I bet I'll find Hernando's land deed there too."

Denise was purring like a kitten by now.

"Can we kiss on it?"

She came up close and placed her arms around Amison's neck, pushed her lips into his and maneuvered him with his back to the open french doors. From where they stood, Amison could see her reflection in the mirror by the bed. He had seen that look before, at the hospital in Fort Lauderdale. The softness was gone and replaced by a steely smile. One arm was around his neck him while the other hung down at her side with two fingers pointed down. He saw a red dot crawling on the wall over the mirror like a bug.

"So, Denise. Now that we're partners and in love, tell me why you murdered Victor and why your sister killed Emilio."

"You fucking idiot," she screamed. Veins began swelling in her neck and a venomous look covered her face as he swung her around with her back to the balcony. He heard the almost inaudible sounds of two toy balloons bursting in the distance, dove to the floor, leaving her standing alone.

Denise swayed slightly and an almost loving smile crossed her lips as she fell over Amison. She lay still and stared at him silently, her arms around Amison as if waiting for a round of sex. Then slowly her arms relaxed. A whimper left her open lips and she closed her eyes. Leroux had wanted her dead. He had his wish fulfilled after all.

Amison got up and peeked out into the street in time to see Calvin running out of Boucher & Salieri. So that was Denise's secret lover. He groaned. He was in the suite and his gun was on the boat.

There was no time to think. Guessing that Calvin would take the stairs, he stood by the door and waited. He was right. Swinging open the door, Amison pulled Calvin into the vestibule, but he was too quick and kicked Amison out of the way. They tumbled into the bedroom where Amison fell on his back. Calvin pulled out a silencer tipped pistol and aimed it at his head.

"Edward!"

A shot rang out.

Calvin Bard's gun arm dropped and he fell next to Amison who blinked and stared at Sid Stone standing over him.

"I thought you didn't do guns," he said.

"I usually don't," said Sid. "Frank and Luis gave me lessons."

CHAPTER 35

▼

End Game

It was time to close in. The volcano was acting up again, dropping hot ash all over the island. Fires were breaking out and lava was flows were sliding down the mountain into the Rio Blanco, slowly engulfing La Fortuna in a crackling, glowing inferno. Early that morning, Amison headed for Erica's store, fighting crowds going in the opposite direction until he found himself in near empty, fire and wind streets that were rapidly filling up with volcanic ash.

He had the address and his GPS in hand, on which was taped a piece of paper with twelve letters arranged in two sets of six each and under each set, a bunch of hand scribbled numbers. But even without the GPS, he knew exactly where to go and what he would find when he got there. And so he kept walking until he stood under a sign on a small two story building reading, Casa Bella.

This was the place. A lemon colored Mercedes Benz was parked in front of the door and store display windows which were all covered with fine volcanic ash. Anxiety gnawed at Amison's stomach and he hoped that the store would be deserted. Wiping clear a section of the display window, he peered inside where he saw a rack of men's suits next to a shirt and tie counter. Hard against the back wall was a large wooden crate resting on a dolly over an old rug.

Near the women's wear racks was a counter upon which blank dummy heads with blonde and brunette wigs were mounted. An imaginary light flashed over Amison's head. Blonde wigs. So, that's how the menorah heist and Victor Duncan's murder was pulled off.

He took a deep breath and walked in. A bell rang, leaving him to stand like a fool and trying to figure out what to do next. He went to the men's rack where his hands accidentally brushed against the sleeve of a brown suit jacket.

"Try the dark blue one, Ruby. You look terrible in brown!"

He spun around as if shot.

"Erica!"

She stood next to the crate, hand on hip, following Amison's every move. "Well. Aren't you going to kiss me hello?"

Amison moved forward timidly and kissed her on the cheek.

"Is that the best you can do, Ruby, or are you running for public office?"

They kissed again, and this time he tried to be more passionate.

"Damn it, Erica. You know why I'm here."

"You're here to propose marriage?" Sarcasm dripped from her voice.

"Not quite," he stammered.

Erica stepped over to the front door and hung up a 'closed' sign.

"It doesn't matter, Ruby. I knew you'd be by."

"You're a good mind reader."

"I try, hon. And you're here in the nick of time. Janice and I are leaving." She pointed to two duffels standing on the floor of an near empty kitchen that had been converted into a store room and which was visible through a doorway at the other end of the store.

"How are you getting out?"

"We were counting on you, Frank and your boat."

"We may have to take Luis. He's on the boat."

"Luis doesn't like us," said Erica.

"He's always suspicious. He's a cop."

Amison chuckled.

"Now, if Luis was here, he'd probably ask if you were taking that crate on the boat."

"Why, are you worried about it being too heavy?"

He lost his smile.

"No. But I want to see what it's standing over."

Erica shrugged her shoulders and said, "Beats me. There's an old rug nailed to the floor under it. So suit yourself."

Without another word, Amison rolled the crate away and ripped off the worn rug to expose a dust covered trap door. He pried it open with a crowbar that he found lying nearby and looked down stone steps with a shelf cut into the rock just under the store's floorboards. On the shelf was a wooden box. He kneeled down and removed the box. Stepping back up into the store, he opened it and removed an old sealed document.

"Hernando's deed to the West Indian Mines property," he exclaimed.

"I never knew about the trapdoor," Erica maintained.

"Probably not," said Amison. "But it doesn't matter if you did. It's not the only reason I'm here. You and Janice are accessories to robbery and murder, aren't you?"

Erica was silent for a moment and pointed to the storage room.

"Tea or coffee?"

Amison followed her into the room. Besides a few empty cartons, all that was left was a stove, a sink with a carving knife in it, and a table against a wall. She filled a tea kettle with water and placed it on the stove to heat. She found a jar of instant coffee, two plastic cups and a spoon in a wall cupboard above the stove and placed them on the table. The social niceties completed, Erica turned to Amison and asked him point blank, "What do you want, Ruby?"

"The truth."

She did not reply and the stillness in the room was broken by the tea kettle's high pitched whistle. Amison parceled out a spoonful of instant coffee in each cup while Erica poured the water and took a sip of coffee.

"When you get right down to it, Ruby. We have to forget the past and start over again elsewhere."

"That's hard when we carry baggage from the past, Erica."

"What do you mean?"

"I'm still stuck on trying to understand what happened at the San Jeronimo jewelry exhibit in San Juan because it dovetails into Victor Duncan's murder."

"I'm sure you've worked it out, Ruby," said a voice from the door. "In case you haven't, Erica and I impersonated Denise and I stole the menorah while she shot Victor in Connecticut."

Janice strolled in with Frank as if she owned the world.

Amison never budged. His eyes narrowed, but his voice stayed low.

"Grand theft and murder. That was the way the cops will put it together. Four women and a make-up artist, Estrella Gomez, and the help of feeble minded heavies like Felipe and Quentin Bates."

"Now that you know, Ruby, what happens?" Erica asked.

"Ask Frank."

Frank rolled his eyes.

"I don't know what happens. But I sure don't want Janice or Erica to go to prison or face murder charges over this. I don't think they really knew what they were in for."

Amison walked out to the crate stood and wheeled it into the storeroom.

"They didn't, huh? I bet that if we opened it, we'd find the menorah inside."

The two women's faces paled as Amison went on.

"The menorah disappeared at about noon on a Monday. Witnesses place a 'woman in red' at the scene who looked very much like Denise. Louis Salieri, when interviewed by Gus Galindez, identified Denise as the 'woman in red.' But he can't talk since he's dead. So is Paul Boucher. Sol Weinberg did them.

"However, witnesses say a person looking like either Denise or Danielle shot Victor Duncan early that evening. Then we have Danielle who was supposedly with Juan Duarte in Washington, standing in for Denise who was in Florida with Emilio, this, according to Emilio and other witnesses like Felipe.

"Now, Tom Clark believes that Victor's shooter was Denise because she was left handed and so was the shooter and the weapon at the scene was designed for a southpaw. Danielle is right handed. So, if Denise killed Victor, she could not have been in San Juan earlier in the day. The travel logistics between San Juan and Connecticut work against that possibility.

"With regard to Danielle, I have no problem with her being in Washington. She was seen by too many people who knew her well. The problem is Denise who could not be in three places at almost the same time. But I think I have the answer."

"What is it?"

Amison began pacing the women, circling them like a big cat circling his prey.

"It goes this way. We have four women, friends in school, who meet years after and begin sharing their problems and desires. Two are unhappily married. They are killers and thieves, looking to murder their husbands and score big. Two are single, needing companionship and money and are totally clueless. A friendship between the two pairs of women is rekindled, much by coincidence, at a party.

"What happens? Our clueless women enter into affairs with the husbands of their friends and become kept women while the killer women look the other way. Their friendship grows and soon the killer women (we'll call them Killer One and Killer Two) involve the clueless ones in their crimes, first as fences and then as accomplices.

"Then one day, our clueless ones are invited to join in a grand scheme, a plot to rob a priceless heirloom, the fabled Menorah of Titus, to be exhibited at the

the San Jeronimo museum by Boucher & Salieri and which just happens to be insured by Centurion. One of our clueless girls will dress up as Killer One and lift the menorah. Why? Because this clueless one has an inside knowledge of the ins and outs of the old fortress. She lives and works close by and happens to be one of the museum's tour guides.

"Our other clueless woman also dresses as Killer One and stays with Emilio in Florida. It works since they're having an affair anyway. Emilio goes along. Why? For any number of reasons. Your guess is as good as mine.

"This leaves Killer One free to be in Connecticut to kill Victor while Killer Two goes to Washington with Juan Duarte. You know the rest."

"Who did Killer Two murder?"

"A good question," said Amison. "Danielle shot Emilio during the attack at the Brittany with a small caliber pistol, leaving fingerprints on the weapon."

"Are you finished?"

"No. Exposing dumb broads as witless accessories to murder isn't my bag."

Amison pulled the hand held GPS out his pocket.

"As you know, Frank, this thing works."

He pushed a button and the GPS screen lit up and filled with numbers.

"I finally solved the letter codes Hernando left me. It was a code designed by a simple man for simple people. That's why it was so hard to decipher.

"Each letter corresponds to a number up to '26', the number of letters in the alphabet, with the letter 'O' used either for the number '15' or Zero. Changing the the first three pairs of letters into numbers, I get the following numbers: 16, 59 and 50, or more specifically, North Latitude16 degrees, 59 minutes and 50 seconds.

"The second three pairs of numbers, 62, 30, and 40, give me West Longitude 62 degrees, 30 minutes and 40 seconds.

"So now I look at the GPS screen and check my position. Lo and behold! I am standing within ten feet of Hernando's coordinates. This is the back way into the mine and why I think the menorah is in the crate. Now, Frank, you should know that the trapdoor leading to the tunnel is in the next room and on a shelf under the trapdoor I found Hernando's property deed.

"But when you get right down to it, I never needed the GPS; nor did I need the coordinates."

"You didn't?"

Amison grinned.

"No. Juan Duarte laid it out for me when he said that Calvin Bard and Max Zimmer hung out at Emilio's place, the house he let Erica live in and work her business. Bard, Zimmer and Emilio, and maybe Juan Duarte, knew from the beginning about the deed and the trapdoor. But they didn't know that it led to the tunnel. They used it merely to hide the property deed, and Juan Duarte put them out to dry when things got tight. Max, Sol, Emilio and probably Victor planned the menorah heist with the girls, Felipe, Quentin and Julio and then started double crossing each other with Sol working the biggest cross of all. "But the biggest loser was Calvin Bard, aka Edward Lawrence. He enlisted runaway players with separate agendas. He never got them to work together and in the end they inadvertently helped bring him down."

"But I must say," said Frank. "He came damn near to getting us killed."

"Yes," agreed Amison. "All because we inherited a few acres of land."

"If you're so smart, how come you're not rich, Ruby?"

It was a strong female voice that did not belong to Erica or Janice. It came from the doorway where a tall, well built blond woman stood with a machine pistol in her hand.

Frank's eyes nearly popped out.

"Danielle!"

"You have a knack for picking the wrong side, Frank. I told you long ago to tie in with me. And you, Ruby, you would have done much better with Denise than with your washed up girlfriend."

Amison began to laugh.

"Is this a family affair or what?"

"It is a family affair, Ruby," said Danielle. "I brought family."

The rear door opened and Max Zimmer walked in, waving a shotgun. Behind him were Felipe and Julio, armed with pistols.

"Max! I never knew. I thought Felipe had a thing for Erica."

Frank crept closer to the teakettle on the stove as Amison talked.

Felipe turned livid and was about to shoot Amison, but Danielle waved him off.

"Not here, stupid. We'll kill them below in the tunnel."

"Denise is my girlfriend," Felipe said.

"Then Max Zimmer must be Erica's boyfriend," said Frank.

"And Calvin Bard was Janice's boyfriend. That creates a problem," went on Amison. "Because Calvin was also Denise's lover. But we'll never know for sure. Denise is dead and so is Calvin Bard."

"You're lying," screamed Danielle.

Amison shook his head.

"No way, woman. They're gone. Are you smart enough to run the world with a few stupid women, Max? Your old cronies are dead, Salva, Bates, Weinberg, all of them."

"I'll worry about that after we kill you," said Max.

"Before killing us, can you tell us about the menorah in the crate?"

Max cursed.

"That damn thing almost ruined me," he said. "It should never have been stolen."

"Why not?" Frank asked. "You hate Jews, don't you?"

"It had nothing to do with Jews. Calvin's goal was to finance a movement to retake the world for the White Christian race. Stealing the menorah was a side show. Cal never knew about it until it happened. I got sucked into it by Sol."

"Enough bullshit, Max," said Danielle. "I don't give a damn about Calvin Bard's ideas. I just want the gold in the mine and the menorah. The tunnel was under our feet all this time and we never knew until Ruby led us to it. So now it's our show. We don't need him, Frank or their women."

"Why us" Erica cried. "We're your friends."

"We don't need you anymore," said Felipe. "We know how to get into the tunnel and the mine."

"I still would like to see the menorah before I die," Amison asked.

"Why not," said Julio. "Open the crate. It's not locked."

Amison swung open the lid and there in the crate lay the menorah.

He removed it out carefully and delicately and held it up to the light for them to see.

"What a dazzling work of art," he exclaimed. "Now, I can die happy."

With those words, he threw the menorah to the floor where it broke into a thousand pieces of plaster.

Frank moved like greased lightening in the crowded room. He grabbed the teakettle and threw it at Danielle while Amison pulled a knife from under his shirt collar and threw it at Felipe.

The kettle struck her on the cheek and threw her off balance. Felipe caught the knife in his stomach, dropped his gun and doubled over in front of Denise.

It was the chance Amison needed. Picking up the carving knife from the kitchen sink, he plunged it into her chest and pushed her up against Julio who tripped into Max as he leveled his shotgun at Frank.

Amison and Frank dove to the floor, dragging down Erica and Janice with them. Max fired but Danielle was in the way and caught the blast point blank. It blew her head off and her body fell like a sack of potatoes.

Max tried to reload but Julio lost his nerve and started backing away. They were both too late.

Two shots dropped Julio and another blast from behind stopped Max cold. Blood spurted out of his stomach and he collapsed face down over Julio with a bloody gaping hole in his back. The barrel of a fifty caliber assault rifle poking its smoking muzzle into the doorway told the story.

"I always wanted to fire this thing," said Harold, holding the smoking rifle.

Next to him stood Leroux and Luis, pistols in their hands.

"I hope we are not too late," said Leroux.

"Jacques, Luis" cried Amison, struggling to his feet. "Where have you been all my life?"

"I owed you for having Denise taken care for me," Leroux answered grimly.

"And this I did for myself," said Harold.

Moving out of the kitchen to the front of the store, they found Jake Santana, Gus Galindez and Tom Clark waiting with the few police who were left in the smouldering city.

"How did you know we were here?"

Luis pointed to the watch on his wrist.

"It's all in our time pieces, Jonesey. That's how Frank found you and how I found the two of you."

"By the way," said Jake. "We were listening outside. It was a great show. I think you solved our murders and the San Juan robbery."

"One thing I'd like to know, Janice," Gus Galindez asked. "Who did help you steal the menorah?"

"Felipe and Quentin did. We made practice runs late at night and had many dress rehearsals, especially when it came to opening and closing the manhole cover over which we knew the menorah table setting would be placed. Felipe also had a remote control switch box to short the circuits throughout the fort and kill the lights. And of course, Julio had a plane waiting."

Tom Clark shook his head sympathetically.

"All that good planning and a great execution for a bunch of plaster."

"It was going to make us rich," said Erica tearfully.

"Why didn't you take it to the mine through the tunnel?" Tom asked.

"I never knew anything about the tunnel," she wailed.

"That's right," agreed Amison. "They never knew. No one did. That's what this hullabaloo was about. With the other mine shafts shut, this was the only way in."

"But if this menorah is a fake, where's the real one?" Tom asked.

"Oh, easy," replied Amison. "Sol worked the ultimate double cross with Paul Boucher and Lewis Salieri. They switched it with a replica that they made for the show in Puerto Rico. The real one is in a crate in Sol's restaurant. I assume the place is still roped off as a crime scene, so it will be there when you get home, Tom. It should be returned to the Louvre museum."

Janice began to whimper.

"Are we going to be arrested?"

A building across the street suddenly went up in flames and the police were anxious to leave. They quickly accepted Jake Santana's and Gus Galindez's explanation that this was a robbery gone bad and took off amidst the jolts and tremors from the volcano.

Outside, a deep rumbling sound grew progressively louder until it became a steady thundering roar.

"We're not being arrested?" Janice asked again as they hurried out into the street.

"What for?" Jake asked. "We solved our crimes."

"I'm going home," said Tom Clark, watching the skies turn grayish black.

"So am I," smiled Gus Galindez. "As far as I'm concerned, this case is over and we're not looking for you."

Amison motioned to the lemon colored Mercedes and winked.

"Nice wheels, Erica. I hope they get you out of here alive."

EPILOGUE

▼

"So, there was no gold?" One of the teenagers asked after Sid finished telling his story over dinner.

"No gold," answered Sid. "The volcano is still active and the entire island of Monte Fuego is off limits. Jonesey has a valid claim to the West Indian Mines property but there's not much he can do about it until the volcano calms down.

But he does own that eatery in Puerto Rico, and one of Dimitri's brothers is running it for him."

"What happened to the menorah?"

Sid laughed.

"Jonesey was right. The police found the real one in Sol's restaurant. It was returned and no insurance money had to be paid out."

"And what happened to Erica and Janice?"

"They did just fine. They returned to Florida with Jonesey and Frank after all and ended up opening a store where Charlie Hand's barbershop used to be."

"How did Juan Duarte and Leroux make out?"

"Juan Duarte ended up being a hero, of course, and Jacques Leroux was promoted. He is now Europol's director of covert operations and he has three new associates, Henry Alstrum, Alex Plotnikoff and Vincent Romaine.

"Bob Byrne also made out. Harold Levy got him a job as the head of a large shipping company in Connecticut."

"What about Jonesey and his friends?"

"Jonesey still manages my hotels and he's catching up on quality with his kids and grand kids. Harold turned Used-to-Be's over to him and another of Dimitri's brothers. Who knows. Maybe he'll become a famous restauranteur in his old age.

He asked Frank to partner with him, but Frank says he wants to find himself a wife first. He might change his mind when he sees those women Jonesey hired to help manage his restaurants.

"Luis is taking care of his family and staying out of trouble. Jake Santana, Tom Clark and Gus Galindez are still cops, and Bienvenido will soon be marrying Rosina. And about once a month, we all get together at Hamburger Haven to discuss old times. Other than that, life goes on."

"But no gold?"

"Not yet. But you never know. Now, how about some ice cream?"

END

978-0-595-39426-5
0-595-39426-4

Printed in the United States
54860LVS00001B/181-189

9 780595 394265